Romantic Suspense

Danger. Passion. Drama.

Colton's Secret Past
Kacy Cross

Protector In Disguise
Veronica Forand

MILLS & BOON

Kacy Cross is acknowledged as the author of this work
COLTON'S SECRET PAST
© 2024 by Harlequin Enterprises ULC   First Published 2024
Philippine Copyright 2024   First Australian Paperback Edition 2024
Australian Copyright 2024   ISBN 978 1 038 92171 0
New Zealand Copyright 2024

PROTECTOR IN DISGUISE
© 2024 by Deborah Evens   First Published 2024
Philippine Copyright 2024   First Australian Paperback Edition 2024
Australian Copyright 2024   ISBN 978 1 038 92171 0
New Zealand Copyright 2024

MIX
Paper | Supporting
responsible forestry
FSC® C001695
www.fsc.org

Published by
Harlequin Mills & Boon
An imprint of Harlequin Enterprises (Australia) Pty Limited
(ABN 47 001 180 918), a subsidiary of HarperCollins
Publishers Australia Pty Limited
(ABN 36 009 913 517)
Level 19, 201 Elizabeth Street
SYDNEY NSW 2000 AUSTRALIA

Cover art used by arrangement with Harlequin Books S.A.. All rights reserved.

Printed and bound in Australia by McPherson's Printing Group

Colton's Secret Past

Kacy Cross

MILLS & BOON

Kacy Cross writes romance novels starring swoonworthy heroes and smart heroines. She lives in Texas, where she's seen bobcats and beavers near her house but sadly not one cowboy. She's raising two mini-ninjas alongside the love of her life, who cooks while she writes, which is her definition of a true hero. Come for the romance, stay for the happily-ever-after. She promises her books "will make you laugh, cry and swoon—cross my heart."

Dear Reader,

Welcome back to Owl Creek! I'm so happy to be bringing you Hannah's story. This story is full of my favourite things: a precocious little girl who is five going on twenty-five, a secret identity, twins switching places, a second chance with a twist and all the Colton family dynamics we've grown to love.

Let me tell you a secret, though. I thought I was never going to finish this book! These people would not stop telling me their stories. Hannah and Archer have so much sizzling chemistry that I hated to make them stop talking so I could end a chapter. Throw in all their baggage, and we had a lot to work through to get to that happily-ever-after. Plus Hannah is a mom of a little girl and I miss my own kids being that age, so I spent a lot of time reliving some of those precious and classic childhood moments whenever Lucy appeared on the page.

(Yes, the part about Lucy not letting anyone skip pages during story time is torn straight from my own experience with two kids who are too smart for me.)

Oh, and there's lots of suspense, as always. No one is sure who to trust, and I had a lot of fun with that too. Thank you for picking up this book and gifting me with some of your time. In exchange, I hope you love diving into this story. Happy reading!

PS: I love to connect with readers. Find me at kacycross.com.

Kacy

Chapter 1

Hannah Colton had more brothers than she knew what to do with most days, but Wade had always been her favorite. That's the only reason she took his phone call despite juggling crepe batter, a hot griddle pan and a five-year-old who had moved to step three in her campaign to convince Hannah to get her a dog. Washington at Delaware hadn't been so determined to win as Lucy was when she wanted something.

This occasion was what God had invented speaker-phones for, if there was ever a doubt.

"Someone better be dying," she called in the direction of the phone and winced at her poor choice of words, considering Wade had been the one to call when their father had passed.

Not that any of them had mourned Robert Colton overly much. Maybe the loss of what could have been, but their father had made his choices long ago.

"Not this time." Her brother's voice floated from the counter as Hannah expertly flipped the crepe to let it cook on the other side for a precise one minute.

Most people only cooked crepes on one side when they were meant to be filled, but Hannah preferred the golden griddle-cooked color to be visible on both sides. It was this attention to detail that infiltrated all her cooking techniques over the years as she'd made her mark catering bigger and bigger events.

"Uncle Wade," Lucy broke in. "Tell Mama about the puppy you saw at Aunt Ruby and Uncle Sebastian's place."

Great. So Wade had been discussing the Great Dog Campaign with her daughter again. "Wade. What is the one thing I asked you not to talk about with Lucy?"

"Hey, Goose," Wade called to Lucy, ignoring Hannah's question. "Did you draw me another picture at school?"

"Oh, I forgot! I have it," Lucy announced and dashed from the room to presumably scare up the artwork in question.

"That was an inspired way to get her out of the room," Hannah told her brother wryly. "I hope it wasn't so you could start in on me about getting Lucy a dog. How much did she pay you?"

Wade laughed, and it did her heart good to hear the sound from someone who hadn't done much laughing until recently. Harlow had done that for her brother, and it thrilled Hannah to know that they'd found love again after giving up on each other in high school.

"It wouldn't kill you to get a dog. Betty Jane is a godsend, and you see how much Lucy has taken to her."

"Betty Jane is *your* dog," she stressed. She left out the part about why Wade had needed a therapy dog in the first place, though her brother's PTSD didn't seem to be nearly as touchy a subject as it had once been. "I'm up to my elbows in crepes for the Women Entrepreneurs of Wake County brunch. Did you have a reason for calling or did you just want to hear my lovely voice?"

"Uh, you called me?" he prompted. "Last night?"

Oh, dang. How could she have forgotten that already? The Great Dog Campaign was about to be renamed the Distract Mom Crusade, and she did not need any more of dog campaigns *or* distractions. "I did. Call you. I was just… I've got all these crepes. Hang on."

As quickly as she could, she plated up the remaining fifteen so she could chill them in advance of adding the mascarpone and strawberries. She had a little bit of time before she had to leave for the brunch at the civic center in Conners, where two of her employees, Judy and Todd, would meet her to help serve. As catering jobs went, this one was on the small side, but Hannah treated them all as if each client was her only one, plus she always managed the entire affair herself, regardless of the magnitude. That's why she had lots of repeat business and a steady stream of new customers via solid word of mouth.

Bon Appetit Catering was hers, and she'd built it from nothing. She wasn't just serving food at the Women Entrepreneurs of Wake County meeting—she was a standing member. She'd earned it.

She slid onto one of the stools lined up at the kitchen island where she did much of the prep work for her catering business, taking the phone off speaker in case little ears wandered into the room unexpectedly. Though it seemed as if Lucy had abandoned the kitchen in favor of her room, likely having fallen into a game or elaborate Barbie soap opera that was far more important than the picture she'd gone in search of.

"Okay," she said. "Hear me out."

"I don't like the direction this is headed," Wade groused, his voice shifting as if he'd found a spot to perch as well.

"What? I am a paragon of virtue and good sense." *Now* she was. Six years ago, no. But she'd done everything she could since then to atone for the unfortunate screw-up named Owen Mackenzie. "I would never bring up something that warrants the suspicion in your voice."

"You'd have to actually spell it out for me to hear it, Hannah Banana," Wade told her with a long-suffering sigh.

Fine. Yes. She needed to come out with her idea, but this was a delicate subject requiring careful wording. Especially if she hoped to convince her family, which was why she'd started with Wade. If she could sell him on it, he'd run interference with everyone else.

"Okay, so here it goes. I'm going to investigate Markus Acker."

"No. You are not." Wade's voice had taken on a hard edge that she imagined had made many a marine sweat during his time in the service. "End of subject."

"Un-end of subject," she countered, rolling her hand to mime lifting the imaginary restriction he'd just placed on the topic. "I need to do my part. Aunt Jessie is mixed up in this church that's really nothing more than a cult—"

"That's why you're not investigating him. He's a criminal. We know that much, but the extent of his crimes... We are not finding out what he's capable of with you as bait. Not happening."

Hannah sighed. So Wade could talk about bringing down Markus Acker but she couldn't? "This is my turn to help. None of the rest of you are caterers. I can easily figure out a way to cater an event for the church and use that as my foot in the door to do some additional investigation into the hold he has over Aunt Jessie."

This was necessary. Critical. Not only did she have a no-brainer excuse to finagle her way onto the Ever After premises, she owed her family for disappointing them. First, she'd married Owen, then she'd failed by not figuring out how to keep him around, at least for Lucy's sake. Sure, it wasn't technically her fault that Owen had turned out to be a low-life scum—her brothers' term, not hers, though she did find it fitting a lot of days.

Okay, maybe sometimes she thought it was *partially* her fault and that was her business. After all, she'd picked him. If she didn't carry that blame, who did?

No one else blamed her. She knew that. Rationally, anyway. Still, it felt like she had some atoning to do, and this was her shot. Wade could step aside.

"I cannot repeat this enough, Hannah," Wade said sternly. "Stay away from the church, don't try to contact Jessie, and for crying out loud, please do not walk up and introduce yourself to Markus Acker. If not for yourself, consider Lucy. She only has you."

"I know that," she countered, her mouth flattening as she internalized his point.

Did she really have the luxury of taking risks? No. If she had someone to help carry the load, then maybe, but that was a daydream she had no business harboring. Single mother forever or at least until Lucy went to college. That was her vow, and she was sticking to it.

But how big of a risk was it to cater an event and keep her eyes open?

"Han, promise me," her brother insisted.

"I promise," she intoned and crossed her fingers. "I won't contact Jessie and I won't accost Markus Acker in the middle of the street next time he jogs by."

"Mean it," he said gruffly, and she made a face at him even though he couldn't see her. Thankfully, Wade didn't notice that she'd left out staying away from the church, and she wasn't about to bring it up.

"I'm getting another call," she lied and then nearly yelped when her phone beeped to signal another call.

Maybe she should buy a lottery ticket since she seemed to be able to predict the future.

"I'll talk to you later, then. Tell Lucy Goosey I said to come over and play with Betty Jane."

She hung up without honoring that subject with a reply and switched to the other call from an unrecognized number, answering automatically because she'd already committed to it after mentioning the call to Wade. Normally she'd let an unrecognized number go to voicemail since it was usually someone wanting a quote for a catering job, which required a dedicated chunk of time to get all the details. She'd just deal with it real time as her penance.

"Hello?"

"Is this Hannah Colton?" the unfamiliar female voice asked. "Formerly Hannah Mackenzie?"

Something flashed across the back of her neck, heating it. She hadn't gone by that name in over four years. Not since Owen had hightailed it out of Owl Creek and probably Idaho as a whole, not that he'd bothered to tell her a blessed thing about his plans or final destination.

"Can I help you?" she countered instead of confirming the answer to the woman's question, because after all, Mackenzie was still Lucy's last name and until she knew exactly what the nature of this inquiry was, she would wait to share any information.

"I'm looking for Hannah Colton who was married to Owen Mackenzie. He's been in a terrible accident."

Hannah drove toward Conners, but not wearing her caterer's uniform, the smart white coat with the entwined *B* and *A* of her logo embroidered on the left breast. Instead, she'd scrambled to get Marcia to cover for her at the last minute at the brunch, dropped Lucy at her mother's house—which fortunately had always been in the cards due to the impending job—and then wandered around in a daze trying to remember how to breathe, let alone the four hundred things she still needed to get done. Because thanks to Owen, she was still a single mom.

Owen Mackenzie. A name from the past that she wished a lot of days would stay there. But she saw him every time she looked at Lucy. Lucy's features favored her mother's, but she had light brown hair, halfway in between Hannah's blond and Owen's dark brown. And she definitely had her father's eyes with her mother's green irises.

What she couldn't figure out was why the hospital had called her.

She and Owen hadn't spoken in years. If he had her phone number, it was news to her because he'd certainly never hit the call button even one time. Had he asked the hospital to contact her?

Okay, there were two things she couldn't figure out— why they'd called her *and* why she'd agreed to go see him in the hospital. She should have hung up and not thought a moment more about him. That's what he'd done to them.

But the lady who'd called indicated that there were complications from the accident and that it would be very beneficial for Owen to see her in person. In Conners. A stone's throw from Owl Creek, where Hannah and Lucy had been living the whole time without one single iota of contact from her ex-husband.

Curiosity, maybe, could be the driving factor here. Was he sorry he'd left them? It would be sweet to hear that. In fact, she had a serious fantasy about that exact thing. The second he saw her standing there, he'd fall to his knees, apologies pouring from his mouth profusely.

Of course, he had apparently been hurt in the accident.

There wouldn't be a lot of falling to his knees, unless he rolled out of the hospital bed inadvertently. Which she would take. She wasn't picky.

Hannah laughed at herself. Yes, she was picky. She wanted a full-bore apology, first to her, then to Lucy second. Then she wanted to spit in his face and turn on her heel to walk out the door so he could see what it felt like to have someone he'd depended on show him their back.

She drove as slowly as possible, telling herself it was due to the heavy snowdrifts on the sides of the plowed highway, but it was really to give herself time to settle. It worked, to a degree.

But when she got to the hospital, nerves took over. It would be a miracle if she didn't throw up at his feet, assuming he was ambulatory. She didn't actually know what condition she'd find Owen in. The lady on the phone had been so vague, continually repeating that the doctor wanted to talk to her in person.

After parking and finding her way to the correct floor, she crept down the hall to the room the receptionist had indicated, feeling like she'd stumbled into another world. One with a hushed sense of doom and urgency. She didn't care for the atmosphere at all.

A plate with number 147 next to a whiteboard was affixed to the wall. Someone had scribbled Owen Mackenzie on the white part with a marker.

The door was open. She forced herself to walk through it, her gaze automatically drawn to the figure in the bed.

Owen. Her fingers flew to her mouth.

His eyes were closed and he had a square bandage near his temple. There was so much white—his gown, the sheet, the bed, the walls. And machines. With beeping.

She scarcely recognized the way her heart was beating, this erratic thump that couldn't find a rhythm.

And then he opened his eyes and fixed them on her. She smiled automatically because *oh my God*, it was Owen. Ashen-faced and obviously in pain, but she had never forgotten that particular shade of brown framed by his lashes, like an espresso with just the right amount of milk to turn it a molten chocolate color.

His hair was longer, spread along his neck, and he should have shaved two weeks ago, but the scruff along his jaw had just enough edge to it to be slightly sexy. No. Not sexy. She slammed her eyes shut and drew in a shaky breath.

"Hello?" he rasped.

"Hi, Owen," she murmured and that was it. The extent of her brain's ability to form words. Her throat's ability to make sounds.

After all this time, after all the scenarios she'd envisioned, the tongue-lashing she'd give him if they were ever in the same room together again—that was all she could come up with? Lame.

"Are you one of the nurses?" he asked, blinking slowly. "Why aren't you wearing scrubs?"

Raising a brow, she eyed him. "It's me, Owen. Hannah. I know I've put on a few pounds, but come on."

Only five! Maybe seven, tops. Plus her hair was the same, since she hadn't changed styles in… Good grief. Had it really been four years that she'd been getting this exact same cut?

"Are we related? The hospital said they were trying to track down my family."

Confused, she cocked her head. "You're kidding, right? We're not related, not anymore, though I don't know that being married is actually the same as being related, come to think of it."

And now he had her babbling, which felt like par for the course. She'd been knocked sideways since the phone call back at home, and being here in this room with Owen hadn't fixed that any.

She had to get it together. This was her chance to make her fondest wish come true—Owen on his knees, begging her forgiveness, blathering about how sorry he was he'd left her. How much he missed her. How big of a mistake he'd made.

Then and only then could she hold her head up high and walk away. Forget this man and the way he'd made her question her judgment every hour of every day, which was not a great parenting skill, by the way.

She'd get that confession out of him or die trying. She opened her mouth.

"Ms. Colton, I presume?" Hannah glanced at the door where a white-coated older gentleman stood with an iPad. "I'm Doctor Farris. Mr. Mackenzie is unfortunately suffering from amnesia. We had hoped that seeing you might jog something loose, but based on what I just heard, that doesn't seem to have happened."

"Amnesia." The concept bounced around in Hannah's head, searching for a place to land, but she couldn't quite connect all the dots. "You mean he lost his memory? That's a real thing? I thought Hollywood made up that condition for dramatic purposes."

"Oh, no, it's very real." Dr. Farris smiled kindly. "It's also not very well understood or studied so a lot of times, we're a little unsure on how to treat it. Conventional wisdom says to give it time, and eventually everything will come back to him."

"Sorry... Hannah?" Owen called, his gaze searching hers as if desperately trying to recall even a sliver of a memory that included her. "I wish I remembered you, but I don't. I don't remember who I am either. Can you tell me?"

Oh, she could. Absolutely. She'd had four years and change to stew about how this man had treated her. He deserved to hear every last horrible thing he'd done to her. Every last tear she'd shed.

But instead, she sat down heavily in one of the bedside chairs and blurted out, "You're the only man I've ever loved."

Chapter 2

The woman in Archer's hospital room was the exact opposite of one he'd have paired with his brother, which was yet another puzzle to solve. But apparently his research had been correct. Owen had somehow hooked up with this hot blonde in a sizzling pink dress and then lost her, like an idiot.

Of course, everything Owen had done in his life had been stupid. Including getting himself killed for a yet-to-be-determined reason by an unknown assailant, though Archer's money was on Big Mike Rossi or someone in his criminal organization. Who would have thought a quiet investigation into the matter would have landed Archer in the hospital with everyone—including Hannah Colton, aka the woman he'd been looking for—mistaking him for his twin brother?

Not Archer. This kind of lucky break didn't often fall in his lap, but he'd jumped on it, instantly coming up with the idea to fake amnesia as a plausible explanation for why he couldn't remember basic things about Owen's life.

It was working out fantastically so far. Other than the stitches and bruised ribs of course.

"We were in love once?" he asked Hannah, infusing his voice with enough confusion to choke a horse, but he had a part to play here.

Looked like that summer at theater camp would be coming in handy after all.

"I can say yes, from my side at least," she said as the doctor's phone beeped and he rushed off with a muttered apology. "But I can't honestly tell you what you felt for me. I came here hoping you'd tell me."

Archer nearly rolled his eyes at that. Figured Owen would screw up even the simplest of relationship staples like telling his wife that he loved her. No wonder she'd left him.

"I'd like to remember being in love with you," he said, which came out a little huskier than he'd have liked given the circumstances.

He had no call to be attracted to his brother's ex-wife, but geez. He hadn't expected her to be so beautiful. Or so… invested.

That was enough for him to put the brakes on anything approaching flirtation. He had a murder to solve, and getting cozy with Hannah Colton, his prime source of information, didn't go down well, especially not when she thought he was Owen. Which was not his original plan, but when he'd woken up earlier, everyone addressed him as Owen, probably because he'd had all his brother's identification in his car, though he wasn't certain why no one had found his real ID. All he was doing was rolling with it.

Hannah peered at him curiously. "You really don't remember anything?"

Shaking his head, he furrowed a brow and adopted the vacant look that Owen used to get when they were kids and he had to think really hard about something. "I don't even know why I was driving around Idaho. They told me I live in Las Vegas."

How was that for irony? Owen had settled in the same city where Archer lived, but they'd never come across each other, even though his brother had obviously dipped his toe in even bigger criminal organizations than before. He hadn't been able to uncover too much before his superiors at LVMPD got wind that one of their back office guys was trying to solve a case on his own.

Then one of his buddies on beat patrol had tipped off Archer that he'd attracted the attention of some very unsavory people high up in Big Mike's organization with his poking around, so one leave of absence later, here he was in Owl Creek. As Owen. It might end up being a great cover for a few days.

"I don't know either," Hannah said and crossed her arms, framing the vee of her blouse, which revealed a lovely slice of cleavage. "We haven't spoken in over four years. Since you vanished."

Archer didn't have a lot of experience interrogating witnesses, but he did have an eye for details and for synthesizing large amounts of data into information. Hannah wasn't comfortable. She sat on the edge of her chair and one foot kept shifting restlessly, as if she couldn't quite figure out where to put it. Her gaze never left him, but she'd seemingly spent the entire time they'd been talking cataloguing things about his appearance, her eyes shifting to his bandage, to his shoulders slightly visible above the sheet.

Did that mean she was telling the truth and hadn't seen Owen recently? He honestly hadn't known what to expect after finding Hannah's address in Owen's desk drawer at his house, but he wouldn't have been surprised if she had been involved in whatever shady dealings Owen had gotten mixed up in. Archer's investigation thus far had turned up a handful of Owen's associations with women, all of whom had their own rap sheets.

Except this one. She was a data anomaly, and anomalies bothered him. Ironing out wrinkles in data—that he enjoyed.

"I'm sorry for vanishing," he told her as sincerely as

possible, hoping if he took the high road, she'd be a little more open with him.

Instead, she stared at him, agape. "Did you just apologize? Now I know you hit your head."

Archer nearly sighed. Owen wasn't much of an apologizer, no, or at least he hadn't been ten years ago, the last time he'd actually spoken to his twin. Full speed ahead, take no prisoners, consequences—who cares? These were concepts that resonated with Owen Mackenzie, not apologizing.

"In addition to losing my memory of people and events, I seem to have forgotten who I am too," he explained carefully. "This is me stripped down, I guess. No telling what I might do next. Maybe actually strip."

The joke fell flat as Hannah eyed him, her beautiful face a mask of uncertainty and suspicion. Well, yeah. He wasn't sure that was a real symptom of amnesia either, but it stood to reason that someone who had memory loss might also forget why they'd acted a certain way. Or what their motivation had been for being a jerkwad to this woman.

So maybe he could right a few wrongs here on behalf of Owen. Archer cleaning up Owen's messes had been nearly a full-time job for a couple of decades, before he'd gotten sick of it and cut all ties. This was one last hurrah that Archer had only agreed to because their mother had wept all over his shoulder, begging him to find his brother's murderer.

He would have done a lot for his mother in the first place, but then he'd discovered that not only was Owen dead, millions of Big Mike's money was missing.

No one had said he couldn't nose around *and* make Hannah feel better about whatever had gone down between her and Owen. She seemed so…genuinely wounded. As if she'd really cared about him. It was a puzzle why she'd fallen for a slick con man like his brother, and maybe she was faking it, but he didn't think so.

"Tell me what happened between us," he insisted gently, catching her gaze to infuse the request with some warmth, so she would know he meant it.

"We got married and you bailed," she said flatly. "As soon as you could, pretty much. I always assumed you had another woman on the side that you ended up liking better than me, but since you never bothered to explain, I never knew for sure."

The number of land mines strewn throughout her statements multiplied as he registered the hurt buried in her green eyes. "I can't imagine that being the case. More likely, I was scared. How did we meet?"

"Through mutual friends. George Kennedy. He was dating my friend from high school, Tory Baker. You surely haven't forgotten George?" she prodded. "You guys were so tight. I think you spent more time at his place than you did at your own."

Probably because Owen didn't actually have a place of his own, but the time frame in question had come after Archer stopped answering his brother's calls. They'd always ended the same way, with a plea for money or for Archer to fix whatever jam Owen had gotten himself into. Since Archer had busted his butt to get a scholarship to UC Davis so he could move far away from the tiny Oregon town he'd grown up in, it was a great opportunity for a clean slate.

"I don't remember George," he said, sure this bit was going to get tired eventually.

"This is so strange," Hannah confessed, her brow furrowed as she studied him like a bug under a microscope. "You're not anything like you used to be."

"How did I used to be?"

She bit her lip. "I don't know. Larger than life. You were such a talker. Free with the compliments, that was for sure. You turned my head in an instant that night we met."

Yeah, that gelled. Owen had always been a fast talker, especially when in the middle of a grift. What had he been trying to scam Hannah out of? Her pants, most likely.

He kept that to himself and gave her a gentle smile, mostly because the situation seemed to call for it. "I am in a hospital bed. Maybe I can get some of my largeness back after I'm not so banged up."

"Oh, my goodness, I am so sorry!" Hannah's hand flew to her mouth, and she poured out of that chair faster than warm syrup on pancakes to hover at his side, her gaze tracking along his face with concern. "Where does it hurt? What can I do?"

She stopped just short of laying a hand along his jaw with what he imagined would be a great deal of tenderness. She had that look about her as if she'd be a fabulous Florence Nightingale for any guy who couldn't fend for himself.

Technically he fell in that category, unfortunately. The amnesia was fake, but the injuries were not, and he did feel a bit woozy due to banging his head in the crash. The doc had mentioned something about broken ribs too, which explained why he couldn't quite catch his breath.

But Hannah might have something to do with that too.

Man, up close and personal, she definitely squeezed a guy's lungs. The scent of vanilla and sunshine drifted over him with warmth more suited for another kind of activity entirely. "I'm pretty happy with you just being here."

Geez, what was wrong with him? Flirting with his brother's ex, who was a suspect besides? Maybe he'd hit his head harder than he'd thought.

She smiled then and he forgot how breathing actually

worked as her green eyes lit up with some sort of inner glow that he suddenly couldn't look away from.

"I thought about not coming," she told him and opted to perch gingerly on the side of the bed, her hip not quite touching his, but close enough that he could feel her heat through the thin hospital sheet and even thinner gown. "But in the end, I couldn't stay away. I needed to see you again, if for nothing more than closure."

"That would be a shame," he murmured. He wasn't done with her at all. And not for the investigative reasons he should be worried about. "Tell me more about you. What are you doing with yourself now? With your life?"

"I run a catering company. I started small, but I've really grown and now have ten employees, four full-time," she stated proudly.

"Wow, that's impressive."

He meant it too. Most small businesses could count themselves lucky if they ever had the dough to hire even one or two full-time employees.

Unless, of course, they were helping Owen launder dirty money through their business. Just because Hannah hadn't physically laid eyes on his brother in several years—assuming she was telling the truth about that—didn't mean she wasn't involved in the shady dealings that had gotten her ex killed.

Money made a lot of people do things they normally wouldn't and there was a lot of Big Mike's missing. He had his suspicions that Owen had been the one to make it vanish, and at the moment, Hannah Colton sat right at the top of his list for the person most likely to know where the dirty money was.

Being laid-up in this hospital bed sucked, but it did provide some unique advantages. Such as a dedicated audience with the woman who might hold all the answers he needed to solve the puzzle of what had happened to Owen. And maybe unravel a few other mysteries as well, like what Hannah's touch would feel like on his face.

"I've done okay with the money you left behind," she said. "I didn't want to use it, but I didn't have anything else, and you'd been doing so well with your investment banking company, I figured I could consider it a loan. But then you never contacted me again, so I eventually reinvested the principal. If you'll give me your banking details, I can have the money wired to you by tomorrow."

Delivered with a steel spine and a defiant toss of her head. She hadn't mentioned the sum of money Owen had given her, but people didn't wire small amounts due to the fees. They just Zelled it or whatever. The fact that she could transfer several thousand dollars at the drop of a hat—and wanted him to know she could—meant something, but what, he couldn't tell yet.

"I own an investment banking company?" he prodded, figuring that might be the best place to start digging.

He bit his tongue on the outright lie Owen had fed her.

"Mackenzie Holdings," she reminded him. "The money you left—it showed up in our joint account, and when I asked you about it, you said you were liquidating some assets, so you might have sold the company. I'm not sure. You disappeared the next day, so I never had a chance to ask."

Owen must have been laundering money even back then. If his dealings with this criminal organization went back that far, it changed things. How, he wasn't sure yet. There would be traces. Patterns. Data. Once he started pulling on it, he'd unravel it fast. Just as soon as Hannah filled in a few more blanks.

But before he could press for details on this mysterious money that had appeared, a uniformed officer wearing a heavy overcoat in deference to the frigid February temperatures knocked on the doorframe.

"Mr. Mackenzie, do you have a moment?"

"Of course," he called, as Hannah shifted to view the newcomer.

Not just an officer. The Wake County Sheriff Archer realized when the man stepped forward to hold out his hand.

"Sheriff Clemmons, Mr. Mackenzie. I'm investigating your accident, and I'm afraid I have some news that might be difficult to hear. It appears someone tampered with your brake lines."

"What? What are you talking about?" Archer did his best to feign shock and dismay, while a grim certainty settled in his gut.

He'd felt the brakes growing squishy, but he'd talked himself out of the slight niggle of concern since he'd traveled almost the entire way from Las Vegas to Owl Creek without incident. Surely whatever was going on with the brakes had been a product of his overactive imagination, which he'd fed consistently on the drive, hashing through the evidence he'd gleaned thus far on the organization Owen had gotten tangled up with.

"Slow leak," the sheriff confirmed. "It's too clean of a cut in the line to be anything other than deliberate and done in such a way that you wouldn't notice the leak right away. A pro job in my opinion. Did you get any work done on the car before you drove up from Vegas?"

An oil change. In preparation for the trip. Man, if Big Mike Rossi had his fingers that deep into the cracks of Vegas... Not that it would take much to pay off the service technician to do the job.

Thankfully, Archer had the perfect excuse—amnesia— and could reasonably deny it. Besides, if he showed all his cards, the sheriff would start asking questions. Big Mike would hear about it and more bad things would happen.

Archer's skin grew a little clammy. If he hadn't left Vegas, would he have been the victim of another, more fatal accident? Had one of Big Mike's goons followed him to Owl Creek?

The sheriff needed to stand down, that much was for sure.

"No." He shook his head slowly as if thinking about it. "I don't think so. But I don't actually remember. I bumped my head and lost a lot of what used to be up here."

He pointed to his temple, and the sheriff nodded understandingly. "I'll be in touch. Are you staying around for a while?"

"At least until they release me," he acknowledged with a smile that he extended to Hannah. "Maybe longer than that."

Pending how things turned out with his brother's ex-wife. If she wasn't involved in Owen's money-laundering scheme, he might be in the market for a little downtime with her. Just for a few days while he kept his cover in place. He could fix the mess Owen had made of her heart and break things off cleanly. Let her have her closure while tying up all these loose ends. Two birds, one stone.

That's when his blood iced over. It didn't matter if she was involved or not. Either way, he'd just painted a big target on her back by coming here. If Big Mike didn't know of her existence before, he would soon.

Archer might have put Hannah in grave danger over his obsessive need to solve the slew of problems dropped in his lap.

Chapter 3

The doctor returned shortly after the sheriff left, giving Hannah no time to ask Owen what in the world was going on. Someone had cut his brake line? Did that mean it wasn't an accident?

A slight throb started up behind her left eye, and if she was really lucky, it would be a full-blown migraine by dinnertime. Of course she'd left her prescription medication at home in her haste to leave for Conners. The fun of this day might never end.

"Oh, good, you're still here," the doctor said to her as he tapped his iPad. "Do you have a moment to speak in the hall?"

With a glance at Owen, who subtly nodded, she stood and followed the doctor from the room. He didn't actually pause right outside the door, opting to stroll to the nurse's desk where presumably they would have a bit more privacy.

From whom, she wasn't sure. Did he not want Owen to overhear their conversation?

"Mrs. Mackenzie, I app—"

"It's Colton," she interrupted, hating to be contrary, but she hadn't gone by that name in years and didn't plan to start. She didn't even know what she was doing here. "Sorry. Owen and I are divorced. I'm not sure why someone contacted me of all people. Did Owen have my number in his phone?"

The doctor's mouth pressed into a thin line as a couple of nurses zipped by at a steady clip. "No, it wasn't that simple. He didn't have an emergency contact on record. In cases like this, we take whatever measures we can to find someone. We asked a few of our insurance people to try to find anyone from Mr. Mackenzie's life to notify of his accident. I apologize for the intrusion. I got bad information that you were currently married to him. Nevertheless, it's critical that Owen have some familiar things or people around to help him regain his memory. Amnesia is a terribly misunderstood condition, and we don't have a lot of data on how to reverse it."

"It is reversible, though?"

The doctor rocked back on his heels as he contemplated her. "I do believe Mr. Mackenzie's amnesia is reversible, yes."

So he'd go back to the way he'd been before. That would be...*awful*. Immediately, guilt panged her chest.

What was wrong with her wishing Owen would stay this version of himself? He was a literal shell of the vibrant, colossally confident man she'd met once upon a time. Early-Twenties Hannah had loved his boldness. He'd marched right up to her and told her he was going to marry her the moment he laid eyes on her for the first time. She'd been so swept off her feet by him.

And then she'd spent the last four-plus years getting back on them.

Slick men with practiced lines didn't work for Late-Twenties Hannah. For Single Mom Hannah. For Business Owner Hannah.

That was a sobering reminder. *No* man worked for her

far better than any specific kind of man, even this brand-new Owen who had the same handsome face but nothing else that even remotely resembled the man she'd married. No matter how intriguing it was to think about getting to know this version of Owen a little better.

But then the doctor continued. "Regaining his memories is going to take time, though. And it would be helpful if he's exposed to things that might jog his memories, like you. I realize it's a bit of a stretch to ask you to spend time with him, given that you're divorced. It's a lot more difficult of a situation than I'd anticipated."

"He doesn't have any other family?"

The doctor gave her a look that she interpreted as—*if anyone would know, wouldn't it be his ex-wife?* Maybe in a lot of marriages, but not hers. He'd never mentioned any family to her, and she'd always assumed he'd been raised by a single mother who had passed. Ashamed all at once that she'd never pressed him on it, she lifted a hand to her burning cheek.

What must Doctor Farris think of her for not knowing basic things about her ex-husband?

"The people we put on finding a contact are pretty thorough since they're usually trying to track down people who have outstanding balances. They couldn't find any trace of relations other than you," he confirmed.

Her heart kind of caved in a little at that. He didn't have anyone. Except her. And he really didn't even have her. How sad was that?

Granted, he'd probably brought his solitary state on himself. He'd alienated a woman who'd loved him and thought he'd hung the moon. Abandoned his own daughter, without so much as a phone call on her birthday, ever. If he could even cite her birthday, she'd stand on her head.

He had no one because he cared about no one.

Stay firm. No sympathy.

She'd come for an exorcism, not a reconciliation. How else could she verify that she was well and truly over him than to face him one final time? Only, she hadn't expected to find herself dropped into an upside-down world where Owen didn't even *remember* her.

Her stupid heart pinged again. If she could get him to remember her, he might regain his other memories. In time. But that would mean she'd have to come back. Probably more than once. She couldn't hop in her car and drive away forever, tossing the man in her rearview with her soul free as a bird.

"Maybe if I talk to him some more, I can help him remember other family," she suggested, knowing in her heart it wouldn't be likely. Insurance people wouldn't miss something like a whole family, but somehow manage to dig up the contact information for a woman he'd divorced over four years ago.

But she had to try. Then she'd be off the hook.

"That would be a good place to start," the doctor said with a kind smile that reached his eyes behind wire-rimmed glasses. "I hope you realize I just want what's best for my patient. That's all."

She nodded. At the moment, that was her. She was the best thing for Owen.

After a deep cleansing breath that did not work to calm the slosh of emotions spilling over her edges, she marched back to Owen's room, determined to make some progress.

When he caught sight of her coming through the door, his lips tipped up in a tentative smile that took out the backs of her knees unexpectedly.

No. Bad Hannah. No reacting to the vulnerable, hot-as-sin man in the bed.

"They said you don't remember any family," she said, infusing her tone with the same no-nonsense steel she used to make sure Lucy knew she wasn't playing around. "When we got married, you said you were on your own. I thought that meant your parents were both gone. Maybe you remember how they died?"

Owen cocked his head, watching her with an expression she couldn't read. "You never met my parents?"

"Does that mean you remember them?" she prodded hopefully, dragging the chair closer to the bed where she could talk to him without getting too close.

"No, it means I'm fascinated to learn about our relationship, and I guess I just always thought that married people hung out with each other's parents, like at Christmas and such."

That was a promising lead if she'd ever heard one. "You have memories of Christmas with a family?"

He frowned, his expression going slightly vague as if struggling to make his brain work. "It's more of a general idea that Christmas is about spending time with people who matter. I don't know if I've ever done that. What did we do at holidays?"

"You worked," she reminded him bluntly. "We were only together for two Christmases, and you spent the entire day on the phone the second one."

He'd complained about Lucy crying for most of it, but she'd been a baby. Babies cried. It had always been baffling to her how hostile Owen had seemed about his own daughter. That was probably at least half of the reason she hadn't mentioned Lucy yet.

What if his daughter brought back all his memories and

he got that look of disgust on his face like in those days after she'd been born? Worse, what if he *didn't* remember her?

"I'm sorry," he said softly. "I have a feeling I have a lot to make up for when it comes to you."

He didn't know the half of it. "You don't remember our marriage at all? Not the wedding at the courthouse? Not living in your swanky condo?"

Owen had insisted that she move into his place in Conners, away from her large family. They'd never gotten along well, which frankly should have been a sign.

"I wish I did remember."

His brown eyes bored into hers, probing, as if he could find all the answers he sought right there inside her and that would be enough for him. She would be enough.

For half a second, she wanted to let him. Invite him in and rekindle the fierceness between them. Things had been so good at first. She'd been so blinded by everything about him that she'd let him become her entire world. To her detriment.

She shook off the odd connection that had sprung up as she stood there in Owen's hospital room. She wasn't twenty any longer. A man would never be her entire world again. About the only thing she had to thank this one for was Lucy and the seed money she'd used to start her catering business, which she would gladly pay back, but had considered due compensation for not insisting on alimony or child support.

Lucy wasn't Owen's in any way except as a sperm donor.

What if Owen remembered her and wanted to be a part of her life? An ice pick stabbed at her eyes from the vicinity of her brain, a sure sign that she'd be spending the rest of the day in a dark room.

She wasn't the same woman any longer and Owen certainly wasn't the same man. He'd have zero shot at wooing her the way he had the first time around.

But *guh*, he'd developed a whole new slew of ways to get her attention, from the deepness in his gaze to the subtle differences in his hair and scrubby beard. Slick Owen had been super gorgeous, sure, but Quiet Owen pinged her in a place deep inside that she was having trouble getting to settle down.

"Try," she commanded him. "Think really hard about your investment banking company. You had an office on State Street, in the Grant building. It was fancy, but kind of sterile if you want my honest opinion. I visited you there a couple of times. Once we had a picnic in the park across from your office. Surely you remember that day."

It was the day he'd asked her to marry him.

Owen shook his head, a tinge of sadness pulling at his expression. "I'm sorry. There's just nothing. I can remember things like I'm supposed to brush my teeth after I eat but there's just blackness where people should be."

What in the world would make her think that pushing him would shake loose a flood of locked-up memories? She'd have to google some information about how to help an amnesia victim recover.

"I'm sorry too," she told him honestly and moved to the bed after all, drawn by the sheer unhappiness she sensed from him.

Probably he deserved to be miserable, but she just didn't have it in her to be the source of it. Sure, it would be nice to hear him say that he'd regretted leaving her every minute of every day, but he'd have to remember her to figure that out, and the odds were slim that would happen today.

He watched her settle, the bandage on his temple a constant reminder that he'd been hurt. And she'd been interrogating him like he'd committed some kind of crime.

"How do you feel?" she asked softly.

"Like I've been hit by a bus," he confessed readily. "I bruised my ribs and I get a little woozy when I stand up, so I've been ordered to stay in bed for twenty-four hours. Then they'll do another evaluation."

He didn't seem too upset about that part of his situation, which was a touch frightening—that a vibrant man like Owen would consent to lying in a hospital bed like an invalid. It would be more in his character to be ripping out the IV needle and shoving aside the sheet with the proclamation that he was fine—everyone quit treating him like he was ninety.

"Hannah?" He blinked up at her. "I'm really glad you're here. It couldn't have been easy to get in the car, knowing you'd be seeing me again after the way I treated you."

Her eyes went wide and she had to blink a bunch to fix the sudden dryness. That was practically an apology and an expression of regrct all in one. The ice pick behind her eyes vanished in an instant. "You really don't remember the way you used to act, do you?"

Old Owen didn't apologize. For anything. He certainly didn't acknowledge that there was anything to apologize for.

"I don't, no. But I have a feeling I was a piece of work. Maybe this is my chance to change that."

Then he did the worst thing he possibly could have. He reached out and covered her hand with his. It was the most innocuous kind of contact possible. Two people touching skin. No big deal.

It was a big deal. And it was far from harmless the way her entire body reacted, heating in an instant.

That was familiar. But also completely different because she recognized it as something separate from her feelings for him. That she *could* separate the two. Being attracted to someone didn't have to engage her heart—in fact, it was far better if it didn't. Twenty-year-old Hannah hadn't possessed that kind of insight. And she still hadn't forgiven Owen for teaching her the difference.

"I have to go," she choked out and nearly fell off the bed in her haste to remove herself from the source of her consternation.

She'd have to move to Mars at this point to accomplish that.

His dark eyes tracked her with a solemnness she had to look away from. "Will you be back?"

Would she? "I don't know. This is just…a lot."

And then she fled before he could do something else to confuse her, intrigue her, light her up inside. All of the above, all at one time. It was overwhelming.

None of it dissipated with distance either. She could scarcely catch her breath, could barely feel the frigid steering wheel of her car beneath her gloveless hands after she threw herself into the front seat of the Honda she'd bought within a year of being in the black with her catering company.

This wasn't over. Far from it. But whether she'd make the journey back to the hospital remained to be seen. She had a business. A daughter. People other than herself who counted on her.

But at the end of the day, Owen needed her too, and she was having a very hard time figuring out why that felt so good. And how to stop it.

Chapter 4

Hannah pulled up to the front of the dark gray clapboard on the lake, a wide swath of property spread out on each side that sloped down toward the water. There was plenty of room for multiple vehicles in the crushed stone half-circle driveway that often hosted at least one guest's car, as it did today.

It was Ruby's. Hannah's sister had recently given birth to her first child, a son named Sawyer, who'd just turned four months old. With the baby's arrival came a new SUV, the kind that could hold the additional kids likely in her future. It was no surprise to find Ruby here since she often dropped by with Jenny's first grandchild.

Lucy was still at that enthralled stage with the first baby she'd been around for any appreciable length of time. Honestly, it was a blessing she'd been after Hannah for a dog instead of a baby sister or brother.

For who knew what reason, that made her think about Owen. Again. Okay, she'd never stopped. It wasn't a crime, and no one had to know that she'd finally admitted to herself that she couldn't hate him like she'd hoped.

"Mama!"

Lucy dashed out of the open front door to throw herself at Hannah. Little girl essence engulfed her and she breathed deep, already missing the baby scent that had faded far too quickly.

She lifted Lucy into her arms, grateful that today wasn't the day she'd realize she couldn't pick her up any longer. "Hey, there. How's my girl?"

"Lu Lu, you can't unlock the door and run out," Jenny called, wiping her hands on a towel as she charged out after her granddaughter, stopping short when she saw that Hannah had Lucy in her arms. "Hi, hon. Did you get your business taken care of?"

"Yeah, I guess so," she mumbled, both glad she hadn't told her mother what she'd needed to drive to Conners for and sorry she didn't have a sounding board.

Jenny's opinion mattered to her, even after Hannah had grown into adulthood. A lot of her friends considered their parents old-fashioned and out of touch, but she'd never thought that way about Jenny, and besides, her mother had been dealt a pretty tough row to hoe when she'd learned— after he passed away—of her husband's secret affair with Aunt Jessie.

Hannah followed her mother inside the house, setting Lucy down in the foyer so she could greet Ruby, then steal the baby from her. There was no human on earth who could resist a sweet face that happily blew bubbles while being held. His Aunt Hannah cooed at him.

"You are the bestest boy ever, aren't you, my darling?" Hannah told the baby and rubbed noses with him. "Any time you want to come visit me and let your mama go out on the town with her handsome husband, you tell her."

Ruby raised a brow. "Sure about that? Because I would totally take you up on it."

"Name the day," Hannah shot back, meaning it. "I would be thrilled to have the baby all to myself. Grandma always horns in when we're over here."

Laughing, Jenny did exactly that, scooping the baby out of Hannah's arms. "Get one of your own."

"One is all I need," Hannah joked back, her throat inexplicably tight as she swung Lucy up into her empty arms, rocking her daughter back and forth, somehow staying on her feet despite the weight difference between her kid and Ruby's.

"Mama, I'm not a baby," Lucy insisted and squirmed free to run over to the TV, plopping down in the swivel chair in front of an episode of *Peppa Pig*, the one with Grampy Rabbit's hovercraft, which was her favorite.

The exchange wasn't out of the norm. Hannah had just been messing around, but the reminder that Lucy wasn't a baby any longer hit her extra hard today of all days, especially after seeing Owen. She'd buried the wound deep, but it had been sitting there festering for four long years, and their marriage wasn't the only thing he'd torn from her.

She'd always dreamed of having a big family like her own mother had. That possibility didn't exist any longer. And it was hard. *So* hard.

"What's wrong?" Ruby demanded, her attention on Hannah since she didn't have a baby in her face to occupy her at the moment.

Thanks, Mom. Hannah swallowed. "Nothing."

"Liar." Her older sister eyed her as if she were twenty years her senior instead of two. "You might as well spill it. You know you can't keep a secret."

That was true. The second she'd agreed to marry Owen, Ruby had been the first person she'd told. A plus sign on the pregnancy test? Ruby. Owen was acting strange and not looking her in the eye? Her sister had been the one she called.

"Because it's not a secret." She let out a long breath that sounded as long-suffering as she felt. She waved them both over to the kitchen where little ears couldn't hear and lowered her voice. "I saw Owen today."

"Owen!" Jenny and Ruby screeched at the same time.

"Shh," she hissed out and jerked her head at Lucy, who was still face first in the TV, laughing at something Peppa had done. "I mean it's not a secret from you guys."

"Start talking," Ruby said grimly as Jenny frowned and hugged the baby closer. "And you better not start out with *it's not what you think*."

What, was Ruby practicing her mind reading? "It's *not* what you think. He was in an accident. He has amnesia."

Both Ruby and Jenny glanced at each other, but it was Jenny who spoke this time. "That's pretty convenient, don't you think? He vanishes and shows back up, trying to worm his way into your good graces again. What better way to avoid having to explain himself or even apologize than to fake being injured?"

Ruby nodded, and the ice pick started up again behind Hannah's eyes. Dang it. Why had she brought this up again? Sighing, she massaged her temples, leaning on the granite countertop of the bar that separated the kitchen from the informal dining area.

"It's not like that. He's in the hospital in Conners. I spoke to the doctor and everything."

"That's where you went earlier," Jenny said with a sage nod. "I wondered why you looked like you'd seen a ghost when you left."

Because that's how she'd expected to feel when she laid eyes on Owen again. Instead, she'd glimpsed something far more affecting. "If he's faking amnesia to get off the hook, he's a much better actor than anyone working in Hollywood today. He's really injured too. He has a gash on his head with a bandage and everything. They're keeping him overnight for observation and maybe longer if the amnesia persists."

How had she shifted into a position where she was *defending* him? Because it felt like her defense too. As if she had to make sure everyone understood that she wasn't about to let him waltz back into her life without some really extenuating circumstances.

Wait, no. She wasn't letting him do anything with her *or* her life. No waltzing. No falling for his slick talk again.

"Not to put too fine a point on it, but why did they call *you*?" Ruby wanted to know. "Did you tell them he's a lowlife creep and to make sure he jumps in Blackbird Lake when he's released?"

"Of course not. He's hurt, Rube. Like really banged-up. Worse, someone did this to him deliberately!" she told them in a hushed voice. "The sheriff came and said someone cut the brake lines."

Jenny's hand flew to her mouth. "Oh, my Lord. You need to stay far away from him then if he did something to make someone angry enough to try to kill him. It sounds really dangerous."

Well, duh. Of course she'd thought of that. But he needed someone familiar to help break through whatever was blocking his memories.

The real question was why she cared.

"I'm fine, Mom. I know how to be careful."

"Do you know how to tell that man to get lost?" Ruby asked. "Because it sounds like you need to practice. A lot."

Boy, her mother and sister had a lot of opinions about what Hannah needed to do and not a lot of faith in her or her judgment, obviously. Her heart sank a little. Yeah, she'd screwed up in the good judgment department where Owen was concerned. But couldn't they give her a little credit for having learned a few things since then?

"Mama, come watch this with me," Lucy called from the

living room, a pointed reminder that the adults might be two rooms away in the kitchen, but they weren't in a vacuum. Her daughter could clue in at any moment that they were talking about her father and start asking questions.

The ice pick stabbed at her eyes again. So what if she did? Owen was *Lucy's father.* Or at least he'd had a hand in creating her. Obviously, he'd opted out of his patriarchal duties years ago, which was why she'd gone to great lengths to make sure he couldn't hurt Lucy by never chasing him down to insist he visit or pay child support.

Everything was a mess. She had no idea what she was supposed to do half the time as it was. Playing the part of both parents was exhausting enough without tossing giant unanswered questions into the mix.

Hannah threw her mom and her sister an apologetic glance and dropped the conversation like a hot potato. Gladly.

Gliding into the living room, she stood behind the swivel chair and stroked Lucy's hair. "This is a funny part, for sure."

Lucy laughed and the sound reverberated in Hannah's chest.

Owen had missed out on every second of this kind of thing so far. As much as she'd been trying to get him to admit he missed Hannah and was sorry he'd left her, a part of her wondered how he felt about his daughter. Had he ever thought about the tiny baby he'd walked out on and mourned the loss of being a dad?

Her hand froze on Lucy's head. What if that's why he'd come back to Owl Creek? What if he'd been sorry about skipping out on being a father and had come back to rekindle his relationship with *Lucy,* not Hannah?

Chapter 5

Being in the hospital sucked worse the longer Archer remained stuck there. The bed could pass for concrete and no matter which way he shifted, something still hurt.

Big Mike would pay for this. Eventually. Archer spent a few glorious moments fantasizing about punching the crime boss in the ribs and seeing how he liked not being able to breathe without wincing.

As if pain was the biggest worry Archer had. Immobilization ranked pretty high on the list too, especially if some goons had made their way north. Passing for his brother might eventually climb a few notches on the list of concerns, but only if Hannah Colton returned to the hospital, and given the way she lit out of here yesterday, he wasn't holding out much hope that he'd ever see her again.

Except the next time he looked up, she stood in the doorway, her beautiful face composed and her hair in a simple ponytail. Her eyes told a different story though. Deep and troubled, they sought him out and nearly walloped him with the strength of her conflict.

She didn't want to be here. That much was clear, especially given the way she hadn't actually entered the room. Her crisply ironed dress hit below the knees, drawing attention to her curves beneath, but he had a feeling that was not the effect it would have on most people.

Archer wasn't most people. He had a very fine appreciation for Hannah Colton that transcended her no-nonsense dress and hairstyle. Maybe even because of it. He had a feeling she'd dressed that way on purpose, to give him the impression she was all business.

But he knew better. No woman who had caught the attention of Owen Mackenzie could possibly be as buttoned-up as this one appeared to be. She must have a whole different side to her, one he'd like to uncover—*after* he figured out whether she and his brother had been working together.

Dang, was it too easy to forget all of that. He and Hannah watched each other, and she finally broke the silence.

"I didn't want to come back," she told him needlessly.

Why she'd been so reticent was the important question. A woman in cahoots with Big Mike didn't have anything to worry about. In fact, she might have been sent to monitor him in a way goons never could.

His gut told him that wasn't what was going on. He'd been fooled before by women in the past, so it was all the more reason to keep her closer than a friend. Nice that cozying up to her fit his agenda too.

He smiled at her, letting it turn genuine because it was easy to do so with her. "But you did. I'm glad."

"I'm only staying long enough to help you work on regaining your memories. I'd still like to pay you back the money you left behind, but I guess I can't exactly wire funds to an account if you don't remember your banking information."

He shrugged and shook his head, squelching the pang of admiration that she'd continued to bring this up. "I have a banking app on my phone, but I guess I'm not the kind of guy to save passwords because I can't get into it."

She didn't have to know that Owen had configured his banking app to allow log-on via fingerprint and his wasn't identical enough to his brother's to allow it to open. Ironic. Facial recognition worked fine but not fingerprints. The technological downside to trying to pass for his twin.

It also didn't matter because all of Owen's assets had been distributed to his next of kin and the bank account closed already, but the logistics of this whole charade fascinated him on an objective level.

"I brought some pictures. I thought they might help."

She strode into the room—finally—and gingerly perched on the edge of his bed, tapping on her phone, then turning it toward him so he could view the screen.

"This is our wedding day."

Oddly struck by her phrasing, he stared at the wide shot of a slightly younger, smiling Hannah standing outside the Wake County courthouse with her hand clutching the crook of Owen's elbow. Except he blinked and it morphed into a picture of himself, as if he'd stumbled over one of those 3D puzzles that flipped perspective if you refocused your eyes.

Just as quickly, it became Owen again, with his much shorter hair and clean-shaven jaw.

A strange ache traveled down his throat as he wondered what his own wedding day might look like. Whether his brother's last thoughts had been of this woman. What he'd lost. The promise shining in his bride's eyes, which he'd thrown in the garbage bin.

It shocked him how much a simple picture affected him.

"Were we happy?" he choked out hoarsely, cursing himself for asking because what did it matter?

Hannah met his gaze then, her eyes liquid and the moment heavy. Neither of them looked away as she got a little misty, and he realized that it did matter. To *her*. And he'd reacted to that at a visceral level.

"I was. So happy," she confirmed with a catch in her voice that thrummed through him. "I thought you were too."

There was so much unspoken in that, he scarcely knew what to do with it. Hannah could be the best actor west of the Rockies, but he'd bet his last dollar that she'd genuinely been in love with Owen.

Then her expression hardened. "That was a long time ago. You've done a lot since then to reverse that. I'm not here to reminisce. I'm trying to help you get your memory back so I can move on. Finally."

Man, his brother had really screwed things up. Hannah's hurt over the way he'd treated her couldn't be more evident.

He made a note to look into Hannah's finances and associations because it was impossible for him to tell fact from fiction when it came to her, especially when she was sitting here by his side, her light floral scent teasing him.

If only he'd met Hannah first, she might have a completely different outlook on how a Mackenzie man treated a woman. The *right* Mackenzie brother.

He shook off that completely unproductive thought.

But it wouldn't go away. All he could picture was his own face in that wedding photo. It wasn't fair that Owen had gotten all the devil-may-care genes, while Archer had been gifted a double dose of responsibility and caution.

Wouldn't it be something if he could settle into Owen's life for just a few days and find out what it sounded like to hear the whoosh of consequences fly by as he ignored them?

"I don't remember you," he murmured, his gaze lingering in places that it probably shouldn't, but his brother had knowledge of her body that he didn't, and he did want to play this part well. "But I want to. What does it feel like to kiss you?"

The question didn't seem to faze her in the slightest and neither did she look away. "I'm not going to demonstrate to see if that jogs anything loose, if that's where you were headed. It was kissing. Just like any other."

Well. That told him a heap right there. Owen was a lot of things, but generous wasn't one of them. Nor did he pay a lot of attention to other people's feelings. Wants. Needs. The lack of flowery, poetic praise of his brother's prowess didn't shock him, no, but his own primal response to hearing it did.

He wanted to give her an experience that would transcend whatever unsatisfying physical relationship his brother had foisted on Hannah. She deserved better.

"It just seems to me that we have a chance for something new and different now," he told her huskily. "I'm not the same man I used to be, Hannah. I don't know how we were before, but I know how we are right now, and if I kissed you, you'd have zero call to compare it to any other kiss."

Her cheeks flushed and he enjoyed that enough to brush off any residual guilt that niggled at him. This was his chance to be the reckless Mackenzie brother. To do what felt good, instead of following the letter of the law.

Besides, he was on leave from the force. This wasn't a crime scene, and he didn't have to analyze one piece of data. Or rather, he'd already examined a lot of the evidence. The more time he spent with Hannah, the more time he *wanted* to spend with Hannah. Plus, it was the best way to keep tabs on her if she did know where Big Mike's missing money was.

And if she didn't, fine. Either way, if he'd found her, so

would Big Mike. That was reason enough to toss out his playbook and embrace the new one that had been handed to him.

"You shouldn't talk like that," she murmured, but a woman who was genuinely uninterested in being flirted with would move to the chair. Or the doorway.

"Because I'm in this hospital bed?" he asked with a glance at the thin sheet covering him, which honestly wouldn't provide much of a barrier at all if she had a mind to snuggle up next to him.

That thought made the bed decidedly more uncomfortable as his body reacted in wholly inappropriate ways that the sheet had no shot at hiding.

"Because of Lucy," she shot back and crossed her arms, staring him down. "I didn't get to the rest of the pictures."

"Who is Lucy?"

Not their dog, that was for sure. Fire sparked from her gaze as she tapped up another picture on her phone and swiveled it in his direction.

The little girl in the photo had her mother's face and her father's eyes. His eyes, with green irises. A blend of them both.

The room spun for an eternity and when it stopped, everything had changed.

Chapter 6

The look on Owen's face as he studied the picture of Lucy scored Hannah's insides with white hot knives.

It wasn't recognition she saw there. If he'd had one iota of an inkling that Lucy existed prior to this moment, she'd eat her very sensible Anne Klein ballet flats.

No, this was a portrait of a man being introduced to something rare and precious. His gaze traveled over the photo keenly as if memorizing every tiny nuance. No detail was too small for him to learn.

"I want to see more pictures," he commanded quietly.

How could she do anything other than comply? This was the whole reason she'd come, to test out whether she should mention Lucy at all. In the end, she had to. He deserved to know about his daughter, if he truly hadn't retained even one small memory of her.

More to the point, this was his chance to prove he was still the same Owen as before. The one who cared zero about his own flesh and blood. Somehow, she didn't think that's what was happening here.

Her hand steady and absolutely not a reflection of the earthquake happening inside, she thumbed through to Lucy's last birthday. Jenny had hosted, naturally, since the multitudes of Coltons wouldn't fit in Hannah's smaller house. There were shots of Lucy blowing out the candles on the cake Hannah had made for her—Little Mermaid, and not the chintzy kind from the grocery store. Hannah had painstakingly cut out a mermaid shape and decorated it with eighteen colors of icing. Her daughter's fifth birthday only happened once, after all.

She had a feeling Owen hadn't even noticed the cake.

His gaze suspiciously shiny, he glanced up at her. "Does she have my last name?"

Hannah nodded. "I kept it for her. I went back to Colton, but she's officially Lucy Mackenzie."

"I want to know everything. Tell me."

Geez. The man had tears in his eyes and steel in his tone. It was overwhelming. Owen certainly hadn't cared one bit about Lucy before, as if she'd needed yet another clue that everything was different this time around.

But for how long?

This was not the way this was supposed to go. He was supposed to casually glance at the pictures and get that vague look on his face, the one that clued her in that his interest had waned. Instead, he watched her with the exact opposite of disinterest in his gaze.

"Everything is a lot to cover," she said with a half laugh. "Lucy is five going on twenty-five. She's around adults a lot and her vocabulary shows it. She spends a lot of time with my mom at her house when I have catering gigs at night."

"Because you don't have anyone else at home to baby-sit her?"

He was wondering if she'd moved on in the man department. It was a subtly asked question, but she didn't think she was wrong. It was also the first time he seemed to realize she could very well have a new husband at this point.

No reason not to be honest about it. "There's no one else

at home. Everything Lucy is and ever will be is due to me and my influence. That's not going to change. Ever," she emphasized, in case he was getting ideas that he might like to poke his nose in Lucy's life.

But he shocked her once again by pursing his lips and shaking his head.

"I'm sorry, Hannah. You shouldn't have been left to your own devices. A man should take more responsibility than that. Should think about things a lot different. A little girl like that is a gift, not an albatross. It's a shame she's missed out on knowing what it's like to have a good father."

Since she couldn't very well say what she was thinking—that Lucy would *never* know what it was like to have a good father due to her mother's terrible choice of husbands—she flipped to another set of pictures. Lucy's first day of preschool. Swim lessons at the public pool, a necessity since Hannah's house sat so near the lake. Random photos snapped when Lucy wasn't paying attention, of her doing mundane things like coloring or turning the pages of a book she was teaching herself to read.

"Is she smart?" Owen asked, his gaze glued to the photo of Lucy at four carrying books in both hands.

"As a whip and a Rhodes scholar combined," Hannah acknowledged with a proud smile. "I'm sure all mothers say things like that, but Lucy is special. She memorizes a story when I read it to her, usually the first time, and she knows if I skip pages."

Owen's gaze swung to hers, his brow furrowed. "Why would you skip pages?"

Spoken like someone who had never been asked to read *Don't Let the Pigeon Drive the Bus!* eighteen times in one night. "She's the master of 'just one more story, mama.' Some days I don't mind but some days, I'm just really tired."

That was literally the last thing she'd planned to confess to Owen, of all people, but he'd asked so earnestly to know about Lucy. Hannah's journey as a mother was so tied up in that question that it would be impossible to separate the two.

And it was hard being a single mom. Owen was 100 percent the reason she'd been forced to be one.

"I would love to read to her," Owen announced with a bit of wonder in his voice, as if it had never occurred to him that such an activity existed or that he'd be in a position to do it.

Not that she planned to give him an opportunity either way.

"Maybe one day," she said evasively, scrabbling to get a handle on this situation before it spiraled out of control.

If her aim had been to get Owen to admit he still cared nothing about his daughter, she'd failed miserably. Actually, she hadn't come close to figuring out what his goal was with his return to Owl Creek, not even a little bit.

"My family helps out with Lucy a lot," she said brightly, lest he get the idea that she might be tired because she had no help. He was the only deadbeat around here. "Do you remember my family? I have a lot of relatives. Oh, I mean, I guess I've lost a couple since we got divorced. My father died last year."

"I'm sorry, Hannah," he murmured. "About your dad and that I don't remember him."

"He wasn't much of a dad." She snorted. "Sometimes I wish I didn't remember him either. He was like one of those guys you see on the news, who had a whole second family that we didn't know about. Worse, he'd shacked up with my aunt Jessie and had a couple of kids. I guess the six he already had weren't enough."

She elaborated a bit about how all this had come out

after her father had died and how she'd met her half siblings Nate and Sarah, but there was a lot of reservation on both sides about jumping into the middle of a relationship when there was still so much hurt to go around.

They were all trying though.

Owen's eyes had widened as she spun the sordid tale. Thankfully, he didn't seem to realize she'd neatly segued the conversation away from Lucy, and she'd gladly spill all these terrible secrets to keep her daughter off Owen's mind.

She and Lucy were a bit alike in that regard—neither of them knew what it was like to have a good dad.

Oh, goodness. What if Owen had new family that he didn't remember either? That was a reality she hadn't considered at all. Her throat tightened. He could be married and have two kids for all she knew!

No, surely not. The insurance people would have turned up marriage records or birth records if that was the case, wouldn't they? They'd called her because they literally couldn't find any other family to notify.

"So then it came out that Aunt Jessie has gotten mixed up in a cult," she continued with a flourish. "The Ever After Church. In Owl Creek of all places, if you can believe it. The head is this real piece of work named Markus Acker and he's cozied up to Aunt Jessie. She contested my father's will, insisting that her kids deserved some of the money, but I think Markus put her up to it. It's just been a mess."

All at once, she wondered how much Sarah Colton knew about her mother's involvement with Markus and the church. Maybe Hannah could have her cake and eat it too if she took a little more initiative to strike up a friendship with her half sister. She could nose around a little to see what she could dig up on behalf of her family at the same time, right? It wasn't a crime.

"The Ever After Church?" Owen repeated and Hannah nodded.

"It's not a real church, not as far as we can tell," she added. "There's a compound where the members live not far from here. It seems to be largely geared toward convincing the members to give the church lots of money."

Owen's brows knit as he seemed to absorb that, but then the nurse bustled in to take his blood pressure and other vitals. He endured it with good humor, another strange factor of his new, improved personality that Hannah would have had to see to believe. He'd always had a short temper and very little patience for people in service jobs, which should have been a much bigger red flag in the beginning than she'd realized.

Late-Twenties Hannah knew the value of people in service jobs since she had almost a dozen working for her now. Never again would she ignore that telling aspect of a man's personality.

Unless of course the man in question seemed to have done a 180-degree turnaround on his stance toward nurses. And Hannah.

As soon as the nurse left, Owen asked a few more pointed questions about the church, an oddity that Hannah chose not to examine too hard when his focus had shifted exactly as she'd intended.

But then during a pause, he hooked her with his warm brown eyes and covered the back of her hand with his. "Can I see some more pictures of Lucy?"

Ugh, she'd thought they were done with this subject. So much for the segue to Aunt Jessie.

With little call to tell him no, she grudgingly pulled out her phone again from her pocket and found some baby pictures. That would be the best test of his memory, to view photos of what Lucy had looked like as he'd last seen her.

But he shook his head and pushed the phone away, his expression crestfallen. "It's incredibly painful to see evidence of how much of Lucy's life I've missed. I want to meet her. Now. In person."

Dismayed, she stared at him, wrestling with the fact that this kind of stance was exactly what she'd hoped for when she'd mentioned Lucy. It was exactly what she'd have wished to hear. Once.

But wishing for it and hearing it spoken aloud—where she'd have to address it—were two different things. "This is not the time to be making those kinds of requests."

"It's not a request," he countered, his mouth set in a firm line. "I'm her father. I have rights."

Oh, goodness. Her soul hurt as the weight of his meaning crushed her. He could fight her for custody. Demand visitation. Insert himself into her life in all sorts of terrible ways. What had she done?

Lungs on fire with the effort to simply breathe, she shook her head. "Not at the moment you don't. You're in the hospital. They haven't released you yet. Maybe once you regain your memories, we can discuss—"

"Bring her here."

Geez, Owen had never been this stubborn before, especially not when it came to relations with another person. "I think they have rules," she suggested calmly, grasping desperately at straws.

He could *not* start up a relationship with Lucy, only to remember in a day, a week, that he despised children, even his own. Especially his own.

As crushed as she felt right now, how would a precious five-year-old feel after opening her heart to the one person in the world she could rightly call Daddy, only to have him callously reject her later?

No. No way. It was a mistake to have even brought it up. Hannah had made the cardinal error of thinking with her heart, not her head—the curse of wanting to do the right thing.

"The doctor said it was critical that I be surrounded by things from my life," Owen insisted. "That's the whole reason they called you. Why wouldn't seeing Lucy be just as valuable?"

"Because you've never seen her as a child," Hannah snapped back, thrilled to have this incredibly important fact to cling to. "The last time you saw her, she was a baby."

"All the more reason to let me get to know her. Hannah," he said, his tone softening. "I've lost so much already."

Good grief. It was as if he'd reached right through her chest and grabbed her heart, squeezing with exactly the right pressure to wring out the maximum amount of emotion. Whether it was empathy, grim determination to get him off this path or panic, she couldn't say.

"I'll think about it," she promised and fled for the second time.

She had a feeling she'd do nothing but think about it for the foreseeable future.

Chapter 7

It was only a matter of time before someone realized that Archer wasn't Owen and that he didn't really have amnesia. Probably due to a monumental slipup, like cussing out his brother in Hannah's presence.

Owen had a daughter.

A bright, beautiful little bundle of joy who had no relationship with her father or her father's side of the family. It was heartbreaking.

Archer's research into his brother's ex-wife hadn't mentioned a kid. That was a pretty big thing to overlook. Of course, the blame for his shock lay squarely in the lap of the deceased and it was a good thing Owen was already dead or Archer would kill him.

It was bad enough that Owen had never bothered to mention that he'd gotten married in the first place, but failing to tell their mother she had a granddaughter—that was unforgivable. Amelia Mackenzie had her faults, and refusing to see Owen's was a big one, but she was still their mother, and she deserved to know her grandchild.

Archer had a little mad left over for himself. Not that he had any clue what an uncle was supposed to do, but finding out he was one meant something to him. Finding out he'd been deprived of this information meant something too—his brother was a jackass of the highest order.

Since the hospital hadn't found a trace of Owen's relatives, Archer could only assume his brother had doctored his records to remove all references to his family—both his birth family and his ex-wife. That was fine. Archer had cut ties with his brother too, but really it wasn't fine, not with Lucy in the mix. He stewed about it for a good long while after Hannah had left.

Of course, the real issue here wasn't what an uncle would do in this situation. He'd somehow managed to become a father in the same stroke that he'd claimed to be Owen. The complications from that one split-second decision had just spiraled out of control.

He could not maintain this charade. He couldn't end it either.

So much for being the devil-may-care Mackenzie brother. That's why he'd never embraced his brother's life philosophy—his conscience wasn't geared to ignore things like responsibility and consequences. And Lucy was one obligation Owen had left behind that Archer would not be able to properly rectify. Not the way he'd like.

Actually, he didn't know how he'd fix this if he could. It was the first time Archer had ever encountered a situation he didn't know how to handle. You couldn't analyze a little girl and put the pieces back together into a whole that suddenly made sense, then move on.

This was a lifetime commitment, no two ways about it. And Archer had zero intention of walking away from it. He just didn't know what his relationship with Lucy—and Hannah—would look like at the end.

The doctor came by and chatted with him for a bit. Archer knew the routine, answered all the questions by rote.

Yes, he felt okay other than the banged-up ribs and the gash on his head.

No, he still didn't remember anything, not even bits and pieces or floaty memories. The doctor had told him that's how it usually happened, that the brain would start releasing blurry, disjointed images first, eventually followed by a flood of stored-up information. It would likely be overwhelming, so the doctor wanted to keep tabs on him here at the hospital.

That was a lucky break, which soon might not be the case. Eventually they'd release him and then he'd have to come up with an excuse to stay close to Hannah, especially after the alarming story she'd told him about the Ever After Church.

As soon as the doctor left, Archer grabbed his phone—a burner his assistant had couriered to him on the sly, along with a credit card, bless him—and did a search for Markus Acker. It was better than being ticked off at Owen and far more productive.

The face of the man who popped up did not give him any warm and fuzzy feelings. He was good-looking of course, as Archer expected from someone who was likely running a solid grift with a lot of moving parts. Acker would be charming in person. Likable and approachable. You'd never suspect a guy like that of lifting your wallet, if you even noticed it was gone, as he dazzled you.

There was only a tiny bit of official information on the Ever After Church, which told Archer a lot more than if they had posted gobs and gobs of propaganda.

This was an organization that liked to keep a low profile.

If only he had access to his workstation at the lab on South Jones, which was nothing like the CSI lab on television shows. He worked in a drab office where dedicated men and women analyzed what was often trace evidence left at crime scenes. There was little glamour, but they put criminals behind bars with hardcore scientific evidence.

And he was good at what he did. Which meant he could cut a wide swath through the layers of Ever After Church ownership and finances in a matter of hours, if he had the right tools. Instead, he had to make do with a phone and busted ribs.

Fortunately, a couple of reporters seemed to have latched on to the church's activities. Archer recognized their by-lines popping up over and over as they linked a lot of shady stuff to Markus Acker and some of his cronies.

One story had multiple hits about Acker's alleged right-hand man, Winston Kraft, though it was clear from the context that the guy's position in the church was "unknown." That was code for "uncorroborated," which meant the reporter was not wrong, just covering his bases.

Dude was a piece of work and a half. He'd been arrested for kidnapping his own grandchildren, supposedly to gain control of the insurance money left to them after the deaths of their parents. Once the children had been recovered, it came out that their grandfather might have been responsible for the car wreck that had killed their parents, one of whom was Kraft's own son.

Archer shook his head. Nice people this church attracted.

And then there were the bodies.

Authorities had found a remarkable number of them buried near the Ever After Church compound, but the investigation had only uncovered a tenuous link to Acker thus far. The link was there, he was fairly certain. Someone would find it.

The name *Colton* scrolled onto his screen. His gut went icy. Lizzie Colton—no mention of whether she was a relation of Hannah's, but surely she was—had been kidnapped and held in a cabin high in the mountains, then managed to escape—good for her—only to wind up unconscious in the woods. During a snowstorm. She was lucky she'd been found by search and rescue so she could finger her assailant, who'd been apprehended. So far, no one had tied the kidnapping to the church, but Archer didn't believe in coincidences.

Something tied these events together. Everything had a pattern: shells, Braille, quilts, seasons, iambic pentameter. He just had to find the telltale slime trail the Ever After Church had left behind as it wormed its way through Idaho. Pick up the breadcrumbs so to speak.

There was only one way to do that effectively. Follow the money.

Of course, he couldn't do it himself and that stung almost as much as his busted ribs.

The nurse wasn't due by for another fifteen minutes and it was a good bet Hannah wouldn't be dropping in so soon after she'd fled the scene. So he felt fairly safe dialing his assistant's number from memory.

"Hey," he said when Willis answered. "It's Mac. I need you to do me a favor."

Quickly, Archer rattled off the details, which Willis would not need repeated, and left his assistant to do some quiet sleuthing into the Ever After Church on his behalf. If this hunch was nothing, fine. There was no way it was nothing, though, and he didn't like the picture these pieces had started to form.

Especially when he was already following the money. Big Mike's missing money, specifically, and there'd already been slime trails heading in the direction of Owl Creek formed by Owen Mackenzie.

Thirty seconds before the nurse was due to stroll into his

room, he wiped his internet search history and did a factory reset on the burner phone, then stashed it back under his mattress. Couldn't be too careful in a public hospital where anyone could come into his room disguised as an orderly or a janitor or even the guy who collected blood samples to take to the lab.

"How are we today, Mr. Owen?" the nurse called as she picked up the electronic tablet from its holder by the door and read over the notes in his medical chart the morning shift nurse had left.

He didn't have to glance at her name tag to know it read Mary Jane Meyer. She'd told him the first day that everyone called her MJ, so he did too. "Fine. I like what you've done with your hair."

She shot him a pleased smile. "You're the first person to notice."

"Ingrates. What, are they blind? You had to have cut off, what, six inches? And the bangs are doing great things for your cheekbones."

His return smile was genuine, mostly because he appreciated the care MJ took when seeing after him. But also because in his line of work, people like nurses always noticed more details than anyone else, so they gave him the best leads.

And you never knew when you would need those details or under what circumstances you might be asking for them. Scoring points ahead of time never hurt.

"Oh, go on," she told him, flapping her hand in his direction. "Flirting will get you everywhere."

If MJ was a day under sixty, Archer would hand in his badge. But if he'd made her feel good about herself even for a few minutes, it was worth his time.

"I hope it'll get me an extra pudding at dinnertime,"

he suggested with a wink and MJ laughed as she took his blood pressure.

"Consider it yours." She noted the numbers on her tablet and leaned over to change the bandages on his head wound, inspecting the stitches at the same time. "Your pretty girlfriend left already? She can stay as long as she likes. I won't tell anyone."

"Thanks, MJ," he said, not bothering to correct her since he couldn't honestly say what Hannah was to him at this stage. Or what he'd want her to be.

He slept fitfully after MJ left, constantly checking his burner phone for messages from Willis. Time crawled.

Near sunrise, Willis finally sent a few cryptic texts that meant he'd found some information that Archer would consider useful, but he'd have to be out of this hospital bed to hear it since he couldn't very well meet his assistant off premises until they released him. Neither could he take advantage of whatever Willis had found.

Being in the hospital sucked. And if he kept saying it, eventually it would help matters, right?

Bored and not a little stir-crazy, he rolled over for the umpteenth time as the sky outside lightened. The next time he looked up, Hannah stood in the doorway of his room, but this time, she wasn't alone.

Lucy was with her. *Lucy.* Her bright, curious gaze sought his and when she locked him in her sights, he felt his soul shift. It was as if he'd opened a vein and poured his own lifeblood into an empty space where nothing had been before and then watched as it became something—this little human who shared his DNA but had the exact same color eyes as her mother.

"Hi," he croaked out since she was still watching him with avid curiosity.

"Mama says you're my father," she told him without any warning and the short sentence tore into him with the force of a bullet fired at close range from a gun in the hand of someone who knew how to use it.

It was one thing to academically understand that the brother he'd decided to impersonate had a daughter. And that pretending to be the little girl's father would be part of the gig. It was another thing entirely to hear that harsh truth straight from her mouth.

She thought he was Owen. Of course she did. Because he'd spent the last few days telling everyone he was and playing the part of an amnesiac to sell it. He'd never regretted that decision more than he did in this moment.

But he couldn't be sorry either.

Lucy deserved a father and Owen would never have been one to her, even if he'd lived. He certainly couldn't change course and decide to be one now. But Archer could.

"Hi, Lucy." He greeted her solemnly and held out his hand. "It's very nice to meet you."

Lucy didn't hesitate in the slightest and stuck her tiny hand in his, her fingers so delicate that it made no sense how they could reach so far inside him, brushing the walls of his heart with such strength.

"Mama said you were hurt," Lucy recited, her gaze wide as she took everything in, sliding to the white rectangle on his temple. "Are you going to be okay?"

Her concern bled through him. She'd met him four seconds ago and her immediate concern was for his health? A testament to her mother no doubt, and he glanced up to see Hannah standing near the door, in the room, but not in the middle of this reunion that she'd opted to allow.

They shared a long glance laden with meaning, but he had no shot at interpreting what this woman was thinking.

Why had she decided to bring Lucy after all? He'd been convinced she'd never go for it.

"I'll be fine," he assured her and before he could say yes or no or get his wits about him, Lucy hopped up on the bed to sit next to him, her mouth curved in a wide smile that revealed a missing front tooth.

She had a stuffed dog clutched at the crook of her elbow, which she held out to show him. "This is Mr. Fluffers. He came in a box, but he wasn't scared of the dark."

"That's very brave of Mr. Fluffers," he said because it seemed she expected some type of response and that one had rolled off his tongue. "What kind of dog is he?"

"A golden retriever like Aunt Ruby's and Uncle Sebastian's dog. He's named Oscar though. Will you let me get a real dog if I come live with you?"

"Lucy," Hannah interjected from the doorway, strangling on her daughter's name. "We talked about this in the car. Your father wanted to meet you first and then we can talk about what happens next. I'm sorry," she said to Archer, her expression full of emotion he couldn't identify.

But wanted to. He wanted to be able to read her, to know they shared this parenting journey and would have each other's backs when it came to something like their daughter asking for a dog. And to presumably stay at his house…in Las Vegas.

Oh, man. He shut his eyes for a brief, fortifying moment that did not work to settle his stomach. This was not the kind of mess Archer normally cleaned up for Owen. Most of the time, Owen's screw-ups involved owing people money he couldn't pay back or having committed to something that he blew off, like picking up Mom from the airport.

How was he supposed to navigate stepping into the role

of father when he didn't even live in this state? Then he had to laugh at himself. Like that was his biggest problem.

"Do you want a dog?" he asked Lucy, partially to give himself breathing room and also because he suddenly craved knowing things about her. All things. Favorite color. TV shows she liked. Did she walk to school?

An objectively fascinating development, this desire to not just meet Lucy, but *know* her. Would he have this same reaction as an uncle—only an uncle with no ability or reason to assume he'd ever be anything else? Or was this yet another step in the chain reaction that he'd unwittingly set off when he first answered to the name *Owen*?

Enthused by the subject of dogs, Lucy nodded yes a bajillion times and tucked Mr. Fluffers back into the crook of her elbow, where he seemed quite at home. "Uncle Wade has a dog too. Betty Jane. She's the best, but I can't play with her sometimes because she has a job. All the dogs have jobs, mostly to find people and sometimes to make sure they're not sad."

He glanced up at Hannah who lifted a shoulder. "K-9 search and rescue, and therapy. She is surrounded by working dogs. I never realized before."

"So you want a dog whose only job is to be yours and to sleep with you and be your friend," he told her with an affirming smile, and Lucy's eyes lit up as if she'd switched on a beacon inside. Oddly, it did the same thing to him.

"Yes, please," she chirped, obviously willing to reveal all her hopes and dreams to the father she'd never known with zero trepidation.

She was fearless and brave.

Owen frequently adopted this slightly hooded expression like he had 147 secrets and he intended to share none of them with you. As if you weren't worthy to be let in on his thoughts.

Right this minute, he hated Owen a little bit. As unproductive as that was. But he couldn't stop himself from wondering yet again what might have been if he'd met Hannah first.

Only he hadn't. He'd met both Hannah and Lucy while pretending to be Owen and now he was good and caught in the lie. Good and screwed too, thanks to his brother, on multiple fronts since he couldn't undo any of this. All he could do was keep plowing through this murder investigation, while ensuring the family Owen had rejected stayed out of Big Mike's sights.

If Archer secretly enjoyed sliding into his brother's life while keeping Hannah and Lucy safe, no one had to know.

Chapter 8

Hannah debated whether to take Lucy to see Owen again the next morning. But really, she couldn't keep them apart. Not in good conscience.

She was flying blind here, going against better judgment, which was her Achilles' heel. On the drive to Conners, she spent a lot of time convincing herself the whole point was to help Owen regain his memories so he could name someone else in his life. Someone who could shoulder the weight of responsibility for his welfare, allowing Hannah to off-load it gladly.

Except that wasn't really the reason anymore.

She'd lost count of the ways her ex-husband was like a different person. One that appealed to her in ways she'd scarcely started to unpack. And she'd gained a reluctant curiosity about how long it would last. A slim hope that he might stay different even after he got better.

Frankly, he had to be. The die was cast, now that she'd introduced him to Lucy. He didn't get to screw up his relationship with his daughter a second time.

When she got to Owen's room, the doctor was there. Spontaneously, she asked if he would clear it for Hannah to take Owen to the courtyard in the center of the hospital. It would be his first foray out of the hospital since he'd come in on a gurney. She hoped he'd appreciate the change of scenery, but she hadn't anticipated the doctor expecting her to roll him out in a wheelchair.

Owen accepted the idea with grace, but he had some trouble transferring from the bed to the seat of the wheelchair. Automatically, she reached out to help him, her hand landing on the small of his back.

Oh my. He hadn't felt like that before, as if he'd hidden a slab of heated concrete under his gown. The long, slow flip in her tummy was not welcome. Worse, it was nearly impossible to ignore. As was his grimace when she snatched her hand back, causing him to land heavily in the seat.

"Are your ribs still bothering you?" she murmured and he glanced up, unfamiliar warmth radiating from his brown eyes.

Great. He'd noticed that she'd reacted to touching him.

"Not so much," he said, but she had the impression he wasn't being completely honest.

Trying to be macho, probably. For her benefit or Lucy's, she wasn't sure, but she could have saved him the trouble on both counts. Lucy had no idea how a father was supposed to act other than what little she might have discerned from her grandfather before he passed, Uncle Buck or her cousin Greg, who had recently gotten custody of his late best friend's kids.

Hannah wasn't swayed by anything Owen could or would do. She'd learned a long time ago to let whatever he said go in one ear and out the other.

They rode the elevator down to the first floor, Lucy jabbering a mile a minute about the two girls she liked best at preschool. To his credit, he listened intently and never interrupted or showed even a smidgen of impatience when Lucy told him the same knock-knock joke twice in a row. She'd figured out that she liked making people laugh and thus, in her five-year-old brain, assumed that everyone would find the same joke twice as funny the second time. Hannah hadn't had the heart to destroy that myth, yet.

Owen actually did laugh both times and it didn't even sound forced. Another point in his favor.

Hannah wheeled the chair into the courtyard, half convinced Owen was going to try to ditch the contraption or at least complain that he wasn't an invalid, but he shocked her into silence once again by asking Lucy if she wanted a ride.

She squealed and immediately jumped up into Owen's lap. He winced as her elbow caught him in the ribs, and Hannah braced for a string of profanities or something else Owen-like, but he just carefully rearranged his daughter and grasped the wheel with one hand to ferry her around the walking path. With the other, he held Lucy tight against him.

Mouth slightly ajar, Hannah watched as Owen stopped near one of the planters exploding with flowers. He snapped off the head of a columbine and handed it to Lucy, who grinned like she'd just been given the whole bouquet.

Well, that was…great. She swallowed. It was. Totally fabulous. They were getting along famously for two people who didn't know each other at all, and for all intents and purposes, hadn't known about the existence of the other a few days ago.

"Mama, look at me," Lucy called and threw up her palms. "No hands."

"I see you, baby."

Boy, did she. Her daughter sitting in her father's lap was a picture she'd never in a million years have conjured up, even in her wildest imagination. It put a misty smile on her face even as it socked her in the gut.

Lucy would never again be just hers. As long as Owen kept stepping up to the plate, of course, and being the dad he seemed poised to become. It was terrible to wish so fervently for something she had a niggling suspicion wouldn't happen and then it would be on her that she'd let him disappoint their daughter. Yet at the same time, she'd have Lucy all to herself again in a catch-22 that made her head hurt.

"Guess what?" Lucy said the next time Owen wheeled her past the place where Hannah had elected to stand out of the way. "Daddy says I can get a dog and keep it at his house!"

Oh boy. Hannah's smile froze but she checked her knee-jerk reaction. "We'll have to discuss that a little more before it's final, okay?"

Lucy crossed her arms and threw her mother a look. "That's what you say when you aren't going to let me."

"It's fine, Hannah," Owen said, his lips curving up in an expression Hannah knew well.

It was the same look her brother Wade got whenever Lucy had conned him into something. *Men.* They were such pushovers when a sweet, diabolical little girl put her evil scheme in motion.

"It's only fine depending on what happens after you get out of the hospital," she muttered, careful not to say too much.

"If you say no, I'll never come out of my room again," Lucy announced with her mutinous face that she rarely trotted out because she knew it wouldn't get her very far.

It still hurt. "I'm not saying anything other than we have to talk about it."

The face didn't change. At least until Lucy turned back to Owen, and then it was all smiles for her dad who had never told her no.

Hannah sighed. Wasn't this great? It was totally fine that Lucy was freezing her out for being the responsible parent, but cozying up to the father she'd known for all of five minutes. Hannah wasn't jealous at *all* that he got to be the fun dad, the absentee dad who lived in Las Vegas and would take her daughter for long weekends, leaving Hannah alone and wondering what her life had become.

Wasn't this just like Owen to swoop in and scoop up Lucy for all the sepia-toned moments he could stuff into a day, skipping over all the bad stuff. The real stuff. The 1 a.m. nightmares and upset tummies that were no match for three sets of clean sheets. He'd skipped out on the things that Hannah had been forced to endure alone.

But he'd also missed out on all the good stuff. The firsts. The onlys. He wasn't there to witness her first steps. The look on her face the first time she ate ice cream. Lucy would never again lose her first tooth and get her first visit from the tooth fairy. At least Hannah could rest assured none of those things would happen when Lucy was with Owen.

Finally, Owen called a halt to the wheelchair ride, his face a bit ashen. His breathing seemed labored, and she caught him wincing as Lucy pouted over being asked to get down.

"Come on, Lady Mackenzie," she called, figuring it was time to step in since Owen had no clue how to handle Obstinate Lucy of the One More Time Clan. "Your dad is in the hospital for a reason, and he's spent more than a reasonable amount of time entertaining you. Give him a break."

Lucy hopped down without further argument, her lips still pouty, but at least she wasn't presenting her case for why she should get an additional fifteen minutes next time. She'd be storing up details on the PowerPoint slides in her head though, for her future campaign.

Hannah wheeled Owen back toward the elevator, both of them quiet as Lucy had a one-sided conversation with Mr. Fluffers about the picture she was going to draw when they got home.

The elevator was plenty deep enough for her to stand behind Owen, but that felt too subservient so she stood next to him. A decision she instantly regretted when he grazed a finger down the back of her hand.

She glanced at him.

"Thank you for this," he murmured. "She's a miracle. I'm not sure if I'm more upset that I missed so much of her life or that even if I hadn't, I wouldn't remember any of it. I want to know everything about her faster than I can absorb it all."

And now she felt selfish and petty for being glad he didn't have any cherished moments with his daughter except for the ones from the last two days. "You're welcome."

She left it at that, because none of this was real. Owen would regain his memories and suddenly, he'd realize he hated kids, as he'd told her umpteen times in the weeks after she'd announced the pregnancy she'd thought they'd both celebrate.

Somewhere underneath all of this was a scam. There had to be. She refused to get caught out again by this man.

Only it was too late. The dad was out of the bag. Lucy had met her father and she'd never let Hannah hear the end of it about the dog she'd been promised.

She could only hope that when Owen pulled the carpet out from under them, she'd have the skills to help Lucy get over her disappointment.

Somehow, she got Owen and Lucy extracted from each other and hustled her daughter to the car, already glancing at her watch and doing mental gymnastics to rearrange her baking schedule for the rest of the day. Bon Appetit had three events coming up, a wedding and two bar mitzvahs.

Just as she was about to put the car in gear and pull out of the lot, her phone rang. The caller ID on her navigation panel announced that it was Wade, so she answered it with her thumb.

"You're on speaker," she warned Wade before he could say a word. "And Lucy is in the car."

"Hi, Uncle Wade," she called from the back seat. "Mr. Fluffers says hi."

"Hi, Goose." Wade's deep voice reverberated from the speaker. "I can call back later."

"I have a superbusy afternoon."

Thanks to taking the morning off to visit Owen, which she refused to feel guilty about. But neither did she want to explain why she was behind. No one in her family agreed with her decision to introduce Lucy to Owen, which was too bad. It would have been nice to have someone on her side. Someone who would tell her it was fine, that she hadn't made a horrible mistake. That she did owe it to everyone to see if things could be different.

"I'll make it quick then," Wade said. "We need to have an emergency family meeting. Soon."

Hannah sighed and it almost came out without the extra drama. "I'm full up on family meetings, Wade."

So far, she'd attended an emergency meeting to find out she had siblings she'd never known about. Then the one where they found out Aunt Jessie had joined a cult. Plus the one where it came out that Aunt Jessie was contesting Hannah's father's will.

What could possibly be left to discover?

"You can't miss it," he insisted. "We've got some important news to share."

"Text me the details," she said without committing to anything she'd regret later.

But honestly, if her brothers had left her out, she'd have words with them. Nor could she stand the idea of ditching the meeting on principle, only to have to wheedle the news out of someone later, when she'd be alone trying to manage whatever bombshell was about to be dropped.

What if it was something about Markus Acker? What if someone else in her family had stepped up to the plate and done the work she'd vowed to do—*and* had discovered something about his church while she'd been waffling around about Owen?

As her phone pinged with the meeting time and place, she had a moment of panic that the meeting would be about someone else picking up her slack on the Ever After research front. Yes, taking Lucy to meet her father had ranked as an important enough task to leapfrog Markus Acker. But now she regretted that she'd made that task into such a priority in the first place, let alone that it had hampered her promise to investigate the church.

When she got home, she picked up her phone and called Sarah before she could think better of it. Voicemail. No worries. She left a message telling Sarah she'd like to connect, squelching the slight guilt that she'd done so under slightly false pretenses.

But not really! She *did* want to get to know her new sister. Half sister. And technically their relationship wasn't *new*-new, like Sarah had just been born. They'd just only learned about each other. Though Hannah knew that Sarah and Nate had known a bit about their father's other family over the years, but had chosen not to reach out until recently. It was a weird situation, and she didn't blame them for preferring to stay in the shadows.

After her aforementioned busy afternoon wound to a close, Hannah threw herself into the nighttime routine of bath and then helping Lucy pick out clothes to wear to pre-school tomorrow, a task that always went better if they did it the night before. Lucy never stuck with her first choice—or second or third—and before Hannah had hit on the idea of letting Lucy pick when they had plenty of time, the ward-robe changes often made them late.

"I want to wear my pink sundress," Lucy announced as she pulled on her pajamas without help, a big girl staple that still managed to puncture a hole in Hannah's heart.

Yes, she academically knew that Lucy would eventu-ally do everything for herself, but as tasks slipped from her grasp, she felt the keen sense of loss. The reminders that the little girl who needed her would eventually grow into a young woman who would move away and leave her mother to chart a life by herself. Thinking about it sliced deeply.

"You can't wear a sundress in February," Hannah told her automatically, falling right into Lucy's trap. That's what she got for letting her attention wander.

"I can if I wear a shirt underneath and leggings," Lucy pointed out.

Since this was still the first round of clothes selection, Hannah didn't see much value in arguing. "Fine. You'll be uncomfortable with a whole second outfit on under a dress that isn't made for layers, but you're the one who will have to wear it all day."

"I want to wear it to go see Daddy," she informed her mother as she pulled the dress, hanger and all, from her closet, draping it over the chair at her desk that would even-tually be used for homework when Lucy hit elementary school, but worked fine as a wardrobe stager.

"I'm not sure if we're going to see your father tomorrow," she hedged.

Hannah had thought they would take a break from the hospital. They'd been two days in a row already. It probably wasn't good for Lucy to see Owen every day. They might form an attachment faster if she did that.

Plus, Hannah really wanted the break too. Seeing Owen on a consistent basis was starting to do a number on her. Making her think about things she shouldn't be thinking, letting phrases like *second chances* and *reunion romance* clog up her brain when she should be focusing on things like braising and basting and baking.

"I want to see my daddy," Lucy insisted as she pull out her purple leggings and laid them by the dress, then frowned at the combo. "He said I could come anytime I wanted. Where are my black leggings?"

And focusing on parenting, Hannah added silently. "Your black leggings are in the drawer where you found the purple ones."

"No, they're not." Lucy pulled open the drawer and proceeded to dump the contents onto the floor to demonstrate that she'd gone through the entire stack.

Hannah stifled a sigh. "Lucy, pick up your clothes and put them back in the drawer. Neatly. I'll check the dryer."

The missing leggings weren't in the dryer or folded into Hannah's own laundry, which was still piled on top of her dresser. Maybe she'd put them into one of her own drawers by mistake. But when she opened the first drawer, the entire thing was in a disarray, as if someone had pawed through it recently. All her drawers looked like that actually.

Returning to her daughter's room, she counted to ten before she let her exhaustion get the better of her. "I've asked you not to go into my room and get into my things without asking."

"I didn't, Mama," Lucy said. "I don't go into your room unless you tell me I can. Did you find my black leggings?"

"You didn't go through my drawers?" she prompted, hoping Lucy would come clean.

Her daughter just shook her head, still distracted by the missing leggings. "I need the black ones in case I get dirty snow on me. The purple ones will show because my boots aren't tall enough."

Hannah bit her lip and forced back the comment on the tip of her tongue about leggings being inappropriate for winter in the first place.

"Can we go see Daddy on Saturday?" Lucy asked right when Hannah had lulled herself into a false sense of security that they'd moved on from that subject.

"Maybe," she allowed, wondering how in the world she'd balance everything when she had an event on Saturday that she absolutely couldn't pass off to one of her employees since it was for a hundred people. The serving logistics alone required a military grade campaign to execute and that was her job.

No wonder she'd misplaced laundry. She'd probably messed up her drawers herself looking for something and forgot, thanks to all the major distractions.

"Wear the purple leggings and pay attention to where you walk. Then you won't get snow on them."

Finally, Lucy moved on to the teeth-brushing portion of their evening routine and then settled into bed for her prayers. The first five sentences were all about Owen in a sweet plea to the heavens to watch over her daddy and help him get better.

Hannah swallowed against the knot in her throat. The

barn door was open and the horse was out. There wasn't much use in closing the door on her daughter's relationship with her father.

And who knew? Maybe Owen would regain his memories and realize he had been missing out on being a father to Lucy. Maybe everything would be fine.

But she had a niggling sensation that she was fooling herself.

Chapter 9

Hannah managed to stay away from the hospital until Sunday, but guilt and curiosity got the better of her by noon. Plus, Lucy had promised to eat all her vegetables for a week if she could visit her dad, and that was too good of an offer to refuse in Hannah's book.

Since she hadn't originally planned to leave the house, a shower was in order. Hannah plopped Lucy in front of an episode of *Peppa Pig* in the living room.

"What's the rule?" she asked as she paused the show, holding the remote out of Lucy's reach.

"Don't move from this chair unless the house catches on fire," Lucy recited with a little bop of her head. "And then I should come tell you so you can call 911."

"Exactly." Hannah unpaused the show and set the remote on the dais next to the TV.

The timer in her head counted down along with the math she knew like the back of her hand. A shower took eleven minutes including time for the water to warm up, a necessity when it was 30 degrees outside. Five minutes for hair and five minutes for makeup, two to slide into clothes and boots. Five episodes of *Peppa Pig* would give her an extra two minutes with conditioner, a luxury she rarely indulged in, but she did have an acute awareness that she'd be seeing Owen later.

When she stepped into the shower, she found herself humming. Until she grabbed the shampoo and dumped some in her hand, only to find that it was body wash instead.

Frowning, she glanced at the row of bottles lined up along the ledge formed by the high window. They were out of order. She always put them back in the same sequence because she used them in a certain order. Plus, they weren't all right at the edge like she'd left them.

Odd. The ledge was too high for Lucy to reach unless she'd somehow dragged a stool into the shower and stood on it without Hannah hearing her. Unlikely, since she'd have to drag it from the kitchen.

The drawers left in disarray plucked at her consciousness. If she'd done that without remembering, she could have easily rearranged the bottles on the ledge without realizing. Probably just an accident due to her extreme level of distraction lately.

Hannah dismissed it from her mind, already having burned through one of her extra minutes by grabbing the wrong bottle. She flew through the rest of her shower and emerged, hurrying through toweling off and drawing her hair up into a simple ponytail. Makeup she took a little bit of extra care to get right, telling herself there wasn't anything wrong with wanting to look nice in public. She could run into anyone in Conners.

But she knew she would be seeing Owen and on the drive over, her nerves let her know about it.

Lucy chattered the entire time from the back seat, repeating, "Blah, blah, blah, that's how daddies talk!" from one of the episodes of *Peppa Pig*, then asking Hannah how come her daddy didn't say *blah, blah, blah*.

By the time they got to the hospital, Hannah was already looking for her sanity. And her migraine medication.

Then they walked to Owen's room, Hannah pausing at the door to knock. Owen glanced over, his brown eyes lighting up with warmth the moment he caught sight of her. Then he smiled, his gaze traveling down to take in Lucy by her side.

All of the air whooshed out of her lungs as she registered his genuine pleasure that they'd come. When was the last time anyone had been that happy to see her? Maybe Betty Jane had occasionally woofed a greeting when she'd dropped by Wade's house. Possibly Lucy's eyes danced occasionally when she spied Hannah in the pickup line at preschool, but she was just as often miffed that it was time to go, announcing that she wasn't done playing yet. Usually she gave her mother a hug, though.

This was different. Owen's joy at seeing them took over his whole face and she had to take a moment to appreciate the fact that he seemed just as happy to see Lucy as he was to see Hannah.

"Hey," he called softly as if afraid to scare them away by talking too loudly. "You're here. I've missed you both."

Unprompted, Lucy scampered up onto the bed and threw her arms around her father. "I wanted to come yesterday, but Mama had an *event*."

"I catered an event," Hannah corrected with a smile as the sight of her daughter entwined in Owen's arms squeezed her heart. "You make it sound like I was invited to the White House for dinner."

"I have something for you, my darling," he said to Lucy and pulled a package from the other side of the bed, handing it to her.

Oh, man. Hannah sucked in a breath, dreading all the ways a gift he hadn't cleared with her could go sideways. The package was almost bigger than Lucy, wrapped in pink paper with giant letter *L*s formed with raised silver sparkles that would likely rain all over her daughter's clothes and then end up in the carpet of Hannah's Honda.

Judging by Lucy's squeal, the package was already a hit and she hadn't even opened it yet. When she tore into the pink paper and raised the lid of the box, both mother and daughter gasped. Lucy pulled the pink raincoat from the box reverently, her eyes shining.

"Mama, it has unicorns," she breathed.

Hannah nodded, unable to speak coherently because what was she supposed to say about Owen buying his daughter a Stella McCartney raincoat that she knew for a fact cost over two hundred and fifty dollars? *Thank you? We can't accept? I've been drooling over this coat for three months and couldn't rationalize spending that much money on something Lucy would outgrow?*

"It's too much," she finally murmured.

Owen just smiled indulgently. "Blasphemy. Nothing is too much. Besides, you haven't seen what I got you yet."

Hannah's brows nearly hit her hairline. Owen had gotten her a present too? "That really is too much."

"Except it's not," he corrected and pulled another box from beside his bed, handing it to her as Lucy hopped off the bed to try on her coat, twisting this way and that in an attempt to see all the unicorns at once.

Automatically, Hannah took the package, noting the heavy metallic rose-colored wrapping paper was almost the exact shade of the dress she'd worn to the courthouse to marry Owen. Because he'd remembered the ceremony or because he'd seen the dress in the photograph she'd showed him?

More to the point, was there some significance to him picking that shade? What was she supposed to take from this?

"Open it," he instructed with barely concealed glee.

"What is this all about, Owen?" she muttered, her gaze on him, not the package. There was an angle here and she refused to miss it while ogling a pretty box.

"It's about me being grateful that you're taking time out of your busy schedule to spend a day with me in the most boring place on the universe," he said, his gaze solemn and deep and full of things she didn't understand but wanted to. "It's about me realizing that I have a lot to make up for. It's me saying thank you for letting me know Lucy."

Hannah glanced at her daughter—and his too—but she was thankfully dialed into the beautiful, impractical raincoat and ignoring them both.

"Open your gift, Hannah," he instructed quietly. "It might be the wrong size and then I'll have to figure out how to send it back when it was an enormous pain to get the hospital to allow deliveries here in the first place."

"Did I get a unicorn raincoat too?" she asked wryly, secretly hoping the answer was yes, because what woman didn't need a beautiful, impractical coat that cost more than her water bill?

"Only one way to find out," Owen told her mischievously as he nudged the box closer.

Rolling her eyes, she fingered the tape loose, hoping to save the paper. It was really nice paper, the kind she could reuse for a myriad of crafts later. When she lifted the lid of the box, she forgot about the wrapping, her suspicions about Owen's motives and possibly her own name.

"This is not a raincoat," she whispered as she gingerly lifted out one of three bottles of twenty-five-year-old Aceto balsamic vinegar from Modena packed in crinkle paper shavings. "Owen, what in the world…"

She could barely stand to hold it in her hand for fear of

breaking it. Neither could she fathom ever putting it down again. The glass cooled her palm, thick and dark to protect the contents from harsh light. The bottle's design alone marked it as something special, never mind what it held.

"This is definitely too much," she insisted as she met Owen's gaze, very much afraid that the slosh of emotions inside had somehow surfaced on her face. "Even one of these bottles runs in the hundreds of dollars. Where did you even find something like this?"

"So you like it?"

"That's akin to asking Santa Claus if he likes Christmas. Of course I like it. Any chef on the planet would kill for access to balsamic vinegar of this quality."

And she'd just been given three bottles. By a man who had no reason to have come up with such a thoughtful gift. She hadn't even been a caterer when they'd been married. She'd developed her love of cooking after that, when she'd been desperate to figure out how to support herself and her daughter, not just on her own financially but mentally and emotionally too.

But this gift wasn't going to go on a shelf in her industrial kitchen. This was a private, personal gift for her as a woman, not a caterer. There was a subtle line between the two and Owen had found it. How had he clued in that she would appreciate this far more than flowers or jewelry?

Before Owen never would have.

The fact that Current Owen paid this kind of attention to both her and Lucy knocked her for a loop.

Before she'd had any time to get her feet under her, the doctor strolled into the room. "Oh, good to see you, Ms. Colton. If you have a moment, I'd like to speak with you in the hall."

That did not sound good. Owen caught her gaze and

tilted his head toward the door, then called out to Lucy in a clear ploy to keep her busy. As if they'd often conspired together to allow Hannah to slip from the room while he occupied their daughter.

It was dizzying how quickly Owen had picked up on the dynamics required to keep a five-year-old busy. And the reasons one needed to.

"Yes, hello, Dr. Farris," Hannah said as she joined the doctor at the nurse's station a couple of rooms down from Owen's.

It was busier than the last time she'd spoken to him. Nurses rushed by in both directions, and the phone next to the empty workstation rang and rang with no one to pick it up.

The doctor regarded her for a brief moment, and she had the impression he was gearing up for something. Bad news? She firmed her mouth, mentally preparing for the worst. Though what that could be when Owen clearly had all his faculties and some extra ones that he'd developed out of nowhere, she had no idea.

"I'll cut right to the chase, Ms. Colton. We're at a point where we can't keep Mr. Mackenzie in the hospital any longer. We're releasing him today, but I have reservations about his ability to function without help."

"What?" Her brain spun in an effort to keep up with what the doctor was telling her. "How can you release him? He doesn't remember anything about his life."

"That's the reason we're having this discussion," he said flatly, his eyes still kind behind his glasses. "Physically, he's fine. His ribs are healing and the stitches in his head will dissolve over time. He needs some basic wound care, and it wouldn't hurt for him to stay on bed rest for a few more days until he's feeling up to more movement. But from a trauma perspective, a hospital is overkill. And he doesn't have any insurance."

Hannah's eyes went wide. "How can he not have insurance? Who has been paying for his stay thus far?"

"We're not monsters, Ms. Colton," the doctor said with an unamused laugh. "We don't just take patients based on their ability to pay. That's the reason the folks in that department started looking for next of kin, actually, and found you. I'm sure they'll work with him to develop a payment plan for the balance owed. We've kept him this long because I had a personal interest in his recovery, but we've done everything we can do for his memory issues. Now it's just going to take time."

"But what is he supposed to do?" she asked as the enormity of Owen's situation worked its way into the cracks of her very foundation. With no insurance, the bill he'd be receiving would likely be backbreaking. "He can't work if he doesn't remember his job or how to do it or even where it is."

The doctor's gaze bored into her, willing her to read between the lines. Well, she didn't like those lines. Or what was between them. And shutting her eyes didn't erase the reality of what he was telling her.

"You want me to take care of him," she stated with zero inflection.

"He needs someone, yes. It would be difficult for him to navigate in a world he doesn't remember, especially while also trying to finish healing. Of course, he can relearn job skills and things of that nature, but he's not back to a hundred percent physically yet. I would recommend he not be left alone. And he needs to follow up with a primary care doctor in a few days."

Which meant the only option was for Owen to stay with her. At her house. So she could be the one to dress his head wound and make sure he didn't overexert himself while his ribs healed. She could cook for him. Fold him into her life. Get used to having someone else around who could sit with Lucy while Hannah took a shower.

It sounded…not horrible.

But how long would that last? How long would she want it to last?

"This is a lot to consider," she said faintly. "What if he doesn't ever regain his memories?"

"That is unfortunately a possibility," the doctor warned her.

But she was busy reveling in how so very wonderful that sounded, to keep this version of Owen around for a good long while, the one that seemed thrilled with the idea of being a father. Who bought them lavish gifts selected with exquisite care.

They could be a family. For real this time.

If that was her reward for taking him in, she'd do it in a heartbeat. But of course, there was no guarantee. And how selfish was she, hoping that Owen never remembered who he was?

None of that mattered in the grand scheme of things. He needed her, not the other way around. What choice did she have but to take him in? Her conscience wouldn't allow her to do anything but that. He had no one else in the world to take care of him other than Hannah. If that wasn't true, they'd have found someone by now.

Even if he one day woke up and remembered he was Old Owen and tore everything to pieces once again, she couldn't walk away from him.

Chapter 10

When Hannah got back to the room, Owen and Lucy were playing tic-tac-toe on a thick pad with the hospital logo in the lower right-hand corner.

She couldn't help but smile. "Who's winning?"

"Me, Mama," Lucy announced and put another *X* in a box, then drew a line. "Daddy sucks at this game."

"We don't say the word *sucks*," she reminded her daughter for the nine millionth time, which was a lost cause because Wade said it, and Lucy refused to accept Hannah's explanation that Uncle Wade was an adult and bound by different rules.

"I'm learning though," Owen said with a wink at Lucy, shooting Hannah a wide smile. "Mostly that my daughter is a shark when it comes to games."

"You didn't bet any money, did you?" Hannah asked dryly, and Owen shook his head. "Highly suggest you don't start. Lucy, why don't you let me talk to your father for a few minutes? If you sit in the chair outside until I come get you, I'll let you play Candy Crush on my phone."

The best treat in her arsenal. Lucy perked up and slid from the bed instantly, a testament to how rarely Hannah used it. Dutifully, Lucy followed her out to the chair in question, taking the precious phone as if she'd been handed the key to Fort Knox.

"What's the rule?" Hannah asked as she covered the screen with her hand before Lucy could start the game.

"No going to other apps. No in-app purchases unless I ask first. No laying down the phone for any reason," Lucy recited, and Hannah smiled in approval.

Calculating that she had about five minutes, Hannah scooted back into Owen's room. It was the first time they'd been alone together in what felt like forever. She had a fine awareness of the way he watched her, so carefully, as if afraid to miss even a single hair.

"What's going on, Hannah?" he asked quietly. "The doctor spoke to you about me being released, didn't he?"

"Yeah, he did." She let out the breath she'd been holding and with it, her reservations. "I'm going to bring you home with me."

It was the right thing to do. But Owen didn't fist pump or grin salaciously. He just let his warm brown eyes focus on her for an eternity until he finally asked, "Why?"

"You're just starting a relationship with Lucy," she said. "She would be devastated not to see you any longer. Besides, where would you go?"

"I'll figure something out," he insisted. "I wasn't planning to leave Conners, if that was your concern."

"No, my concern is that you don't have anyone else who cares what happens to you, Owen."

And by default, that meant she did. He caught the point too, judging by the way the warmth in his gaze spilled over to encompass them both like a blanket.

"Are you sure this is a good idea?" he murmured. "I was a pretty crappy husband. I can't imagine that you have many fond feelings for me."

"Let me worry about that." Especially since she'd already gotten a jump start on that, wondering what in the world she was doing inviting her ex-husband to stay with her in the home she'd made with her daughter after losing everything by his hand the first time. "It's only temporary. Until you get on your feet again. Over the next few days, we'll have plenty of time to talk about what happens next. Whether you want to continue to have a relationship with Lucy going forward. How we facilitate that."

Owen caught her hand in his, lacing their fingers together in a surprise move that felt completely foreign— and she'd held hands with this man before. Lots of times. Granted, it had been years ago, and some days she felt like she couldn't remember being Early-Twenties Hannah at all.

She stared at their entwined fingers as the warmth he'd enveloped her in expanded and grew, becoming quite a bit more heated.

"Thank you," he said quietly. "For trusting me enough to say something like that."

Okay, now she was staring at him, trying to convince herself she hadn't misheard him. Before Owen would have never even realized she'd expressed a great deal of trust in him. That the very act of marrying him had been a gift of trust. And he'd trampled it.

"Everyone deserves a second chance," she said.

Checkout took far less time than Hannah was expecting, and before she could fully acclimate to this new reality, Owen had allowed himself to be tucked into the passenger seat of her Honda, seat belt arranged carefully across his healing ribs.

Lucy was thrilled to pieces that her daddy was coming home with them. Hannah had explained that he was still sick, so she'd offered to help take care of him so he could be closer to Lucy whenever she wanted to see him. With her freakishly keen insight, Lucy had added that this way, she wouldn't have to work around her school schedule to see him either. Which Hannah wished she'd thought of. It did make things easier all the way around.

Except for the weird things it was doing to her heart rate to be seated this close to Owen. Their elbows were practically touching over the center console. The flush of awareness spread across her skin, and she was afraid he might realize she was blushing.

It was stupid. She wasn't a blusher.

Shrugging it off, she put the car in gear and drove, painfully aware that Owen didn't even have a coat to his name. The few belongings they'd handed him at the hospital hurt her heart. "I can take you shopping sometime if you like."

Owen nodded. "I would appreciate that. I don't seem to have packed for a long trip."

Another reason this was a very bad idea. That telltale sign probably meant that he hadn't intended to stay in this area. The accident had forced him into a much longer stretch than he'd been planning. If—when—he regained his memories, he'd probably confess that he was just driving through. The fact that Hannah and Lucy lived near Conners may have never crossed his mind.

If he regained his memories. It was still a big *if.*

Nerves loosened her tongue, and she babbled about the sights the entire drive home to Owl Creek, pointing out Blackbird Lake as it came into view, Wade's house as she passed the drive, the new barbecue place that had opened not too long ago.

"This is your house?" Owen asked, surprise tinging his voice as she pulled into the driveway of the bungalow she'd bought from her brother, Chase, for a discount that she'd argued about until their mother had intervened, insisting that Hannah buy the dang house and let Chase help her afford it.

But she didn't go into those details. Her family had closed ranks around her after Owen had left, and she loved them for it. Regardless, the actions of Old Owen had no place here, at least not at the moment, and she'd like to forget about all of that. Start fresh. Like she'd told him—and she wholeheartedly believed it—everyone deserved a second chance, and she intended to give him one.

"Home sweet home," she confirmed lightly. "And yours for at least a few days. I hope it's okay."

"I just didn't picture you as a living in a house by the lake," he said. "It's better than okay. This is charming. It's a house I would have picked out for myself."

Looking at it with fresh eyes, she did have to admit the place was stunning, with the views of the lake and modern touches that set it apart from the rental properties closer to town. Wade's cabin lay just a quarter of a mile away, visible through the trees now that winter had stripped them of their leaves. Her place had come with a storage shed down by the water where she kept Lucy's floaties and some of the bigger equipment for her catering business.

"It's more than a home," she admitted. "It's a refuge. I hope you come to think of it as one, as well."

He caught her gaze, an emotion she didn't recognize spilling into the space between them as Lucy took Hannah's key and ran inside, leaving the adults standing on the driveway. She should be chilled given the temperature, but it turned out that the heat from sitting next to him in the car had seeped into her bones. Liquefying them. Her knees nearly buckled but she locked them and somehow managed to keep herself off the crushed shells beneath her feet.

"You're a very generous woman, Hannah," he told her sincerely. "I've never met anyone like you."

She laughed without meaning to. But this was all so absurd. "You mean you don't remember meeting someone like me. I'm still the same person you used to be married to, Owen."

"Somehow I doubt that. Maybe you have amnesia too," he teased. "But I see how you are with Lucy, and I have a feeling she's at least partially made you into the person you are now."

That was true and not an insignificant point. Everything that had happened to her since Owen abandoned her had worked to transform her into someone new. Someone she liked. She'd worked hard to provide for Lucy and be a good single mom, which she should honor instead of sweeping under the rug.

It was so odd for Owen to be the one to point that out.

"You're right," she admitted. "I have changed. I'm not who I was when we were married."

The way he was looking at her made her feel blushy again.

"I'm happy to meet you, Hannah Colton," he murmured and held out his hand. "Do me a favor and call me Mac. Maybe that will help us both feel like we really are meeting for the first time."

Mac. Short for Mackenzie. It was fitting somehow, and she did not want to examine how thrilling it was to think of him this way. As someone new, someone she'd never met. Someone she was astonishingly attracted to.

Without thinking through the consequences, she reached for him, allowing his fingers to wrap around hers. The jolt that traveled through her felt as foreign as it did electrifying. Why had she taken off her gloves?

Quickly, she pulled free, immediately missing his warmth. "It's chilly. We should go inside."

Owen—Mac—nodded as if nothing significant had happened.

Nothing significant *had* happened. She was being silly, thinking that it was so momentous for Owen… Mac…to have recognized that they were essentially strangers at this point, as if they had never met.

But she couldn't get it out of her mind that on Mac's side, that was his reality. He didn't think of himself as Owen, didn't remember Owen. But Mac? That was the man he was now.

What if because of that they could have a brand-new start in the very best way? As if they had no history? No bad stuff between them. It was a do-over on steroids that only she could facilitate.

Mac followed her into the house, commenting on everything from her large, well-appointed kitchen, to the floor-to-ceiling glass in her living room that overlooked the lake. Lucy popped up to show Mac her room, a reprieve Hannah took with every fiber of her being.

Blowing out a breath, she hung up her coat in the mudroom and slipped off her waterproof boots in favor of her house shoes that she'd never thought twice about.

But she'd never had a man in her house who would be looking at her feet. The serviceable brown slippers were a little worn-out but more to the point, might have graced the cover of Octogenarian Magazine. She might have to rethink her wardrobe choices in addition to how to feed another adult when she was so used to cooking for one adult and one very picky eater who turned her nose up at vegetables.

Mac returned from the back of the house, Lucy's hand

in his, as she towed him around showing him the entire place, apparently.

"And this is where I watch cartoons," she explained as she pointed to the couch. "You can watch with me."

"Your father is probably not a *Peppa Pig* fan," Hannah called. Poor guy was probably overwhelmed by Lucy's excited chatter.

"How would he know if he hasn't watched it yet?" Lucy returned with her typical eerie five-year-old logic. "Plus, you said he was sick. Cartoons are for when you're sick. They'll make him feel better."

"Can't argue with that," Mac said cheerfully and allowed his daughter to haul him over to the couch, settling in with remarkable grace as Lucy expertly cued up an episode of the show using her kids' profile on the streaming service Hannah preferred.

He looked quite at home, laughing as Lucy pointed out all her favorite characters. Oh, goodness. Hannah put a hand to her fluttering tummy, willing it to stop acting like *that*.

She had no call to be reacting to the sight of her exhusband spending time with their daughter. Lots of people co-parented without dissolving into puddles of goo when they spied a father and daughter watching a TV show together. What was her problem?

The problem was that he didn't resemble her ex in any way, shape or form. He was Mac. She desperately wanted to grasp that fact. It was a lifeline at the moment. A way to balance her feelings for him that didn't interfere with the past.

It was a *good* thing that he was here. Good for Lucy. Good for Mac.

Her problem was that it was a bad thing for her state of mind. Not for the reasons she'd thought, though. But because she couldn't stop thinking about how different things could be this second time around.

At the end of the day, she couldn't call herself altruistic if she had an ulterior motive, could she? Inviting him here was about exploring this new Mac, bottom line. What could be. What this unexpected blessing of amnesia had done for them all.

Her problem was that it could have always been like this. If he hadn't left. If he hadn't been the type of guy who couldn't stick. They'd lost *years*.

And she had a slim sliver of hope that they could reclaim some of that time lost, that it could be like this all the time. Forever. As long as he didn't recover his memories.

Chapter 11

This charade had gone on *far* too long.

Seriously, how had Archer ended up at Hannah's house, still answering to the name Owen? So he'd fixed that by switching to Mac. Everyone at work called him that. It wouldn't be difficult to answer to.

Except it was ridiculous that he'd let it get to this point whether she called him Mac, Owen or Howdy Doody. He had to tell her the truth. Immediately.

Okay, granted, he'd thought maybe it would be excusable to give himself one day. *One day* to play Lucy's father, to try to make up for a whole lifetime of her being disappointed by Owen Mackenzie. Lucy deserved to have good memories of the man who had sired her, and only Archer could give her that.

But then he'd walked into this home and felt the love that had built it. Seen how Hannah parented her daughter, how bright and special Lucy was. Something had physically scored him inside, and he couldn't stand to keep lying to this wonderful woman and amazing little girl his brother had screwed over.

Except he'd never gotten even a second alone with Hannah from the instant they'd crossed the threshold. Until now.

"Hannah," Archer called the moment Lucy disappeared

into her room to fetch the stuffed dog she called Mr. Fluffers. "I need to talk to you. It's important."

Hannah paused, midchop, peering at him from behind the long island/bar combo that separated the living area from the kitchen. "I can listen and julienne bell pepper for this catering job at the same time."

"I mean *privately*," he stressed.

He couldn't in good conscience blurt out the truth where Lucy might hear him. Part of this confession would entail asking Hannah the best way to handle his exit, which needed to come sooner rather than later.

Hannah laughed. "We have a five-year-old daughter. There is no privacy unless she's at school, which won't happen for another fourteen hours."

"What about after she goes to bed?" he asked, ignoring the pang that accompanied phrases like *we have a daughter*.

He didn't have a daughter. He didn't have anything other than an overinflated sense of responsibly to fix the stuff Owen broke.

But he wanted to be the other half of the "we" in Hannah's statement.

Man, was it ever hard not to insert himself in the middle of this cozy scene and run with it, claiming Lucy as his own. He'd never thought about being a dad before, never wondered what it was like to shop for presents and watch with barely concealed glee as the little human he'd helped create discovered what was in the box.

Now he knew. It was like nothing else on the planet, and he wanted more.

But this was not his life, and he had no right to steal his brother's. Or let his brother's former wife keep thinking Archer was Owen.

Hannah laughed again, a sound he should not like so

much. Particularly since he had a feeling it was at his expense.

"You have clearly never put a five-year-old to bed. There's always a fifty-fifty chance we'll be graced with her presence six times between the last story and when we finally pass out from exhaustion after fetching her a glass of water, fixing the curtains so they don't look weird, tucking in Mr. Fluffers again because he's cold—" this she accompanied with exaggerated air quotes "—and who knows what all she'll dream up as an excuse to get out of bed one last time. Especially with you here. I fully expect to be told there's a leprechaun under the bed and only Daddy can make it go away."

Mouth ajar, he blinked. "That's all going to happen in one night?"

"More than once," she promised, still chopping away while talking, as advertised. "If it can't wait, I can send her to Wade's down the shore. She loves to hang out with Betty Jane. That's a dog," she supplied helpfully. "But it will have to be after dinner because he's not home right now."

"That's…who's Wade?" he thought to ask, even though he knew Wade Colton was her brother from the research he'd done on her family. It seemed like a thing Owen would have forgotten, though.

"I thought I mentioned him. He's my brother," Hannah called from the depths of the pantry. "I have two others and two sisters. Six of us total. Oh, and Sarah and Nate. I really didn't mean to leave them out. It's just—you know, new. I have to keep reframing my family to include them."

"It's fine," he said. "If you think Wade wouldn't mind, that would be great."

"Sure. We do need to talk about…things," Hannah said as she came back into the kitchen from the pantry, empty-handed, her expression perplexed. "Lucy? Where are you? Have you been in my kitchen?"

"What's wrong?" Archer asked.

"Some things in the pantry have been rearranged and a bottle of oil is missing. I need it to sauté these peppers." Hannah frowned and opened one of the cabinet doors, then another one. "Some of the dishes in these cabinets have been moved too. It's like my dresser drawers all over again. This is so weird."

Archer's gut pinged and his senses sharpened to full-alert mode. "What do you mean, like your dresser drawers? Some things were rearranged in your dresser too? The one in your bedroom?"

Hannah nodded, biting her lip. "I thought it was Lucy, but I just remembered that my shampoo bottles were out of order. I probably did that, though. I'm just so distracted lately…"

She trailed off, but he knew she meant because of him, which did not ease his guilt any.

"Can you show me your shampoo bottles? And the dresser? I'd like to see everything that you've noticed is different, no matter how small of a change you think it is."

"What? Why?" Now Hannah's expression veered toward alarmed and she scrubbed at her neck as if agitated. "Do you think something is wrong?"

Yeah, something was wrong. Someone had been searching her house, pretty methodically too and on more than one occasion, by the sounds of it, but not carefully enough to avoid detection. His blood chilled as he thought about the implications. Big Mike had fingers in a lot of pies. There was absolutely no reason to believe Hannah had skated under his radar—and a lot of reasons to believe that he'd already known about her because she'd been working with Owen.

No. He couldn't picture Hannah in that role any longer. There was no way she'd been Owen's accomplice. Or was that his emotional response instead of the analytical one?

Archer nearly sighed out loud. When he couldn't remove his own prejudice from the equation, how could he rightly call his conclusions unbiased?

Hannah might be involved. He didn't know for certain.

But even if she wasn't, that didn't mean she hadn't popped up on Big Mike's People of Interest list. Five million dollars was a lot of money to be missing in the first place, but if it could be traced to a crime organization, Big Mike had more than a vested interest in recovering it, regardless of whether there was an innocent little girl in the mix.

"Nothing's wrong," he assured Hannah, or at least he hoped he'd used his most reassuring voice.

Archer was an analyst, not a comforter. But he'd dang well better learn how to smooth over his tendency to be business first since he clearly wasn't going anywhere.

His plan to tell Hannah the truth evaporated as his mind instantly chopped through the data with the same efficiency she'd applied to make short work of the peppers. The sooner she knew he wasn't Owen, the sooner it would get out to someone in Big Mike's organization. And it was far better for everyone to think that the hitman assigned to take out Owen had failed.

For now. At least until Archer could get some more facts.

"Nothing's wrong," he repeated. "I'm just curious. I like to figure things out and if I can help ease your mind about what's going on around here, I'd like to."

That much at least was true.

Seemingly mollified, Hannah asked him to wait while she put Lucy to bed, a mysterious ritual he wanted to know more about. In time, he hoped he'd get to be involved.

A solid thirty minutes later, Hannah led him to the back of the house via the hallway to Lucy's room. The guest room Hannah had shown him to earlier lay in the opposite direction, off the kitchen. He didn't assume it was an accident that the rooms were so completely separate, and he appreciated the reason.

But if it came down to it, he couldn't protect Hannah or Lucy if he was so far away. Archer suspected he might eventually be sleeping on the floor outside Lucy's door pending what he discovered regarding the not-so-invisible fingers who had searched the house.

The moment he crossed the threshold to Hannah's bedroom, he realized his mistake. It smelled like vanilla and sunshine, exploding with colors and light. Exactly like the woman. He could scarcely look away from the bed where he could easily imagine Hannah sleeping in something scanty and…way off-limits. A guy like him shouldn't even be fantasizing about her clothed, let alone anything else.

She didn't even know his real name.

Archer swallowed. "You said something about shampoo bottles?"

Hannah nodded and let him into the bathroom that was even smaller than the bedroom. He could reach out and pull her into his arms with no effort whatsoever from this distance. Which was an idea he quite liked. And also needed to stop thinking about.

"I line up all my bottles on that window ledge." Hannah pointed at the long rectangle that sat about six feet off the shower floor. "I don't like them on the floor, and shower caddies always slip off the showerhead, so I stopped buying them."

Too high for Lucy to be the one who moved them around. Kudos to whoever did rearrange them though—checking for hidden keys and other important things inside random bottles was exactly what he'd have thought of too.

"Makes sense," he said, curious why she thought she had to justify her own personal organization system.

"You always got so mad when the shower caddy wouldn't stay put," she told him, biting her lip in the way he'd started to think of as her Owen face. Anytime she recounted something he'd done in the past, she always looked like she wasn't sure if she should be talking about this stuff.

"I was a jerk, Hannah," he told her bluntly. "You don't have to sugarcoat anything for me. I can take whatever you want to dish out about how I used to act. I need to hear it. I don't ever want to be that guy again."

That was literally impossible, but he also appreciated the lessons on how not to be like Owen if he ever had a doubt about whether he was his twin's polar opposite.

"When you say things like that…" Hannah hesitated, her gaze flitting between him and the floor.

Unable to help himself, he reached out and tilted her head up with his thumb, fanning out his fingers to cup her face. "What? When I say things like what, Hannah?"

Her skin warmed his hand as she stared at him. "Things that make me think you're serious about being different. Serious about being a father. It's overwhelming."

"I mean every word," he said gruffly, and it was the truth. At least as much as he had the ability to make things better for her. To fix the things Owen had broken.

Of course, Archer was in the process of creating a whole new set of difficulties the longer he stood here with his hand skating along Hannah's jaw. Because he couldn't seem to pull away. Or make himself stop staring into her eyes, willing her to see *him*. Not Owen.

"I don't know what to think half the time," she murmured. "It's like you're two different people."

Archer's heart stuttered. "What do you mean?"

She let her lips drift upward. "In my head, I refer to you as Before Owen and Current Owen. It's like Before Owen vanished, and Current Owen is who showed up in his place."

That, he could work with. It was better than her realizing he wasn't Owen—he could be a hybrid version of himself. "We can thank amnesia for that, I guess. Since I don't remember who I was, I'm doing whatever feels natural. Maybe this me was always trapped inside and I just needed a swift punch to the head to uncover it. It would be nice if you could forget Before Owen, too, and I'm sorry I can't figure out a way to help with that."

Was he a horrible person for reveling in Hannah's focused attention? His brother had messed up his relationship with this woman and all Archer wanted was a redo. A way to set things right and maybe slide into something that seemed like it would be amazing at the same time.

There was no way the universe would be so cruel as to ensure Owen had screwed it up for Archer too. Who better to give Hannah this second chance than someone who knew exactly what it felt like to be betrayed and disappointed by Owen Mackenzie?

Besides, Hannah had a steel core that Owen would never have recognized. A sense of humor Owen would never have understood. A warm personality that his brother would not have appreciated.

But Archer did. On all three counts.

"What are you doing, Mama?" Lucy called as she strolled into the bathroom rubbing her eyes. "I heard a noise."

Archer dropped his hand before Lucy could clue in that

he'd been about half a second away from reeling in her mother for a very long overdue kiss.

Thank goodness for interruptions. Kissing Hannah would have been a very bad idea for a multitude of reasons, none of which he could think of at the moment.

"Hey, Lu Lu," Hannah called brightly and stooped down to engulf her daughter in a hug, despite the fact that the little scamp should be in bed. "Sorry we woke you."

Witnessing the two of them entwined put a lump in Archer's throat. Hannah and Lucy loved each other so openly and easily. His relationship with his own mother was complicated by her inability to see Owen for the scammer he was. She loved her sons equally and thought it was a virtue, failing to see that not holding Owen accountable for his sins devalued her love for Archer.

Yet Archer still did as she asked, chasing after Owen's killer, desperate to win a little more of that love over to his side. Where it should be.

"If I had a dog, I wouldn't be worried when I hear voices," Lucy announced slyly, her gaze full of wide innocence as she slid it over in his direction, likely because she'd already figured out he was the easy mark.

Archer had to laugh. "Is that so?"

"Or," Hannah interjected lightly, "you could think to yourself, oh, that's right, my daddy is here now and there's nothing to worry about because he's going to take care of me."

That sentiment put a whole lot more than a lump in his throat.

"I will definitely do that as long as I am physically able to, Lucy Mackenzie," he said, the catch in his voice wider than the Grand Canyon.

"You don't have to say my whole name at home, Daddy," she told him with a lofty toss of her head.

"Well, the thing is, I've never said it," he told her truthfully. "And I like saying it because it's my name too."

Lucy grinned. "We can be twins."

Well, that was a sobering—and telling—reminder if he'd ever heard one. As cozy as this stolen family time was, he had no right to be wishing he'd been the one here with Lucy this whole time, tucking her into bed every night for the last four years. His brother had really missed out on something great.

"Back to bed, Ms. Thing," Hannah said and scooped up her daughter to carry her out of the bathroom.

Leaving Archer behind. Because he wasn't part of their routine. Not yet. Probably not ever. He was living on borrowed time in the first place. If Big Mike did figure out there was a man living in Hannah's house who looked like Owen Mackenzie and answered to that name, Archer's life would be in jeopardy.

He took himself off to bed, settling into the guest room that he imagined Hannah had decorated herself with earth tones and shades of peach that were a perfect balance between masculine and feminine. It was ironic. This place felt more like a home than the one he lived in every day, and he'd only been here less than six hours.

Chapter 12

In the morning, Archer taught himself how the coffee maker functioned and had a pot brewed before Hannah emerged from her wing of the house. She came into the kitchen wearing a long quilted robe that would have been dowdy on anyone else.

On Hannah, it made his mouth go dry.

"Good morning," he choked out hoarsely and cleared his throat.

Moron. The long talk he'd given himself about letting his slight crush on Hannah get out of hand clearly had not worked. It was just so hard not to think about how his brother had basically done whatever he'd wanted his entire life with no regard to consequences, and his reward had been Hannah and Lucy. Who he'd promptly abandoned.

And Archer's reward for doing the right thing his entire life was the opportunity to lie to this woman about his identity and pretend to be Lucy's father. All so he could figure out a way to repair the damage Owen had done, plus investigate who had killed him. Oh, and look for the millions of dollars of missing money in his spare time, while keeping his eyes open about a potential threat to this precious family he'd stumbled over.

No problem.

Was it too much to ask that he get a little bit of something good out of this whole deal? A very brief shot at feeling like this family belonged to him, even if only for a couple of days?

Completely oblivious to his internal angst, Hannah crossed to the coffee pot and inhaled the rich aroma. "There is no better scent in the world than freshly brewed coffee. Thank you. I used to preprogram the machine to brew it before I got out of bed, but when Lucy was a baby, she had a lot of digestive issues. More often than not, the coffee would sit on the burner for an hour, sometime two, before I could actually take the time to drink it, so I quit doing that. It was just easier to make the coffee fresh in the morning when I was ready for it. It's nice to have someone else make it for once."

Fascinated in spite of himself, he took his own mug and slid into one of the barstools at the long kitchen island. "Tell me about Lucy as a baby. Start at the beginning. Don't leave anything out."

Hannah laughed and it was as nice of a sound in the dim morning light as it had been last night. Maybe better because Lucy was still in bed asleep. As far as he knew anyway. He'd never appreciated Hannah's warning that they'd have zero privacy more than he did at the moment, because he'd like nothing more than to back her up against the counter and see what it felt like for her to laugh against his mouth.

Right. Because *Lucy* was the biggest obstacle to that fantasy.

"That's a tall order," she countered lightly, sipping her coffee. Then she moaned and let her eyelids flutter shut. "This is amazing. What did you do to this?"

He was too busy stuffing away his inappropriate reaction to her coffee-drinking that he couldn't answer for a beat. "I put grounds in the filter and turned it on."

"Liar," she accused with a smile. "I do that, and it comes out okay. This is a whole other level."

"I'm heavy handed with the scoop, I guess." He shrugged, ridiculously pleased that she liked something he'd done for her enough to comment on it. Moving on. His reactions to Hannah's reactions were a dangerous subject. "Back to Lucy. If you can't tell me everything, at least some highlights. Anything. I'm not picky."

Hannah joined him at the breakfast bar on the backside of the island, but she didn't sit in a chair. Instead, she leaned a hip on the counter, facing him, and he tried not to think about how easy it would be to swivel his chair with the sole intent of pulling her into his lap. Or between his legs for an embrace that would feel far too intimate for a kitchen.

Though this island did have a very large, very solid white marble top that could be put to a lot of uses that had nothing to do with chopping vegetables.

"Since you deserve a medal for this coffee, and Lucy stories are my favorite, I guess I can come up with a couple." She warmed to her subject, riffling through the file folders in her brain for whatever she might deem worthy of sharing. "You see how good she is at tic-tac-toe. It's not just that one. She learned to play card games at three. Slap Jack is still her favorite, but she picked up Uno this past Christmas from Wade, along with three or four others, all of which she will kick the pants off you if you play with her. She's so competitive. I have no idea where she gets that from."

Owen. No question.

His twin made everything a competition, from who could finish eating first to who could pick up a girl the quickest at a bar. That one had gotten old fast, especially when Owen had been a champion at identifying the one Archer had noticed first, and then swooping in to pluck the girl away with his charm.

That had been one of many reasons Archer had cut off contact with his brother ten years ago. It was just too much.

Still was. The pattern had obviously continued, with Owen beating Archer to the punch once again with Hannah. Only this time, Owen wouldn't be coming back around for a second try. This shot was all Archer's. If only he could figure out whether there was actually a shot to be taken here.

"I'd love to play with her," he told her honestly. "I am a very good loser."

Hannah laughed like he was kidding, but Archer was the opposite of competitive. He'd had to be growing up with Owen. Someone had to be second and it was never his brother, so that left Archer to learn how to be okay with never winning. It was how he'd gotten good at analyzing a situation.

When you weren't focused on beating everyone else, you could take a step back and notice details. See the lay of the land, so to speak. Take time to put pieces together and take a top-down view to what the whole looked like.

"It's your funeral," Hannah said, her mouth lifting at the corners in a tiny smile that was somehow better than her normal one. As if they were sharing a secret. "Like I said, don't bet any money you don't want to lose. She is a shark when she scents candy money coming her way. My brother, Fletcher, walked away ten dollars poorer last week, and I'm fairly certain he thought he was going to let her win as a courtesy, only she beat him fair and square. Four games of Uno in a row."

"I'm not sure if that should make me proud or terrified," he admitted.

"Exactly," Hannah said with another of the tiny smiles that were quickly becoming his favorite. "That's one of the things they don't tell you about parenting. It veers between making you gooey inside over your little person's accomplishments and worried you're not going to be able to guide them toward using their powers for good instead of evil."

The underlying stress and uncertainty beneath her joke came through loud and clear. Would he ever not insert judgment on his brother's stupid decisions? How could he avoid it when Owen had skipped out on standing side by side with this amazing woman to help her raise the human being they'd made together? It was unconscionable.

"I'm sorry, Hannah," he said sincerely, also wondering how many times he'd have to apologize for Owen's bone-headedness before he felt like it was enough. "I should have been here, helping you figure out how to keep Lucy from turning into a pool hustler before the age of twelve."

Hannah didn't laugh that time. Okay, so he wasn't as good with the jokes yet, or it was too soon. He wasn't sure.

But then she shocked him by covering his hand with hers. "You're here now, Mac. That's what matters. The past is the past. Let's move forward."

The grace radiating from this woman… It humbled him. And pricked at his eyelids enough that he had to blink a bunch to avoid a show of unmanly tears.

"I can get on board with that," he agreed readily, since leaving the past in the past was the only way he could move forward. "And before we go too much more forward, I do want to say thank you again, for inviting me to stay here. For being so willing and open to give me a second chance with Lucy. It means a lot to me."

She went dead silent for a beat and then nodded once. "I'm choosing to trust you. Because it means a lot to me that you want to be here. That you want to have a relation-ship with Lucy. Don't disappoint me on this. Or her. She deserves to know you."

"I completely agree," he interjected fiercely. This was the one thing that was nonnegotiable, no matter what happened. "I'm not going anywhere this time. When I say I want to be her father, I mean it."

This part at least crystallized for him.

He'd figure out what his promise looked like once everyone knew the truth later. He'd…adopt Lucy. Or something. Whatever made it legal for him to be her daddy from now on, he'd do it.

But first, he needed to get square with Big Mike's agenda, whatever it was. Get the trigger finger who had offed Owen behind bars. Find the money. At this point, he'd take finding a flipping clue in lieu of the money. As long as he could call it progress toward the end of this charade.

On that note, now that he wasn't hampered by being in the hospital, he could do a lot more low-key nosing around. "If it's okay with you, I'd like take a tour of the town. I didn't get to see too much of it as we drove through. It's called Owl Creek, right?"

Hannah nodded. "Do you want me to play tour guide or explore on your own? We lived in Conners before, when we were married, but my family is from here. I've got a few roots, to say the least."

Once again, he was struck by the fact that she'd uprooted herself to move to a new city with her new husband. Had Owen even realized how difficult that must have been for her to be a newlywed with a baby in a city an hour's drive from everything familiar?

"If you have time, I'd love for you to show me around,"

he said, immediately scrapping his plan to do some investigating.

He'd rather spend time with Hannah, given how fleeting
those opportunities were. And how quickly the possibility
would dry up as soon as he confessed his crimes, of which
there were many.

She certainly wouldn't look at him the same way as she
was right this minute once she found out he wasn't Owen.

Hannah's phone buzzed and she rolled her eyes at the
text message. "I forgot my mom is having a get-together
this afternoon. You're invited, of course. Can we do the
town tour another day?"

"Why do I get the sense this invitation has an ulterior
motive?" It did, of course, and he didn't even need the
giant neon sign of her expression to explain that as her
gaze flicked over the text message that had just come in.

"My family is understandably concerned about your reappearance in my life," she said delicately.

No punches being pulled here, obviously. "So this is a
chance for everyone to check out what's happening."

"Pretty much. Is that going to bother you?"

Normally, yes. Archer wasn't much for being on display,
and he liked being examined like a bug under a microscope
even less. But he got the point. Owen had hurt Hannah
once. He'd abandoned his daughter. Anyone who loved them
would stand between them and the man who had wreaked
the destruction. He respected the notion, if not the reality.

But this was his reality and he'd signed up to be Owen
for the foreseeable future, however short that may be.

"It's your family's right to be sure you're safe and happy,"
he told her sincerely. "Besides, I would like to meet them,
especially the famous Uncle Wade. Lucy talks about him
so much that I feel like I already know him."

Hannah was looking at him strangely. "It's a little shocking to hear you say something like that, even after everything that's happened. You and Wade never got along."

"My fault," he returned, because it was a sure bet that Owen was to blame. "I'm doubly eager to set things between us on the right note, then."

More like Archer would be spending an hour or two convincing Hannah's brother that he wasn't on the take. The man was a vet, former marine—Special Forces to boot—from what his quick research had revealed. Odds were high that Wade had scented Owen's less than savory nature from the first. If so, Archer would start out their rekindled acquaintance already highly appreciative of Wade Colton's opinion of his brother.

Hannah shook her head. "I cannot get over how different things are with you this time around. I might have accidentally on purpose forgotten the get-together, which I swear my mom was already planning before I decided to bring you home from the hospital. But I will admit, I was a tiny bit worried about bringing it up. I thought for sure you'd refuse to go. Or worse, agree to go, and then throw some kind of tantrum once we got there so I'd be the one who insisted on leaving early."

"Did I do that a lot before?"

Dumb question. Of course Owen had been a real class act when it came to spending time with Hannah's family. It didn't surprise Archer a bit that his brother had forced Hannah into the role of being the bad guy when it would have been so much more of the decent thing to do to have made an effort to get to know his extended family by marriage.

"Honestly, I need to stop talking about what you did before," Hannah said and dusted her hands off as if to say she'd already moved on. "I literally just said the past should be in the past, and I'm the one who keeps dragging us back there. I'm sorry. It won't happen again."

"Hannah."

Before she could pick up her coffee mug again, he snagged her hands in his and did exactly what he'd been trying not to do for a million years, pulling her into his space. Because he wanted to be close to her. Because he had to make sure she understood this was all about Archer, not Owen and their complicated history.

She stared at him, caught in the same draw between them that he knew she felt. It was in the very molecules of the atmosphere around them, tiny electric sparks that made everything brighter, sharper.

"Hannah," he murmured again. "It's okay if you want to compare the me I am now with who I used to be. It's okay if you don't. There are no rules. This is a strange, unprecedented situation. Please do and say and be however you want with me. You've earned it."

She gave a watery laugh that did nice things to his insides even as it scored his heart to realize she was fighting back tears. Because he'd given her permission to do what felt natural? How had she felt like Owen expected her to act before?

Archer shook his head. He had to get out of that mindset. It wasn't like he could ask Owen exactly how much of a jerk he'd been. He knew. Now his job was to repair the cracks his brother had caused.

"Amnesia is a gift," he told her sincerely, and he believed it with every fiber of his being. "To us both. You deserve to have a partner in this life as much as Lucy deserves to have a father. You've had to do all of this alone for so long. I can't begin to make up for the time we've both lost, but please don't spend what time we have second-guessing a single thing. I'm just happy being here."

She nodded, shaking a tear loose, and he fought the urge to wipe it away for her. They didn't have that kind of relationship. Not yet. Maybe not ever, but here in this moment, he had everything his brother had thrown away and it felt like he'd found a much greater treasure than Big Mike's missing money.

Archer planned to enjoy it for as long as he could.

Chapter 13

Fletcher, Chase and Wade stood side by side at the end of the crushed stone driveway. They were three formidable figures in any circumstances, but Hannah knew they were waiting to greet Mac properly. She just hoped it wasn't so they could dismember him and hide the parts in the lake.

"Ugh, I'm sorry about this," she murmured to Mac, who was holding Lucy's hand as they walked up the drive from the street where they'd found a place to park two houses over.

When the Coltons came together, they were not a small bunch. And they took care of their own. She loved that her brothers had cared enough to close ranks. But she was equally glad she wasn't the one on the other end of their glares.

Fletcher and Wade were cut from the same cloth, both wearing their Serve-and-Protect-and-Possibly-Rip-Your-Face-Off personas like jackets. Though Wade with his eye patch was the one she'd bet most people wouldn't want to meet in a dark alley. Chase had a whole other kind of intimidation factor. You could take the man out of the suit, but he still looked like he could buy and sell a small country before breakfast, while discreetly instructing the many people at his beck and call to end you.

"It's fine, Hannah," Mac murmured to her quietly over Lucy's head. "I would expect nothing less than the inquisition followed by boiling oil and the rack if I answer any questions wrong. It makes me feel better to know that you've had your brothers in your corner this whole time."

That put a little lump in her throat because yeah, she did have a great family, one that she'd grown a lot closer to since she'd become a single mom. They'd told her the first time that Mac—Owen as she'd called him then—was bad news and she hadn't listened. Maybe this time she should open her ears a little wider, because they certainly hadn't been quiet about their intense dislike of both her ex-husband and the fact that he was staying at her house.

"So," Fletcher called, "the weasel has come home to roost."

"Fletch, behave," she called with the same warning note that she used when Lucy tried to sneak an extra cookie. "We're just here to relax and have fun."

"*You're* here to relax and have fun." Chase's crossed arms didn't hide his clenched fists, but then she didn't think he was actually trying to keep them out of sight. "We're here to get a few answers from Lover Boy about where he's been for four years."

Mac threw up a hand to stop the flow of Hannah's protest, which he'd somehow guessed she was about to make. He didn't flinch at the glares aimed in his direction, which earned him points. With her at least.

He stood there taking the brunt of her brothers' hostility with grace and determination. As if he truly understood he'd hurt her and running this first gauntlet was not only warranted but necessary. Something he wanted to do to prove himself.

"Take Lucy inside, Hannah," he told her calmly. "Your brothers and I have some air to clear."

Biting her lip, she glanced between them, wondering if

she should get a fan to blow away all the testosterone wafting around out here. Probably that wouldn't help. Instead, she opted to at least throw down another warning. "Owen doesn't remember where he's been for any number of years, no matter how hard you press. So maybe keep it friendly. And he goes by Mac these days."

Wade, who managed to pile twice the condemnation into his expression despite the patch covering one eye, grinned. No one could possibly mistake it for amusement. "We're all friends here. Right, guys?"

On cue, Fletcher, Chase and even Mac chorused their agreement. Men. Ugh. She was so done here. "Fine, y'all have at it. Let me know if I need to call the paramedics."

Fletcher showed his teeth in a mirror image of Wade's. "I'm trained in basic triage. We're all good here."

Turning her back, she grabbed Lucy's hand and flounced into the house, leaving them to their Y-chromosome convention. So much for the "family meeting" that Wade had texted her about. Obviously *she* was the subject of the meeting.

"Why does Uncle Wade look like he's about to pee in his pants, Mama?" Lucy piped up with her question as Hannah dragged her up the front steps and through the front door. "I didn't even get to say hi."

"He'll be inside in a minute, Lu Lu," she promised through gritted teeth, wondering if she could say the same about Mac. If her brothers scared him off, she'd personally punch every single one of them in the nose.

"Where's Rabbit Boy?" Ruby asked the moment Hannah hit the foyer.

Her sister stood halfway between the kitchen and the living room, bouncing Sawyer on her hip. Hannah shot her a withering glare. First Lover Boy from her brother and now this. "Rabbit Boy?"

"Because he runs the second he gets spooked," Sebastian, her husband, filled in as he took the baby from Ruby, crooning to his son in a way that told everyone exactly how he felt about being a dad.

"This is *my* life, you guys," she called to the room at large, knowing full well that she was the only one here who thought that meant they should butt out.

But then, this was her family calling her judgment into question. As they'd been doing for over five years, since she'd first hooked up with Mac. She didn't blame them, honestly. She didn't always make the best decisions.

Still. There was no proof she'd made a bad one this time. Not yet.

"It's a little bit of a suspicious situation, sweetheart." Jenny bustled out of the kitchen, Frannie right behind her. "You have to admit."

Kiki, her brother Fletcher's fiancée, wisely stayed in the kitchen but called out a distracted greeting from the counter where she was mixing something. She and Fletcher had been keeping a low profile with their relationship, but had recently announced their engagement. Hannah liked the woman her brother had fallen for. But man, how was it fair for that much gorgeous skin to be given to one woman?

Hannah's sister, Frannie, gave her a quick hug. Apparently, she was solo today as her other half, Dante, didn't seem to be among the judgment crew already lining up to give her even more opinions about how to live her life. Chase's girlfriend, Sloane, also seemed to be absent today. Too bad. Hannah needed all the newcomers to the family on her side. Surely they would be a little more reasonable since they didn't have the history.

"It's not suspicious, Mom," Hannah told her, shooting Jenny a wide-eyed look and a subtle head jerk at Lucy.

Fortunately, Harlow Jones was one of the newcomers who seemed to be on the right wavelength, which might have more to do with how long they'd known each other—since before she and Wade got involved again. She appeared from the depths of the kitchen where she'd been helping Kiki and greeted Hannah with a hug before bending down to speak to Lucy at eye level. "Betty Jane is in the back. Want to come say hi with me?"

Lucy lit up at the mention of her favorite dog and willingly followed Harlow out of the living room toward the deck that comprised most of the backyard, which sloped toward the lake. Since Lucy had spent so much time at Wade's house, she'd developed a natural affinity to Wade's significant other. The fact that Harlow was a Dog Mom had a lot to do with that.

"Bye," Hannah called out with only a touch of sarcasm at her daughter's retreating back. At least Lucy stopped to wave over her shoulder instead of ignoring her completely.

With the half-pint out of the way, Hannah crossed her arms and stared at her family.

"So," Frannie said.

"What are you doing?" Ruby asked a little more pointedly. "Did you seriously let Owen *move in*?"

"His name is Mac now. And he's recovering," Hannah corrected, shooting her mother a look. "You must have left that part out when you told everyone."

"Recovering. Also known as gearing up to leave again?" Jenny put her hands in the pockets of her apron, rocking back on her heels. "We just don't want you to get hurt by the same man."

Or make another bad call. Yes. She got it. She'd disappointed her family in a very significant way by marrying Owen in the first place.

But this was a whole different ball game. That's why she'd agreed to bring him before the firing squad. She'd told Mac that the past was the past. It was time to start putting her money where her mouth was and see how he fit into her life this time around.

Otherwise, it was just paying lip service to her agreement that he could have a role in Lucy's life. *This* was Lucy's life. These were her relatives too.

The problem was that she couldn't force them to accept Mac. She was having a hard enough time figuring out which end was up herself, let alone asking someone else to do so, someone who hadn't seen the way Mac watched Lucy sometimes when he didn't know Hannah was paying attention.

The man had changed. There were no two ways about it. Sometimes she thought he even looked different, but people did age in unexpected ways. She didn't look the same as she had in her early twenties either. It was time to see what the present looked like without the burden of the past.

"I appreciate everyone's concern," Hannah began but was interrupted by the sound of voices as her brothers escorted Mac inside.

He was still in one piece, thankfully. And he hadn't hightailed it away from Owl Creek after the interrogation. Everyone got points for both.

"He can stay," Chase said gruffly and ruffled the hair on Hannah's head like she was the same age as Lucy.

She ducked away from him with a tiny smile of thanks that she only meant for him to see. Because he was still her big brother at the end of the day, and whatever the Colton boys had orchestrated to ensure Mac didn't leave a gaping hole in her heart, she appreciated.

"He's solid this time," Wade murmured to her as he passed through to the kitchen, clearly looking for Harlow.

Fletcher bumped her arm and gave her a quick nod. Just once, and no accompanying verbal approval, but the nonverbal one was reflected in his gaze.

Hannah swallowed the lump in her throat. Everything got a lot more real in an instant. If Mac had passed whatever test her brothers had put him through, that meant she hadn't made a bad call this time. That they saw what she'd seen—a man who was sincere about his second chance.

What did that mean? For her? For Lucy?

Mac moved into the circle to stand by her side, quiet, but definitely sending her family a message that he intended to be present this time. He'd had no clue what he was walking into here—honestly, she hadn't realized it would be a series of tests either—but he'd passed with flying colors.

So far. He still had to get through her sisters and Jenny.

"Hello, again," Mac said to her mother. "You must be Hannah's mom. I apologize if we've met before. I don't remember. But I wanted to thank you for having me in your home, despite what must be serious reservations on your part. I want you to know I'm not going to disappoint your daughter or your granddaughter this time."

Jenny nodded, her assessing gaze roving over Mac as she processed what he'd said to her. "See that you don't, and you'll always be welcome here."

And that was that. The welcoming committee broke up into smaller pieces as Hannah introduced him to the rest of her family, including the tiny addition named Sawyer, the most popular guest at the party by far. Finally, everyone's focus snapped away from Mac and back to various party tasks. He'd been accepted, pending future bad behavior.

Hannah let out the breath she didn't know she'd been holding. Mac immediately turned to her, his hand grazing her arm.

"You okay?" he murmured.

"I should be asking you that question." She stared at him, drinking in this man who had willingly faced down a wall of Coltons to gain access to the inner sanctum, then managed to disarm her mother with one impassioned speech. "What did you say to my brothers?"

"The truth. That I may not remember Lucy, but the moment I knew she existed, pieces of me physically shifted places to make room for her and now she's there permanently."

Hannah's heart did a slow swan dive as she internalized the way he'd simplified something so vast and far-reaching. "That's how I felt when I first found out I was pregnant. I'd always hoped we'd share that feeling."

"Now we do," he told her, his gaze warming as they stood there in a bubble where only the two of them existed. One that he'd created by focusing on her so intently that she felt like the only other person in the room. The world.

Oh, goodness. She put a hand to her flaming cheek. What was she doing here? Falling into a fantasy where she and Mac were in sync, partners in parenting. Perhaps even more than just parents.

It was dangerous ground. A place that she hadn't foreseen she'd find herself solely by bringing him to her mother's house for a low-key get-together.

Nerves clamped down on her lungs, turning her breath shaky. How did she navigate the rest of this day?

Mac didn't seem to have the same confusion. He smiled and took her hand, which did absolutely nothing to calm her nerves. The opposite. Her heart rate shot into the stratosphere.

Mac even *felt* different. She'd never have said they had *sparks*. But the fireworks going off along her skin said otherwise. Of course she'd been in love with Before Owen. Probably. Sometimes she wondered if it had been more like an infatuation.

Because she'd never felt like this when he'd touched her before.

Was this part of starting over? Learning about each other, but as the people they were now, not who they had been? What else would be different?

The blush that heated her cheeks this time didn't escape his notice. "What are you thinking about?"

Nope. Not going there. "How I have no idea what I'm doing right now."

"You're at a party," he reminded her gently. "You're the one who said it. We're supposed to be having fun."

"I may have forgotten how."

"Step one. Hold on to me and I'll be right here, reminding you that everyone here cares about you. Forget whatever is waiting for us outside these walls and enjoy yourself for now."

Shockingly, that seemed to do the trick. She got hold of herself and straightened her spine. She was Hannah Colton. She could handle whatever this was. "We're just going to call you the Hannah Whisperer from now on, okay?"

His smile ratcheted up the heat, dangerously so. Making her think about things she shouldn't be thinking about.

Oh no. *Nonononono.* That was not happening, not now, maybe not ever, not that easily, not without a lot of groveling on his part. Tossing her head, she smiled back with a lot of teeth.

He'd have to earn it this time around. And she would not be so easily swayed by his looks and his money. That's how she'd use her head, not her heart.

Okay. The drama was over for today. She could relax,

have fun with her family now that it seemed they were going to accept Mac at face value, and see how things went. Simple.

There was a knock at the door, and everyone turned simultaneously, glancing at each other while doing their own mental head counts. Had Sloane decided to join them after all? Judging by the look on Chase's face, he wasn't expecting her.

"You all going to just stand there or answer the door?" Jenny dried her hands off on a towel and tromped toward the foyer. "Never mind, I'll get it."

When Jenny opened the door, a petite brown-haired woman stood there, her face a mask of nerves and trepidation as if she hadn't quite figured out whether she was going to be eaten alive by the owner of the house right there on the porch or invited inside so the crime could happen behind closed doors.

"Sarah," Jenny said warmly. "You came."

Sarah.

Hannah shared a long look with Ruby and Frannie. Their mother had invited their half sister to come to the house where Jenny had lived with Sarah's father?

The party's drama quotient had just escalated a billion notches.

Chapter 14

Some family get-together. Archer wasn't sure who Sarah was, but her arrival seemed to have put a pin in the forehead of every one of Hannah's siblings. None of them was moving, talking, breathing. It was almost as if they'd been frozen in place by nothing more than the presence of this diminutive woman.

Obviously there was a story here.

Instinctively, he slipped a hand around Hannah's waist and pulled her closer, wincing as he stretched the area of his torso where he'd cracked a rib. She didn't protest and in fact, seemed to curl into his side, as if seeking protection. Something hot and bright bloomed in his chest as his instincts bellowed to take care of whatever was bothering her.

"Are you okay?" he murmured. "I take it whoever Sarah is, she was an unexpected addition to the guest list."

"You could say. Sarah is my half sister," she explained, a tiny sentence with about a half ton of explosives lining the underside. "Remember I mentioned it? My father had an affair with her mother. Who is also my aunt."

Archer whistled one long low note as he called up all the details Hannah had spilled at the hospital. "My short-term memory doesn't seem to be a problem. So that's her?"

"Yeah. My mother's own sister. I mean, it's not Sarah's

fault. But she is a big neon flashing reminder of what a dirt-bag my father was. It's a little surprising my mother would be fine with having her around. And vice versa. Sarah's mother is not the person highest on our list of favorite people right now."

Filing all of this away alongside everything else he'd learned about Hannah's family, he hung back to watch whatever was about to unfold. The Ever After Church had sucked in Sarah's mother, no doubt, and there was a possibility that Sarah had likewise become a member. If so, it was a fortuitous bit of timing that he'd managed to score an invite to the same party with the woman.

Willis had turned up enough about the church to put Archer on higher alert than he'd like to be at a party. But he'd already been subjected to a lovely chat with the male half of the Colton clan and then been sized up and spit out by Hannah's mother. He'd been warned, in no uncertain terms, that screwing over Lucy or Hannah again would result in some very unpleasant consequences.

Yeah. He got it. Owen wouldn't have cared, but he did.

That was the irony. Archer would never have stacked up those dominoes in the first place. If he'd been the one to meet Hannah all those years ago, he'd be five, six years into his relationship with her, and her family would welcome him with open arms.

He'd be lucky to escape with his skin intact once they learned the truth.

Sure, he hoped he could keep being Lucy's father, but he was savvy enough to know that he wasn't the one who got to make that decision, regardless of his intentions.

No time to wallow in self-pity. Archer swallowed his angst over things he couldn't change and people he'd never have a chance to know at a deeper level, pasting a smile on his face as Hannah bit her lip.

"That's some messed-up history," he muttered, turning his head so his comment didn't drift toward the newcomer. "But Sarah must be seeking her own answers, or she wouldn't be here. Introduce me. She might need someone on her side who isn't a blood relation."

Hannah squeezed her eyes shut and when she opened them, the emotion he saw there nearly knocked his knees out from under him.

"Thank you for that," she whispered. "You can't begin to know what that means to me. She's my sister. But not, if you know what I mean. I want to love her, but it's…well, it's a mess."

Oh, he knew exactly what she meant. It was like wanting to resurrect your twin so you could murder him all over again. A love-hate relationship that could never be reconciled now. The best Archer could do was learn how to do some serious posthumous forgiveness and move on. Live his life and swallow the regret. Fix the mess. Be present for this woman and her daughter since Owen couldn't. Baby steps.

Hannah grasped his hand, a sweet, unexpected move that filled him to the brim with what he could only call joy. Then they were on the move, headed toward Sarah. The first of her siblings to step forward—he was proud of Hannah for taking the lead.

And not a little exhilarated to be at least partially responsible for the genuine smile on her lips as she greeted her sister.

Sarah, for her part, seemed at least open to Hannah's brief hug. She had Hannah's eyes, he noted, the same as Lucy's. They must have all three inherited that lily pad green from Hannah's father. It was a tenuous link that he hoped Hannah would take positively, as opposed to a re-minder that her father had shared his genetic heritage in a selfish and hurtful way.

"I'm Mac," he said as Hannah turned to him, and left it at that since he had no idea how to qualify his presence here. Was he Lucy's father? Hannah's ex-husband? Hannah's current rehabilitation project? Something more?

Boy, he'd love to know what that might be.

Sarah met his gaze with a touch of warmth and shook his outstretched hand. "Nice to meet you."

"Likewise."

He sensed Hannah's siblings breaking free of their stupor behind him and took advantage of the opportunity to get a bit of his own agenda into the mix before they remembered their manners. "I'm the outsider here. If you need a friendly face, come find me later."

Sarah's smile had a hint of Hannah in it too. "I appreciate the offer. Please take it in the spirit that it's intended if I say I hope I won't need to."

"I do," he assured her. Having been on the receiving end of the welcoming committee already, he hoped for a good reception for her as well.

His brief bonding time with the daughter of the woman rumored to be Markus Acker's girlfriend ended abruptly as Hannah's sisters, Ruby and Frannie, muscled their way in to say hi to Sarah.

The party jumped into full swing then as the Colton boys fired up the grill outside on the deck. Archer found himself hustled out with them, holding a plate of hot dogs. Wade shoved a beer into his other hand, which he sipped slowly enough that he couldn't even taste it, but he'd never been a big drinker. Plus, he needed his wits about him.

Sarah, he noted, had gravitated to the area below the

deck where Lucy was playing with Harlow and an enormous husky—Betty Jane, Harlow had called her. The main source of Lucy's dog wishes. She was a beautiful creature, clearly well trained not to knock over his daughter, which he appreciated.

Er, Owen's daughter. Sure, he had to be completely error-free at referring to her as his daughter out loud, but there was no reason to be thinking of her as *his* in his own head. Well, none other than the fact that he hadn't been overstating what he'd told all of Lucy's uncles. Lucy was wedged inside him so tightly that he couldn't imagine ever yanking her free. Or wanting to.

His brother had been a piece of work all right.

Archer managed to do the impossible and relax as he and Hannah sat on the deck and ate hot dogs with her family. It was an idyllic setting, one he'd have never pictured himself enjoying. And not just the view out over the lake, which was spectacular, but the company too. Hannah. Her siblings. Even her mother had a quick smile and kind eyes that she spread around to everyone in attendance, Sarah and Mac included, neither of whom would be welcome at many other matriarchs' homes.

It spoke to the kind of people Hannah came from. He could not fathom why Owen would ever have been interested in someone like this strong, capable woman by his side. She wasn't at all his type. Which got Archer's senses humming. He was a huge fan of the Occam's razor brand of investigative analysis—ten times out of ten, the simplest explanation was the right one.

In this case, that meant she must be involved in Owen's scams. Somehow. He just couldn't figure out the link.

After the mountain of hot dogs had dwindled, Betty Jane gladly wolfed down the last as a treat from Wade when he thought no one was watching. Archer wasn't the only one with his eyes on the dog, though. Lucy's face had rarely turned from the husky, and he recalled his throwaway statement to her from earlier that she could have a dog at his house in Las Vegas.

That had been a mistake to offer, clearly. How would that even work? Once Hannah found out he wasn't Owen, the odds of her agreeing to let him play the adoring uncle would be zero. And if she really was involved in Owen's illegal activities, he might be arresting her and taking her away from Lucy entirely. No one would let the little girl within five hundred miles of him then.

It put a bitter taste in the back of his throat. Sometimes doing the right thing sucked.

Sarah had been equally quiet during the Colton clan's raucous conversation. No doubt she still felt a little uncertain about her place in the family, which he totally understood. Neither was it a surprise when she asked Wade if she could walk Betty Jane down by the water. It wouldn't surprise him if she'd deliberately looked for a way to separate herself for a regroup session.

But shockingly, after Wade agreed, Sarah turned to Hannah and asked if Lucy could walk with her. There was no way Hannah would have been able to resist the "Please, please, please" from her daughter in a sweet, wheedling tone, and the beseeching puppy-dog eyes put the icing on the cake.

Hannah laughed and told them to go on ahead, but the glimpse of how hard it was to parent a cute little girl gave Archer hives. How did Lucy not get away with literally everything when she knew exactly how to pour on the charm? It was eye-opening and would likely get worse the older she got. She was half Owen's daughter, after all.

Wade watched Sarah double loop the leash around her wrist and take Lucy by the other hand, then pick her way down to the water. To say his sharp gaze rivaled a hawk's wouldn't be an understatement, and only having one good eye didn't seem to be a detriment.

"I'm keeping them in sight too," Archer murmured to Wade, though it was fifty-fifty on whether Hannah's brother would welcome the extra vigilance.

Wade didn't shift his glance even an iota. "I would expect no less from Lucy's father."

For some reason, the sentiment settled heavily in his heart. Owen would have taken it as criticism or worse, Wade trying to tell him what to do. Archer saw it as the double-edged sword it was meant as—a condemnation of the past and a pat on the back for the present.

And maybe a third edge. He wasn't actually Lucy's father. Continuing to pretend he was wouldn't end well.

He should tell Hannah the truth. It was as simple as that. The longer he kept this secret, the worse things between them were going to be. Tonight. He should tell her as soon as they left the party. Swear her to secrecy. Trust that she wasn't involved with Big Mike and continue with his investigation, except Hannah wouldn't be in the dark.

When Jenny picked up some plates and headed for the kitchen, Kiki and Harlow followed her, leaving Hannah's siblings and Ruby's husband Sebastian sitting on the deck. Just as Archer wondered if he should volunteer for dish duty, Chase cleared his throat.

"Now's a good time to have a very quick emergency family meeting," Hannah's oldest brother said, which had the effect of silencing every conversation in an instant.

"You should stay," Hannah said as she pulled her chair in

closer to Archer's, settling his internal debate about whether they expected him to excuse himself.

Chase's gaze roved over his, assessing, but he didn't contradict his sister. "You should all know that we don't think Dad's death was due to natural causes."

Obviously, this was no ordinary family meeting. Or was this how they all went?

Hannah gasped, clutching Archer's hand automatically. He squeezed back in support, though it didn't seem she even realized she'd done it. That seemed to answer his question—no, they didn't generally drop such bombs when Jenny disappeared into the kitchen.

"What are you talking about?" she demanded. "You think someone killed him?"

"Not someone. Jessie," Wade confirmed grimly. "She had a lot to gain from it."

Fletcher, who was on the job with the Owl Creek PD, nodded, which lent the most credence to the statement in Archer's book. If the lawman thought it too, it was likely the truth. But Jessie was Sarah's mother, which meant she'd killed the man who had fathered her children. It was a bold claim.

And Archer hadn't put enough pieces together yet to understand why the Coltons had chosen to include him in this announcement. Earlier, he'd heard Chase talking about his real estate business, which seemed to be quite far-flung and lucrative. Every bit of this got the motor in his brain whirring.

"You're serious," Hannah said, her gaze flitting back and forth between her brothers as she absorbed what they were telling her. "But the coroner ruled his death as a stroke. You can't force someone to have a stroke. Can you?"

Her brothers exchanged glances, but it was Fletcher who

spoke. "There are ways you can introduce certain factors that could cause a stroke, yes. Emotional upset for one. Stress. Asking someone to lift something heavy."

There were more sinister ways as well. Archer kept his mouth shut though, as it would be highly suspect for Owen to know a blessed thing about ways a person could induce a stroke in someone.

"We're not a hundred percent sure Jessie acted alone," Chase said, his expression grim as he warmed to the subject. "Or even orchestrated it. Markus Acker could just have likely done the deed with Jessie helping him. He had more to gain than she did if she'd managed to get the will changed."

"But she didn't," Hannah supplied, which was information Archer didn't have. "And we don't know for sure that she would have given Acker any of Dad's money if she'd gotten control of it."

"Yeah, we do," Wade countered. "She's already given him all her own money, and we suspect that she's coerced the members of the church to cough up a lot of cash. The woman is bad news, despite being family."

Archer's senses moved from tingling to full-on lightning strikes. Any time a lot of money was at stake, all bets were off. If Hannah's brothers thought their father had been murdered, odds were high they'd found at least a shred of truth buried in the middle of what most folks would call coincidence.

There were no coincidences. Not in a police investigation, not in life. Not ever. Especially not when he was already on the trail of a lot of money. The odds of there being two different sets of "a lot of money" was 12 percent. Give or take a half percent because he was doing the math in his head.

In other words, the odds were low. There was a link

between the Ever After Church, Hannah's father's death, Sarah's mother and Owen Mackenzie. Archer would stake his life on it.

Though he had a pretty good feeling he already *had* staked his life on it.

And he had Owen to thank for putting Hannah and Lucy in the middle of it.

Chapter 15

Mac had asked if he could help put Lucy to bed and Hannah couldn't see any reason not to let him read a story or two. It was a legit request and Lucy ate up her father's voices, which Hannah had no idea her ex-husband could even do.

But he proved to be a master at changing his timbre for each character in Lucy's current favorite book about narwhals. Plus, he didn't try to skip any of the pages, even though the story had a lot of tiny text and kind of dragged in the middle.

Rushing ahead was a trap. Lucy had the book memorized and she'd call you out if you so much as accidentally on purpose acted like two pages had stuck together.

Hannah hung out by the door, at loose ends since she hadn't had a second free for five years at bedtime. What would she even do with herself if she didn't spend all her time filling the gap that Mac—the Owen version of himself—had left? Playing the part of both parents had been so much a part of her life that she didn't even think about it most days.

Except for a day like this one. Mac had not only picked up his own slack, he'd rendered her redundant in the equation. Lucy hadn't glanced in her mother's direction one time thus far. And why would she? She had her father's undivided attention, and he'd probably honor each and every request for "read it again" or "one more story" or "tell me one you made up."

Honestly, Hannah's attention kept drifting to Mac. This was an unprecedented chance to study him without his knowledge. He made such a dear picture sitting on the edge of Lucy's big-girl bed holding the narwhal book in his gentle hands.

She'd always loved his hands. Some women might like a man's hands to be rough, and sure, that was fine for a romance novel where the heroine fell for a bad boy, but this was real life. She'd never wanted anything more than a man who treated her well.

Yeah, that had worked out.

Except she'd promised to put that behind them, and she really was trying to see Mac in a new light. In fact, the more she studied him, the more differences she could pick out. Maybe it was the car crash or the distance of time, but his face seemed slightly less refined. Before Owen had polish. A layer of shine that she'd swooned over.

Now she knew better than to fall for a pretty face, which was why she might be slightly fixated on the fact that Mac's appearance didn't have the polish it once had. Probably it was the scraggly beard that he'd been growing since the crash. She didn't want to bring it up since the bandage he still wore over his stitches might make it awkward to shave.

Before Owen wouldn't have left the bathroom without ensuring he'd done everything in his power to look his best. Mac had let his hair grow out. It practically brushed his shoulders and framed his face in a way that she had to admit gave him a bit of a dangerous edge that she didn't hate.

Maybe there was more to the bad boy fantasy than she'd given credence.

And man, when had it gotten so hot in here?

Hannah fanned her face and ducked out to wait in the living room before Mac saw her acting so weird over him. It was *Owen*. She'd been in love with him, sure, but he'd never… revved her engine like some of her friends talked about.

Since she had nothing but time, Hannah's brain got busy coming up with its own entertainment. Not Mac-related! Her inner vixen seemed determined to push the envelope though, so she focused on the revelations her brothers had dropped at the party.

Her father's death might not have been due to natural causes.

Hannah could not get over the strange turn of events that had embroiled the entire Colton family since one of the members of the Ever After Church had tried to run Sebastian Cross off his property. Ruby had been right there in the middle of it and almost killed by a crazed Markus Acker disciple. The couple had managed to escape with their lives and fallen in love in the process, then immediately started their own family with the birth of sweet Sawyer.

So it hadn't been all bad news.

Just not nearly enough good news.

She still wasn't quite sure where Nate and Sarah fell on the spectrum. It wasn't every day that you learned about half siblings you hadn't known existed. If Aunt Jessie had been responsible for Hannah's father's death, it certainly wasn't the first decision she'd made that had sent shock waves through the very foundation of the Coltons.

The next time Hannah looked up, Mac stood in the doorway of the living room, his gaze resting on her. The expression on his face raised goose bumps on her skin as if he'd actually touched her, when in fact, he hadn't moved from his casual lean against the doorframe.

"Lucy's asleep," he murmured softly.

Because that's how you spoke in a house with a sleeping five-year-old. There was no call to be imagining that he'd adopted that low, silky tone in deference to the atmosphere, maybe to deliberately heighten the underlying sense of anticipation.

That happened anyway, whether he'd meant to lace the space between them with tightly wound tension or not.

"Thank you for reading to her," Hannah responded, her own tone matching his out of habit. No one wanted a cranky five-year-old out of bed after a long day at Grandma Jenny's.

Mac rambled across the room to where she was sitting on the couch, and she thought of a lot of other reasons it would be highly beneficial for Lucy to pick tonight to sleep like the dead.

He perched on the couch next to her, his frame slightly taut as if he hadn't quite figured out if she welcomed his presence in her space.

She'd have told him if she'd rather have been left alone. Or she could have retreated to her bedroom, effectively cutting off the rapport that had grown between them almost overnight. Co-parenting, even for such a short period of time, had proven to be a much greater bonding experience than she'd have guessed.

But no mother on the planet could remain unaffected by the sight of a man reading to the child they'd created together. Not to mention the dozens of other scenes she had in her head of the two of them together. Lucy had zero reservations about her father—she had just thrown open the walls of her heart and sucked Mac in.

Hannah didn't have the same luxury. She had to think with her head.

"Are you doing okay?" he asked, his gaze gently probing hers as if he truly cared.

The fact that he'd even thought to ask spun her a bit. "I've been better."

Honesty. She hadn't seen that coming either. Normally she put on her big-girl panties and showed the world that it couldn't break Hannah Colton. But this was the other part of being a single mom that she'd missed. The personal support of her, as a woman. As a partner. Having someone to unwind with at the end of the day who cared.

Mac cared. It was there in the lines of his expression and the way he'd turned his whole body toward her as if there was nothing else in the room he'd choose to focus on but her. It was going to her head.

"You've had a bit of a shock, I would imagine," he murmured and reached out to finger a stray lock of hair away from her cheek in a move that somehow weakened her knees even though she was sitting down.

Before Owen had never done anything like that. If she was being candid, he usually had been too concerned with his own appearance to even notice if she had hair in her face or behind one ear or on the floor because she'd cut it off.

Mac's attention was doing something to her lungs because she couldn't catch her breath.

"Apparently the shocking events are still on the agenda for the evening," she muttered, cursing herself when he dropped his hand.

It was for the best.

"Sorry. I sometimes forget that we're not still together," he said and then shook his head before she could form the question he'd likely guessed she would ask. "Not that I'm saying I remember before. It's just that I feel so comfortable with you. It's like I already know how to be with you deep down in my soul. If that makes any sense."

Oh yeah, she got it all right. It was the same for her, despite not having that frame of reference from the first time either. Sure, she *should*, but it was so not the same. There was a whole other vibe going on this time, as if they'd slid into a space where they made sense together instantly, clicking like a key in a lock.

"It's okay," she told him. "If I didn't want to be here, I wouldn't be."

"Talk to me about what your brothers said," he prompted, instead of launching into a practiced seduction routine. "About your dad. If you want to. I can tell it's bothering you."

It set her back for a moment, even as she appreciated his segue. She didn't know if she was ready for something to happen between them, not so soon. But he seemed totally in tune with that, expertly transitioning back to his original query. He really did want to know how she was and not so he could get her clothes off.

"You really have changed," she said flatly as she stared at him. "You're definitely not the same man anymore."

Mac shifted uncomfortably and she felt bad for saying such an insensitive thing when he didn't remember anything about his life, let alone who *he* was.

"It's a good thing," she murmured, thinking how great it would be if *she* had amnesia and couldn't remember Before Owen either. It would be so much easier to let herself indulge in the quiet, intimate atmosphere that had sprung up around them.

"I'm trying to change the subject and you're not letting me," he said with a wry smile. "So I'll blurt it out. Do you think Jessie killed your father?"

"I don't know. I mean, I knew her a little when I was growing up, but she left my uncle Buck and their children a long time ago." Hannah dug a little deeper into the couch in search of a more comfortable spot, turning in toward the middle to face Mac. "She got sucked into this church business and showed up ranting and raving about the will out of nowhere. The weird part is that the will was already being split seven ways. Why kill my dad over it? Nate and Sarah's part wouldn't have been *that* much money."

"Some people kill other people over a pair of hundred-dollar basketball shoes with the right logo on them," Mac countered grimly. "Have you ever heard that alcohol amplifies someone's personality? Money does too. The amount rarely matters. If you don't value human life in the first place, the line you won't cross gets further and further away. But that doesn't mean your aunt is guilty. Only the court can decide that."

While the sentiment didn't give her any warm fuzzy feelings about her aunt, she did appreciate Mac acting as a sounding board. Talking to her brothers would only get her riled up since they were already set in their minds that Jessie had been involved.

To what end? They didn't have any evidence that she knew about.

But they might if she could get a toe in the door with Sarah. Her investigation had fizzled, that was for sure. If by fizzled, she meant never started in the first place. The party would have been the perfect place to cement a new friendship with Sarah and instead, she'd stuck close to Mac's side in case her brothers had decided to pull any shenanigans.

That didn't mean she couldn't use the party as an excuse to talk to Sarah. And only the guilt she felt at not having come up with anything useful thus far could tear her away from Mac.

"I think I'm going to turn in," she told him. The less he knew about her plan to befriend Sarah in order to pump her for information, the better.

Mac looked pretty disappointed when she stood up, but he didn't say anything other than good-night, allowing her to escape with all of her faculties intact.

When she got to her room, she called up Sarah's name in her contacts. It still startled her a bit to see two new names under the *C*'s. Colton, Nate, and Colton, Sarah, interspersed between Max and Ruby, who would always be Colton Cross in Hannah's phone, whether her sister went by that name or not.

Hannah hit Call before she could change her mind, fully expecting Sarah to send the call to voicemail. But she answered on the first ring. Surprised, Hannah gaped for a second and then repeated her half sister's hello.

"I just wanted to say thank you for playing with Lucy today," Hannah finally blurted out. "At Mom's house. I mean Jenny's house. I know she's not your mom."

Smooth. Hannah rolled her eyes at herself.

"You have a great daughter," Sarah murmured, obviously in a forgiving mood. "You've done a fantastic job teaching her manners."

"Oh, well." Flustered, Hannah waved that off, but couldn't avoid being thrilled that someone had complimented her little girl. Who was brilliant and amazing, of course. "Thank you for saying that. She can be a handful, so it's nice to know she remembered to act civilized in polite company."

Sarah laughed graciously and for some reason, that hit Hannah wrong. Sisters shouldn't laugh graciously at each other's jokes.

"I'm really calling because I think it would be nice to get to know you," Hannah announced, as if Sarah had won a prize in a sweepstakes.

But Sarah didn't seem to notice Hannah's weird tone. "I'd like that. I've never had sisters before. I have this pie in the sky idea that they're meant to be like best friends who are also blood relations, so it's extraspecial. And now I can hear you backing slowly away—"

"No," Hannah cut in, thinking it was fate that they were both kind of awkward. "That's exactly what it's like. I've had it my whole life with Ruby and Frannie, and I'm sorry you haven't. I can fix that for the future though, and I'd like to."

"That would be nice," Sarah said a touch wistfully. "It's a little difficult right now since I live in Boise, but maybe we can connect by phone occasionally?"

Disappointed that she'd forgotten that important factor, Hannah nodded. "You bet. But I insist that you come visit me some time."

Maybe after Mac left. Hannah's heart twinged at the thought, but he couldn't stay here forever. There was no scenario where he'd still be in the guest room in a few weeks. Sarah could come then.

Of course, the investigation couldn't wait. They needed answers about what Jessie had been getting up to with the church, and even more so, what Sarah knew about Markus Acker. He was the linchpin in all of this, she just knew it.

Jessie couldn't necessarily have been called a good mother before she'd joined the church, but Acker had corrupted her, no doubt. He needed to be stopped. Maybe if he was out of the picture, Jessie would realize the error of her ways and return to her family. Families? Goodness, what did that matter if she really had helped murder Hannah's father? How terrible all of this must be for Sarah and Nate.

"I'd like to see your home," Sarah said a touch more enthusiastically, having now come a little further out of her shell over the course of the call. "Thank you for reaching out. It means a lot to me."

Hannah swallowed against another way of guilt, this

time because she'd basically struck up a friendship under false pretenses. But not really! She did want to get to know Sarah. This was multitasking. Using her head instead of her heart, which never worked out.

And who knew? Maybe she really would get a new sister out of the deal, one who wouldn't give her grief about Mac and would be nothing but supportive when—if—she decided to see what Mac and Late Twenties Hannah looked like together.

But first, she had to figure out what she was waiting for.

Chapter 16

Archer's ribs hurt. It wasn't the bed's fault, but he didn't have a handy scapegoat otherwise, so he whacked the mattress a time or two to unleash a bit of his frustration that it was 4:00 a.m. and he couldn't sleep.

Okay, some of that had to do with Hannah and his inability to stop making excuses to get closer to her. Mentally and physically. His crush on his brother's ex-wife had blossomed into a full-bore attraction that he couldn't shake.

Yet despite having met the Coltons a few days ago, he still didn't know if Hannah—and possibly her family—had some connection with Big Mike and/or his missing money, which were two different factors that he hadn't considered enough. It was one thing to be in cahoots with a known money launderer and another thing entirely to have helped Owen steal and conceal five million dollars from one of the nastiest crime syndicates around.

And he needed to make some headway on whatever link might exist before he fell in any deeper with Hannah.

Despite the hour, he made a call to Willis, who wasn't too pleased to be woken up.

"It's an hour earlier in Vegas," his assistant complained in lieu of a greeting. "This better be good."

Archer didn't bother with hellos either. "What have you found out?"

"Acker has a long history of founding churches that front as scams. Buy-your-way-out-of-hell kind of vibes."

No big surprises there. The real story was how he'd evaded the law thus far. "No history of arrests? None of his previous congregation members has ever turned state's witness?"

"Not that I've turned up. He's slippery. One of the cleanest track records I've seen for a criminal of this caliber. His assets are pretty layered, but it wasn't too difficult to track a few of his accounts offshore. I got a couple of feelers during my searches, so I stopped digging, but simple math would dictate his net worth is somewhere north of fifteen million."

Archer bit back the whistle. That was a lot of bought-and-paid-for redemption. No wonder Willis had hit up against someone else's feelers. "It could be his people monitoring."

"Could be. Could be internal too."

It wasn't a throwaway comment. Archer's blood ran a little cold. But it wasn't out of the realm to be dealing with dirty cops who were working with Acker. "Stop researching. I can pick it up from here."

Willis's eye roll came through the line loud and clear. "Gee, thanks, buddy. You couldn't have told me that at, like ten o'clock?"

Chuckling, Archer ended the call. Well, he was good and awake now. No point in trying to find a comfortable spot on his mattress, so he got up and did a few half-hearted sit-ups that made everything worse, including his mood.

When he picked up his burner phone, he saw that someone had texted him a series of numbers along with the phrase "Whatchu talkin bout?"—Willis's call sign when they were trying to stay on the down-low. In a few minutes, Archer had worked through the cipher, which resulted in another series of numbers. The kind that could have been texted unencrypted.

Willis was such a comedian. Payback for waking him up.

The numbers were coordinates. When Archer punched them in on his offline map, the street view narrowed in on a warehouse here in Owl Creek, which public record cited as being owned by Colton Properties. Chase was the CEO, a fact Archer had learned somewhere along the way.

He frowned at the data. Why would Willis put this in front of him? Not solely to give him grief. They'd been working together long enough that his assistant knew exactly how far to push that envelope and encoding a set of numbers inside another set of numbers was the hard limit.

This meant something. Archer stared at the aerial photo of the warehouse until his eyes watered, examining it from as many angles as the satellite cameras would allow.

And then he realized.

The date of purchase coincided with the date of Owen's death. Given his view on coincidences, this was a bombshell. Surely this didn't mean that someone in the Colton family had been working with Owen and double-crossed him, taking the five million for themselves. Real estate purchases didn't execute that quickly—unless it had been originally orchestrated as a joint purchase put into motion well before someone decided to take Owen out of the picture.

Archer turned this over in his head, letting the camera in his brain do much the same type of examination from every angle as the satellite had done on the warehouse. It was so common to use real estate holdings to launder money that it was almost cliché, which was one of the reasons this information tripped him up.

Big Mike wouldn't have set this up. He was way too savvy to try to push money through a shell company to clean it. Some years ago, Big Mike's syndicate did a lot of fancy revaluations of property around Vegas, then took out loans against the equity, which they paid back with dirty money. Slick work, unless you had someone like Archer on the job who followed every paper trail there was until he put all the pieces together. In a series of mistakes too convenient to be legit, the DA had screwed up the evidence, so there was no conviction, and Big Mike had never tried that particular scam again.

But that didn't mean someone else hadn't thought of it.

More research needed, stat. The fact that Willis hadn't already done it meant something too. This was one of the money trails his assistant would have gladly followed, except someone had noticed him nosing around. It was much safer to pass the baton to Archer, as long as no one realized he wasn't Owen.

The dilemma this created put an itch across the back of his neck. How could he tell Hannah the truth now? There were too many unknowns that needed to become known asap.

He had to talk to Hannah. Feel her out. Without tipping her off.

He waited until dawn and wandered into the kitchen to put on a pot of coffee, which had become his norm over the last few days, a routine that soothed him and hopefully endeared him to Hannah. The warm smile she gave him as she padded into the kitchen in her so-unsexy-it-was-sexy robe said that she did appreciate the coffee. And him.

Man, he needed to tone down his reaction to her. The odds of her appreciating it if he acted on the thoughts running through his head were probably in the negative numbers at this point. Owen had behaved like a class A ass to her, probably for the entire length of their relationship. He didn't blame Hannah one bit for categorizing him firmly in the "ex" category. But the fact that she seemed to so enthusiastically embrace putting him in the "father of her child" category spoke to her character.

And that was as attractive as anything else about her. Which put him back to square one and the cycle continued.

"Morning," she murmured and breathed in the aroma of coffee emanating from the mug she clasped in both hands under her nose. "I could get used to having you around."

"Could you?"

She glanced at him, clearly not expecting him to jump on the offhand comment, but dang—you couldn't throw a starving man a piece of bread while holding the remainder of the loaf in your hand and not expect him to slaver after the rest of it.

"Well, I mean, yeah. Lucy is taking to you like a duck to water. If she didn't want anything to do with you or I had evidence that you were mistreating her in some way, things would change faster than a heartbeat. But it's going pretty well and I'm happy you're finally in her life, despite the circumstances."

He nodded, used to her defaulting to Lucy as the reason he was here in her home. It made sense that she would put Lucy first, and as her temporary/fake stand-in/whatever-his-title-was father, he approved. "I'm happy that you're enabling us to have a relationship. We should probably talk about what that might look like down the road."

Hannah sipped her coffee, her gaze downcast as she contemplated that. "I want to say that's premature, but it's not. I'm letting her build up expectations that will be disappointed if we're not fully clear on how to move forward."

He threw it down. "I'd like her to come for visits in Las Vegas. I have no interest in dragging it through court, and they'd probably deny me any motions for joint custody anyway, so this is all dependent on you and your good graces."

Which would likely change as soon as she found out the truth, but he wouldn't budge from his stance that Lucy deserved a father. He'd like it if Lucy would think of him as hers, even once Hannah determined it was appropriate to tell her that Archer was really her uncle.

"I'm strongly considering it, Mac. Please know that," she implored him. "But it's a lot to take in, a lot to consider. She's never been on a plane, and I can't take unlimited time away from my catering business to drive her."

"I'd pay for any airfare costs incurred," he interjected, though he realized that wasn't Hannah's objection. In fact, she probably had more money than he did given what he'd discovered during his research of Colton Properties and the cost of housing in Owl Creek, especially on the lake.

She smiled. "I wasn't worried about that part. My catering business does okay. Speaking of which, I still would like to pay you back for the money I used to start it."

"Keep it."

He waved that off. Not only did he not want her money, what little money Owen had legally to his name had already gone through probate and had been distributed evenly between Archer and his mother. He'd make a call to reopen the case as soon as it was physically safe for him to do so, now that a legitimate heir had been located. It was his role as the executor of his brother's estate—a ridiculous word for a few thousand dollars and a handful of furnishings—to ensure that Lucy got everything of Owen's, including any new property that he came across. In short, Hannah would just be paying that money back straight into Lucy's account that, as her mother, she would have conservator control over.

Geez, this was a convoluted mess. One he needed to straighten out, pronto.

"Besides," he continued. "You said I had a lot of money before. I'm sure I still have a lot of money."

Hannah cocked her head. "You don't know?"

"Amnesia. Remember?" He lifted his lips in acknowledgment of the ironic joke.

"Oh, goodness. I never thought of that. You can't access your bank accounts, can you?"

He shook his head, stomach squelching at the outright lie, which he hadn't been forced to do too many times, thankfully. "If you can't remember your PIN or what you set as your security questions, banks aren't overly inclined to take your word for it that you have amnesia and should be given access anyway."

"But you could go to the bank with your driver's license and gain access to your account that way, couldn't you?"

Archer nearly gave it all away by rolling his eyes at himself for falling into that trap. Faking amnesia was harder than they made it look in the movies. "Sure, but it's a regional bank in Las Vegas. I'd have to travel there to do that."

Good. Believable.

In reality, Owen's bank account had been closed and the money distributed to his estate. It had been such a laughable amount that it was a safe bet Owen had money stashed other places, most notably the five million he'd assuredly lifted from Big Mike. That's what Archer needed to be concentrating on, not Hannah's laugh.

"I'll drive you there if you need me too."

"You literally just said you didn't have time to drive to Las Vegas to bring Lucy to see me," he pointed out and shook his head as she scowled. "No, it's fine. I, uh…had some cash in my wallet and I have a credit card that doesn't require a PIN. Plus, I'm keeping a tally of what you've done for me so far. I'm the one who will be paying you back."

Good grief, he sucked at interrogation. So far, he'd failed to mention the warehouse purchase, but somehow elicited an offer from Hannah to repay the money Owen had left her and then dodged an offer for her to drive him to get his own money.

"We can square up later," she said with an enigmatic smile that he shouldn't be interpreting in quite the way that his gut was trying to.

"Speaking of finances," he segued as casually as possible. "Did you end up with a stake in Colton Properties when your father died? There was all that talk about the will, but I didn't quite understand how the estate was divided."

Hannah sipped her coffee, watching him over the brim, her gaze a touch too alert for his liking.

"That's a strange question. Are you really trying to figure out how I get along with my family since you don't remember?"

Suddenly feeling like he'd stepped in quicksand, he shrugged it off. "Maybe. I don't even know if I have a family."

"You certainly never mentioned any relations to me," she offered, which she'd told him before, but it still irked him that Owen had acted like an orphan when he had a really great mom and a brother who'd bailed him out of trouble more than a few times.

"Tell me more about the business I owned," he said instead of going down his original path in the direction of Colton Properties, which probably wouldn't have gotten him very far anyway, even if she'd answered his question.

Owen's investment banking company—in huge air quotes—was a thread he should have pulled on long ago, but he'd gotten distracted by the Colton money floating around.

Hannah slid into a seat at the island breakfast bar, near where Archer was standing, and he liked the intimacy of it, which had been instantaneous from the first day.

"I don't know very much," she said in a tone that told him she felt guilty about it. "You didn't really talk about it much. You didn't have a very high opinion of my ability to understand it, so you gave up after a few times."

"Explain it to me the way you understood it."

Cautiously, she sipped her coffee again, likely as a stall tactic, which told him a lot about how badly Owen had made her feel about her comprehension of his "profession." Jerk.

"Well," she said. "It seemed like you used person A's money to give person B a loan, and then you charged a monthly fee, kind of like interest. I always thought it was strange that you didn't do anything with stocks or capital for investments, but when I asked about it, that's when you got frustrated and told me I didn't get it."

"Seems like you understand it just fine," he said flatly. Definitely a money-laundering operation. It wouldn't shock him to find out that Owen had been working with Big Mike way back then too. "And for the record, fee-based loans are not what typical investment banks do, so your question was legit."

Her gaze shone with the light praise, which hooked him in the gut. Did no one in her life tell her how smart and beautiful and amazing she was on a regular basis? Obviously not if she'd lit up like that over what amounted to a condemnation of Owen more than anything.

"That's the real reason I wanted to pay you back," she

admitted. "Because I thought you'd appreciate that I really did get it. It was capital for my business and an investment. You should reap the rewards of that. I've more than qua-drupled that money."

"Hannah."

He shook his head and bit back some of the more ef-fusive, flowery phrases that sprang to his lips instantly, things that would accurately describe how blown away he was by her. But this wasn't the time and place to indulge in the fantasy running through his head of finding out what Hannah slept in that required such a heavy robe to conceal.

Instead, he opted to cover her hand with his, marvel-ing at how easily hers was swallowed up. And that's what Owen had done to her, then spit her out. It was miraculous that this woman even chose to speak to him, let alone re-paying him a dozen times over with kindness and grace.

She didn't move her hand, simply stared at him from under her lashes, as if she'd grown shy in the last couple of minutes, when he knew for a fact, she was not.

"I'm sorry," he murmured. "It's small and mean to make you feel inferior or unable to understand financial concepts. Especially given how you've created a thriving business. It's impressive. Don't ever let anyone tell you differently. I'm really proud of you."

"I have to confess a dirty secret," she said with a half smile that did things to his insides that might not even be legal in some states.

"Tell me," he urged her, moving in a little closer to where she was perched on a barstool at the kitchen island.

"It's so bad," she teased, her smile growing a tad wicked. "I've dreamed about the day when I could tell you that my business is worth double what you unknowingly invested in it. And then I started doing pretty well and realized I was past that mark. And I started dreaming about telling you I'd tripled it. Today I was able to say I quadrupled that money, and your expression is so much better than in my dreams. I thought I was going to be rubbing it in your face. I never in a million years expected you to tell me you were proud."

That put a catch in his throat that he couldn't swallow. Or speak around.

No, she hadn't come right out and said she wasn't working with Big Mike, though he wouldn't be the slightest bit surprised to learn she could outearn him with a legit business. But he'd stake his life on his assessment that she was clean.

Her character shone through with every word out of her mouth. She was a good mother. She came from a tight-knit family full of law enforcement—not that he automatically trusted cops and veterans, but if there was anything Archer excelled at, it was taking bits and pieces of seemingly random information and forming a whole out of it.

The Coltons were solid people. And there was no way Hannah had any idea that she'd married a two-bit criminal, nor that he'd expanded his illicit career horizons after he'd left her.

And if that was true, odds were high she had no idea where the money was.

Chapter 17

Hannah had to work an event that night, so Archer made a move to leave the kitchen, but she stopped him on his way, inviting him to stay as long as he liked. Since there was no place he'd rather be, he slid onto the same barstool she'd just vacated.

It was still warm.

As Hannah chopped sweet potatoes for what she informed him would eventually become curried sweet potato soup, they talked. And talked. It was as if getting to live out her fantasy of telling Owen that she'd made something out of herself had uncorked her.

He liked the uncensored version of Hannah. A lot. She had a wry sense of humor he appreciated, and she could do her job with her eyes closed, clearly, since she'd scarcely glanced down at the sharp knife in her hand.

She was so different than his brother's usual type that it was baffling what qualities Owen would have ever been attracted to in this woman. Unless…he'd used their marriage as some kind of front for his operation without her knowledge. He made a mental note to do some checking into whether his brother had ever put any assets in Hannah's name. Or even Lucy's. It was an angle he hadn't considered until now, and it bothered him that he'd missed it.

Hannah ducked down to root around in the cabinet built into the island. She stood, hands on her hips, gaze darting around the kitchen as if searching for something. "Drat, I really thought my ceramic soup tureen was in the house. It must be in the shed. I'll be right back."

"Want me to get it?" he offered. "It sounds heavy."

"Nah, thank you." Her smile was the kind of shy one from earlier, which was quickly becoming his favorite. "That's the only exercise I get these days."

"Cold out there," he commented mildly, unsure if this was one of those times she'd prefer chivalry to letting her be an independent woman who didn't need a man to lift a ceramic pot.

"Hence the 'drat' in my statement. Also, you're not supposed to be lifting anything heavy. Sit there and drink your coffee like a good boy."

She pulled on her coat and boots in the mudroom and exited out the back door before he could insist otherwise. Not that he could have done it. She was right about his ribs and carrying a soup tureen a hundred yards back up a hill from the shed by the lake wouldn't be on his doctor-approved list of stuff he was allowed to do.

Still, it didn't sit well with him to leave her to do the heavy lifting. Maybe he could volunteer to clean the house for her as part of his compensation for her kind care and for basically letting him freeload in her home.

When she came back lugging the white ceramic tureen, she was out of breath and he felt like a heel and immediately jumped up to wrestle it from her grasp. "At least let me take it from here."

"Thanks, that hill gets steeper every year, I swear."

"What's wrong?" he demanded as he caught the flicker of something in her expression.

"Nothing. I just thought I locked the shed the last time I used something out of there. It was open."

Carefully, he set the tureen on the clear counter space near the stove and made a show out of arranging the lid so she didn't see the alarm that had likely just climbed all over his face. "Does anyone else use that shed? Like Lucy?"

"No, she's not allowed down by the lake without adult supervision. Wade does sometimes, but that's usually during the summer, when he needs a life vest or something."

"When was the last time you remember going down there?" he asked casually, but Hannah was having none of that.

"You think this is connected to all the other stuff going on around here. The misplaced items."

When he turned, she'd crossed her arms over her coat and leaned back against the island, but he wasn't fooled into thinking it was because she'd relaxed. She was holding herself in.

And he'd done that to her. Scared her.

But maybe it was time that he gave her a few clues about what was really going on around here. He couldn't be with her or Lucy all the time and whoever had fingered her as a person of interest had resorted to breaking into her shed to look for the money. But whether it was because he'd shown up here masquerading as Owen or because Big Mike had figured out the connection between Hannah and the man who had double-crossed him, he couldn't quite say yet.

"I think it would be a good idea to stay vigilant," he said evasively, desperately sorting through the data in his head to see what might be the safest thing to tell her. "It's possible it's just a homeless person looking for a warm place to sleep."

"There are no homeless people in Owl Creek," she countered flatly. "There's an excellent shelter in Conners that takes people in."

Great. Yeah, there was a reason they didn't let him out of the lab very often. "Fine, then I think we should talk about getting Lucy a dog."

"A dog!"

The little voice behind him lifted his heart right out of his chest and he'd just seen Lucy mere hours ago when he'd read her a story before bed.

The voice-owner herself popped around a corner holding Mr. Fluffers, wearing a robe that matched her mother's, which was adorable. He had a sudden urge to buy them a bunch more outfits that would signify them as a set, his part in the deal to shower them with compliments and wear a smug smile because they were his family.

Speaking of fantasies…

"You're getting me a dog?" Lucy repeated, her face glowing with expectation that he'd move a mountain not to erase.

"You bet," he said, letting the smile on his face match the one on the inside. "Seems like you mentioned that you had your eye on one from your aunt Ruby and uncle Sebastian's training place."

"Lu Lu, let's get you some breakfast," Hannah cut in brightly and shot Archer a look from behind Lucy's back as she hustled her daughter to the table, then produced a bowl from a shelf above the countertop. "Cheerios or oatmeal?"

"Cheerios," she announced decisively and fetched a big purple box from the walk-in pantry herself. "Can I name the dog myself? I already decided to call her Misty Princess Pants."

"Brilliant," Archer told her. "I love it."

"Mac," Hannah called through gritted teeth as she plunked

a carton of unsweetened almond milk on the table next to Lucy's bowl. "May I have a word with you?"

Brooking no argument, she clamped a hand around his wrist and hustled him from the room, apparently intending to allow Lucy to finish preparing her own breakfast.

"You can't do that," she whispered heatedly, keeping her voice low since they were just in the hall outside the kitchen, where they could still see Lucy. "Now she'll expect you to follow through."

"I plan to follow through." The fact that she didn't think he would spoke volumes. "I don't know what I have to say or do to get you to understand that I'm in this for the long haul, Hannah."

Or at least as much as this woman would let him keep his vows.

She scrubbed at her forehead as if the subject had given her a raging migraine. "That's not the point I'm trying to make here. This is all new. For both of us. I get it. But this is a classic case of not checking in with her other parent before you offer something that may not be okay with the other parent. Me. I'm the other parent here, and this is my house. I don't have the time or energy to handle a dog."

Archer started to get the feeling he'd screwed up. "I'm sorry, I didn't think about that."

"Why do you think I haven't gotten her one so far? News flash. It's not because I don't want her to have something she's asked for repeatedly with that desperate little girl wheedling that knifes right through me. And then you swoop in with promises to give her everything her heart desires, and I look like the bad guy."

The pain in that statement did its own number on his gut, pairing nicely with the squelchy sinking sensation that he'd blundered far more badly than he'd intended. "Geez,

Hannah, I definitely didn't mean to do that. Please back up a second. Let's work through this. Breathe with me here."

He was supposed to be fixing Owen's mistakes, not making a bunch of his own! If she started crying, he'd be done.

But she didn't. Without an ounce of protest, she did exactly as instructed, matching his deep, even inhales and exhales. When the mottled red faded from her cheeks, he risked lifting a hand to one, brushing it gently in a nonverbal apology that definitely didn't fit the crime.

"I'm sorry," he murmured again and dropped his hand since he didn't have permission to touch her like he wanted to. "I should cut to the chase and print that on a T-shirt. This is so far out of my realm of experience that I might as well be on a different planet. Parent World, where the quicksand doesn't just trap you, but everyone else too."

"I know. I get it, I really do." She lifted her lips in a tiny smile. "I'm thrilled that we're having this conversation in the first place. It's been rough being the only one on Parent World who can reach the top shelf."

"We're doing this together now," he informed her, the emotion in his voice roughening it unrecognizably. "You keep telling me when I'm doing it wrong, and I'll fix it. I'll learn. I want to be Lucy's father, and it's worth it to me to get it right."

The more he said it out loud, the more he felt it in his bones. Owen was gone, but he'd never been meant to be Lucy's father in the first place. No coincidences. Archer *wanted* the job. Didn't that count for something? In his mind, it counted for everything.

"Okay." Hannah nodded. "I'm not sure I'm the best teacher, but I'm all you've got."

"It's enough," he murmured. "I like the idea of being partners with you in this."

"I'm glad." She tipped her head toward the kitchen. "Now about the dog. It's one thing to vaguely promise she can get one to keep at your place, but—"

"That's what I'm saying. I want to give her this, Hannah. Let me be the one to teach her to take care of the dog. It's something we can do together. No burden on you. I'll handle all of it. The dog can come home with me, and it'll be something familiar for her in a place you're not. Assuming you're open to visits and we can work that out somehow."

Oddly, his impassioned speech seemed to sway her. She nodded again, her expression softening. "Okay. I like that idea."

"Okay?" Speechless, he stared at her. "Did we just have a mature conversation where we listened to each other and settled a major issue without bloodshed?"

She laughed. "You say that like that doesn't happen very often."

"You were at the same party I attended where your brothers not so subtly helped me to understand all the ways my leg bones would be broken if I so much as breathed on you wrong, were you not?"

Her grin widened at his comical grimace. "Point taken. We'll just make it a thing between us. Clan Mackenzie rules. We'll be mature about everything."

His heart stuttered as he absorbed what she'd just called them. *Clan Mackenzie.* Man, did that do unexpected things to him to be included in something so…intimate. She must have clued in on the gravity of the moment because her smile slipped from her face, and everything got heavy in a heartbeat.

"Sorry, that was little too much," she murmured.

"No." He shook his head, clasping her hand in his in case she had a mind to flee. "It's perfect. I love the thought of being in Clan Mackenzie with you. It's exactly right, exactly how I feel too."

Everything he hadn't known he was looking for.

He couldn't have been more drawn to this woman if they'd both been made of magnets. As if it had become a foregone conclusion, she swayed into his space, her grip on his hand tight, as if she needed to hold on to him before she lost her footing and slipped to the floor. He knew the feeling.

"Mac," she murmured, and it sounded like a plea.

If he didn't kiss her, he feared he'd never be whole again.

"What are you guys talking about?" Lucy popped into the hall, Mr. Fluffers in hand and a curious gaze fastened on the adults.

Archer sprang away from Hannah faster than a teenager caught by his mother in his room. "Nothing."

He'd forgotten Hannah's warning from the other day about total lack of privacy until Lucy went to college. Dang. Parenting was not for the weak.

Hannah was a little quicker on her feet. "We were talking about getting you a dog. Which we decided would be fine."

Lucy's squeal should have busted out all the glass in Hannah's house, but the panes stayed miraculously intact. Not so much his eardrums. "I take it that means you're excited. We can go look tomorrow since you don't have pre-school on Tuesdays."

"We can't go today? Aw, man." Lucy pouted, her arms crossed over Mr. Fluffers, who was getting squished into oblivion.

"Sorry, darling, you mom has to work tonight, and school comes first," he told her as he smoothed out her messy hair, which had come loose from her pigtails overnight. When he glanced up, the emotion in Hannah's gaze weakened his knees.

She wasn't giving him back-off vibes. Quite the opposite. Her body language had a whole lot of "we'll pick this up later" in it.

"Thank you," she mouthed, which set off a glow inside him that didn't fade for the rest of the day.

Chapter 18

The catering gig went flawlessly, thanks to Hannah's employees. It certainly wasn't due to her own contributions, which consisted of "gah" and "whu?" when someone asked her a question.

She had too many brain cells with Mac's name carved all over them to concentrate on anything approaching speech, how the soup ladle worked, walking without tripping. Complex stuff like that.

Not for the first time, she appreciated the fact that he'd asked her to call him Mac. It had contributed to the ease with which Clan Mackenzie had rolled off her tongue earlier in the kitchen, sure. But it also separated him in her mind—her ex-husband was Owen.

This new guy in her life was Mac. They had no history. She liked him. He made her feel things she hadn't felt in... well, ever. All of this was new all right, and not just the co-parenting journey they'd agreed to embark on together.

This was *different*. In her head, Mac had an ocean of possibilities wrapped up inside him and she wanted to explore them all.

But first, she needed to get her head out of the clouds and drive home from the party location on the other side of the lake, one of the giant custom-built mansions that seemed to be so prevalent in the resort town of Owl Creek. She'd liked the town a lot better when it had been a quiet place for families, but if it had stayed off the map, she'd have no business. So it was a good thing that people had moved into this area who didn't sneeze at one seventy-five a head.

Could she charge less? Absolutely, and she did if it was a resident who had been around for a while. But everyone else got the Bon Appetit going rate, which was worth it because she delivered excellent food and service.

Most days. Today wasn't a good example of her giving a top-tier performance, but the client had paid the balance in full before she'd cleared the driveway, so she'd call that a win.

She navigated—carefully—through the layer of snow that had fallen while she'd been inside the client's house, trusting her winter tires not to send her straight into a ditch, but that only worked if she didn't drive like a maniac. It took twice as long as it might have at another time of the year, but she didn't mind. Price of doing business.

As she unlocked the front door of her little house by the lake—a stark contrast to the one she'd just left—it occurred to her that this was the first time she'd ever left Lucy with someone other than a family member when she worked a catering gig.

Only Mac was *Lucy's* family. Clan Mackenzie. It was even Lucy's last name.

Neither Lucy nor her father were in the living room, which boded well since it was way past Lucy's bedtime. But surely Mac wasn't still reading to her.

She followed her instincts to Lucy's bedroom. Mac sat on the floor outside her room, hands resting on his drawn-up knees, his head thrown back against the wall. He gave her a sheepish smile when he caught sight of her and held one finger up to his lips like she wasn't fully aware that talking right outside her daughter's bedroom when she was asleep would be a bad idea.

Mac climbed to his feet and led her out into the living room, still wearing a sheepish expression. "I was listening to her breathe."

Oh, man. That hit her right in the heart. "I do that sometimes too."

"I was just thinking about how I'm not going to get to do that when I go back home to Las Vegas."

Even in the low light of the living room, she could see the angst climbing through his expression, feel the inner torment in the set of his shoulders. He didn't want to leave his daughter.

"We can work it out," she murmured, determined to make it true. "Whatever it looks like. She needs her father, Mac. But more to the point, you need to heal. Until your ribs are better and you have more than the memory of a goldfish, you're not going anywhere."

The brief smile he shot her tingled her toes. "I was worried I'd started overstaying my welcome when the dog situation happened."

"No hard feelings on that. I mean it."

And she did. She'd resisted a dog for a variety of reasons, but first and foremost because she'd already dealt with enough loss in her life. What if the dog didn't work out? What if this was another example of Hannah thinking with her heart and not her head, when she could have avoided the fiasco by not giving in to Lucy's heartfelt pleas?

But with Mac here, everything felt different. As if she could handle anything a little bit better, smarter. Even a dog.

"Good night, Hannah."

She laughed at the unexpected end to their conversation. "Is that my cue that you're about to turn into a pumpkin?"

"It's your cue that you might not want to be here with me in this room while you're laughing, and the lighting is set on romantic." The hoarse thread in his voice definitely didn't make her feel like laughing any longer. "So I'm giving you an out. If you want to stick around, nothing would make me happier, but that choice comes with a warning that I'm having a hard time keeping my hands off you."

So much for being able to handle anything life threw at her.

Especially the way the vibe had gone hot so very fast, as if the heater had blasted the room to ninety degrees instantly.

Her brain turned to mashed peas as they stared at each other, and she tried to sort out whether she wanted to stay or flee. Or rather, which one she wanted more, because both were true simultaneously, and wasn't that the exact issue?

"I think I should go," she murmured, and his expression mirrored the crushing sensation in her chest. "Mostly because I'm not sure and I want to be sure."

He nodded. "That works for me too. I am not a fan of kissing a woman who isn't sure she wants me to be kissing her."

He didn't stop her as she dashed from the room, her face flaming as she contemplated all the ways that scene had made her feel gauche and unsexy. Surely she'd just killed any romantic feelings Mac might have had about her by fleeing from him when the moment had gotten a little too steamy.

But this was a prime example of a time when she needed to use her head. And getting involved with Mac physically wasn't smart. It just might feel really, really good and that might be enough of a reason to do it, as long as she could keep her heart separate. Huge emphasis on *could*.

* * *

In the morning, she stayed in her room instead of joining Mac in the kitchen for coffee like she had the last few mornings. Yes, it was cowardly, but she didn't have her wits about her yet, and she didn't think the lighting in the living room made all that much difference as to whether she might take him up on the offer to let him put his hands on her.

And they had a dog to add to the family today.

When Hannah finally did emerge, Lucy and Mr. Fluffers sat at the table with a half-eaten bowl of cereal in front of them, Mac sitting in the next chair sipping coffee and nodding intently as his daughter told a story at warp speed.

Hannah had to pause for a moment, hand on the doorframe, until her knees stopped feeling like jelly. Lucy was Mac's daughter. Through and through. She had half of his DNA. It was so strange to think like that, to see evidence that he was taking his paternity so seriously, as if he hoped to make up for what he'd missed over the last few years.

She liked unexpectedly stumbling over them together. Much more than she'd have thought. It put dangerous ideas in her head, ideas about ways to resolve the issue of Mac not being able to listen to Lucy breathe in her sleep at some point in the future—and none of them involved him leaving.

Enough daydreaming.

"Good morning," she called brightly. "I see someone is so excited to get her day started that she's eating breakfast without me."

"It's Dog Day," Lucy announced. "Princess Misty is going to love it here."

"It's Princess Misty now?" Hannah asked wryly as she poured some coffee into a travel mug.

She'd texted Ruby yesterday to ensure that Crosswinds still had the dog that Lucy had latched on to a few weeks ago. Sometimes they had dogs slated to undergo therapy training, but they didn't quite have the temperament, so those dogs had to be rehomed. It would have been a bad scene if Princess Misty had already found another home, but that wasn't the case, so full steam ahead.

Whether Hannah was ready to be a Dog Mom or not.

"Misty Princess Pants is a dumb name," Lucy announced as Mac and Hannah glanced at each other.

If someone at Lucy's preschool had said one nasty word to her daughter about her choice of name…

But Lucy breezed past it as if she'd come up with the idea of changing the name, so Hannah didn't press her. They piled into the car and Mac sat in the passenger seat, enduring the chatter from the back seat with no visible grimaces, which won him lots of points.

When they got to Crosswinds, Sebastian personally greeted them at the door and led them to the area in the back where trainers worked with several dogs who seemed to be in varying stages of progress.

Sebastian paused at a row of large kennels and spoke to one of the volunteers. Lucy was about to come out of her skin, bouncing like a pogo stick from foot to foot as the volunteer led a black-and-white Border collie from the depths of the kennels, then held out the leash handle for Lucy to take.

"Look, Mama, Princess Misty is already so good," Lucy announced proudly as the dog sat at her feet, ears perked for the next command.

"She is a good dog," Hannah said with a smile and a nod at Sebastian. "What do we say?"

"Thank you, Uncle Sebastian," Lucy singsonged. "You're my favorite uncle ever in the whole wide world."

Sebastian laughed. "You be sure and tell your uncle Wade

that next time you see him. Maybe mention it a couple of times."

Yeah, that would go over well, but Hannah just rolled her eyes since he was kidding. Probably. She pulled out her phone to send Crosswinds the money for the adoption fee, waving off Sebastian when he tried to tell her it was on the house. He did good and valuable work here that she was proud to support financially, especially when he'd already invested money in Princess Misty's care thus far.

That's when she noticed Mac bend down to the dog and pat her gently on the back, murmuring to Lucy. Lucy mimicked his movements, glancing between Mac and the dog, her excitement nearly palpable. Hannah had no doubt he'd already started the dog ownership education process.

But the vibe had a lot of something else in it. A father and daughter bonding. Mac's face bled tenderness and his small smile had a touch of wonder. As if he couldn't believe he got to witness this first meeting of a girl and her dog.

Well, he could join the club. Hannah was getting to watch Mac and Lucy interact with the dog, and it was seriously melting her heart.

How much more of this could she actually take? It was like waiting for the axe to fall when you knew it was up there, suspended. Just waiting on the right sequence of events to drop and sever everything in two.

Except she wasn't so sure that's what was going to happen.

"Hey," Ruby called as she strolled down one of the aisles from the back, where she'd been doing a wellness checkup on a few of the dogs.

Hannah grinned as Ruby joined her in viewing the scene unfolding before them. Her sister's role as a veterinarian had long made Hannah proud and baffled that she came from the same stock as someone who had the chops to get through the rigorous course work required to get a degree of that caliber.

"You sure this is a good idea?" Ruby murmured with a head tilt toward Princess Misty, father and daughter, so it wasn't entirely clear which part she'd questioned.

Hannah chose the less complicated of the two as the subject of her response. "I'm going to do my best to make it work. Lucy would be sorely disappointed if I didn't."

And that's when she realized she hadn't actually picked one or the other because the sentiment applied to both. Lucy needed Hannah to make things work with Mac, probably even more so than she needed the dog to become a member of their family.

How either of those happened depended on Hannah.

"I know he's her father," Ruby began and held up a hand when Hannah started to protest—likely because they both knew what she was about to say. "Give me a sec to make this point. I don't like the way he treated you when you were married. I don't like how he's treated you since then. You can't erase six years of someone behaving like a complete and utter jackass."

"I'm not trying to erase it," Hannah countered hotly. "I'm trying to forgive and move on. I can't erase my daughter's genetics either. He's a part of her, period, whether he chooses to embrace what that entails or not. Get back to me when Sawyer is five and tell me whether you wouldn't move heaven and earth to ensure that Sebastian is in his life, even if your marriage doesn't work out."

"That's totally different," Ruby scoffed. "Sebastian is noble and good and kind. Plus, he didn't leave me."

"Didn't he?" What was good for the goose was good for the gander. "Seems like I recall a period of time when you were pregnant and alone, Ruby. It wasn't all hearts and flowers for you either, but you gave it a chance and it worked out. Give me that same chance."

The hard cross of Ruby's arms said she had more to say, but she shut her mouth, so Hannah did too, her spine relaxing a touch when Mac caught her gaze and they shared a long look full of emotion. Only some of it had to do with Lucy and her tangible delight with Princess Misty. The rest? Well, she wasn't sure, but she did know that the next time Mac caught her in the kitchen with that heavy intention weighing down the atmosphere, she wouldn't be so quick to leave.

As they bundled Princess Misty into the travel crate Sebastian had loaned them, she had a sudden flash forward of the three of them—make that four—doing things like this all the time. As a family. Clan Mackenzie. Maybe they'd add a few more members to the clan. More dogs. More children.

Her throat went tight and hot as she lived in that moment for a few seconds. It was a dream she never thought she'd let surface. How could she? She'd vowed to sacrifice her own personal life to be Lucy's mom, but deep inside, it was a fear of a repeat broken heart that had kept her away from the dating scene. Since there had been zero immaculate conceptions for over two thousand years, she'd assumed Lucy would be it.

Was this the start of a real second chance with Mac, who had yet to hurt her, yet to abandon her, yet to disprove his claim that he'd changed? There was only one way to find out.

Chapter 19

Archer had never had a dog before. But to be fair, he'd also never had amnesia, a daughter or an ex-wife, so he was pretty much winging everything on a minute-by-minute basis. What was one more thing to add to the pile?

He helped Lucy get Princess Misty—the name that seemed to be sticking—get oriented in Hannah's house. They showed the dog how to politely ask to go outside by bringing the leash to Lucy, which Princess Misty mastered relatively fast, thanks to the training she'd already received at Crosswinds.

That was some high-class operation. The fact that Princess Misty hadn't made the cut felt highly suspect given how the dog never barked, never scratched at anything and seemed to be constantly waiting for the next command. Archer wondered if Lucy's aunt and uncle hadn't finagled their inventory of dogs a bit to create the illusion that this Border collie wasn't slated to become a therapy dog.

If so, he was doubly glad that he'd pushed as hard as he had to get Hannah to accept the idea. She might not have ever made the decision to adopt Princess Misty otherwise, and then Lucy would have missed out on a rite of passage no kid should go without. It was humbling and gratifying to be a part of giving his daughter something that he'd never gotten to experience.

Owen's daughter, rather, but it got harder and harder to qualify that in his own head, let alone in reality.

Lucy was amazing and brilliant and while Owen had a head for finance, his mind didn't work nearly the same way as Archer's did, and he caught glimpses of Lucy's brain making sharp calculations that far eclipsed any logic Owen had ever exhibited.

Was it terrible of him to imagine that she might take after him in some small ways?

The next day, Hannah had a catering job and Lucy had preschool, so Archer took a rare opportunity to do some recon in town at the library, where he used Hannah's account to research the death of her father.

Stroke. Or at least that was how the coroner had ruled it. As Hannah's brothers had mentioned, there were some ways to force someone into a stroke, but it might be really difficult to prove that. Reading through the news articles he could find yielded nothing new or interesting, and it was a gamble to do too much heavy lifting on a public computer with a tie to Hannah's name, so he quit.

Archer wandered around town for a bit, at loose ends. This was the first time since taking the job at the LVMPD that he didn't have access to his lab or his computers. Having to sort through data strictly in his head was causing him a great deal of discomfort, especially considering he still got headaches occasionally from the accident. It might help if he could write some things down, but he didn't want to risk Hannah finding his notes.

Or worse, someone else.

To say the investigation wasn't going well would be an understatement. Thus far, he'd ruled out Hannah's involvement in Owen's dealings, then and now, but he couldn't quite strike the rest of her family from the list. Particularly Chase.

The timing on that warehouse transaction still bothered him, as did the assertion made by her brothers in his presence that their father had been murdered. The situation with Jessie Colton factored in, plus he hadn't begun to make a dent in sorting out the misplaced items at Hannah's house—which surely meant someone had their eye on her and likely him too.

And then there was the fact that he'd made zero headway on the thing he'd come here to investigate. The missing money. Find that, find the trail to Owen's killer.

Something needed to break soon. Especially since he couldn't keep up the amnesia act much longer. In fact, he'd like to come clean with Hannah sooner rather than later, preferably before something irreversible happened, like his will to keep his hands off her shattering into a million pieces.

Archer finally gave up doing anything productive and drove Hannah's car back to her house instead of staying in town for another two hours until it was time to pick up Lucy from preschool. He'd planned to go straight from the library to the preschool near the fire station at the west end of town, then spend some time with Lucy until Hannah's event ended. This was a life he could get used to…except for the lack of purpose and meaningful work to do.

Not for the first time, he tested out in his head what things could look like going forward. How often he could come back to Owl Creek to visit Lucy. And Hannah. He could not deny that mother and daughter had started to feel a bit like a package deal. At least that was how he wanted to see them.

How Hannah felt about that remained to be seen.

Parking the car in the driveway, Archer got out and flipped the key fob ring around his index finger as he strolled toward the house, then froze as he registered the slight crack in the front door. The not-closed front door.

Archer slipped the key fob into his pocket and glanced around for a makeshift weapon of some sort, settling on one of the umbrellas sticking out of a colorful pot to the left of the door. If nothing else, he could stab an intruder with the metal tip, but discretion would definitely be the better part of valor in this situation.

Cautiously, he eased the door open, umbrella raised, which would have been slightly comical in any other situation. It wasn't like he normally carried a gun in the first place; he wasn't that kind of cop. Nor had he expected to run into trouble at Hannah's house, but in retrospect, that had been a rookie mistake. Hadn't he just run through that data point not fifteen minutes ago?

This was his break. The one he'd asked for. Archer was about to catch the intruder in the act. With an umbrella as his only defense against someone who very likely might be carrying.

As silently as possible, he slipped over the threshold and slowly swung the door back to its original cracked position. No point in alerting the intruder that someone else had entered the house. Archer still had the element of surprise on his side.

Nothing out of the ordinary stuck out in the living area, so Archer toed off his sneakers, stowing them behind a chair so he could traverse the hardwood floor in his sock feet. Hannah kept the house on the chilly side so the wood creaked a little as he walked, but blessedly, the heater kicked on and covered the noise.

Experienced at being stealthy he was not.

The kitchen was empty of sketchy intruders. Archer padded to the wing with his bedroom and ducked low to peer inside. Nothing. No one in the bathroom either. He remembered at the last second to check behind the shower curtain, umbrella poised in case the prowlers had watched a bunch of bad slasher movies in preparation for the shake-down of Hannah's house.

Empty. He huffed out a breath of relief.

That left Lucy and Hannah's bedrooms. As he passed back through the kitchen, he swapped the umbrella for one of Hannah's pricey knives, pulling the biggest one from the butcher block and rolling his eyes at himself for not think-ing of that earlier.

Not that he thought he'd have a chance against a well-aimed bullet. But someone might think twice about jump-ing him if he had some hardware that could do a lot more damage than poke an eye out. Plus, he had righteous in-dignation on his side.

He hefted the knife higher as he headed to Lucy's room. Mr. Breaking and Entering better not have touched a sin-gle thing in his daughter's room or everyone would find out exactly how motivated Archer was to defend his own.

The intruder wasn't helping himself to Lucy's stuffed animals, though. That left Hannah's bedroom. The logical place for someone likely employed by Big Mike to spend the most time since she'd been married to the guy who'd stolen his money.

But it was also thankfully devoid of criminals with neck tattoos. Archer lowered the knife and took a moment to let his heart rate return to normal. Had he left the door cracked when he'd left to take Lucy to school and Hannah to her event, then? Could all of this have been a figment of his imagination? Surely not.

Now that the imminent threat had dissipated, Archer combed the house, looking for clues. There. The lamp in the living room sat a quarter of an inch to the right of where it had been this morning. Visually, he could see it was off-center against the lines of the end table. The sofa cushions had been lifted and returned to their former positions. The one on the end stuck up a little higher than the others, though, and it was the one he'd sat on earlier to tie his shoes.

Cataloging what was changed or moved in every room didn't take long. Unlike the first couple of times the house had been searched, this was a pro job, with few mistakes. Nearly undetectable if you didn't know what to look for since a lot of the examined items had been put back exactly as they'd been. You had to have an extreme eye for detail with above-average spatial perception to be this precise.

Someone had called in a higher caliber of talent. Expensive talent. The kind you didn't mind using when the payout promised to more than cover the outlay of cost.

Archer's stomach turned over as he considered the implications. This was no longer a bunch of random criminals doing a rush job to find a double-crosser. What it was, he didn't know.

But the thing at the base of his throat was slick, black fear, no question.

Archer's *family* was being threatened. Hannah and Lucy were in danger. What if they'd been home and the intruder had decided to add a felony or two to his repertoire?

His phone buzzed, shoving the slickness into his mouth. Swallowing, he glanced at the screen. Hannah. Text message. She'd finished her event early and was asking if she could go with him to pick up Lucy.

Yes, yes, she could. She wasn't going *anywhere* without him for the foreseeable future.

Thankfully, they'd elected to enroll Princess Misty with a doggie day care to give her other dogs to play with when no one would be at home. Otherwise, the scene he'd stumbled onto here at the house might have been a much different one.

Which begged the question in his mind—the five-million-dollar question, which he already knew the answer to. How had this professional talent known that no one would be home? Someone was watching them, obviously.

Archer strolled to the car as if nothing had changed. Because the worst thing he could do now would be to tip off his unknown adversary. It might already be too late, but hopefully whoever was watching wouldn't think anything of Archer taking an umbrella into the house. He slid behind the wheel of Hannah's car, adjusting the rearview mirror casually to cover himself as he checked out the woods across from the house for the glint of binoculars.

A flash. Bingo. There was someone in the woods and he'd make an assumption it was the less bone-chilling option—binoculars—and not the scope of a rifle.

He started the car and backed out of the driveway, white-knuckling the steering wheel as he braced for anything. A shot to ring out or a tire to blow.

Nothing happened. He might be letting his imagination run away with him. But he hadn't manufactured the evidence that at least two different individuals had systematically searched Hannah's house. For what? That was the question he *didn't* have the answer to.

What data did someone else have that Archer didn't?

Hannah waited for him outside the library where they'd agreed to meet. She slid into the car, her cheeks rosy from the cold and a smile on her face. "Thanks for picking me up."

"You could have waited inside." *Should* have waited inside, he corrected silently, but he couldn't tell her why it was necessary. "It's cold. I would have texted you when I got here."

"I didn't want to make you sit here and twiddle your thumbs. I wasn't out here that long and besides, I'm from Idaho. We have to build up our fat layer to survive here."

She laughed, and it had the odd effect of making Archer's spine relax. "It gets cold in Las Vegas too at night. Sometimes."

The undertones of the conversation—the reality that they lived in different cities—tugged at his heart again, the way it seemed to constantly do lately. He hated that they weren't having completely different conversations about the future, but he couldn't make one single decision about what would happen once he'd dumped Owen's murderer behind bars. Plus, she deserved to know the truth.

"Hannah—"

She shook her head. "I know what you're going to say. I don't want to worry about what's going to happen when you go back home yet. We'll work it out. Somehow."

"I believe you. But—"

"No buts." She reached over and mushed his mouth together with her thumb and forefinger. "New subject. Ask me how my catering event went."

"How did your event go?" he mouthed against her glove-less fingers, playing along as he reeled in his wholly inappropriate reaction to her touch.

She chattered for a solid three minutes about how well it went and how cheerfully her employees worked together, while he envisioned the words coming out of his mouth. *I have something to tell you. I'm not who you think I am, Hannah.*

Then he thought about how her expression would change. How she'd be upset. Disappointed. Maybe furious. Maybe she'd refuse to let him see Lucy and wasn't that a bucket of cold water? He had zero rights, morally or legally, to pursue a relationship with his niece. No matter how much he thought of her as his daughter already.

It didn't matter. Everyone needed to know the truth. The words burned his tongue, but he couldn't spit them out. Not yet.

This equation didn't have a lot of positive outcomes, not that he could calculate. But he could do the easier math, the story problem that went something like: once Archer tells Hannah the truth about his identity, what are the odds he'd be kicked to the curb, leaving her and Lucy in the house by themselves with nothing other than a Border collie named Princess Misty for protection?

He couldn't tell her anything. She could accidentally— or even on purpose—tip off the wrong people.

Worse, his days of keeping a low profile were over.

The best way to draw out the eyes in the woods—and the employer of that surveillance crew—was to use himself as bait. He had to make some noise. Get some attention on his presence here.

The thought of putting Lucy and Hannah in those crosshairs squeezed his heart until he feared it might actually burst. But what choice did he have? Magically come up with the missing data he didn't have on why someone had targeted Hannah's house as the most likely place to contain fill-in-the-blank?

He also couldn't leave. It would be far preferable to stick that target on his back and walk out the door. Go back to Vegas and let the goons come after him. But it was a huge assumption that they'd lose interest in Hannah's house when he wasn't even positive they knew who Owen was. Or that whoever was calling the shots wouldn't send a second set of guys after Archer, leaving the first set here.

This was a chess game with far too many moving pieces.

And he'd leave Hannah and Lucy here to fend for themselves over his own dead body.

Chapter 20

Mac had been quiet since they'd picked up Lucy from preschool, but Hannah more than made up for it with her own chatter. Nerves, mostly. Could he tell?

Oh, goodness. She put her cold hands to her flaming cheeks as Mac stowed Princess Misty's travel crate in the hatchback of Hannah's car, praying he hadn't noticed her telltale face.

It wasn't every day that a woman decided it was time to seduce her ex-husband. Okay, that was not exactly what she'd decided. Maybe it was more of a conscious decision to open her heart to letting something happen between them. A full-bore Lady in Red routine wasn't her wheelhouse. Nor did she think that would go over very well.

What did a woman even do if that was her goal? Buy some sexy lingerie and wear a trench coat to dinner?

Yeah. This was helping her cheeks calm down.

Mac drove them home with Lucy twisted backward the whole way as she told Princess Misty all about her day. Which was more than Hannah had gotten. Lucy had barely even said hello before she'd asked if she could take Princess Misty to Wade's house for a visit so she could introduce her new dog to Betty Jane.

Lucy's mile-a-minute conversation with the Border collie covered the fact that Hannah had run out of things to say. More to the point, she was imagining that trench coat and having a serious crisis of confidence about her decision. Maybe she *should* be thinking about ways to move things forward. A signal that she was ready. Not lingerie. But something.

Or maybe she should abandon the whole idea and pretend nothing had changed.

Hannah made dinner in a daze, scarcely recognizing the ingredients she'd thrown into the wok for the crispy stir fry on the menu. Mac helped her serve and then took his customary place next to Lucy, which meant he was across from Hannah. So she could look at him without it being weird.

Except it was weird, because she'd started thinking about what it would be like to kiss Mac. It wouldn't be like kissing the same man she'd been married to, or at least that's what she'd been telling herself. The whole point of putting a stake in the ground meant discovering how things worked between them as the people they were now. She'd changed. She had to believe he had too.

But her nerves wouldn't stop kicking her butt.

After dinner, she cleaned up and then stopped Mac with a hand to his arm as he started to follow Lucy down the hall for bath time, grimly determined to figure out which way she'd go. "If you don't mind, I'd like to read Lucy stories tonight. Just…you know. The two of us."

Mac's lips lifted a touch. "You haven't had much girl time lately, have you?"

Relieved that he actually understood, Hannah nodded. "That's it exactly."

"I'll get Mistress Mackenzie bathed and then you can take over, okay?"

She grinned at his nickname for Lucy. That had been far too easy. Why she'd been expecting resistance, she couldn't say. But she did get that Mac's time with Lucy might be limited and that he'd of course want to spend every second he could with his daughter. Only he hadn't made a peep about that, content with the part she'd allotted him.

They were really gelling with this parenting thing. Shockingly.

When it was time to read, she passed Mac in the hall, exchanging a relaxed glance as if they'd often tag-teamed bedtime. It spoke to his desire to make this work too.

As she breezed through the doorway to Lucy's room, she paused to take in the sight of Princess Misty snuggled in next to her daughter, who already had a book in her hand. She was reading to the dog. Who was intently listening.

It was precious.

"Which book is Princess Misty's favorite?" she called.

Lucy rolled her eyes. "Clifford. Duh."

Hannah made a face. "Do we speak to others sarcastically, Lucy Louise Mackenzie?"

Lucy lifted a brow, looking so much like Mac in that moment that Hannah's knees nearly gave out.

"Only when the question is dumb," Lucy announced. "Then it should be fine."

Instead of continuing the teachable moment, which clearly would fall on deaf ears, Hannah sat on the pink comforter, careful not to disturb Princess Misty's tail. "Can I ask you a serious question that isn't dumb even though it may feel that way to you? I need an honest answer."

Her daughter cocked her head, hopefully clueing in that her mother's tone meant business. "Is this one of those times I should pay attention to someone else's feelings besides my own?"

"Bingo." Hannah stroked Princess Misty a couple of times, which soothed her far more than she was expecting. Wasn't petting a dog supposed to make the *animal* feel good? "So the question is, what do you think about meeting your daddy?"

"He's the best!" Lucy exclaimed instantly. "He got me a dog and lets me play with the bubbles for as long as I want at bath time."

An indictment of her mother's strict bathroom schedule. Because if she let Lucy linger, it put Hannah behind, and she often had prep for a catering event after her daughter went to bed. That tracked. Mac was all about fun and games and new experiences. But she'd already assumed that would be the case and had chosen to let them bond instead of being a stickler about rules.

"What if he was around all the time? How would you feel about that?"

Her face lit up. "Does he want to be in our family?"

Clan Mackenzie. Hannah swallowed at the sudden ache in her throat. "I don't know. Maybe. The grown-ups need to talk about it, but I wanted to get your thoughts on it first."

"It's a big decision," Lucy said with eerie wisdom. "He might want two slices of Grandma Jenny's chocolate cake at my birthday party, and then someone else might not get any."

Hannah laughed. "If you're good with having your daddy around on a permanent basis, I'll gladly make a second cake. We will always have enough food for everyone who wants to be at our table."

As metaphors went, it wasn't a bad one to embrace. As long as Mac wanted a place, she should do her part to ensure she made room for him. Regardless of what happened between the two of them. That was how adults did things.

"I drew a picture at school today." Lucy jumped out of bed and grabbed her backpack without asking permission, but Hannah let it slide. "Do you think Daddy will like it?"

She took the picture Lucy handed her and absorbed the stick people with surprisingly detailed clothing and shoes. The important thing was the number of people: three. Not two like Lucy had been drawing for quite some time.

She'd included her dad.

That was answer enough for Hannah, though it changed everything whether she was ready for it or not. "I think he'll love it."

"Give it to him," Lucy instructed, before settling back under the covers and handing Hannah a book. "Don't skip the part where the monkeys jump on the bed."

Hannah huffed out another laugh, though it broke against the emotion in her throat. She swallowed again and set the explosive stick-drawing picture aside in favor of story time. Much to Lucy's delight, she made a point of reading the monkey book twice, all the way through, no skipping. Small price to pay for getting her head on straight.

Once she had girl and dog all tucked in and had turned the light off, she tiptoed down the hall to the living area, praying Mac was still watching TV where she'd left him. It would be par for the course for her to have made a monumental decision to try some variation of whatever Lady in Red ambush Hannah could cobble together, only to find an empty room.

It wasn't empty.

Mac glanced up as she came into the room, a slow smile spreading across his face as if he'd somehow picked up on her vibe. Oh, goodness. Had he? Something fluttered in her midsection that she hadn't felt in a very long time, and it wasn't the stomach flu.

"Lucy asleep?" he murmured as she stood there frozen, four steps away from the island that separated the kitchen from the living room.

"That or plotting a coup to take over the pantry so she can eat an entire package of Oreos single-handedly." Mac laughed, a warm, buttery sound that brushed across her skin. That felt so nice, she cast about for something else funny to say so he'd do it again, but then she remembered the picture. "She made this for you."

His expression instantly a heartbreaking blend of awe and surprise, Mac took the heavy construction paper from her outstretched hand, his gaze zeroing in on the figures. "Is this me?"

She nodded, not trusting her voice to actually work. He glanced up, his gaze meeting hers, so full of unvoiced emotion that she desperately wanted to understand. That was enough to get her mouth moving. "She wants a family. Not a dad who lives in another state."

The gauntlet had been thrown. Or something a little more sexy.

Mac stood, crossing the ocean of carpet between them that suddenly felt like mere inches the closer he got. He placed the picture on the island behind her, his presence wrapping around her in a way that shouldn't be so encompassing when he hadn't actually touched her yet. Wait. Was he going to touch her?

Then he did, his hand cupping her face as he guided it upward to gently force her to look at him. "What do you want, Hannah?"

"I want to know what's going to happen when you get your memories back," she blurted out. A statement also known as the number-one mood killer available on the market today.

But she needed to hear him say the words. Even if it meant he'd remove his hand from her face—and she quite liked the brush of his thumb over her cheek.

Except he did drop his hand. And his whole body. To his knees, capturing her hand in his on his way down. She stared down at him, prostrate at her feet.

"Hannah," he bit out hoarsely. "I'm so, so sorry about what happened before. I can't erase it. I wish I could, but please know that I can't imagine hurting you again."

"That's not an answer."

He nodded, not the least bit cowed. Which went a long way.

"It's not an answer. Because I don't have one. I've never been in this situation before. That I know of," he amended with a slight eye roll that made her lips tip up in a half smile. "But I do know that I'm not going to lose my memories of what precious little time I've had together with you and Lucy, here in Owl Creek. You're my family. Forever. I want to be the one to take pictures of Lucy's first day of school and help you put candles on her birthday cake. If you let me, I'd like to do this parenting thing alongside you. Holding your hand."

"And sleeping in my bed?" she added bluntly. Maybe there was a course you were supposed to take on how to be a Lady in Red before you actually tried it.

But the look on Mac's face drove that thought right out of her head, along with all of the other ones.

"If that's part of the equation, yes," he murmured. "I would be blessed ten times over to be given a chance to prove that I mean what I say. I'm not going to disappoint you this time."

No, she didn't think disappointment would be anywhere in her future if she let Mac into her bed. But she did recognize that he was giving her the choice. Instead of sweeping her off her feet and snowing her senses with what she knew would be an amazing kiss if she gave into the heated vibes swirling between them, he was letting her take the lead.

And she wasn't sure she could make that choice. Not yet.

"I can't talk about that right now," she told him honestly. "But I do want to be clear that what happens between you and I is not in any way a factor in you being Lucy's father. Show up for her. No matter what."

He nodded, squeezing her hand. "I plan to. It's not an option for me to walk away from her. Not now. Not ever."

Despite the fact that he was saying all the right things, she couldn't let her guard down long enough to figure out how to let him in. To his credit, he allowed her to slip away and didn't try to follow her when she fled to her bedroom.

The next morning, she skipped Mac's coffee and left the house early for an appointment with a potential client in Conners who wanted to throw a huge wedding that bordered on a party. If she booked with Bon Appetit, the profit would equal Hannah's entire annual forecasted income in one gig.

The future bride and Hannah hit it off instantly and by the time she left the woman's home, she had a signed agreement in hand, with a hefty deposit already sitting in her bank account. Riding high on the success, she pulled out her phone to text Maria, one of the moms she'd befriended on the last preschool trip she'd chaperoned for Lucy's class, thinking it might be fun to meet for coffee.

She had several missed texts and calls from Owen. She'd never switched the name label to Mac in her phone, and it was a bucket of cold water to see his real name paraded across her screen so succinctly. Calling him something different had worked to a degree to get her to stop thinking about the past, to stop instantly assigning him to the old places of her heart.

But he was still Owen underneath. A new name didn't change that, or at least that's what her brain kept telling her.

Her heart wanted her brain to shut up. To believe. To feel him in the new places, the ones he'd created since that first moment when she'd seen him in that hospital bed and every moment since then. Especially the ones with Lucy. Whoever said that it was sexy watching a man be a good father had been onto something.

In case his messages were urgent or related to Lucy in some way, she read them, relieved to see he was just asking her where she'd gone and when she'd be back. Well, she didn't answer to him. Though it was a little sweet in one of the messages where he mentioned that he'd missed having their early morning alone time together.

Honestly, she'd missed it too.

She couldn't think about all of this. It was too much. She edited his contact entry to Mac and saved it, then hit the text symbol for Maria, asking her if she had some time free to chat.

Maria responded instantly that she'd love to have Hannah drop by. Feeling free as a bird since Mac would take care of Lucy all day if Hannah asked him to, she accepted. Maybe some people might call it avoiding an explosive issue, but Hannah preferred to call it waiting to address the situation until she had her feet under her.

Besides, Mac—Owen in this particular case—owed her. She'd been a single parent for four years, five technically since he'd never lifted a finger to help out for the brief period after Lucy had been born. If she took a few hours for herself after a great client meeting, that was what fathers were for.

Maybe after coffee with Maria she'd feel more like putting down some ground rules for what things would be like going forward. Probably it would be a very bad idea to get involved with Mac again. They should take a giant step back and figure out how to co-parent as two single adults.

Maybe at some point in the future things would be able to gradually change.

When she got to Maria's house, another vehicle sat in the driveway, so she parked on the street and walked back, dodging some ice patches on the walkway to the front door. Just as she got to the front porch, the door swung open and Ana Sophia, Lucy's friend from preschool, came out holding the hand of a man who looked so much like her, he could only be her father. Ana Sophia waved at Hannah and her father nodded his head as he passed, guiding his daughter to the car in the driveway.

Maria appeared behind them, her gaze on Ana Sophia as she watched the girl's father buckle her into the car seat on the second row of the newer SUV. The mother's expression was heartbreaking.

"Hannah," she called, finding a smile, but it seemed to be a bit hard-won. "I'd hoped Ramon would be gone before you got here. He was running late, but when is he not? You'd think spending time with his daughter would be something he'd be early for, but no."

"I'm sorry if I'm intruding," Hannah began but Maria cut her off.

"No, not at all. Please, come in. It's great timing. It's Ramon's day to have Ana Sophia and I'm always at loose ends when she's gone. The company will be nice."

"I'm sorry," Hannah murmured. "I didn't realize you and Ramon had separated."

"It's somewhat new." Maria led her into a cheerful kitchen decorated with bright colors. "We're trying to figure out how to manage, but honestly, most days, I just wish we could be a family again. It's so hard on Ana Sophia to have her parents living in two separate places and arguing about parenting decisions that we should be making together."

"I could see how that would be difficult."

And she could. In real time, in her head, as she imagined how the next few years would go as she and Mac tried to co-parent Lucy through text messages and brief snippets of time at the front door as they transferred their daughter between them.

"If it's not intrusive," Hannah said as she accepted the coffee mug from Maria with a brief smile, "is there any chance you'll work it out? Be a family again?"

"I would love that," Maria said grimly, her eyes growing misty. "But Ramon doesn't want to. This is all his decision, and I had no say in it."

Hannah absorbed the sentiment as if Maria had flung it at her, beating her over the head with the words. Because it was her own story, in reverse. She was the one holding back. She was the one who was going to tell Mac there was no chance and that he had no say in the decision.

And honestly, that's not what she wanted.

She didn't want to tell Mac that he had to see Lucy on his designated days, when she'd have to watch them both walk away to be father and daughter some place she wasn't. She didn't want to tell him there was no chance for them.

Clan Mackenzie. That's what she wanted. It was what she'd always wanted. This might be her one and only chance to make it real.

Chapter 21

When Hannah finally texted Archer to let him know she'd been at a friend's house, but she'd be home soon, he took his first breath of the day. Since he'd awoken this morning to find Hannah's bedroom door wide open and the woman nowhere to be found, a pair of giant hands had grabbed his lungs and squeezed.

Sure, he'd checked the garage and found her car missing. Probably she was in it, driving some place. *Probably.* But she hadn't mentioned anything to him about an event today, so naturally he'd assumed the worst—Big Mike had kidnapped her and forced her to drive her car to a remote location in the mountains, where he'd finish her off. Or she'd dashed out for milk and had been run off the road by someone employed by whoever had pulled the same crap with him.

So his brain got busy recounting the other hundred bad scenarios that could have happened while he texted her and called for a clue as to her whereabouts, pulse pounding in his throat. No answer. Meanwhile, he'd worn out the carpet in front of Lucy's room, checking and rechecking on her to ensure she'd slept through the worst couple of hours of his life.

She had. Then she'd bounced out of bed to announce that she and Princess Misty required pancakes for breakfast, and since Hannah wasn't home and wasn't responding to his texts, he decided that pancakes sounded fantastic. So he'd pulled out all the ingredients and used Hannah's fancy cookware to make a dozen of the fluffiest pancakes in existence, awed at how much nicer it was to cook in a well-appointed kitchen.

After breakfast, they'd watched *Peppa Pig* for an hour and then Archer had declared they'd had enough brain rotting for the day, and moved Lucy on to coloring at the table.

When Hannah breezed through the door near lunchtime, he had to physically restrain himself from sweeping her into his arms to kiss her senseless and then personally check every inch of her body to ensure she was in fact still in one piece.

"There you are," he said gruffly instead, stuffing his hands into his pockets. Obviously she was fine. And not lying in a ditch.

Man, did she wear that windblown, rosy-cheeked-from-the-cold look well. She might be the most beautiful woman he'd ever met.

"Mama, see what I did," Lucy commanded, and Hannah crossed to the table to ooh and aah over the drawings in question.

"I have a surprise for you, Lu Lu," she said brightly and glanced at Archer. "What would you say to a sleepover at Grandma Jenny's? Princess Misty is invited too."

Lucy cheered and raced Princess Misty to her room as her mother called after her to remember to pack pajamas and her toothbrush.

"A sleepover?" Archer asked, trying to catch up. Was this a regular thing that Lucy and Hannah did together?

"I hope you don't mind," Hannah said once Lucy was out of earshot, a delightful splotch of color climbing into her cheeks. "I thought it would be nice to have a night to ourselves."

Dumbfounded, Archer stared at her, his brain sliding into a place that it shouldn't be without a whole lot of clarifications. "Are you asking me on a date?"

"Um, yes?"

He clutched his heart in mock cardiac arrest to cover up the fact that she had in fact nearly knocked him over with the admission. "I'm crushed at how unsure you sound. Maybe try again without all the question marks."

"Mac, would you like to have dinner with me tonight?" she responded dutifully but whacked him on the arm playfully, which worked for him and then some, because it allowed him to grab her hand and pull her into his arms.

Progress. In more ways than one.

"I'm practicing," he informed her when she blinked up at him with one eyebrow askew. "For later. I was making sure my ribs would be up for it if your dinner ended up being so good that I needed to thank you with a hug."

"How's that working for you?" she asked, her tone wry. But she didn't pull away.

In a shocking turn of events, she slipped her arms around him in kind.

He squeezed her closer, as if testing, wobbling his head in indecision. "I'm not sure. I'm definitely going to have to do this again to figure it out. Maybe several times."

That was the only way he could ever get his fill of her. His heart thrummed as her scent filled his head. Whatever had turned her *I'm not sure* into *sure*, he was a fan of it.

"If you're expecting an argument, you won't get one here," she murmured. "Maybe let's pick this up later, though."

"Yes, ma'am," he said with far less enthusiasm than the

words deserved. "How fast can we get Lucy to your mom's house?"

She laughed, making it very difficult to release her as he'd absolutely intended to do. But then Lucy came back in the room dragging a pink overstuffed suitcase with the Little Mermaid printed on the flap, so it kind of became necessary to give Hannah her mobility back.

"Mama, I can't get it zipped," Lucy complained, apparently not the slightest bit concerned that her parents had been wrapped around each other in the kitchen mere moments ago.

Good. Hopefully that meant she would continue to be unconcerned about such events, because Archer planned to repeat the casual affection as often as possible. His arms had already cooled far too much, and Hannah had only been absent from them for about ninety seconds.

Hannah bent to help Lucy rearrange what looked like half of her room dumped haphazardly into the cavity of the suitcase. Together they pulled the zipper closed—barely. But in no time, Lucy allowed Archer to heft the suitcase into the hatchback of Hannah's car. Princess Misty's travel crate went in next to it, then Lucy dove into the back seat to get clicked into her car seat, jabbering to the dog about all the fun things Grandma Jenny would do with them.

Archer went with them to drop off the kid and dog combo, and the moment they got back into the car for the return trip, the silence was so deafening that he almost asked if they could get Lucy back.

Almost. This was the first time he and Hannah had been truly alone, and unless he'd somehow misread all her cues—unlikely—this was a momentous occasion to be marked with adult activities. This was his one and only chance to make it memorable for both of them since he had the worst feeling that time was running out.

Archer was not a slouch in the female department, but this was different. He wanted Hannah with a fierce sort of possessiveness that he didn't recognize, and he was worried that it would come across as creepy instead of flattering. She deserved to be romanced. What would Owen do?

"Do we need to stop at the store to get anything for dinner?" he asked. Smooth. That had romance stamped *all* over it.

Hannah didn't seem to notice his lack of skills. But she did smooth hair back from her face a bunch of times as she stopped at a traffic light, as if nerves might be getting to her too. "I do actually. Do you want to go with me?"

"You bet."

It was a homey sort of task that a married couple might do. So maybe he had channeled Owen a little bit better than he'd thought he had, though he doubted seriously that his brother had ever accompanied a woman to the grocery store.

It turned out to be fortuitous though, because it allowed him to select a bottle of nice red wine to go with the steaks Hannah added to their cart. Her eyes widened a bit at the price, but he shushed her and also managed to beat her to the credit card machine at checkout, so she wasn't the one footing the bill in the first place.

"Mac," she protested as soon as they cleared the sliding glass doors at the entrance to the store. "I invited you to dinner. I was supposed to pay."

"You're cooking," he countered firmly. "Everyone knows that means that it's my job to pay. Besides, you charge your catering clients for the food. This is no different."

"You're not a client."

No, he was not. The reminder somehow managed to cast

another silencer spell over the car and he couldn't think of a blessed thing to break it. Maybe they'd built this up too much with all the back-and-forth.

Plus, he had a heightened sense of the unknown variables between them. Like the fact that he wasn't Owen. That was probably 90 percent of the problem on his side. But that didn't account for what was going on on her side. And he wanted to know.

As soon as he'd carried the groceries into the house, he stopped Hannah from immediately spinning into a cooking dervish with a hand on her arm. "What is this all about, Hannah?"

She glanced up at him. "Dinner?"

"No, *dinner*. It suddenly seems to come with a lot of expectations or something that have gotten us wholly uncomfortable with each other. I like spending time with you. I like laughing with you. You have a wry humor that I appreciate. I'd rather go get hamburgers at Dairy Queen than drink expensive wine if it means we can get back to where we were before."

"You like my sense of humor?" She seemed dazed by this admission and more than a little pleased. "You never did before."

"I was an idiot before," he growled, suddenly not the slightest bit interested in playing the part of Owen, who was actually the one responsible for the vibe between them.

The real question was: What would Archer do?

"Hannah," he murmured. "Obviously I haven't told you nearly enough what I think about you. And I think about you often. Everything about you appeals to me. You're an accomplished business owner. An excellent mother to my daughter. As beautiful inside as you are outside."

"Really?" she whispered, and he couldn't take the distance any longer.

Pulling her into his space, he cupped her jaw with one hand, tracing the lines of her cheek as she met his gaze without flinching. Something had changed in her head that had led to tonight and he didn't want to stumble over it. "Really. But I think you already know how I feel about you. The real question is how you feel about me. About this. About what it feels like is happening between us."

Without warning, Hannah's mouth fused to his. The moment the kiss registered, he scooped her closer and breathed her in, reveling in the sensations of her taking control of this. Whatever *this* was. He couldn't wait to find out.

She got a little bolder and he let her explore to her heart's content, jerking back his immediate response of pushing her up against the counter to take his own tour of her mouth. The little noises she was making drove him to the brink and he groaned in kind as everything got intense.

Her hands spread across his back, heating everything in their path. There was so much more of him she hadn't touched, so much of her he wanted to kiss. Her lips worked across his jaw, finding a hollow near his throat and the sensations threatened to overwhelm him.

This was not supposed to happen. Not like this. He needed to…think. Or something.

"Hannah," he growled and set her back a solid six inches. "You have to slow down or there will be no eating in our future."

"Oh, you're not hungry?" she asked, seemingly disappointed, her green eyes searching his.

"Yes, I am," he bit out succinctly. "And in about three seconds, you're going to find out what I'm hungry for. So

I'm suggesting we take a breather. Have some wine. Before I lose my mind."

Her lips tipped up in a smile that had a bit of wonder in it. "You're...um, that attracted to me?"

His brain malfunctioned. There was no other word for it. It simply couldn't compute an answer to a question that ludicrous. He thought about all the graphic ways he could demonstrate that with a little show and tell but forced himself to breathe. At least until he could be reasonably sure he wasn't about to spontaneously combust.

She needed to know a few things before this went any further.

"You're the most intoxicating woman I've ever met," he ground out. "I can't think when you're touching me. When you're not touching me, all I can think about is the next time you're going to touch me. And then I think about me touching you and the cycle starts all over again. I'm not the kind of guy who reads a lot of poetry or spends time coming up with flowery phrases, so I can't exactly say what's going on inside me other than it's big and bright and strong and beautiful and it has your name all over it."

Okay, those were not the things he'd meant to tell her. They'd just spilled out. And judging by the look on her face, he'd scored some points in his clumsy attempt to communicate.

"That was pretty good," she murmured. "For someone who didn't come up with that ahead of time."

"Hannah," he growled again as she lifted her hands to his chest, spreading her fingers wide to nip in, as if holding on.

"Shh. No talking. Not right now. The future can take care of itself. Just kiss me like you think I'm intoxicating again. That's the first time you've ever said anything like that. I'm having trouble accepting that you're talking about *me*. Before—"

"There's no before," he cut in roughly and caught her up in his arms, dragging her into his embrace with fierceness that she couldn't mistake. "Only now. You make me feel lost and found all at once. Nothing exists except you."

And then he proved it to her with a searing kiss that drove all rational thought out of his head. She didn't know how he felt about her. That was a *travesty*. So he poured every ounce of his raging attraction to her into the mating of their mouths. It was an onslaught and she more than met him halfway.

This was no tentative exploration. It was a volcanic eruption, the kind that only happened once every thousand years, the kind that decimated everything in its path with a river of heat.

He lifted her effortlessly to slide her onto the counter so he could access even more of her. She went willingly, wrapping her legs around him in an embrace so intimate that his eyes crossed.

Yes. This. Now.

The future could take care of itself. That was a concept he could get on board with.

Nothing else mattered but making this woman his. Not Owen, not Archer's investigation or his need to protect Hannah and Lucy. The only problem he wanted to fix in this moment was the one where Hannah was too far away, and she hadn't heard nearly enough about the way she made him feel. The way she made him believe in good things. The things she did to him inside, where no person should be able to reach, but she'd burrowed beneath his skin to take up residence.

So he told her. For hours. As they christened the countertop, her bed. As they ate the dinner she finally cooked. As they drifted off to sleep, well sated with each other.

Chapter 22

What had started as a simple dinner with Mac to tentatively push things forward, move them in the right direction so to speak, had turned into something far more explosive. A stake in the ground. A demarcation to end all mile markers.

The man had slayed her.

Not that Hannah had a lot of experience to draw from, but she'd never felt like that. Ever. She'd be hard pressed to find evidence that she'd even *believed* a woman could feel like she had with Mac.

It certainly eclipsed any experiences she'd had with him before. In fact, if she didn't know better, she'd swear up and down that before last night, she'd never so much as kissed the man she'd spent the night with last night. Everything felt different. New. Better.

So much better.

The morning unfolded much like the night before had. Languid. No agenda. Just two people enjoying each other. At some point, she'd thought this dinner idea might be a precursor to seeing how Mac fit into her life. A test.

He'd passed. He fit into her bed so well that she'd woken up seriously contemplating ways to keep him there permanently. A lover suited her to the ground, but also made her giggle because she'd never thought of herself as the kind of woman who could have a man so intently devoted to her.

Mac lifted sleepy eyes in her direction, his dark hair spread over the pillow in a wholly appealing way that had her thinking the opposite might be true—he could snap his fingers and she'd become devoted to his every need.

"I like your laugh," he told her huskily.

"I like that you make me feel so bubbly inside," she informed him truthfully. "I guess I should be coy and act like I'm worldly and unimpressed. But if I'm being honest, those games irritate me, so I'll lay it out instead. I'm not the kind of woman who flits from bed to bed. This is it for me. And you're Lucy's father. I'm sure I don't have to tell you that one false move can set a child into a tailspin. No tailspins. Promise me."

He lifted her hand to his mouth, grazing her fingers. "I love Lucy. I would hope you already realized that. If I have it in my power to keep her from ever being hurt or disappointed by anything in her life, I will do it. Whatever it is. I promise you."

Good grief. And she'd thought he couldn't possibly say anything more perfect than the lovely words he'd whispered to her last night. "Okay."

"Okay." He smiled and pulled her close to lay a sweet kiss on her temple.

Could it really be that easy? Her heart stretched a little then, like a flower seeking the sun's warmth, only the sun looked an awful lot like Mac. She'd kept her tender organ packed away, or at least she'd thought she had. This man had somehow lifted away the foam peanuts where she'd buried her heart and revealed things she'd thought she'd never feel again.

Of course, they were still walking a line called amnesia. Though somewhere along the way, she'd stopped worrying about what would happen when he got his memories back. If anything, the gentle, appreciative man he was today would probably work doubly hard to make it up to her, when he realized how much he'd hurt her back then. She could handle a dozen roses every day for a month if he had a mind for it.

Not for the first time, she blessed the accident that had given her something so unexpected and precious. It was a terrible by-product that he'd been hurt, absolutely, and she hated that part. But she couldn't change it, so she was choosing to focus on the positives—and there were many.

Looping her arms around Mac's neck, she snuggled into his warmth and then looked at the clock. "Ugh, is that time for real?"

"Yeah." He nuzzled her ear. "You have a date?"

"I'm supposed to get Lucy before noon. And I have a brunch tomorrow that is going to take a serious amount of pre-prep. Ramona was supposed to do it, but she broke her arm skiing. So the boss gets to pick up the slack," she explained with a half laugh, half grimace.

"I'll help you. Let me pick up Lucy so you can start doing your dazzling chef-things," he suggested. "Then you can stay right where you are for another forty-five minutes."

The wicked thread running through his voice left no question as to what he planned to do during that time. But she didn't lean in immediately to get started on the implied premise. Instead, she pulled back to meet his gaze.

"What's going to happen after that?"

He didn't pretend to misunderstand. He let his embrace loosen but didn't drop it entirely, which had a lot of undertones she wasn't sure how to interpret. "This is the part where we talk about the future, isn't it?"

It sounded so awful the way he said it. That axe still hung over their happiness, waiting to sever everything good and new and exciting between them. While she may not be as concerned about him regaining his memories anymore, she couldn't ignore the other complications—namely, that they lived in different cities.

Some days, she wished her driver's license didn't say she was an adult. Then she could stick her head in the sand and just put her own needs first instead of worrying about every last nuance. "We kind of have to."

Mac brushed a thumb across her cheek. "Whenever you're ready. I want you to hear that. But maybe we can wait until later. It won't hurt to shut out the rest of the world for a few more minutes, right?"

Oh, she did like the sound of that. "You drive a hard bargain, but I'll take it."

Forty-eight minutes later, Hannah threw herself in the shower after shoving Mac out the door to get Lucy before Jenny started calling. When she stepped onto the bathmat after the world's shortest shower on record, her phone was already ringing.

It was Wade, though, not their mother. "Hey, Wade."

"Tell me you didn't start investigating Markus Acker after I told you not to," he demanded.

"I…" *Didn't.* But maybe did to a degree? Did talking to Sarah count? She had no idea which way to answer, especially since Wade sounded pretty mad already. "Why don't you tell me what you think the answer is?"

"I'm hearing rumbles that someone has been looking into Acker's finances."

"How would I look into his finances?" she returned hotly. "Besides, how do *you* hear rumbles about something like that? How does someone even find *out* that someone is looking into finances?"

This whole conversation made her head hurt.

Wade didn't immediately answer the question and in the

pause, she got a pretty good idea who one of the someones was. "It was Fletch. Wasn't it? He's got some fancy police equipment that detected it?"

"Don't be ridiculous. Owl Creek PD doesn't have that kind of money." Another pause. "He still has some contacts in Salt Lake City. They're quietly investigating Acker for some shenanigans he pulled when he joined the Church of Latter-day Saints some years back."

"So that's a legit thing? You can tell if someone is looking into a suspect's finances who isn't you?"

Wade's grunt confirmed it. Fascinating.

"You're not answering the question," he insisted. "Are you still trying to investigate him?"

Hannah stood in front of the mirror dripping, guilt gnawing at her insides. Her face had a well-loved glow that she didn't recognize, and her body bore a couple of marks that secretly made her quite proud when she recalled about how she'd gotten them. Of course, that made her think about Mac and anything else pretty much drained from her mind.

He'd been a distraction since day one. Even more so now. She'd almost completely abandoned her quest to find out more about Markus Acker, even after finding out it was possible he and Jessie had killed Hannah's father. That should have been motivation enough to make it her top priority once she'd found out her brothers suspected it.

Instead, she'd volunteered to help Mac get back on his feet and then jumped into bed with him.

She put her phone on speaker and dried off, then pulled on clothes as she answered.

"Yeah, I am," she told him. Intent counted. "I don't know how to look into his finances, but if I figure it out, I will be. Thanks for that tip, Waderkins."

"That wasn't meant to be a how-to, Hannah Banana,"

he said, defaulting to her nickname in retaliation for her using his. "Stay away from Acker."

"No argument here. I have zero plans to get anywhere near him."

Sarah, on the other hand, was a different story. She had every reason in the world to spend as much time with her half sister as she wanted to.

And should. It was a great reminder that she needed to get her mind off Mac and back on her real life. Whatever was going on with her ex-husband, she couldn't afford to fall for him again. That's how she'd messed up the first time—letting her heart lead instead of her brain.

Brain first this time. It made sense to cultivate a relationship with Mac for Lucy's sake. It made sense to let him do all kinds of delicious things to her after hours because it felt good. There was nothing wrong with reveling in an attentive man who deserved a gold medal for figuring out her feminine buttons with zero memories to guide him.

For once, she was grabbing something nice for herself. It was a lovely coincidence that what was good for Lucy worked out for Hannah too.

This was every bit using her head. She wasn't Heart-First Hannah any longer. And if in her heart she wanted Clan Mackenzie, no one had to know. Wanting something didn't have to be the thing that forced her decisions.

"Speaking of people you shouldn't be getting anywhere near," Wade threw in casually and she knew instantly where this was going, "how's Lover Boy?"

"Don't start, Wade. My relationship with Mac is my own business."

"Calling him a different name this go-round doesn't make him less of a heel."

"Also none of your business. And you have no clue what you're talking about."

It did make a difference. A huge one. He was starting over, and she believed him when he said he was not the same man. Why not commemorate that with a new name? It was a time-honored tradition. A form of rebirth. Muhammad Ali had done the same, along with a slew of other celebrities who were definitely more well-known by their new names than their old ones.

Besides, it helped her reframe their relationship and right now, she and Lucy needed that. Head talking. Not heart. Wade could shut his mouth.

"I just don't want him to hurt you and Lucy again," Wade said gruffly, and she gave him a break.

"I get it. Thank you. I know you're looking out for me, and I appreciate it. But please hear me. He's Lucy's father. When you have kids, we can talk about this again because then you'll understand that sometimes we have to make choices that hurt because it's best for them. Right now, I'm focused on her and what's best for her relationship with her father."

Mostly.

She wandered into the living room just as Mac strolled through the front door with Lucy in tow and when he smiled at her, her tongue went numb. Everything else woke up and danced the Macarena, especially the parts that were still pleasantly raw from his beard sliding across her skin, a sensation that was wholly unique to this version of the man.

"Wade, I have to go," she told him, her gaze fastened on Mac as they shared a glance full of things no one else could possibly understand.

She didn't even fully understand it.

When she set her phone down, Lucy rushed over for a

hug, babbling about all the things she'd done with Grandma Jenny.

"Do you have a mom, Daddy?" she asked out of the blue.

Mac visibly recoiled, and she rushed to fill the gap. "Daddy has some problems with his head since he hit it, and he doesn't remember his mom. So he needs you to love him extra hard to make up for that."

Lucy's gaze swept her father, as if seeking assurance that no other strange phenomenon existed that she'd been previously unaware of. They hadn't told her anything about his medical conditions and probably Hannah should have checked with Mac first before spitting out something like that, but he relaxed, so she figured it had been the right move.

"Do you remember me?" Lucy asked with her typical five-going-on-twenty-five shrewdness.

This was one he'd have to take himself. And he didn't hesitate to kneel down next to her.

"I remember that you like pancakes in the morning and that *Don't Let the Pigeon Drive the Bus!* is your favorite book," he said and straightened the cuff of her jeans where they'd gotten caught on the Velcro straps of her pink glittery *Peppa Pig* high-tops. "I remember that your friend at preschool is Ana Sophia, and that Jack Harper pulls your hair on the playground. I remember that I gave you permission to deck him if he does it again."

Hannah smacked a hand to her lips before the protest slipped out. Permission to hit another child was definitely something they'd be discussing behind closed doors. Assuming she could get a word out edgewise when she had a feeling he'd be claiming her mouth for other activities the moment they shut the door.

Lucy nodded as if all of this made perfect sense to her. "And you gave me dogs."

Mac cocked his head with a vague smile. "Princess Misty is definitely sprightly enough to count as two dogs, that's for sure."

"I meant Mr. Fluffers too. He came in a box, but he wasn't scared."

Something clanked with a distinct metallic edge and reverberated through the kitchen. Hannah and Mac jumped at the same time, both dashing toward the mudroom. Mac twisted her behind him in an impressive move that simultaneously made her swoony and also put a knot in her throat.

Did he think someone was in the house? Like the intruder who had moved stuff around?

Mac stopped her from entering the mudroom with a hand to her chest, presumably so he could check out the room first, then dropped his arm.

"It's the water dish," Mac announced, his relief evident. "Princess Misty turned it over by accident."

The dog in question hung her head, clearly ashamed.

Hannah stepped over the threshold and reached above the long wooden bench seat to the cabinet where she kept old towels. "It's okay. That's why we set up her food and water dishes in here where there's lots of tile meant for muddy snow boots."

While she mopped up the water, Mac stroked Princess Misty's fur, which seemed to help her realize she wasn't in trouble. Lucy called for her, and the dog perked up, dashing from the room to meet her mistress in the living room.

"Crisis averted," Mac said as he took the wet towel from her, then helped her to her feet.

When she rose, he caught her up in his free arm, careful to keep the other away from her so the towel in his hand didn't transfer water to her clothes. It was a nice detail that made her a little weak in the knees.

"I missed you," he murmured and laid a fiery kiss on her upturned lips.

"You were only gone for thirty minutes," she protested with a pleased laugh, but it died in her throat when she met his heated, intense gaze.

"I've been gone a lot longer than that," he told her with quiet fierceness. "And I have a lot of making up for lost time to do. Starting with kissing you in the mudroom because I cannot physically stand to be apart from you right this moment."

Oh my. That was definitely not her head squeezing so tight it felt like it might burst.

Chapter 23

The high wire Archer had started walking across when he'd woken up in the hospital with everyone calling him Owen had just reached impossible heights. And he was afraid to look down to see just how far away the ground was.

The splat was coming, though.

The Dinner Date, cemented in his mind in capital letters, had been over a week ago. He and Hannah had never picked up their conversation about the future. His fault. He'd only wanted to put off reality for a bit longer, and she'd pounced on the opportunity. Every time he started to bring it up, he thought about Big Mike and how vulnerable Hannah and Lucy would be without him here.

They needed his protection. He needed to keep being Owen for just a little while longer, until someone took the bait. He'd turned up so little to connect the Ever After Church with Big Mike and Hannah, but he knew the three were somehow linked. He could feel it.

Eventually the pieces would click into place, and he'd be able to see the whole picture. Until then, he had to sit tight.

But the voice inside laughed at all his justifications. He was still here with Hannah because he wanted to be.

She turned over and caught him watching her from his side of the bed. The one he'd claimed a week ago and hadn't given up yet. She hadn't asked him to go back to his room on the other side of the house either, and he wasn't about to bring it up.

"Is the door locked?" she murmured.

He answered her with a slow smile. "I never unlocked it earlier."

Hannah smacked him on the arm without any heat. "That's one of the unbendable rules. What if Lucy wanted one of us?"

Man, he'd never get used to the idea that a little girl might possibly seek him out in the middle of the night for comfort and cuddles. That she'd choose him, maybe even over her mother. It was almost enough for him to slide out from under the covers and flick the lock open. Almost.

Instead, he slid Hannah closer, wrapping his arms around her. "If she comes to the door, I'll put on my pants and open it. She's old enough to understand that she doesn't get free rein over all the rooms in the house. The double-edged sword of having a brilliant child, my darling."

Hannah stuck her tongue out, laughing. "That's half your fault. I like it when you call me things like that, by the way."

"What, darling?" he murmured, enjoying the feel of it leaving his mouth.

It seemed like something his brother would say, and he'd gotten in the habit of trying to please Hannah through that lens. After all, she'd been in love with Owen once. It didn't take a rocket scientist to assume she'd liked aspects of his personality, and frankly, Archer didn't figure there was a lot about a numbers guy like him that she'd appreciate anyway, so it was easier to adopt a bit of Owen's persona.

Especially since that's who she thought he was.

Misery coated the back of his throat as he took another step along that swaying high wire.

If someone had ever told him he'd fall for his brother's ex-wife, he'd have signed them up for psychiatric evaluation. If they'd told him he'd fall for her while posing as his brother, he'd have signed himself up.

"Yeah," she whispered. "It makes me feel shivery."

That made two of them. It was going to be hard to give her up when the time came, but that's where this was headed. Especially when she found out the truth.

Not only would she be furious—she wasn't even in this for the long haul. Look how carefully she'd qualified that he wasn't allowed to walk out on Lucy. It hadn't escaped his notice that she'd never elicited a similar promise from him about their own relationship. Obviously, she didn't have nearly the same attachment to him that he did to her.

It was fine. He didn't get nice things for himself. That was the unwritten rule about being the good Mackenzie. His job was to clean up Owen's messes, not collect musthaves for his own life. Besides, he lived in Las Vegas, not Idaho. He had a job, a team. A condo that Willis had been going by every few days to collect the mail.

The more he contemplated what the future actually looked like, the bleaker it seemed. Was it so horrible to sink down into this place he'd unwittingly landed? To spend a few precious moments living a life he'd had no clue would fit him, let alone become something he desperately wanted?

It was working. For now.

He'd deal with the consequences later. It was the most Owen thing he'd ever done in his life.

In the morning, he almost started whistling as he padded down the hall to wake up Lucy for preschool today, as had become his habit over the last few days. He'd fought Hannah for the privilege of driving their daughter to school, which served an excellent double purpose of ensuring mom got some alone time. He also intensely disliked Hannah and Lucy being in the car without him when he couldn't shield them from the dangers of the world that he knew lurked out there.

Sometimes he had a bad moment when he thought about Hannah being alone in the house by herself, but he couldn't be in two places at once. So far, whoever had their eyes on them hadn't made their presence known. It was highly likely the goons were under orders to observe and not approach. That's what he kept telling himself anyway.

At the doorway to Lucy's room, he had to pause for a moment as she came into view, her gorgeous light brown hair a stark contrast to the pale pink pillow case. Brown, not blond like Hannah, thus likely from Mackenzie blood. His blood. By a circuitous route, no doubt, but it still counted.

He'd make it count. There had to be a way to keep Lucy in his life, even after Hannah found out the truth. He didn't have a lot of hope she'd have any interest in keeping the intimate portion of their relationship intact, but surely he'd proven he meant to stick with Lucy.

Princess Misty sensed him and lifted her head from her preferred spot at the end of Lucy's bed. He liked the dog there. Just in case.

Sebastian had trained Princess Misty to bark if Lucy needed anything but otherwise, the dog never made a sound, a trick Archer appreciated. The more he got to know the individual members of Hannah's family, the more he liked them. Especially since Sebastian had kept quiet about the fact that he'd earmarked the Border collie for Lucy from the first, something Archer had learned when he'd had a side conversation with the Colton brothers while Hannah had been distracted.

He had Wade to thank for voicing that tip, which Hannah's brother had grudgingly shared at Jenny's get-together. All of Hannah's brothers were good people who cared about their sister and their niece. It made him feel a lot better that so many Coltons would be between Hannah and Lucy and danger if—when—the time came that Archer couldn't be around to make sure they were safe.

All in all, he could count his foray here in Owl Creek as a success if for no other reason than the family he'd come to think of as his was happy and safe. Clan Mackenzie. It would be the first time he'd fixed a mess Owen had made and come out better for it himself too.

His stomach hurt when he thought about what it was going to be like not to see Lucy every day. To watch her learn. Grow. To see her as a six-year-old, a seven-year-old. Hitting double digits, Princess Misty by her side. Cobbling together time with her as he and Hannah split parenting duties across state lines, if she'd let him continue to be Lucy's father even though she wasn't his birth daughter.

Today, he didn't have to worry about any of that, and they'd be late if he kept standing here watching Lucy breathe. He touched her shoulder, and when her green eyes blinked up at him, so much like her mother's, he couldn't stop the slick, hot emotion that poured down his throat, tightening it.

"Hey, Lu Lu, time to get up," he murmured hoarsely, shocked his voice had worked at all.

"Hold Mr. Fluffers," she commanded as she sprang out of bed, a bundle of energy despite having been deep asleep mere moments ago.

Wryly, he took the stuffed dog from her hand as she bounced over to the pink plastic table and chairs in the corner of her room where she set her backpack each night before bed.

"I'm wearing pajamas today," she announced as he tucked the dog into the crook of his arm, amused at the picture he probably made.

Not that he could even contemplate who he'd share a photo with. His mother? He hadn't mentioned to her yet that he'd found Hannah and Lucy during his investigation of Owen's murder. She'd want to meet them and that wouldn't be helpful in this scenario. Maybe after everything shook out, Hannah might be willing to introduce Lucy to her paternal grandmother.

But the explanation for why Hannah didn't know Owen's mother existed would come tangled up with the additional surprise existence of Owen's twin brother. A subject better left for another time, when it would be less dangerous— and complicated—to untangle.

"I think you have to wear normal clothes to school, Lu," he commented mildly, far too used to her announcements to worry too much about handling the potential showdown.

The sly look she shot him didn't faze him either. "Sometimes we get pajama day."

"Is that today?"

She pouted for about five seconds. "No."

Smart girl. "I'll buy you new pajamas for next pajama day. How about that as a deal for why you're going to get dressed in regular clothes without any arguments?"

Her sunny smile back in place, she dashed to do as he suggested, wisely realizing it wasn't optional. These were some of his favorite times with Lucy, when it was just the two of them and he wasn't as worried about doing or saying the wrong thing. Not that Hannah's presence felt judgmental, but she'd been doing this a lot longer than he had, and she made it seem so easy. She never questioned herself or made mistakes, whereas he constantly had to think about how a parent should respond to situations, instead of his first inclination, which was—why not wear pajamas to school?

With a minute to spare, he got Lucy bundled into the car. March weather would nip some of the cold back, but not by much. That was one thing Las Vegas had going for it. Better weather. At least until summer when it got hotter than Hades.

Archer parked at Lucy's school and unbuckled her from her car seat, then helped her hop down out of the back seat of Hannah's hatchback. Lucy slipped her hand in his as they waited at the edge of the crosswalk for the monitor to stop the traffic, his throat getting tight again at the casual way this little girl had incorporated him into her heart with no questions asked.

It was a testament to Hannah, no question. Owen would have probably never even considered driving Lucy to school, let alone actually doing it. His loss. In more ways than one. Owen would never know this family, know what it meant to belong to them. Never know what he'd walked away from.

Archer knew exactly what he was giving up and it was killing him.

Lucy dashed off at the door of her classroom and her teacher waved at him as he paused for one last look, never sure if today was the last time he'd see her. On a razor's edge emotionally, an unfamiliar place he didn't like to be, he didn't notice the car following him at first.

But when he turned toward the lake to head to Hannah's house, the grey sedan turned too, not even trying to stay hidden. It was quite clear the car meant to keep pace with him and also to ensure that Archer became aware of his tail.

Just like the watcher in the woods hadn't bothered to hide

the glint of his binoculars. The goons were either sloppy—not likely—or employing a subtle intimidation game.

Archer wasn't the average law-abiding citizen though. He had extensive training in recognizing patterns and putting pieces together that ordinary people might overlook. Yet he still didn't know who was behind all of this. It was bothering him at a cellular level, as if someone had figured out how to get beneath his skin and writhe around, making him wish he could peel it off.

The sun glinted off the windshield, preventing Archer from getting a good look at the driver. It took all of thirty seconds to memorize the license plate, make and model of the car, though, and would take Willis about that long to find out the registration information, once Archer texted it to his assistant.

But he couldn't do that and drive *and* keep an eye on his tail. Plus, it might be prudent to lure the sedan away from Hannah. Sure, odds were high these goons and their employer already knew he was living at Hannah's house, but there was a huge difference between being academically aware of a fact and leading someone who likely had a loaded weapon strapped to his waist right to a person Archer cared about.

He turned left instead of right at the road to Hannah's house. The sedan kept pace. Good. Archer glanced in the rearview mirror every few seconds, hoping to get a glimpse of the driver, but the sun was too bright this morning in a cloudless sky.

This was ridiculous. The car never sped up or slowed down, just kept following him. As a scare tactic, it didn't work. All it did was make Archer increasingly agitated. Another emotional response to something that he should be approaching with coolheaded logic. That's why he'd gone into forensic analysis instead of putting on a uniform and chasing down criminals in the street—he didn't have the juice for this kind of cat-and-mouse game.

Nor did he have a weapon, an oversight he needed to correct pronto.

Archer led his tail halfway around the lake, past the turnoff for Jenny's house, well past the marina. He thought about heading into the mountains toward Crosswinds, but the odds of being able to lose his shadow on the narrow roads turned his blood cold. So he kept on this same track, his brain turning over a hundred scenarios so he could plan his next steps, just in case the driver decided to finish off what someone else had started during Archer's drive out to Owl Creek all those weeks ago.

But instead of ramming him from behind as Archer had braced for, the gray sedan suddenly peeled off and vanished down a side street.

Regrouping? Trying to cut him off at some indeterminate point ahead?

Archer pulled over to the shoulder and did a quick U-turn, praying he'd shoot past the side road the sedan had taken before the driver got his car flipped around. If that had even been the goon's goal. At this point, nothing would surprise him.

No gray car appeared. Archer's heart rate didn't slow until he'd doubled back to Main Street, inserting himself into the middle of the normal Owl Creek traffic. That had been close. And not close enough to make any kind of progress on his to-do list.

All of this was coming to a head faster than he'd like. He had to tell Hannah the truth eventually, but would she be safer if she knew now? Or safer if she had no clue until he could unravel the truth?

He was still waffling on his mental flower-petal pulling—*I tell her, I don't tell her, I tell her*, et cetera, et cetera, for an hour—when he got back to Hannah's house. When he turned from stomping his boots off in the mudroom, she was waiting for him, her face ashen.

His blood froze as he realized the gray sedan might have been trying to lure *him* away from Hannah's house.

"Hannah? What's wrong?"

He reached for her automatically, yanking her into his arms as he held on to her, trying to get his galloping heart under control, at least until he figured out what had her so concerned since it was so very clear something had.

"You were gone so long," she croaked out, likewise clinging to him as if she couldn't fathom letting go. "I was worried."

Archer cursed. *That's* what he should have taken the time to do—text Hannah. "I'm so sorry, darling. I didn't mean to scare you."

"I thought something had happened to you and Lucy."

"No," he said gruffly, which wasn't a lie, but neither was the truth as innocuous as his simple denial made it sound. "Nothing happened. But I thought… Well, it's probably my imagination. But I thought someone was following me."

She made a noise in her throat. "The same people who searched the house?"

"I don't know," he admitted, which sliced at something inside—he was far more used to being proficient at his job.

Except he wasn't doing his job. He was pretending to be Owen because it seemed like a good cover to do some snooping around, only he'd done precious little of that and had instead done the one thing he shouldn't have—fallen in love with Hannah and Lucy.

"You left your phone," she said into his shoulder and

lifted her face to his. "That's what got me so worried. I couldn't even text you to see where you were."

"I didn't forget my—" *Phone.*

He swallowed the word because he hadn't forgotten *his* phone. He had, however, left *Owen's* phone in his room. And hadn't thought about it one time in weeks. Because it was useless to him once he'd combed through the contacts.

Curious that she'd picked up on the fact that he wasn't carrying it, though. Had she gone through his things? Why? Not that he was trying to hide anything—well, except everything—but it sat on his shoulders crossways.

He released her and stepped back, missing her warmth immediately.

"How did you...did you find my phone somewhere?" he asked cautiously, feeling as if he'd just walked out on ice that had started to crack.

"It was ringing," she said and held it out to him like it was nothing, just a phone, and not a ticking time bomb. "Over and over. There's like 35 missed calls."

There were only two reasons someone would call the phone of a dead man—they knew Archer had Owen's phone or they thought he was Owen. Who wasn't supposed to be alive.

A big gaping hole appeared in the ice, and he plunged into the frigid depths.

Chapter 24

Why did it seem like Hannah had stepped out on a ledge and looked down to see she'd somehow ended up outside a window on the seventieth floor of a high-rise in a bustling downtown area?

Not that she'd ever been on the seventieth floor of anything, but the sense of one wrong step signaling a very big fall wouldn't abate, and the look on Mac's face wasn't helping.

"Mac?" she whispered. "Should I be asking you what's wrong? Who called all those times? Do you recognize the number?"

Mac stared at the phone still clutched in her fingers as if he'd never seen it before, nor did he make a single move as if he meant to take it from her.

"I don't recognize the number," he murmured in a voice that sounded far away. "Because it's not my phone."

She cocked her head, taking in his beautiful face and the shadows that had sprung up in his eyes. "What? Of course it is. I picked it up from your bedside table myself. I heard it ringing from the kitchen and I was going to ignore it. But they kept calling, and well, I'm sorry, but it was annoying."

Was that the problem? He was upset she'd gone into his room to retrieve the phone? Obviously he'd left the ringer on, which she personally found a little unusual, but some people did that because they were expecting a call and didn't want to miss it. If that wasn't the case, why leave the ringer on? And forget to take the phone with you?

"You don't understand, Hannah." Mac sucked in a deep breath, still not looking at her, his gaze locked on the phone screen. "It's not my phone. It's Owen's. I didn't want to tell you this way, but honestly, there was never going to be a good time to come clean."

"Come clean?" she whispered as something clutched at her lungs until she couldn't breathe—and she didn't even know what these words were that Mac was saying to her. Only that oxygen didn't exist in this place. "What are you talking about? How can it be Owen's phone but not be your phone?"

"Because I'm not Owen, Hannah," he said. "He's my brother. My twin brother."

A taut thread wrapped around her heart and yanked, slicing into the tender parts as she registered the truth of his statement in one irrevocable flash. Her soul knew it instantly. Of *course* he wasn't Owen. That explained everything.

Even so, in the next moment, inexplicably, denial rose to her lips. "No. That's not possible."

"It's not probable. But it's absolutely possible." His lips didn't lift at what might have been a joke in another life where this wasn't happening.

The man in front of her wasn't Owen. How could the man in front of her not be Owen?

Twin, he'd said. Her ex-husband had a brother he'd never mentioned. A keening sound hummed in her throat, and she choked it back because Coltons didn't fall apart when someone ripped the very fabric of their existence in two.

"I don't understand." *Good*. Firm. Her voice didn't really

even crack. Too much, anyway. "Who are you if you aren't Owen?"

Like that was the most important question she could be asking here.

Oh, dear Lord. She'd slept with this man, and she didn't know his name. Actually, names constituted critical information all at once. She wasn't that woman, who fell into bed with a man she didn't know…except she had done exactly that.

Because he'd lied to her.

"I'm Mac, Hannah," he said softly, as if he'd sensed that she'd gone to a very dark place. "That part was always true."

"No," she said with a half laugh. A very unamused one at that. "No, you are not Mac. Mac is the name of the man who came into my life and clicked all the pieces into place. Mac is the guy I trust and who trusts me too. Mac is Lucy's father."

Her eyelid slammed close as she internalized that. Let it roll around inside and cut her and make her bleed a bit more. She'd let a stranger into her house and into her bed and into her *daughter's life*.

"Yes," he countered with quiet fierceness. "That is who I am. I'm Mac, short for Mackenzie. It's what they call me at the precinct."

"The…the *precinct*? Is that what you just said? You're a *cop*?" Why that struck her so hard the wrong way in the midst of everything else, she couldn't say. But this whole conversation bordered on ridiculous anyway, so she rolled her fingers, steeling herself. "Come on. Start talking. I need to hear everything else right now, whoever you are. Where is Owen, by the way? Does he know you're here? Was it his idea?"

Owen's twin. That much was obvious. One she hadn't even known existed. Didn't twins love to tell people they had a clone walking around? No, not the one she'd married and definitely not the one standing in her kitchen.

The Mackenzie brothers liked to switch places and dupe a stupid, stupid woman into falling for them. Not once, but twice.

What was left of her heart rolled over and then fell into ash somewhere near her ballet flats.

"Hannah, Owen is dead," Mac told her, his mouth hardening into a line. "He was murdered. I came to Owl Creek to investigate."

It hit her then. The million-dollar question. "You never forgot a blessed thing. You don't actually have amnesia, do you?"

She'd tacked a question mark on the end, but she knew already, even before he shook his head.

Oh, for the love of Pete. No wonder he'd kissed her like it was the first time. No wonder she had the sense she'd never touched this man, as if she'd been gifted something rare and precious, like a real second chance that actually felt very much like a first chance with a man who had been reborn. That's how stupid she was.

Only Hannah Colton could fall for a trick like this. She'd left her brain in her other coat and never bothered to retrieve it, obviously.

"Why?" she whispered. "Why would you do this to me? To Lucy? Was this all a game?"

He didn't reach for her and the distance between them spoke volumes. It was a testament to how hard and fast she'd fallen for him that the absence of his touch felt like a layer of skin had been ripped off.

"It was never a game." He shook his head. "It was an accident. Or rather *the* accident. I woke up in the hospital and found out the sheriff had unwittingly gifted me the perfect cover to gather hard evidence against whoever killed my brother. It was never my plan. I just went with it."

"Is that supposed to make it better? You're a liar *and* an opportunist. I see." She folded her hands over her stomach, right where it hurt the worst. "You should have told me the truth a long time ago."

At least then she would have had a chance to stop the train before it left the station. Now it was too late. She knew what it felt like to be loved by this man. And it was *painful* to find out the nirvana she'd found with Mac was all a flimsy house of cards.

"I still don't know your name," she whispered, terrified the keening sound was going to start up again.

"Archer," he murmured. "Archer Declan Mackenzie. I… you can still call me Mac."

"No, I'm fairly certain I cannot," she said with more wryness than she would have expected to be possible. The name Mac was so wrapped up in other indescribable things that she just didn't think she could force her tongue to make the word.

Archer. That didn't feel right either. It was even more foreign and now she regretted asking.

Deep breath. There was so much more conversation that needed to happen, but her energy level had started to flag. How much more of this was she going to have to take?

"Just for fun—keeping in mind that none of this is actually fun and also that I don't know how much I'll believe— but why are you telling me all of this now? You didn't have to. You could have jetted back to wherever you came from and never breathed a word about any of this."

He nodded as if he approved of the segue. "I could have. I could have made a decision to tell you sooner, but I thought I was protecting you. The less you knew, the better."

The snort came out automatically as she processed that. "Protecting me from what? Knowing the truth?"

"Hannah."

His voice came out a touch flat, but it was enough for her to realize he was struggling with his emotions. Because she'd started picking up on his subtle cues over the last few weeks. It was something she'd rather have not become an expert in, but wishing she hadn't jumped in with Mac—Archer, rather…and no, that would never stop being weird—didn't make it go away.

Owen had never been like that. He wore his emotions right out in front where everyone could see them and be forced to deal with them. Overly dramatic to the core. Everything had always been about Owen.

He and his brother were nothing alike. Stupid. The theme of the day. Of course this man wasn't Owen, and the fact that he'd had to *tell her* was sobering.

She'd seen what she'd wanted to see. A man who had changed. One who had fit the narrative in her head, who had finally figured out what he'd missed by leaving, who had made a conscious choice to be involved in her life and Lucy's.

Except he wasn't Owen. Owen hadn't made those choices.

And one tiny little corner of her heart had room to be utterly grateful that she at least hadn't been monumentally stupid enough to fall for Owen again.

No, she'd made a whole new set of mistakes with the wrong Mackenzie twin.

"I know it doesn't make a bit of difference, but I'm sorry it happened this way, Hannah," he said. "But the things going on outside of this house are real and dangerous. Someone killed Owen, and it wasn't an accident. Neither was the car crash that put me in the hospital."

It hit her then. Owen was dead. The steel in his brother's voice convinced her, even as she had a few brain cells left to question whether he was actually telling the truth. Head-First Hannah needed to be in the driver's seat for a good long while.

"If I google it, will I find evidence to support your claim that Owen is dead? I mean, as far as I knew, he had no family. Maybe you're one of those people who finds their doppelgänger online and poses as him to scam people out of money."

Oh my, was she in danger *inside* this house? Her heart rate shot through the roof. She had no assurance that Archer—Mac—wasn't the one who had searched through her things.

Dang it. He was still Mac in her heart and she couldn't seem to make herself transition to calling him Archer.

"There's an obituary online if you search for the *Las Vegas Sun*. Also, you can look up death records for Clark County and order a copy for yourself if you would like. I would recommend it as Lucy will be entitled to his effects, but I'll take care of transferring everything the department is aware of over to her as soon as I'm able to get back home."

Home. In Las Vegas. Where he'd return to, but not as Lucy's father—as her uncle. It was baffling to her that he'd played his part as a devoted father so well and easily when Lucy wasn't even his biological child.

But then, Owen was her biological father and he'd never cared one whit about reading her stories. A migraine threatened, the likes of which she hadn't had in some time. Not since Mac had stormed into her life.

Head aching, she ignored it in favor of verifying everything Mac had said. Her internet searches came up exactly as he said they would, and while a really savvy criminal could probably do some kind of fake website thing, it would have to be a pretty elaborate setup for no reason she could think of.

But that was the problem, right? She wasn't a criminal and therefore had no expertise in all the reasons why someone would have posed as their own twin brother in order to gain access to a family. To charm his way into her heart without even trying. To fight with her over who got to put Lucy to bed.

"I still don't understand why you did this," she whispered. "What possible reason could have been good enough in your mind to scam us into believing you were Owen?"

Mac lifted his hands. "The people Owen was involved with are dangerous, Hannah. They ran me off the road on my way here. I do think they meant to leave me for dead, but I'm a little bit better of a driver than they'd counted on. I didn't know about Lucy, either, for the record. We'll circle back to that huge investigative miss on my part later. I couldn't undo the fact that everyone was calling me Owen when I woke up. It seemed like a gift that I shouldn't pass up, especially when I realized there were links between the criminal organization I know in my gut ordered the hit on Owen and the Ever After Church."

Oh, so this *could* get worse. Hannah's vision tunneled and went black. For her next trick, she'd hit the floor. But Mac's strong hands caught her by the forearms, holding her up. That was not okay. But neither did she think she could wrench away without her knees buckling, and if she fainted, he'd probably just catch her.

What was wrong with her that her heart soared at the thought?

"Hannah?" Mac murmured. "Are you okay?"

She blinked, and it turned out she was in his arms after all. Something was definitely wrong with her because it still felt like she fit there. "Not even a little bit."

Mac didn't release her either, choosing to tighten his grip. "I'm sorry. It's my fault. I should have trusted you with the truth a long time ago, but I wasn't sure… I am now, no question. But you have to understand that I didn't know why Owen never told you about his family. He was fully aware I'm a forensic analyst for the Vegas PD. I couldn't be sure you weren't working with him. At first. I know now."

Hannah sucked in a breath and then another until her vision cleared enough to steady her knees. There was an odd ring of truth in the idea that Mac had suspected her of something nefarious, solely because of her association with Owen.

With one last cleansing breath, she regained her feet and stepped out of the odd paradox that had engulfed her inside of Mac's embrace—a weird mix of being so angry with him but still having the immediate reaction of relief, of *thank goodness he's here.*

"Owen was involved with big-time criminals, wasn't he?" she asked.

But it wasn't really a question when it was obvious that's where all his money had come from—now that she thought about it. Current-Day Hannah had a bit more wisdom and a lot more practice at reading between the lines. Lucy was Owen's daughter after all, with his wicked sharp intellect and a keen sense of how to use it to get what she wanted.

Mac nodded, his expression serious but still devoid of anything approaching the tenderness she'd become so accustomed to seeing there, especially when he looked at Lucy. Could he have faked all of that? Sure. But she didn't think he'd been acting.

Not that she'd call herself a great judge of character or anything. *Ugh*. This whole situation reeked of a Hannah Special, one her brothers would have a heyday with.

"He was, yes. Money launderers," Mac confirmed. "The same ones I'm pretty sure the Ever After Church is using. It wouldn't surprise me to learn Owen was the go-between."

And there it was. All roads had led to this. And here she'd been berating herself for letting Mac distract her from her own investigation into the church. It was almost laughable. They should have been working together the whole time.

"That's who you think has been searching the house," she said with a grim nod. "The money launderers. Because if you wondered whether Owen had involved me in his schemes, someone else would too."

Mac's lips lifted into a brief smile. "I definitely should have been talking to you about this sooner."

A noise near the door distracted them both. A man stood there. A stranger she'd never seen before. And he held a gun.

"This is all so sweet," he snarled. "But I don't think I can stand to listen to another word of this gibberish. I need the key to Owen Mackenzie's safety deposit box now, and you're going to get it for me."

That's when he leveled the gun at Hannah's head and cocked it.

Chapter 25

Everything slowed in that moment. Hannah's throat froze as Mac stepped in front of her, his hands raised. Talking. Mac was talking to the man.

But more importantly, he was standing *in front of her*. Shielding her from the potential bullet that the man might fire at any second. What was he doing? He wasn't bulletproof.

Her heart squeezed as he backed up a few tiny steps. Closer to her. To provide even more of a cover. This was Mac being heroic. And stupid.

"Let's just calm down," Mac said, his voice even, but it was also a tone she'd never heard before. "You don't want to do this."

"Oh, you're right, Mac," the man with the gun said in a singsong voice. "I forgot. I *don't* want to do this. Why didn't I think of that before I came in here? Shut up. I'm talking to the girl."

Girl? He meant *her*? She almost couldn't swallow the hysterical giggle that threatened to bubble to the surface, but her tight throat wouldn't have let it go anyway.

"She's not talking to you," Mac shot back before Hannah could figure out what she was supposed to say in response when none of this made any sense. "Whatever you want to discuss, I'm the guy."

"Sure, whatever. Fine. You get the key then, and we'll call it a day."

The stranger motioned with his gun toward the back of the house. Hannah and Lucy's wing. Because he knew that's the direction they should go to get this mysterious key he kept referencing. Or was it merely a throwaway gesture?

"What key?" Mac asked, reading her mind. That was her question too.

"Don't play innocent," the man said with a smirk. "You've been here all this time getting cozy with the lady of the house. You know where it is."

"I don't," he countered immediately.

Hannah one hundred percent believed he didn't know where this key was, since it wasn't something she had any knowledge of either. But on the heels of everything else, it wasn't a stretch to assume he had been playing her to get close so he could find it.

At least, that was the narrative her head kept repeating. Her heart stubbornly refused to get in on that action. After all, he'd stepped in front of her to face down a man with a gun. Willingly.

"What is this key you keep mentioning?" Hannah croaked out the question as she peeked around Mac's shoulder, the first time she'd spoken since she'd first noticed the gun in the stranger's hand. "We can't help you if we don't know what you're talking about."

She tried to gauge exactly who this guy was that they were dealing with. Midforties, probably. Average height and build. He had a nondescript look about him, as if he'd tried extra hard to blend into the background, but his gaze was sharp. Probably he didn't miss much.

The guy rolled his eyes. "Nice try. We both know you're in on it. Why do you think Mac showed up here in the first place? It's not because of the side benefits, though I'm sure he's enjoying those too."

"That's enough, Barnes." Mac's voice whipped out, low and lethal.

Wait—he knew the guy's name? Hannah stared at the back of Mac's head as it registered that the stranger had referenced him by name as well, but she'd assumed he'd heard it during their conversation. Now she wasn't so sure.

"You know each other?" she whispered, but didn't need his nod to put it together in that moment.

He'd told her the other people at his precinct called him Mac. The guy on the other side of the trigger must work with him. Was Barnes a cop too? Oh, man. That was bad for many reasons, but first and foremost because it meant he was probably a pretty good shot.

Mac's heroism suddenly felt a lot more like a suicidal move. He'd known all of this and still stepped in front of her.

"You want to know why I came to Owl Creek?" Mac asked in the sudden silence. "You're right. It was because of Hannah. I thought she might know something about Big Mike and his organization. Silly of me when I could have just strolled into the bullpen and chatted you up about it."

"Yeah, silly. This thing where you're trying to keep me talking in hopes of distracting me is not going to work." Barnes motioned with his gun again. "I've been waiting patiently for you to do your job and we see how that's turned out. Now we're going to do things differently. Starting with me shooting your girlfriend if that key is not in my hand in fifteen seconds."

Barnes started counting and Hannah's body went into fight or flight mode. Both at the same time, unfortunately, so her muscles had no idea what to do. And she was still behind Mac.

The kitchen island beckoned, where she had more than one cooking implement that could be used as a weapon. It made her heart hurt to think about using her beautiful Mauviel copper pasta pot as a blunt instrument.

She would do it regardless. This was life or death.

The pot was behind her though. At least eighteen or twenty steps, which would mean she'd have to move away from her cover and dash out of the mudroom before Barnes could level his gun and pull the trigger.

She had to try. Using Mac as a human shield sat wrong with her anyway.

Mac raised his hands higher and took a step toward Barnes. "I can't produce a key I know nothing about. Stop counting and let's discuss this. Brainstorm. We can figure this out together since you clearly have information that I don't. What makes you think there's a safety deposit box, much less a key that Hannah would have?"

Barnes stopped counting, which did wonders for the pulse point hammering in Hannah's throat.

She edged toward the island. One tiny shuffle. Then another.

"I'm starting to think you're even less good at your job than I was expecting," Barnes snarled. "That, or you're a very good actor, which is more likely since you fooled Blondy here into thinking you were Owen. Nice touch, by the way. If it had worked. So let's pretend you're telling the truth and you have no clue that Mackenzie sent his ex-wife a package three days before he met an unfortunate end. Does it jog your memory for me to mention that fact? Maybe make you think twice about trusting her?"

The blood in Hannah's head rushed out, leaving her feeling woozy.

"That's not right," she managed to croak out. "Owen

didn't send me anything. I haven't heard from him in years. I don't have any idea what you're talking about."

She'd have remembered something so explosive as that.

Especially since Barnes had just made Mac's point about why he wouldn't have immediately trusted her with the truth. Had he thought Owen sent her something too? Everything had flipped over on its head instantly and she needed to sit down. Or duck her face under the faucet and let a stream of water cool her burning cheeks.

"Or, you're lying because you were in on it and want the money for yourself," Barnes countered conversationally as if they were having a lovely chat about the weather. "This is why we're doing things my way now. Waiting around for Mac to do his job got old. Neither one of you Mackenzie brothers ended up being all that smart in the end."

"Is that why you killed Owen?" Mac asked in the same conversational tone. "Because he wasn't smart enough to see the double-cross coming?"

This man was Owen's murderer?

Hannah peeked out from behind Mac's shoulder, desperate all at once to see how Mac's accusation struck Barnes. Was it true? Would Barnes confess to them right here, right now?

Barnes just laughed, which told her more than he might have realized. Namely, that he was unhinged.

"Look at you trying to change my mind about how truly dumb you are," Barnes taunted. "He died because he tried to make off with Big Mike's money. No other reason."

"You mean he succeeded," Mac corrected evenly. "Or else you wouldn't be here. You think the money is in this safety deposit box?"

Obviously. Hannah didn't need to see Barnes to know that Mac had just pieced it all together. And done the impossible—put her firmly on his side. He'd been telling the truth earlier. Owen was dead. Killed by this dirty cop who must be working with the money launderers Mac mentioned.

Mac couldn't have created a better exhibit A for why he'd thought she might be in danger. She hadn't fully bought into his story before, but there was no way she could deny now that he'd acted according to the information he had in the moment.

The keening sound rose up in her throat again, but she couldn't figure out fast enough what part of this situation had cut her so deeply. The fact that Mac had so easily stepped between her and a gun—or that her daughter's father was indeed well and truly dead? Owen would never have a chance to change his mind and get to know the special little girl he'd helped create.

Maybe she should be most concerned about the gun still trained on them both. Right this second anyway.

One thing she did know for certain. She and Mac needed to have another very long conversation, this time with nothing between them but raw honesty. *After* they'd removed the threat of death and additional criminals darkening her doorstep, of course.

"You killed my daughter's father," Hannah screeched and took advantage of the stunned silence to grab an umbrella from the rack to her right, launching it at Barnes's face.

Mac sprang toward the threat, instantly taking advantage of Barnes's flinch. A shot rang out, shoving Hannah's heart into her throat.

Both men fought over the weapon. In an impressive show of strength, Mac wrenched the gun from the other guy's hand, pointing it at him. Just like that, Barnes sank to the ground, holding up his hands in a similar pose to Mac's a moment ago.

Hannah forced herself to breathe.

"This is not over," Barnes announced succinctly. "Big Mike's organization is vast and clever. Someone else will be along soon to pick up where I left off."

"Yeah, but it will give me a great deal of satisfaction to know that you'll be rotting in jail when that happens," Mac told him, and without taking his eyes off Barnes, he called over his shoulder. "Hannah, can you do me a favor and retrieve the bag from my room? It's the one by the door."

Dutifully, she dashed to his wing and found the bag in question, wondering if she should call 911 on the way back. But given the fact that there were already two cops in her house, she wasn't sure the addition of more would help. Better probably to let Mac handle it. And wasn't that a kicker to realize all of her anger from earlier had drained.

When she handed him his bag, he pulled two long black strips of something—plastic?—from its depths and then passed the gun to her. Wait, what was she supposed to do with this?

She nearly bobbled the weapon, but Mac's encouraging nod steadied her hand.

"Just keep it pointed at our friend here and everything will be fine," Mac advised her. "Pull the trigger if he moves the wrong way."

Efficiently, Mac yanked the guy's hands behind him and pulled the plastic tight around his wrists. Oh, it was a zip tie. That was ingenious. Mac levered Barnes to his feet and took possession of the gun again, thankfully, shoving it into his prisoner's ribs. Then, he marched him out of the house, calling over his shoulder that he'd be right back.

In a flash, Mac returned, gun still in his hand, but as soon as he cleared the mudroom door, he clicked a few things and then stuck it in the waistband of his pants at the small of his back, his expression grave as he crossed the mudroom floor in two long strides.

"Hannah, are you okay?" he asked, concern a physical force that nearly overwhelmed her.

"There's a bullet hole in my wall," she said and heaved a shuddery breath. "But I'm physically fine if that's what you mean. What did you do with that guy?"

"He's cooling his heels in the storage shed." Mac's smile was fleeting but it felt like a flower blooming in her chest. "Forgive me for not asking first and for borrowing your key. I called Fletcher to come sort this out since it's a local matter of armed breaking and entering at the moment, but I'm sure we can add some other charges once my guys do their investigation into Barnes's ties to Big Mike's organization."

"Do I want to know who Big Mike is?"

"If you do, I'm happy to tell you anything you ask. No more secrets between us."

Mac held up his hands in much the same way he had earlier, when protecting her from Barnes. In fact, he'd been amazing under pressure. Calm. Authoritative. He'd literally saved her from a ruthless gunman in her own home.

This was a man she wanted to get to know better. What a strange paradox to already have such intimate ties to someone who was a virtual stranger. But then again, did he really feel like one? He was looking down at her through the same eyes as before. She'd pushed her fingers through that same hair falling down on his forehead.

Now that she knew he wasn't Owen, she could see subtle differences between him and his brother that she'd attributed to aging and maybe her own faulty memory. But that didn't change the fact that he *wasn't* Owen—and that actually awarded way more points in his favor than she'd have said earlier.

She hadn't been so colossally stupid as to fall for Owen twice. But who had she fallen for? *That* was the secret she wanted to unravel. Except that sounded a lot like Heart-First Hannah talking.

All of this was aggravating her migraine. "Maybe we should focus on this key that guy kept talking about."

Mac nodded. "It would be best to have that squared away. That must be what whoever searched the house was looking for. Are you sure you didn't get any packages? Maybe Owen didn't include a return address so you didn't know it came from him."

Shaking her head, she started to deny it again when something tickled at the back of her brain, coming into focus sharply. "When did Owen die? What was the date?"

"In August. The seventeenth. Why? What do you remember?"

She bit back an incredulous laugh. "He didn't send the package to me. He sent it to Lucy."

That's what this was all about? The mysterious package that had shown up here addressed to Lucy right before school had started for the year? Hannah had assumed Wade sent it via a third-party shipping company that had forgotten the card, but he denied it when she asked. At the time, she'd blown it off as her brother being cagey because she'd literally just spoken to him the day before about how much he spoiled Lucy.

"What was in it?" Mac asked.

"You're not going to believe this." She motioned him into Lucy's room and cast about until she spied the familiar brown fur, snagging it and holding it up for Mac to see. "Mr. Fluffers. That's what was in the package."

Dawning disbelief drifting over his face, Mac sank onto the bed and nodded to the stuffed dog. "Feel around inside him and see if you can tell if there's anything there. We can do a surgical extraction to preserve him as much as possible if you find something."

Good grief, could the man be any more earnest about saving Lucy's favorite stuffed animal from being destroyed? Her heart wasn't so lucky—he'd reached inside and squeezed it without moving a muscle.

Hannah perched next to him, carefully running the stuffing between her thumb and forefinger, her pulse thudding in her throat. Nothing, nothing, nothing...*something*. The barest prick against the pad of her finger.

"I think...this is it. It's here," she told Mac breathlessly as she worked the hard thing a little closer to where the dog's head attached to his body. "I have a seam ripper that will do the trick."

In seconds, she'd retrieved it from her sewing kit and sliced a few stitches until the silver tip appeared in the opening.

"Hannah, you found it," Mac murmured. "You know what this means, right?"

"No more secrets." She held up the key and then handed it to him. "And this means I trust you with it. I'm angry you lied to me, but it doesn't erase everything that happened between us."

"Hannah." Mac shut his eyes and when he opened them, she no longer thought he might sweep her into his arms. Instead, the iciest chill seeped into her bones as he stared at her. "I didn't tell you the truth because I thought there was a happily-ever-after in store for us. I told you because there's not."

Chapter 26

Paperwork might very well be the death of Archer. And if it wasn't that, the huge hole inside where Hannah and Lucy used to be would probably do the trick eventually.

He hoped it would be sooner rather than later. Because being without them sucked.

The look on Hannah's face when he'd told her he was going back to Las Vegas had nearly ended him then. But he needed her to be safe and he was not the man to ensure that, not anymore.

The best way to draw every goon away from Owl Creek was to lie to Hannah and tell her that he didn't care anything about her. That they had no future—well, that part wasn't a lie. He didn't get nice things and he'd long ago accepted that.

Especially after Hannah told him he couldn't be Mac to her any longer. That she'd trusted him and he'd broken that irrevocably. He could still hear those words echoing in his head, neatly severing everything he'd held dear.

Of course that was what had happened. What would always be the result of his actions. Loss. He'd started out his relationship with Hannah and Lucy with a lie, so it seemed fitting to end it with one, especially since he'd had to shut down the conversation she'd started. The one that felt like she'd been about to insist they talk it out.

He didn't deserve to talk about anything.

Besides, he couldn't do forensics on the key from Hannah's house without any of the equipment in his lab. What would he do, bake its origins out of it?

Funny, Owl Creek still had snow on the ground, but in Vegas, it was early spring already with the days getting longer. Yet the place he'd called home for years felt like Antarctica. So cold he could hardly stand it. And his condo had zero warmth even with the heat set on seventy-eight degrees.

That's why he'd spent most of his time in the lab at his office, Willis sulking around as if afraid Archer might bite him given the opportunity. Yeah, okay. His mood hadn't been the best, but this was a forensic investigation, not a pool party. They needed to trace down what bank this key had come from. Owen clearly had expected to drop by Owl Creek and retrieve it himself, so he hadn't bothered to communicate this information to anyone.

Maureen, the department coordinator, knocked on the door of Archer's lab and jerked her head toward the front. "Visitor for you."

Hannah. Archer's heart did a slow dive before he could catch it. And then he had to get hold of himself. Hannah wouldn't have come to Las Vegas to see Elvis Presley back from the dead, let alone to see Archer.

The person waiting for him wasn't a woman anyway—it was a man in his midfifties who had *cop* written all over him, but the stilted kind who worked a desk and had for years.

"Bob Mitchell. Internal Affairs," he said and stuck out his hand for Archer to shake. "Wanted to catch you up on the charges against Jonathan Barnes since you're likely going to be tapped to testify."

Archer nodded. "Appreciate it."

"At the moment, we're looking at attempted kidnapping, false imprisonment, assault with a deadly weapon and official misconduct. Would be nice to tie it up with a bow and add federal money-laundering charges or collusion."

"You haven't found a link yet between Barnes and Big Mike Rossi," Archer guessed, tempering his frown. That wasn't surprising. Barnes would have been smart enough to cover his tracks internally. "Will my testimony allow a judge to at least issue a warrant to look closer at Big Mike?"

"Unlikely." Bob tapped the tablet under his arm. "What you relayed in the affidavit is not a confession. Barnes never admitted to pulling the trigger on your brother, nor that he had any significant dealings with Big Mike. We need something else."

The money.

That was the link to end all links. He knew in his gut that Owl Creek lay at the heart of this. Owen had been headed for his former digs, no question, especially since he'd sent the key ahead. But only to keep on the down-low? Or was there more to it—like the presence of the Ever After Church and Markus Acker?

Somehow the money would tie all of this together. Finding it had just gotten a lot more critical.

Mitchell chatted at him for a few more minutes, but Archer didn't mistake this visit for what it was. Apparently, IA had bubkes on Barnes other than what amounted to a few years in prison for whatever they could get on him internally—misuse of police equipment and data, etc.—plus the assault charges from when he'd held Archer and Hannah at gunpoint. Mitchell was unofficially asking him to get more, which he technically couldn't do because Archer had already been told not to investigate.

For the first time, he started to wonder if Barnes wasn't the only one in the Las Vegas MPD with ties to Big Mike. And if Archer might be in a little bit more of a precarious position than he'd assumed by coming back home.

Ironic that the biggest threat had come from an inside job. Barnes had been feeding Big Mike information the entire time. In fact, it wouldn't surprise him to learn that everyone had known he wasn't Owen the entire time.

This was far from over.

He closeted himself in the lab, kicking Willis out just in case someone came by looking for trouble, and locked the door behind his assistant. No point in taking chances this close to the end.

A few hours later, he had nothing. Only the serial number on the key, which didn't match any of the known records he had access to via the LVMPD's web of information. Granted, he'd limited the searches to the surrounding areas. Surely Owen hadn't carried five million dollars in cash to a bank across the country.

But then again, it was Owen. Who knew what his brother had been thinking?

He stared at the key, running a finger over the serial number, thinking it looked vaguely familiar, like he'd seen the number before. Likely just a function of having keyed it into searches so frequently over the last few hours.

It kept niggling at him though. And then he remembered. He'd seen it in Owen's phone once, fleetingly. Archer grabbed the phone, rolling his eyes at all the game apps and sheer disorganization of everything. Where had he seen this number? In a note app? No, nothing there, though how anyone would be able to find an iota of useful information in this mess was beyond him.

Contacts. It had been in the contacts section, a weird

anomaly where the phone number had seemed too long but Archer had blown it off as possibly a foreign configuration that he wasn't readily familiar with. But he saw it for what it was now—the serial number of the key and a name. B.D. Starke. A quick Google Search had him nearly dancing out of his seat.

B.D. Starke wasn't a person. It was a bank. In Conners, right down the street from the hospital, no less. Because of course he'd been a stone's throw from the money the whole time, while he'd been busy faking amnesia and falling for his brother's ex-wife.

Archer rolled into Owl Creek near lunchtime, still questioning the wisdom of turning right instead of left to go to Conners. It was like he couldn't help himself. He was so close to Hannah. Was it so bad to want to cruise by her house and make sure she was okay? And maybe to see her for a second, just to assure himself the brief shining few moments she'd been his weren't a figment of his imagination.

He'd eventually like to call Lucy and tell her he was thinking about her. But his relationship with the little girl he wanted nothing more than to call his daughter might be a casualty of his bad decisions too. It was Hannah's choice, not his, and it was too soon. For a lot of reasons—first and foremost that he didn't know which direction the danger might come from.

He'd chosen this path and now he had to walk it.

What had Hannah told Lucy about Archer's absence? Had she caustically instructed the girl to never think of him again? Coldly told Lucy that Archer wasn't her father after all and that he'd lied about it for far longer than any decent person would have? Because all of that was true.

He only meant to swing by the house and just…make

sure it was still standing. Maybe peer through the window and give his heart one good long last look.

Except Lucy was playing in the snow outside by the driveway, Princess Misty chasing snowballs as her mistress threw them. And Hannah stood next to them, laughing. Until she turned her head and caught his gaze through the windshield.

And then it was too late. It would be weird to drive off as if he hadn't seen her, his tail between his legs, wouldn't it? So he rolled to a stop and sat there for a minute, completely out of his element.

Hannah lifted her hand and waved, somehow conveying a bundle of nerves and unease in that one spare movement. Lucy had no such reservations. Her face split into a huge grin and she raced toward the car, calling, "Daddy, Daddy, Daddy!" at the top of her lungs.

The prick behind his eyelids nearly undid him, but he wasn't about to waste the positive energy, so he flung open the door and caught Lucy as she launched herself into his arms. Everything righted itself inside as he breathed in little girl scent mixed with snow.

"Mr. Fluffers had surgery and we baked cupcakes to make him feel better," she announced, settling into his embrace as if she'd done it a million times. "And Mama let me take Princess Misty to school for show-and-tell. She was so good, my teacher said I could bring her back. And—"

"Whoa," Hannah said with a laugh and pulled Lucy free, setting her on her feet with a tiny push toward the house. "Can you give me a minute to talk to your father before he goes deaf? Take Princess Misty inside and watch *Peppa Pig* until I come in to make lunch."

Dutifully, Lucy waved at Archer and darted off, leaving him standing there with his brain buzzing. He shouldn't be here. But something akin to hope exploded in his chest and he couldn't squelch it. No matter how much he knew he should.

"You didn't tell her," he said. It wasn't a question because obviously she hadn't. Why hadn't she told Lucy the truth?

"Tell her what?" Hannah's cheeks were rosy with the cold but he barely felt the temperature as her face turned up towards his. "That you had to go away for a few days but that you'd be back? I did. And you did."

"You're sugarcoating it," he muttered and shook his head, trying to untangle what he *should* say with what he wanted to say. "You shouldn't call me her father in her presence like that."

"Why on earth not?" she said, clearly incredulous. "You've been more a father to her in the last few weeks than her biological one was in the whole of either of their lives."

"That doesn't make it true." It also didn't make his heart stop hurting any less to hear her praise. Because it didn't matter if he was good at it or wanted to be Lucy's father with a fierceness that eclipsed anything he'd ever yearned for before. Except Hannah.

She stared at him for a second. "You told me you were in this for the long haul. Did you mean that?"

"I said that when I thought… It doesn't matter," he told her brusquely, aching over the words he'd meant but couldn't honor. "I can't be Lucy's father."

Not now. Not when he'd made them a target by coming here. The whole time he'd been playing house, he'd shone a spotlight of attention on both of these people he loved. On all of Hannah's family. He'd fooled no one with his charade except himself.

"I'm trying to understand what's happening, Mac," Hannah said, wrapping her arms around herself. "Why did you come back if it's not because of Lucy? Spoiler alert. There is a wrong answer."

He started to respond with a comment about making sure they were okay and it got caught in his throat. She'd called him Mac. Casually. As if maybe she'd said some things she didn't mean in the heat of the moment and he shouldn't be so quick to dismiss the forces that had driven him here.

He didn't deserve her forgiveness. But he wanted it more than anything.

"I don't know," he choked out hoarsely. "I didn't mean to."

That much at least was honest.

"You didn't mean to pose as Owen either, to hear you tell it," she said, her voice driving into him with staccato beats the equivalent power of a nail gun. "Maybe it's time to take some credit for your actions. Do what you mean to do."

Like sweep her into his arms and tell her he loved her? That would ruin things faster than anything else. He stood there, running a hand through his hair, unable to believe that there was any chance Hannah could love him back. Those scales wouldn't balance in his head no matter what he did because at the end of the day, she didn't really know him.

If she had any feelings for him whatsoever, she'd developed them when she'd thought he was Owen. He'd never been himself around Hannah.

"I came by because I couldn't stay away," he murmured, his throat aching with it. "I found the bank. The one that goes to the key. It's in Conners. That's where I should be but instead I'm here, wishing for things that I lost the chance to have before being given the chance to have them."

Her expression softened. "Who said that? Not me. You're the one who left, and I gave you that space because I can't force you to be here with me and Lucy. There's no magic to this, Mac. Just two people who have a lot of unsaid things between them because both of them are scared."

"I'm not—" *scared*. But that was the one lie that he couldn't seem to spit out, apparently. "What are you scared of?"

Better. Focus on her instead of the myriad of emotions rioting in his chest. Cold seeped into all the cracks of his body as he waited for her response.

"You," she murmured. "Us. That you're such a good and decent human being that you won't take this chance that's been given to both of us, solely because your sense of propriety won't let you move past the way we met."

"I don't understand." His fingers rubbed at a raw place near his temples that had sprung up from the sheer friction of the repeat motion. "There is no us. You never—when you asked me to promise I wouldn't walk away from Lucy, that was the extent of what you wanted from me. A father for your daughter. And I was happy to take it."

"Were you?" she countered with raised eyebrows. "Okay. That's fair. I never asked you if you were interested in more. My mistake."

"Wait."

He grabbed her hand and drew her closer so he could see the things swimming in her green eyes for himself. The truth. Whatever that truth happened to be. There needed to be a lot more of it between them.

And yeah, it was terrifying. For more reasons than one.

"You don't even know who I am," he told her, and it came out a lot more like an accusation than he'd intended.

But she didn't seem overly bothered by it. Just shook her head and let her lips lift into a small smile. "Because you hid behind your amnesia. Behind Owen. He's gone now. Let's let him go and take some steps toward whatever this is."

"You could do that?" He stared at her skeptically. "Forgive everything and just…move forward? Get to know each other with nothing else between us?"

"I don't know," she admitted. More honesty. "Owen's ghost has been a part of my life longer than he was. I have some work to do too to banish him, same as you do."

"How do we… Is there a way?" he asked, genuinely perplexed that such a thing could be possible. That he'd be standing here in the snow with a woman struggling to deal with Owen's death the same as he was. "I've been living in Owen's shadow for a long time. It doesn't feel like such an easy thing to pick up where he left off. Step into his place in this family."

Hannah's smile grew a lot warmer. "Owen never had a place in this family. The spot you filled was one you created."

Well, he wasn't quite sure how that was possible. Owen had far more right to this family than he did. But Owen was gone. Archer was not. And Hannah was saying she was open to seeing what it looked like if he didn't walk away after all. From either Lucy or her.

For the first time in his life, he didn't know how all the pieces fit together. And he wasn't going to have the luxury of stepping back to analyze before plunging in. It scared him. It scared him that Hannah had picked up on his fear. It scared him that none of that was enough to stop him from aching to take this shot.

"I don't know what to do next," he admitted as his heart threw open the doors to the possibility that his story with Hannah and Lucy might not be over.

"You said something about a bank in Conners?"

Chapter 27

Hannah kept trying to sneak glances at Mac as he drove toward Conners, but he kept catching her. How was she supposed to secretly study him if he wouldn't at least pretend not to notice her sweeping his expression for clues as to what was going on inside his stubborn head?

"What?" he murmured, shooting her a small smile.

It was the only kind of smile she could seem to muster too. It was like her heart could only let her be slightly joyful when so much hung in the balance. Undecided. But there was nothing that could stop her from getting tingles when her arm brushed Mac's against the center console.

"Nothing," she told him, and he let her get away with that for the second time since they'd climbed into his car after dropping Lucy at Wade's.

Her brother had given her the side-eye when he'd seen Mac standing silently behind her, but he hadn't said a blessed word, thank goodness. She'd told her family nothing, so as far as they knew, Mac was still Owen and still slightly suspect in their eyes.

Oh, the irony. When she told them the truth—and she would, pending how much she and Mac decided they needed to know—he'd probably shoot up in their estimation. And he'd been so lost in his own head about owning the blame for lying to her.

Granted, she'd had a full head of steam about it when he'd told her. But she'd had a lot of time to think after he'd gone back to Vegas, and she didn't see another way this whole thing could have unfolded. The problem wasn't whether she could forgive him. It was that he couldn't forgive himself.

And he was the one who had to figure that out.

At the moment, all she could do was come along for the ride.

"You're trying to catalogue the differences between me and Owen," Mac guessed with a lot more insight than she'd have credited.

"I've been doing that since day one," she admitted. "I just didn't know I was."

"Really?" He took his eyes off the road for a brief second as he glanced at her.

"Come on, Mac. You can't be serious."

Where would she even start with the list of things she'd subconsciously internalized that split the two brothers into completely different halves of what looked to be a whole to an uneducated outsider?

But it felt like an evolution of their relationship that she verbalized it for both of their sakes.

"Your face is totally different, for one." She ticked it off on her finger. "You have a kindness that softens the lines. It's in your eyes too. Your voice. Your mannerisms. Owen spent twenty-four seven focused on Owen. That's not something you could have ever hoped to emulate, even with months of practice because it's not who you are."

He pursed his lips. "So you're saying I'm a terrible actor."

She had to laugh at that. "Yeah, I'm afraid so. At least

when it comes to playing the part of your brother, who probably couldn't have told you his daughter's middle name at gunpoint."

It was a sobering reminder that she hadn't meant to introduce. They'd both been held at gunpoint, and she was painfully aware that the dangers hadn't been completely eliminated yet. If even slightly. Whatever they found at this bank in Conners would open the floodgates.

At least she hoped so. Everything hinged on the contents. It had to lead to the Owen exorcism that she and Mac desperately needed. The elimination of the feeling that she still had a target on her back. The fear that whoever Owen had been tangled up with would target her family. All of it could be solved with the key Mac had handed her for safekeeping while he drove his rental car toward Conners.

The place where everything had changed. If she'd known what would be in store for her when she'd walked into that hospital room to visit the man she'd thought was her ex-husband... It was mind-boggling.

"It's Louise," Mac murmured. "I pulled Lucy's birth certificate. Louise is my mother's name."

Speaking of mind-boggling. "Your mother is alive?"

Well, of course she was. Probably Owen's father too, and a host of uncles and other siblings maybe. How selfish of her not to even ask these questions about Lucy's paternal relatives, now that she had exhibit A on how Owen had hidden these parts of himself from her.

And then suggested his mother's name for Lucy's middle name. It was baffling why he'd do that.

"She is. Alive and well and living in Las Vegas. She's going to be thrilled to find out about Lucy."

"You haven't told her yet?" Good. She wasn't the only one still trying to figure all of this out.

Mac shook his head. "I'm investigating Owen's murder at her request. I figured I should have that solved before I told her anything."

A heavy silence filled the car and Hannah picked at the thread on her seat belt, weighing what to say. "It's going to be tough to remove the specter of Owen, isn't it?"

He flashed her a brief smile as he signaled to go around a slower driver in a minivan. "Hard when you'll see him every time you look at me."

"But I don't, Archer." It was the first time she'd said his real name out loud. She let it settle into the cracks of her heart, filling them. "That's not something I can prevent *you* from thinking about, but I stopped seeing Owen a long time ago. In my head, you're Mac."

Oh. That's why he'd asked her to call him that. Because he knew at some point she'd find out the truth, and it would be very difficult to segue from Owen to something else. Which she appreciated on levels she hadn't fully examined yet. It spoke volumes about his intentions. And they weren't to vanish from her life.

Did he even realize he'd been two steps ahead even back then? He had to. Then why all the hesitation and stoic resolve to stay detached from what she'd so clearly offered—a second chance?

"You loved Owen though," he said simply, this time not looking at her. "That's a difficult thing to get past."

"Well, I can understand that," she said sinking down in her seat, but minimizing her profile didn't stop the barbs from flaying her insides. "I'm not too fond of my decisions on that front either, so I can see how it would be a problem for you—"

"No, Hannah, not a difficult thing for *me* to get past," he corrected gently. "For you. He's the one you married and had a baby with. It's totally understandable that he'd hold a special place in your heart and that I might not measure up."

"Uh, no, Mac, he doesn't." As if. Had she not told him enough times what a loser Owen was? How he'd left her and Lucy, *never* to return? "There's no measuring up you should ever worry about."

He went quiet for a beat. "Then why were you okay with it when I walked away?"

Her mouth fell open and practically cracked at the hinges as missing parts of the big picture came into focus. And the enormous mistake she'd made. "Are you being serious right now? You think I was okay with it? I cried for hours. But you needed that space to sort your head out. I needed that space. So we could both be sure this is real. I love you, Mac. You. Not Owen. *Because* you're not Owen, not in spite of it."

The whole paradox was almost laughable, but she didn't feel like laughing all at once as Mac pulled into the bank parking lot and rolled between the white lines, throwing the car into Park. He turned his whole body to face her, his gaze searching hers with intensity that she hadn't seen since the last time he'd kissed her.

It felt an awful lot like he might do it again and she was not planning to stop him.

"You're in love with me?" he murmured, his fingertips reaching for her cheek with a hesitation that felt almost reverent, as if he couldn't believe he had the latitude to make such a bold move.

She nodded, pushing her jaw into the palm of his hand. "If you sensed any hesitation on my part, it was because I was terrified you'd get your memory back and realize why you'd left in the first place. Finding out you're not the man I was married to is everything to me. And one day, it'll matter to Lucy too. You're the man he should have been but never could be."

Something lifted from her shoulders then—the weight of her eternal debate about whether she should lead with her head or her heart. And of course the answer was both. Intellectually, she knew there would be hiccups, but in her heart, she also knew this was worth it.

Archer Declan Mackenzie was worth it.

And then he did kiss her, unleashing so many unverbalized things between them that she forgot they were in a car, forgot there were ever any problems, forgot her own name. This was what love tasted like, what it felt like under her fingers. *Mac.* The answer to every question, the echo of every heartbeat.

He lifted his lips, and she squeaked in protest.

"We're overdue for some serious repeats of that kiss," he murmured a tad breathlessly and wasn't that glorious, to know she'd been responsible for it. "But first, I need to tell you that I love you too. And that we are in a parking lot, so while I am a huge fan of where your hands are, the locale is maybe not the best one for it."

Laughing, she held up both hands and then cupped his face with them. "We have a safety deposit box to check out and then yes to kissing some more while hashing out logistics, like whether you still want the same side of the bed or not."

His grin lit her up inside as she internalized that it was the first one he'd given her since he'd confessed he wasn't Owen. "Safety deposit box first, yes. And I don't care as long as you're saying you want me to have a place in your life. I meant everything I said when we were pretending I was my brother. I'm in this forever. I want to be Lucy's father, if you're okay with that."

"You already are," she told him softly. "It would be a lie to say differently."

"I'm still not clear on how we got to this point, though," he murmured as he nuzzled her cheek, then her mouth. "You're supposed to be furious. You're not supposed to love me when all I meant to do here was make up for the crappy way Owen treated you."

Was *that* what he'd been doing this whole time? Her heart melted and reknit itself into a whole that felt ten times better now that Mac had a permanent place in it. She drew back and smiled at him. "But that's *why* I love you. After all, you came back."

Somehow they made it out of the car and into the bank before it closed for the day. The clerk led them right back to the vault and pulled out an innocuous-looking safety deposit box, then left them alone for privacy. Sure, there'd been a moment it could have gone the other way when the bank employee had asked for ID, but Mac pulled out Owen's driver's license, and that was that. The last time, God willing, he'd have to pretend to be his brother.

So easy. Easier than she'd expected. It almost didn't seem real, as if she'd wake up and realize all of this had been a dream.

"That was too easy," Mac muttered, reading her mind. "This isn't going to be the answer, is it? It's going to be another dead end. You'll still be in danger, and I'll never be able to sleep until I know for sure that you and Lucy are safe."

"That's why you left," she said with dawning certainty. "You thought you could draw off the heat from Owl Creek if you went back to Vegas."

"The heat?" Mac shot her a grin. "We don't really talk like that. But yes. It was one of many reasons."

They could talk about that later. It didn't matter. Whatever was in this box had led Mac to her and to Lucy. It was a blessing, regardless.

"This is a big box. Right?" She glanced at Mac for verification, who nodded. "This whole time, I've been thinking—what in the world could Owen have put in a safety deposit box when they're so small. But this is an extra-large one. Maybe for a reason."

"Only one way to find out."

Together, they slid the key into the lock and it was moment-of-truth time. Mac lifted the lid. And there it was. Stacks and stacks of money. Hundred-dollar bills in neat piles. Her heart stuttered.

This was real. This was a lot of money. In a flash, any lingering doubt about any of the events that had transpired this far vanished. Mac had made every decision in the interest of keeping people safe. No other reason.

"How much money did he supposedly steal from the money launderers?" she croaked.

"Five million dollars," Mac said grimly and tapped each stack, mouthing numbers as he went. "And that's exactly how much is here if it's hundreds all the way through."

Agape, she stared at him. "You did that math in your head? That might be the sexiest thing I've ever seen in my life."

Mac chuckled, a pleased, but slightly embarrassed, smile gracing his lips. "Lots more where that came from."

Beneath the money, she spied something that wasn't the color of a hundred-dollar bill. Curious, she shifted some of the stacks out of the box and pulled the manila folder free, opening it. And then nearly dropped it when she read the name scattered throughout the paperwork.

"Mac," she whispered and held it out to him. "Is this what I think it is?"

He flipped open the cover and scanned through the files, his expression growing more and more astounded. "It is. It's a link between Owen, Markus Acker and the Ever After Church. This is explosive evidence, Hannah. I'm sure this is what got Owen murdered. I can use it to put the FBI on the case. He may have saved us all."

And with that, the ghost of Owen fizzled and faded away as Mac pulled Hannah into his arms.

Epilogue

Mac glanced over at Hannah as he rolled to a stop at the only red light between their house and Jenny's. And no, it never got old to think of it as "their" house, even though Mac's name hadn't officially been added to the paperwork yet.

She'd been a little busy making up for lost time. Lucy had gotten to spend the night at Ana Sophia's for her first big-girl sleepover as a result, which worked for everyone.

She caught his gaze. "What? Do I have something on my face?"

"You're the most beautiful woman I've ever seen," he murmured. "I can't believe you're mine."

Oh, well. *Now* she had something on her face—a lot of color and heat and some of it was leaching down into other parts at an alarming rate. "Stop that. We're on the way to my mom's house and I do not want to have to sit there thinking about what I'd rather be doing."

"Sorry not sorry," he teased and tore his gaze from hers in favor of watching the road, which she appreciated. "Did you figure out what you're going to say about us?"

"Mom, it's not going to work out with Owen. I met someone else."

Mac laughed and then did a double take at Hannah's expression. "That's not what you're really going to tell her, is it?"

Hannah stuck her tongue out at him and hummed happily. "It's the truth. And I have to tell everyone *something*. We can't call an emergency family meeting to explain everything that's happened and just leave out the part where you're going to be sticking around permanently."

Every day was the best day ever since Mac had resigned his position at the LVMPD. The badge in his wallet read Owl Creek as of yesterday and she owed Fletcher a huge hug for facilitating the transition so quickly. Mac's assistant, Willis, had happily relocated as well and Hannah had recently introduced him to Ana Sophia's mom, Maria. They seemed to be hitting it off, and Hannah appreciated that her friend smiled a lot more lately.

"What if we tell them I proposed to you on the way over and you said yes?" Mac suggested as he parked behind an SUV that might belong to Chase and Sloane but she had no idea because her vision had just gone gray.

"What? You're asking me to marry you? Now? Here?"

Mac turned to her and snagged her hand, bringing it to his lips in a shudder-inducing move that did nothing to increase her ability to breathe or think or figure out if this was really a dream she'd wake up from before the good stuff happened.

"I don't want to wait, my darling," he told her. "I want you to be an official member of Clan Mackenzie. As much as I like your family, there are already too many Coltons. Be a Mackenzie with me and Lucy. Forever."

"Oh, well, that's an offer I would be a fool to refuse," she said with a watery smile that matched his more closely than she would have credited.

She loved it when he got emotional and didn't hide it from her.

"Is that a yes?" he asked, his expression so hopeful that her heart soared.

"Well, hold on a minute," she said, one brow raised. "We haven't talked about kids outside of your adoption petition for Lucy. Is that it for you or are you—"

"Is that it?" His voice rose almost an octave. "Have you bothered to google the definition of the word 'clan' recently? You may need a refresher. We're having at least five more. Maybe six or seven, pending whether or not Chase can score us a much bigger house. Don't argue with your laird."

That got a genuine laugh out of her, the kind that mixed well with the misty tears his sweet proposal had already generated. "I wouldn't dream of it. Sounds like we're on the same page then. Very well, I'll marry you."

He matched her smile and produced a ring box from somewhere. Maybe by magic. When he flipped the lid, she practically melted out of her seat. The ring was nothing like she'd expected. Low profile. A simple band with channel set diamonds. "Mac, it's perfect. Exactly right. I can wear it when I'm baking or serving and it won't snag on anything."

He lifted a brow. "You say that like it was an accident or maybe I didn't already think about that when I picked it."

And then he slid the band onto her finger and of course it fit. Just like he did, in every way.

"I love you," she said.

"I love you too, but you have to stop crying or your brothers are going to jump me before I even get over the threshold."

"I can't help it when you're making all my dreams come true."

Sniffling, she tilted her hand to let the diamonds catch

the low light. Was it terrible to be so happy when there was still so much unsettled? The Internal Affairs people had caught the other three dirty cops inside the Las Vegas Police Department, the ones who had been working with the money launderers, thanks to the testimony of that terrible man who had held them hostage.

The FBI had gotten involved once Mac turned over Owen's files, quickly tracing links between her ex-husband and the Ever After Church. It was enough to start investigating Markus Acker, and the federal presence in town had helped take attention off Hannah and Lucy, so Mac breathed a little easier.

From the files, Hannah had realized Owen hoped to cozy up to her and then use her brother's real estate business as a cover when he took over handling the money laundering from the church. Big Mike hadn't been too thrilled about the idea of losing that business, as best they figured, and likely had taken out Owen as a result. They couldn't prove it—yet—so Mac had put a bug in the FBI's ear. It was keeping the crime boss pretty busy, so Hannah and Mac ducked out of that mess, opting to focus on each other.

As a married couple apparently.

"Hannah," Mac said, caressing her name the way he always did, the way she liked best. "You're the one making my dreams come true. I came here to expecting to fix whatever Owen had screwed up and instead, you fixed me. I got all the rewards this time. You and Lucy."

He kissed her and she saw stars. Not the migraine kind—she didn't get those anymore—but the kind she'd never get tired of. This was *her* reward for finally figuring out she could use her head and her heart. Together. Finally whole.

* * * * *

Don't miss the stories in this mini series!

HE COLTONS OF OWL CREEK

MILLS & BOON

Protector In Disguise

Veronica Forand

MILLS & BOON

Veronica Forand is the award-winning author of romantic thrillers, winning both the Booksellers' Best and the Golden Pen Award for the novels in her True Lies series.

When she's not writing, she's a search and rescue canine handler with her dog, Max.

A lover of education but a hater of tests, she attended Smith College and Boston College Law School. She studied in Paris and Geneva, worked in London and spent several glorious months in Ripon, England.

She currently divides her time living between Philadelphia, Vermont and Cape Cod.

Visit the Author Profile page
at millsandboon.com.au for more titles.

Dear Reader,

I'm so glad you're here for the first book in the Fresh Pond Security series. I love writing underestimated heroines, women who are far more capable than they first appear.

Fiona Stirling, a petite novelist, learns that her deceased husband did not die in an overseas military assignment. Not only is she furious he lied to her, but his reappearance puts her and their son in jeopardy. Jason, on the other hand, learns his wife had once been a government assassin, taking down government targets across the globe. Thrown back together in the middle of chaos, they have to learn to trust each other again while dodging bullets and rescuing their son.

This book is dedicated to my father, who died only a few days ago. He embodied the best kind of hero, one who valued his partnership with my mother and parented my brother, Steve, and I as a mentor, not an authoritarian. He allowed me to find my confidence and strength while always having my back. The novel's hero, Jason, learns to embrace those same qualities as the story unfolds.

Grab your favourite beverage, give a quick toast to the hero in your life and enjoy the story.

Best wishes,

Veronica Forand

DEDICATION

For Dad

A man who preferred history and political books
but read every one of my romances.

Chapter 1

Fiona Stirling's first blind date in the five years since becoming a widow would be the death of her. Death by boredom. The elegant restaurant overlooked Boston Harbor with its seagulls and sailboats and a steady stream of aircraft landing across the water. While the intoxicating aromas from the kitchen encouraged diners to try some of the best seafood in the city, her companion, George, preferred roasted chicken and a beer, and had berated the waiter for not allowing him to order from the lunch menu. Fiona asked for the roasted sea bream and a glass of Sauvignon Blanc from South Africa. Based on the first few minutes, she might need an entire bottle. For an appetizer, they agreed on an order of artichoke dip. She was starving when it arrived. The scent of melted cheese with a touch of white wine filled her with a dozen memories of meals with friends and family. Before she had a chance to taste it, George bit into the French bread, toasted to a perfect warm tan, and spit the bite into his napkin. He waved down the waiter and sent the whole dish back to the kitchen before Fiona could say a word.

"Are you okay?" she asked, her patience evaporating each minute she sat across this man who would never measure up to her dead husband.

He gestured with his hand while he found his voice. "I expect a certain level of quality while dining. This isn't it. The bread is stale."

Fiona bit back the remark burning on her tongue. The Oceanside Grill was her favorite restaurant. She ate there at least once a month with friends or her son or her literary agent, Janet, when she was in town. The bread was never stale. "Was the bread stale or toasted?" she asked.

His expression froze, then he straightened his back and resumed his focus on all the other patrons of the restaurant. "Toast can be stale."

Fiona had a very low tolerance for rudeness. If George acted like a recalcitrant toddler with a piece of bread, how would he deal with more serious issues in life?

Her phone vibrated. She glanced at the text from her son, Matt.

I'm home. Found the lasagna. Thanks.

Although thirteen years old, Matt conducted himself like a seventy-year-old man. He was the kid most mothers wanted their own children to hang out with. Solid grades, a skilled athlete, mild-mannered, preferring an at-home movie or game night to wild parties. Despite all that, Fiona worried about him every second of every day. After already losing one man in her life, she would do everything in her power to keep her son safe.

The waiter brought over a bread basket and placed it on her side of the table. He returned with another glass of wine only moments later. She owed him a very large tip for reading her mind.

As the dinner dragged on, two other guests came

over to the table to ask for an autograph. She smiled, signed a napkin and posed for a selfie. George nodded toward the other guests as though he were harassed by fans all the time. Perhaps he was. A college professor in molecular genetics, he had an impressive résumé and bragged about his soon-to-be promotion to department chair. Fiona asked him about his work, but he dismissed her as though she would never understand such complex issues. Her platinum blond hair and 34D chest precluded intelligence for many people who had imbibed the stereotypes thrown at them for decades. Fiona's deceased husband, Jason, had been the exception. He'd been her biggest champion and a perfect husband in looks and everything else that mattered. To be fair, George was attractive, in a lawyerly sort of way, with his blond hair swooping over his blue eyes like a Wall Street Ken doll. Quite the opposite from her *type*. Jason had sported a permanent three-day beard on his chiseled jawline. His dark hair, dark eyes and intensity had sent Fiona into a sexual meltdown every time he looked into her eyes. In the sixteen years she'd been with him, he'd never said a mean word to her or to anyone around him. He'd been her anchor. Even five years after his death while on a military assignment in Colombia, the grief bowled through her, sending her mind into a glum and restless place.

"…sex on a train?" George was talking about something Fiona wasn't sure she wanted to hear.

To avoid being rude, she snapped out of her memories. "What?"

"The sex scenes you write. Where do you get your ideas?" George lifted his second beer and winked at her.

"Oh." She forced a smile. Her thriller novels often

had one or two sex scenes in them. It spoke volumes that those scenes would be George's focus. She now saw how the rest of the evening would go if she didn't separate him from his assumptions. She leaned forward on her elbows, her arms pressing her breasts together and causing George's attention to drop in anticipation of the rest of the night. "I make up the sex scenes from things I read in books or watched in movies," she said in a low purr. "The murder scenes, however, are carefully orchestrated and practiced. I can slit a throat without breaking a nail." She was a bit rusty, but she was sure she could still handle the task with a three-and-a-half-inch Benchmade blade.

He choked on his beer. It was the first time she laughed all evening.

Her phone rang. Matt. He never called. Ever. "Sorry. I need to take this. It's my son." She pressed Answer. "Hey, honey, what's up?"

"Someone is sneaking around the back of the house." Matt whispered the words. "I saw him by the back hedge after the motion light turned on."

Everything inside her went still. "Where are you?"

"In my room." His nerves traveled to her phone like a high-voltage surge. She always told him to always trust his instincts and she would too.

A wave of panic crashed over her. Nothing mattered to her more than Matt.

She checked the cameras she'd installed around the house. In the backyard by the hydrangeas, a shadowy figure tried to hide, but his solid dark pants and shirt didn't blend into the nuances in the background. "If you hear a window or a door break, run to Meaghan's house.

Otherwise, don't come out until I get home. I'm on my way. Call the police and stay on the phone with them." She stood up and grabbed her purse. "I need to get home. My son needs me."

George finished eating a bite of chicken, then stood too. "Rushing off every time your son has a problem won't prepare him for the real world."

"Fuck off, George." She threw down three twenties to pay for her half of the bill. Her best friend, Meaghan, would be hearing from her about her insistence that George was her *perfect match*.

Once in the parking garage, she scanned the parking lot full of Mercedes, BMWs and Teslas for her ten-year-old Jetta. It may have been smaller and not as luxurious as the cars surrounding her, but it was cheaper to run and could move surprisingly fast. The tires squealed as she circled down three stories of concrete and exited onto the street. As usual, the Saturday-night traffic shuffled along State Street. Fiona couldn't wait. She swerved around several cars and managed to slip through a light as it flickered orange, keeping everyone behind her stalled at red.

Matt's voice pushed her to maneuver like a Formula One driver. He tended to remain calm in most situations, like his father. Tonight she heard apprehension.

She used Alexa to call Meaghan so she wouldn't have to slow down.

Meaghan answered on the second ring. "You better be calling to tell me you just had the best sex of your life."

"Not even close. George is an ass."

"He can be, but he's gorgeous. Couldn't you just ignore everything he said and enjoy the ride?" Meaghan said with a chuckle.

"No. My mind has to be as seduced as my body for me to enjoy sex."

"That must lead to some pretty lonely nights."

"George is not why I'm calling." Fiona wasn't in the mood to discuss her sex life when her son was in danger.

"What's wrong?"

Meaghan was a no-nonsense kind of friend, the only kind of friend Fiona could tolerate, so she just burst right out with it. "Someone is trying to break into my house, right now."

"Oh. My. God. Are you okay? Is Matt okay?" Meaghan, a person who never showed a wide range of emotion, sounded stressed.

"Can you get over there?"

"I wish I could. I'm with a client in Rockport, but I'll tell them I have to go."

"Don't bother. I'll be there before you find your car."

Fifteen minutes later—after a lot of near misses and some angry exchanges with annoyed drivers—Fiona arrived home without a speeding ticket. Their simple one-story ranch house had no lights on, not one. Her neighbors had power and the streetlights still cast a bright ring on the road every hundred yards or so. Fiona rushed to the side door, her eyes scanning her surroundings as she unlocked it. The kitchen was dark with only the external lights casting enough of a glow to make out objects on the counters. The large glass casserole of lasagna she'd made for his dinner sat uncovered on the stove, half-eaten.

"Matt?" She stepped inside, her only defense the keys

in her hand and her small leather purse. She'd never been so unprepared for something in her life.

Before she could call out again, a large arm wrapped around her and covered her mouth. She fought to get free, but another arm locked her body tight against a brick wall of a chest. Her assailant had the physique of a bodybuilder. A burglar? Where were the police? Where was Matt?

The man pushed her forward toward the family room. Fiona twisted and tried to slam the back of her head into his face. No such luck.

They passed the edge of the counter. The darkness hid the colors and details of the interior, but this was her space. She reached behind her and took the ballpoint pen she'd left by her grocery list. One stab to the neck and he'd not only loosen his hold on her, he'd be headed to the morgue, but she'd promised herself she wouldn't kill unless absolutely necessary. So she hesitated, and his grip on her tightened. Before the bastard could crush her ribs, she smashed the pen into his thigh. He stepped back, and she slipped through his arms. Clasping both hands together, she rammed a double fist straight up into the man's groin. He fell forward in pain, but recovered faster than she expected. He grabbed a stool from the table and swung it into her. The hit launched her against the oven, and she dropped to the floor.

Headlights outside the house brought some light into room. The man, his large form coming into focus, wavered. Fiona scrambled back from him. Without a better weapon she stood no chance. But he surprised her. Instead of rushing toward her, he sprinted out of the house into the backyard. Fiona pulled herself up, swallowed her nerves and raced down the hall.

"Matt?" she called out, pushing open his bedroom door. Turning the flashlight on her phone on, she scanned the room. No sign of him. He could have escaped through the window and been safe at her neighbor's, but she paused and waited.

A muffled sound came from under the bed. She dropped to her knees and looked underneath. Behind two flat sweater bins, her son's beautiful brown eyes peeked out.

He pushed his way out of his barricade and stood—he was already a few inches taller than Fiona. She wrapped her arms around him and held him tight as her heartbeat slowed. Having someone invade her space in such a violent manner while her only living relative was home alone shattered the sense of security she'd built around them.

"Are you okay?" She examined his face, his arms, until he pulled away, annoyed enough at her actions to decrease some of her tension. She never should have left him alone. There were too many things that could have gone wrong.

"I'm fine," he replied, "but your nose is bleeding."

She turned away from him and wiped her nose with her sleeve. "Let's get out of here before the beast returns."

"He's still in the house?"

"He escaped out the back door, but I have no idea why he was here so I have no idea if he's coming back." She pointed to the door. "We'll wait out front until the police arrive."

He remained silent as he followed her to the front yard. They stood next to the streetlight, but remained partially hidden by an oak tree on the Murphy's front lawn. Just in case.

It took over ten minutes to hear the sirens. Matt waited with his hands in his pockets, slouched against the tree trunk. He'd always been a calm, levelheaded kid. He had to be deeply processing everything that had happened. In the dark, he looked like a thinner version of his father. If only Jason was still with them. She shook her head. This wasn't the time to be drawn into what-ifs. The *what-is* was too pressing. Someone had broken into their house while her son was there alone. Fiona had never for a moment felt unsafe in this neighborhood, but now, the house where she'd lived these past five years had a shadow over it, one that wouldn't lift. The police arrived, and two officers came out of their car, hands on their revolvers. She announced herself before moving around the large tree in case she surprised them. Matt followed behind her.

The police officers looked past her to Matt, and the older one, about forty-five years old, spoke first. "I'm Officer Dunlop. Did you call 9-1-1?"

He nodded and turned to his mother. Fiona squeezed his arm and stepped forward. "Someone broke into the house and attacked me."

"Where is he?" Dunlop glanced over her shoulder toward the house.

"I don't know. He ran away after I stabbed him with a pen. His blood should be on the floor."

He sent his partner, about ten or so years younger, toward the house. Fiona gave the officer as complete a description of what happened as she could. Matt offered little help as he'd hidden immediately and remained hidden while the man rummaged through several rooms.

She was proud of him. Had he tried to stop the man, he would have been seriously injured or worse. The man who had attacked her was not playing around.

A second police car arrived. The additional blue lights swirling through the neighborhood brought out several neighbors.

The lights flickered on inside the house, which meant her tormentor had only flicked a switch. She'd been so concerned about Matt that she hadn't checked the circuit breaker. Several minutes later, the younger officer returned alone. He strode over to Dunlop and Fiona. "The scene is clear. The circuit breaker was switched off."

Several officers present spread out and searched the neighborhood for "A male suspect, approximately twenty-five years of age, over six feet, black T-shirt, Caucasian, dark hair," as Dunlop had reiterated what Fiona told him.

She looked around. A maze of streets created an easy escape for someone who had left a car one or two blocks over. "You should be able to get his DNA off the blood on the floor."

Dunlop's partner shook his head. "There's no sign of any forced entry and nothing in your house looks disturbed."

"I stabbed him in the leg. There had to be blood on the floor or on the pen. I dropped it after he hit me with the stool."

"Can you show me inside?" Dunlop asked.

Fiona hesitated. She didn't want to be ambushed again, and despite the police officer's presence, something felt off. She told Matt to remain outside with the other officers as she reentered the premises with an armed guard.

The entire scene appeared quite mundane under the five cool-toned track lights illuminating every surface in the kitchen. After her eyes adjusted from the dark, she scanned the room. Not a drop of blood anywhere. It was as though her brain had malfunctioned and now everything was back in order. Even the stool had been placed back next to the island. Officer Dunlop remained beside her, watching over her shoulder, glancing in every direction she looked.

The kitchen floor was cleaner than it had been when she'd left for her dinner date. The man who had assaulted her didn't do this. It would have been too much detail work for someone with an injury. The first officer didn't have time to turn the room over in the five minutes he was in the kitchen before coming outside. Someone else?

"Where's the lasagna?" she asked.

"Lasagna?" Officer Dunlop shook his head as though he were being baited.

"There was a half pan of lasagna on the stove. Right there." She pointed to where she'd seen it when she walked into the room. It wasn't in the sink or the re-frigerator. Her stomach twisted as she opened the trash can. Not there either. Even more than having a stranger in her house trying to harm her and her son, the loss of the lasagna scared the hell out of her.

Chapter 2

Jason spent years setting up a perimeter around his wife and child to protect them in case someone from his past came looking for revenge. He wiped the sweat from his brow. Even with every safeguard he could think of, someone came close enough to kill them. The thought of what could have happened tonight burned. For five years, his family had lived unaffected by his past, and he'd let his guard down. He never would again.

For now, Fiona and Matt were safe. He took a deep breath and leaned back against the passenger seat of the delivery van he'd repurposed for surveillance. Regret never fixed anything. He'd take the information learned and up the security around them. He'd also have to face the consequences of withholding the truth from his team.

After returning to the States from a military deployment in Colombia, he'd been permanently removed from his military position—not really discharged since it had been agreed that his family would be safer if he died on the mission. Awarded a small stipend and new identification to start an alternative life, he created Fresh Pond Security, a security firm specializing in the protection of individuals at risk who were entitled to little or no protection from regular law enforcement units. The company started as a front to keep his own family protected, but the enterprise expanded into something fairly profitable. He only employed the best of the best. Men and women who were highly skilled and unable or unwilling to continue their work for the government. They risked their lives to protect their clients and they had the right and the need to know and understand Jason's past in order to provide the best protection possible for Fiona and Matt.

He rubbed the place where his wedding band had once been. The cool fall air reminded him of the first time he'd met his wife. A graduate student in Global Affairs at the Fletcher School of Diplomacy, Fiona had a parade of admirers following her about like pathetic ducklings. She dismissed most of the men who wanted a place in her orbit with an apologetic smile and the excuse of a schedule too busy for dating. Jason, however, saw obstacles as opportunities. After watching her from a distance for a week or so, he came across her in the library, trying to study, her blond hair twisted at the nape of her neck, her focus on a twenty-pound geopolitics textbook. Two aspiring diplomats sat across from her, peppering her with questions about her time in Belarus. Her frown at their constant interruptions gave Jason an excuse to finally meet her.

"Guys, I would appreciate you annoying someone other than my girlfriend." He sat in the empty chair next to her, pulled out his laptop and proceeded to ignore her while he finished a term paper in his Contemporary Spanish Literature course. Her classmates left, leaving Fiona and Jason to study in companionable silence. If she didn't have any interest in him, she had the option of packing up her things and leaving, no explanation necessary. Instead, she remained. After an hour, she invited him for coffee. They had remained together ever since...until the day he "died."

He carried three other memories of her with him everywhere he went, anchors to a past he never wanted to lose. The first was the moment Fiona stepped out to walk down the aisle on their wedding day. Dressed in a stunning black gown with her blond hair curled into a 1950s siren's bob, she dazzled. Despite protests from her parents, she'd refused to dress as a virgin and pretend an innocence that wasn't there. Instead, she radiated confidence, sex appeal and an independence that kept him happily caught in her web.

The second memory involved the thirteen hours of labor and physical exertion Fiona went through at Matt's birth. She had ten pounds and three ounces of complaints to use against him and she did curse quite a lot, but not once at Jason. They were a team even in the worst of times.

Then there was her lasagna. Double the ricotta and beef, and half the tomato sauce of a regular recipe, but enough sauce to fill each bite with a perfect tang. She always broiled it for five minutes at the end to turn the mozzarella golden brown. She could easily seduce a man into her bed with that dish. He shouldn't have taken it, but he was a man starving for a taste of his past. If he couldn't have a relationship with Fiona or Matt, the lasagna would have to do.

"You could have shared." Steve, Jason's business partner, stared at the empty pan.

"Not a chance. You almost blew the whole operation with your insistence on running into the bathroom."

"You pulled us into this assignment at the last minute. I didn't have time before I was shoved into the van."

"Always prepared?" Jason echoed his partner's favorite catchphrase.

"Sure. I even cleaned the blood off the pen. I have to give Ms. Fiona Stirling a lot of credit. She looks like Marilyn Monroe and fights like Ali. She nailed that guy. Almost took him down without a hair out of place. Now that's what I call a mother bear."

Fiona always drew attention with her movie star looks, light blond hair veiled over one of her bright blue eyes. Her appearance was a weapon, disarming everyone around her. That's what had made her so exceptional at her job at the State Department negotiating international trade agreements.

The intruder stirred and tumbled forward on the van floor. Steve pushed him back toward his seat. The man fell against the side of the van—not that he'd be going anywhere. They'd put handcuffs on him before they cut the phone cords and pulled him into the van in the street behind the house just as the sight of the police lights caught the neighborhood's attention.

Jason called up to the driver, Finn. "Any word on our passenger's identity?"

"The photo you took of him wasn't the best quality since his eyes were closed and his nose was broken."

Steve bent over to look closer at their passenger's face. "He had a gash in his forehead and his leg was bloody from the pen, but his nose was fine when I caught up to him."

"My fist must have accidentally hit him while I was moving him to the van," Jason said, feeling the impact on his knuckles. He would have done far worse to the person who had threatened his family, but the information in the asshole's head was more important than letting his rage fly.

They turned the corner into a garage under a storage facility one town over from Fiona's house. The proximity allowed them to arrive and disappear before the police pulled up. Jason had monitored her house from the moment she'd moved in.

He went to his office to wait for the suspect to wake up. The asshole had better be willing to speak or he'd have a very uncomfortable night.

Two hours later, Finn, one of his best security consultants, contacted him with an update on his family. Jason had pulled him off an assignment protecting the CEO of a pharmaceutical company, leaving only Sam protecting him. Sam could handle the job while Finn watched over Jason's family. Although they'd been too late to prevent the break-in in the first place. Despite all his preparation for just such an event, he'd failed. He shuddered to think what would have happened if she hadn't been able to fight off the intruder. She'd been so lucky to have gotten away with only a bloody nose.

"Hey, boss."

"What's their status?" Jason didn't have time for pleasantries.

"They packed up and headed to the Seagull Hotel."

"You're kidding me." They were sitting ducks if someone was truly after them and not anything in the house. The Seagull Hotel was so named not from a view of the ocean, but for the throngs of birds circling the local Walmart parking lot next door.

"Wish I was. The police think she's safer there for the night, but don't have the resources to watch over them. They're calling it a bungled burglary."

"It doesn't matter what the police do. We're going to keep them secure." An absence of actual police presence was for the best. Jason wanted to limit their involvement until he understood the exact risk. Any press would place a spotlight on Fiona and Matt. She'd already brought too much attention to herself with her skyrocketing book career.

"I agree. I checked into the room next door and have been keeping an eye out for anything unusual, but I've been working on both assignments for over twenty-two hours combined. I'm ready for a replacement." Finn prided himself on his eagle eye and sniper-perfect shot, which meant he demanded rest when he needed rest.

"Noah's on the way. Thanks for keeping an eye on them. Can you send me the room numbers?"

"Sure."

"And Finn?"

"Yes."

"Thanks for switching assignments so quickly."

"That's my job."

Jason closed his eyes when he hung up. Part of him wanted to drive down there and tell Fiona she had to go into hiding to protect herself and Matt from his past, but he knew she wouldn't listen. Her stubbornness was her biggest asset and most annoying quality. She'd survived his *death* and raised their son into a strong and competent soul. She left her government job because of its heavy travel schedule and her need to be closer to Matt. Then she published a whole series of thriller books and made a name for herself. She deserved the recognition and the income helped her where his life insurance couldn't, but it also brought attention from the wrong people. Hiding her would be near impossible unless she agreed to tamp down her personality and become average. Fiona was anything but average.

His phone rang. He picked it up on the first ring as he always did for Kennedy, an analyst in the NSA who assisted him.

"DJ?" she always asked, as though someone might have compromised his phone. Jason used DJ as his alias to keep his name as buried as his former life.

"Go ahead."

"Great news. My sources identified the guy's mug as a Robert Harper." Her sources were unmatched in the field.

"That name means nothing. Who is he?"

"A hired gun for Federated Security. They have many clients, some not so aboveboard. They have a reputation in the field as being outside the law and are more than willing to do anything if the money is right." The constant tapping on her keyboard was her official soundtrack, digging down under layers and layers of security walls to find out what they needed.

"Thanks. Let me know if you learn anything else."

"Will do." She hung up, leaving him staring in silence at the wall.

The news reinforced the urgency to find a safe place for Fiona and Matt until Jason could eradicate the risk. His past might have finally come for his family.

He strolled into the back room, a place with no windows, one door and a whole lot of safeguards. Mr. Harper was on the floor gaining consciousness. He'd be remaining here until Jason figured out what he wanted with Fiona.

Although Jason had lost his wife's companionship five years ago when he'd faked his own death, he'd never given up looking after her. His love hadn't faded one bit. If anything, by watching her from a distance, he'd only fallen in love with her more. She aged like a fine wine, more complex but in a mellow way.

And Matt? He couldn't imagine loving a person more. He looked out for his mother, received good grades, used his strength to protect people from bullies in school and broke enough rules to make Jason assured that he'd never be a pawn for anyone. Not like his father had been.

The memories sent a surge of regret through him. He leaned back in his black leather chair and squeezed his eyes shut. It wasn't enough to orchestrate their safety— he longed to pull them into his arms for as long as he could.

Steve walked in without knocking, eating one of the energy bars he always seemed to have in his pockets.

"I'm going to replace Noah in a few minutes," Jason said. "He was pulled from another assignment like Finn, and I want them both to have a break."

"I can do it if you want."

When he started this business, Jason didn't trust anyone. Money and power could transform someone from loyal to backstabbing. Yet, over the years, the team showed more commitment and reliability than any group he'd ever known. His deception, if they knew about it, could burn the entire operation to the ground. But it was time to come clean.

"I've got this," Jason said. "Before I go, we need to talk about Fiona Stirling."

Steve nodded. "Sure. What's up?" He sat down in the chair across the desk.

Jason took a deep breath and told him everything.

Chapter 3

The sound of cars rushing down Route One outside her window did nothing to ease the stress hammering through Fiona. At three in the morning, both she and Matt should be asleep. They weren't. Back-to-back-to-back reruns of *Law and Order: SVU* allowed them to sit in their respective beds without speaking to each other. Her duffel bag and Matt's backpack with his homework in it rested on the table.

Her mind ran over everything they'd done in the week and month prior to the break-in. She'd had her share of readers targeting her after something she wrote, but all the harassment came in the form of social media bullying. She'd never experienced anyone physically threatening her as an author. Matt had no known enemies, especially men who probably had ten to twenty years on him. Her writer's brain had all sorts of reasons they were attacked. An obsessed fan, an everyday burglar, someone from her husband's world or maybe someone from her own sordid past.

While Jason had thought she had a respectable job at the State Department, she actually worked as a specialized skill officer in the CIA's Special Activities Division. She acted as an employee of the State Department in order to move in normal diplomatic channels, a deadly weapon dressed in navy suits and carrying a briefcase. She enjoyed acting as a diplomat who wined and dined business executives all over the world, but her actual assignments had more sinister ends. She had handed over a piece of her soul for a large sum of money to pay off her student loans. It was a decision that took her outlook from sunny and optimistic to stormy and destructive. They trained her to take out the most villainous men with the most minimal fanfare. Her techniques had become so refined that her targets often didn't die until long after she departed whatever country in which she had delivered her death sentence. Only she and a few higher-ups knew her actual objectives. Even Jason had been excluded from her inner circle. After giving birth to Matt, she could no longer handle the work. She wanted out. Jason's death gave her the perfect excuse. She had to raise her son alone. She couldn't travel anymore. She had lost her touch. It was for the best that she left the government all together. An old friend from college encouraged her to write a book based on her past. She couldn't, but she could make things up. Her first novel had no plot and no character development. Her next one? Better. Three attempts later, she was a published novelist making up stories for a living. She never wrote about or looked back at her former occupation.

If her past had been outed, they'd never be safe.

After another hour of television, Matt fell asleep, to the drama of the night. With him sleeping soundly, she had a chance to think about everything that had occurred. She pulled out her notebook and looked at the notes she'd jotted down. The names of the police officers who had responded to the call, the assistant district attorney who wanted to meet with her the following Monday, and the phone number for a victim assistance agency. One page had a hastily drawn sketch of her assailant. The police took a picture of it to compare to databases. Regrettably, the blood all over her clothes was her own.

When she had gone back into the house to pack, she had examined every nook in the cabinets and on the floor. Not a drop of blood found. She had even picked up the pen and opened it up. The inside was damp as though someone had taken the time to rinse the blood away, but didn't have time to thoroughly dry it.

Questions raced through her head. Wiping away the evidence of a crime scene was the stuff a hit team would do or someone in organized crime. It didn't make sense. If someone wanted her dead, they could have waited for her to get home, taken a perfect shot with a .22 and a silencer to keep the sound to a minimum and driven away, changed cars a few streets over and have been long gone by now. Heading into the house added risk. From what she'd seen, nothing besides the lasagna had been taken. Which meant they were after people, not things.

She shook her head at her detailed assessment of the best way to kidnap or kill her. Old habits never died. It bothered her that such an analysis was necessary. She hid in the bathroom and called Meaghan. They'd left text messages back and forth, but hadn't connected otherwise.

Meaghan answered on the first ring. "Are you okay? Is Matt okay?"

"We're both fine. Matt hid under a bed and only came

out when I went looking for him. I might have a black eye from the assailant's punch to my face, but he's worse off. I stabbed him with a ballpoint pen in the leg before he escaped."

"That's insane. Were you in heels?"

"Seriously? That's what you want to know?" She shook her head.

"It would be wicked hard to take out a guy in heels and if you did—damn, girl." She paused, then said more seriously, "Who was he?"

"No idea. But that's not the weird thing. I'm sure there was blood on the kitchen floor when I left. When I entered again with the police, the whole kitchen was immaculate. Like someone had scrubbed the scene. There's no way he cleaned up the kitchen on his way out the door, but someone did. I looked like an idiot to the police."

"Sounds like one of your novels. Do you want to come over?" The offer was wonderful, but someone might want to hurt her, and she couldn't drag Meaghan into it too.

"Thanks, but we're okay for right now. Matt's already asleep. I might stop at your house tomorrow morning for some coffee or maybe a Bloody Mary. You can help me pick out an outfit for the book signing next Saturday."

"You're not going after all of this."

"I've planned this for months. I won't let my fans down."

"Your fans? What about your stalkers?" Meaghan asked.

"I'll be better off doing something to keep my mind from obsessing over this, and I'll bring Matt with me so he isn't at the house alone."

"Fine. I couldn't change your mind anyway. If you're

going to be stubborn, I'll go to keep an eye on your son while your fans worship you."

Fiona laughed. "I bet he'd love your company." Matt enjoyed hanging out at Meaghan's house. She was the only person Fiona knew who could kick Matt's ass in *Call of Duty*. She'd been lucky to find a neighbor like Meaghan. A person she could share her parenting worries with even though Meaghan wasn't a parent. She'd also made an awesome babysitter when Matt had been younger.

Fiona hung up and sat on the toilet, staring at her reflection in the mirror. Remnants of her date makeup had smeared together, giving her face an impressionistic look. The wave in her hair had flattened into something that looked as though she'd woken from a ten-year nap. Not her best look. The whole evening had been one disaster after another.

Dressing up to meet her readers had always brought her joy, but going out on dates? Not so fun. Especially when that date had been George. At thirty-eight-years-old, she preferred nights at home reading to going out to meet new people. She could hear George's voice in her head snickering over the sex scenes she'd written. The life of a spinster seemed far preferable to having the companionship of the wrong man. *Spinster* had once been a pejorative word, but now, it was more of a badge of honor. When a woman happy in her own existence chose to spend time with someone else, that someone else had to be extremely special. George was not special. He was more the kind of guy who expected a single woman to be grateful for whatever crappy treatment he was willing to give her. Fiona didn't have the desire or the ability to kiss the ass of an ass.

It was all Jason's fault. He'd been too perfect, and truth be told, he became more perfect with each passing year. His flaws diminished and his personality took on superhero attributes. If he walked into her room at that exact moment, she would be putty in his hands. Hands that were large and strong, but so gentle when they needed to be. Her body heated up at the thought of his touch. She stood up and rinsed her face with cool water. This was not the time to get all hot and bothered over the ghost that haunted her dreams.

She found a nip of Bombay Sapphire in the minibar. A bit of ice would make this the perfect nightcap to an otherwise crappy day. She grabbed the key to her room and slipped into the hall. On her way back from the ice dispenser, the door next to hers opened and a man stepped out in a tweed coat. He seemed like a young professor who spent his free time competing with the football team for time in the weight room. Lost in thought, he barely acknowledged her.

Fiona glanced into the man's room, never one to ignore her surroundings. Another man, tall, dark, muscular, calmly stood up and disappeared into the bathroom as the professor type closed the door. She dropped the ice bucket. Ice scattered across the hall. She didn't care. The man in the room looked exactly like Jason.

It was impossible. Jason was dead. She remained frozen staring at the closed door.

"Are you all right?" the other man asked, kicking the scattered ice to the side of the hallway. His demeanor softened as he picked up the ice bucket and handed it back to her.

"This has been a long day. I should just go to bed." She waved and turned back to her own door. It had been a very long day.

She had to stop her obsession with her husband. She'd thought she'd seen him a hundred times since his death. But he was dead. And the man next door wore his hair in a long ponytail, not the crew cut from his last family photo. That sliver of his profile, however, displayed Jason's best features, the nose, broken only slightly from a college football incident that never healed quite right, and intensely alluring lips. Lips that fit hers so perfectly, they could kiss for hours, all night long, and never be sated.

Shutting the door, she sat on the edge of her bed. If Jason had been home, the pen in the intruder's leg wouldn't have been the worst thing that happened to him—he'd probably be dead at the hands of a very competent army captain. But Jason had died in Colombia. The military claimed it was an accident, although her research through her government connections revealed questions that no one could answer about the incident. The military handed her son a folded American flag at his service. His ashes were over her fireplace mantel in a wooden box inlaid with black onyx.

She'd made her peace with his death years ago. Yet, seeing his doppelgänger threw her memories back to the last time they'd seen each other. He'd been playing soccer in the backyard with Matt, never letting him win, because in Jason's opinion, Matt had to fight to beat him or what was the point. He hugged her and their son before he grabbed his gear and headed to his car. Matt didn't cry. His dad left all the time. For him, this was another goodbye with a reunion guaranteed in a few weeks. But he never returned. Matt had waited by the window for months, just staring. Fiona restored Jason's car, a 2000 red Mustang convertible, adding a few more safety features like a back-up camera and integration with Matt's phone. They drove it around town and on brief trips to the mountains. Eventually, she wanted to give it to Matt. It wouldn't bring his father back, but might provide a connection to a man who would have been such an amazing influence in his life.

She took a sip of gin and savored the taste. As of tonight, she had to step up her security. There were too many loose ends from her past that she'd taken for granted. Trying to hide from what she'd done only placed Matt more at risk. She downed the rest of the glass and poured herself some Jack Daniel's, staring at the wall to the next room as though she could see through it. Without seeing his entire face, she no idea who that man was. She took a sip, then another. She had to scrub any thought of Jason's potential resurrection from her brain.

Her obsession with seeing Jason again had led her to create his resurrection in her last book. For months she'd written about a beautiful world where a military mission gone wrong had left her heroine's husband unable to remember who he was. Although they thought he was dead, he was very much alive. When his memory returned, he rushed home to be with his family. It was a complete fiction, more of a fairy tale. She wanted to understand why her husband never returned home. Her government contact had shared classified details on Jason's death that the military had left out of the story they'd given her. He'd been delivering military aid to the Colombian government, the truck was ambushed, everyone died. She rewrote that story, changing some details, but having her hero survive an ambush and eventually reunite with his family. The hardest part of the story was typing "The End" and leaving her hero behind to begin a new book.

Yet, this entire line of thought was ridiculous. Obsessing about Jason coming back to her only exacerbated the heartbreak she couldn't escape. Her son needed a strong presence in his life, not a grief-stricken parent who couldn't get out of bed in the morning. Perhaps a few more dates with men who weren't George would provide some solace to her broken heart. Doubtful, but why turn down an orgasm from some handsome and generous soul? She smiled. Maybe a five-year dry spell was long enough.

Matt stretched his arms over his head and turned his face toward the pillow, his arm resting over his ear. She was so proud of the way he'd handled the whole situation. He'd remained calm, found a safe place and called the police. At the police station, Matt had recapped the entire incident step-by-step three times to three different officers. He had a good mind for details, like his dad.

Swallowing the last of the whiskey, she leaned against the pillow, grateful he'd come out of this unharmed and that she had a mere bump on her nose and the beginning of a black eye. Now if she could only figure out the identity of the intruder and what he wanted with them.

Jason clenched his fists to keep from slamming them into a wall. Of all the bad moments for Fiona to leave her room, she had to choose the exact time when Noah left theirs. This whole situation was a nightmare. He'd spent the last five years hiding himself as close as he could to Fiona and Matt. Too close and he would trap them inside his nightmare. Too far and he'd have missed the attempt on Fiona's life. Now he needed to find out why she was a target and if it was related to the ambush in Colombia.

He should have had Steve keep an eye on his family at the hotel, but it was Jason's family. While Steve had been understanding of why he'd hidden his identity, that didn't stop his anger toward Jason for placing the rest of the team in a dangerous situation by not giving all the facts of the assignment. It would take time to earn his trust again, if ever. So far, however, Steve remained on the job. Jason didn't know how he'd make it up to him, but he would. Jason had met Steve when some loser at a restaurant had hit on his wife and wouldn't back down. Jason stepped in and blocked the idiot from ruining Steve and Olivia's anniversary dinner. They invited him to join them for a drink to thank him. They'd been friends since, which made the deception even worse.

They didn't have the chance to tell the rest of the team that the secret client who paid to keep Fiona and Matt safe was Jason himself. By withholding that key information, he had placed his team at a disadvantage protecting them. That one omission could implode the whole organization. Trust was the keystone of everything they did, and Jason had blown that right open.

He called Noah, who answered on the first ring.

"Did Fiona say anything to you?" Jason asked.

"Nothing of importance, but at one point, she stared past the door into our room. From the look on her face, something spooked her, and it wasn't me. Maybe if you stopped dressing as one of the Hell's Angels, you wouldn't get such a drastic reaction from women. She'd just fended off an attack by a thug in a black T-shirt. It would make sense that she'd fear another guy in a black T-shirt in the room next to her."

"Are you sure she saw me?" he asked, but knew damn well she had.

"I'm sure of it. You were on the bed, then walked over to the bathroom."

If Jason was lucky, it wasn't his identity that concerned her but the black T-shirt, as the intruder was wearing black as well. He returned to the exact spot he'd sat on the bed when the ice bucket went down. An image of his face in the window reflected back at him, not super clear, but enough to give a good indication of his facial features. And she'd have seen his profile when he walked to the bathroom. What the hell was he thinking? He should never have come over here.

"Next time, I'll wear a golf shirt."

"Something with color to bring out that sparkling personality of yours." Noah's voice dripped with sarcasm, which was fine. Jason gained more insight into their cases when everyone could speak freely. Ass-kissing only led to unimaginative teams and lots of conflict between employees. The team was a family, trusting each other in life-and-death situations. Except Jason hadn't done his part to protect them. Once they found out he'd hidden his identity from them, the trust and camaraderie he'd built up over the years would disappear.

"Point taken. See you back at the office in the morning. Ask Steve if he can replace me. I need to get out of here."

"On it," Noah replied and hung up.

After a few minutes of beating himself up, he had to shut down the urge to go to Fiona and comfort her after such a long, hard day. She'd remained so strong over the past five years and here she was caught up in the middle of a nightmare. If the attacks continued, he'd gladly sacrifice himself to keep Fiona and Matt safe. For now, he had to understand exactly why she'd become a target. He opened the hotel door, standing half in the hall, half in his doorway. If someone approached their room, he'd be there. If she opened her door again, he could step inside before she saw him. Steve had better get his ass over here soon.

Fiona woke to the television blaring across the room. "What the…"

"Sorry, I didn't know the volume was so loud." Matt turned the television off and sat on the bed. Half his hair stood straight up and the other half pressed into his skull.

"Don't worry about it." She stretched but didn't sit up. The sun was already awake, offering a sliver of light from behind the curtain. "What time is it?"

"Nine o'clock."

"I never sleep this late."

"You were up late talking on the phone."

"How do you know that?"

"I heard you."

"You did?"

"You aren't exactly quiet when you talk to Meaghan."

He was right. Meaghan and Fiona got on so well, their voices increased with the enthusiasm for whatever topic they were on. Meaghan was the sister Fiona never had and the family she needed after her tiny family unit had broken apart. She also provided Matt with an adult in his life who didn't carry parental expectations. She loved him exactly as he was and didn't care what he did with his life as long as he was happy. Fiona was different. She wanted him safe, financially secure and able to find a partner who would care for him the way Jason had cared for her.

"We should head out. I want to make sure the police closed up and locked the house after they left. Then I need to get some work done."

"We have time." Matt tended not to worry about anything, although after last night, his brows remained furrowed as he packed up his things. Should she take the day off and let them rest on a mental health day, or should she plow on with her schedule? The slightest smile appeared on his face as he texted a friend. It would be okay. Maybe it would be best to carry on without focusing on what had happened.

She headed to the bathroom. "Let me wash my face, and we can eat breakfast at Meaghan's." She paused and before she shut the door, she turned to him. "Is that okay?"

"I guess. Am I going with you?"

"I would prefer it. Last night freaked me out."

He nodded. "Me too. Okay, I'll go."

"That's what I love about you. You're the best kid ever." She ruffled his hair until he pulled away. The furrow over his eyes disappeared during their interaction, and mild amusement took its place.

An hour later, they sat in Meaghan's kitchen enjoying

freshly baked blueberry muffins and omelets. Meaghan, all five feet ten of her, had dressed in cargo pants and a white tank top. Not her usual wardrobe. She typically wore tailored pantsuits and had her hair just so. Not this morning. Her hair was up in a ponytail and if Fiona didn't know better, she'd think Meaghan was headed into battle. She bustled around the kitchen, looking at her phone, her watch and even scanning the windows now and then. No doubt the break-in next door also upset Meaghan's sense of security.

"You spoil us," Fiona said to break the tension.

"It's nothing. Besides, I feel bad I wasn't here last night."

"Why would you feel bad for working? It's not like you're paid to wait by the phone for my panic calls."

Meaghan sighed and took a sip of her coffee. "Do you want me to go with you to your house?"

Fiona waved her request away. "You have a million things to do today—you told me yesterday before I went on the date from hell. Go. We'll be fine, won't we, sport? It's broad daylight. I doubt someone's waiting in the closet for us." She brushed back Matt's hair.

He shrugged, still looking at his phone. "Can I go over to Sarah's house for the afternoon?"

"Absolutely. First, let's get the bad vibes out of the house so I can lock myself in my office for the day without looking over my shoulder."

He thought about it and then nodded. "Deal."

When they got to their front door, Matt hesitated.

"Everything okay?" she asked.

"Are we sure there's no one in the closet?"

"No, but I'll do a quick sweep to make sure. You wait here."

She went inside and looked around. This time, she expected someone to come from behind her and was mentally ready. Just to be safe, she also grabbed one of the fillet knives from the kitchen counter. She checked the coat closet in the foyer. Clear. The living room and bedrooms were untouched. When she returned to the kitchen, the spotless floors annoyed her. Someone was hiding something. She wasn't sure whether to blame the police, the intruder or someone from her past, but she knew a cleanup job when she saw one. Looking around, she didn't see anything else out of place.

"All clear," she called out to her son as she placed the knife back into the wood holder.

Matt came in and looked around. "Will I ever feel safe in here again?"

"I think so. I'm going to install some extra security cameras this afternoon, including ones inside the house. Maybe you can help me. We'll link them up to both of our phones. If anyone comes close to the house, we'll see them. Nothing is foolproof, but a security camera might have caught the man sneaking in."

"That works. What time do you want me home?"

"Two?"

He nodded and headed back out the door.

"Also, can you answer the phone whenever I call just for today?" she called out to him. "Just so I know you're safe."

He turned around. "Okay. You do the same."

She pulled him in for a hug and watched him take off for Sarah's, only six houses away.

After he left, she walked the perimeter of the property and found where the man entered the yard. The damp grass showed footprints under her hedges. She followed them back into her neighbor's yard to the edge of his garden and found one nicely preserved footprint caught in the damp soil. She placed her hand next to it and took a photo from two different directions to get the shading of the large imprint better, which was more like a sneaker than the shoes and boots most police officers wore.

She searched closer to her house to find his exit point, but the police had added significant traffic under all the windows and out the doors. It would be nearly impossible to track him under so much visual noise.

In need of more coffee, she went back into the house, poured a hot cup of black coffee and retreated to her office. With the help of her computer and a credit card, Fiona located and bought several security cameras for the house, the kind that ran off batteries and recorded video both wirelessly and with a copy saved on the camera. She also contacted her closest ally at her former agency for any potential leaks that had occurred recently. Nothing. That was expected as the agency had a near flawless record of getting their jobs done and leaving without a trace. But it only took one mole to bring a whole organization down.

When done trying everything in her power to protect her son, she went to put her cup into the dishwasher and nearly dropped it on the floor. Taking up the entire bottom rack was the lasagna pan, rinsed clean.

Assembled in the conference room at a round table that could seat ten comfortably, five members of the team waited for DJ, the founding partner, to go over what had happened with Fiona's case. There were a few team members, including Meaghan, still out on assignment. Jason would follow up with them later. Steve sat next to him, looking every bit as uncomfortable as his partner. After Jason had told him the truth earlier, Steve shook his head and told him he'd expected more from him, especially since his lie had directly affected the team. While Jason believed Steve would have done the same to save his own family, he probably would have come clean eventually. Jason should have opened up about it. Coming clean now, after Fiona was attacked, was too late as far as he was concerned.

The trust Steve had placed in him years before didn't fall to the wayside easily. But Jason assured him that he would do everything in his power to earn his full trust again. Steve had slapped him on the back and reminded him of the Maxwell case, where Jason pushed Steve out of the way when someone began shooting at them. As far as Steve was concerned, he owed Jason his life after that, and the least he could do was forgive him for this omission. Jason wouldn't argue with him although Steve had saved his ass in many situations as well. The gesture kept their partnership and friendship intact.

He looked over the team, all waiting for what might seem to them a normal group meeting to go over what had happened and to plan for the future. While that was true, what had happened would take a lot of explaining. He hated the prospect of losing anyone. Each person employed by Fresh Pond Security deserved a seat at this table. The only one who didn't was Jason himself. Finn and Noah chatted about their weekend plans, while

Sam and Calvin, their computer expert, focused on coffee and the doughnuts Jason had brought in to keep the mood lighter. Not that his bombshell would land softly.

Jason hesitated, so Steve broke the ice. "We're meeting together because the Fiona Stirling case has issues that have come to light that need to be clarified and understood before we can carry on as an organization."

Steve's words had the team members, all former members of the military or law enforcement, sitting up straighter and turning toward Jason. This was going to be so much harder than he'd anticipated, yet he also blamed himself for not having had the guts to come clean to them years ago. Whatever happened from this point forward, he would never leave out information that could hurt the team.

He looked over the group. Steve Wilson, his partner, stood out with his red hair and scattering of freckles more noticeable after years of weekend boating trips. He'd been FBI, not the sleek gun-toting type who rescued kidnapped children but more a bean counter who could track down missing funds in tax havens and other financial black holes around the world.

Sam Dempsey sat as though he were still a first lieutenant in the US Marines. With his bronze skin, crew cut and a wrinkle-free button-down shirt and khakis, he could blend in as a billionaire's bodyguard or a country club tennis pro. He'd been dishonorably discharged from the Marines for ignoring his command and rescuing a civilian. He had more integrity than the whole group combined.

Across the table sat Finn Maguire, dressed in a pair of well-worn jeans and a comfortable sweater. His light brown hair, carefully brushed back in a style that appeared to have demanded an excessive amount of time and effort, failed to hide the reddish scar slashed across his pale cheek. He left the military in disgrace as well, a pawn in a powerful game that protected leaders and let the smaller guy take the fall. His issue was trust. But despite his casual appearance, he rarely cracked a smile while at work. The scar on his face symbolized the price he had paid for his misplaced trust in a system that had ultimately let him down.

Mild-mannered Noah Montgomery seemed more prep school teacher than bodyguard—a former intelligence analyst who could handle himself in most any situation. His clean-cut look gave him an advantage when doing surveillance. Calvin Beckett came from the NSA. He could create magic with computers and what information he couldn't obtain from certain secure systems, Kennedy could, as she was still inside the government. She was more of a shadow member of the team and never came to meetings.

They each brought their own special skill set that supported everyone else. They also called bullshit when they saw it. Jason braced himself to receive the blowback from his omission. Whatever happened, he deserved it.

After a tension-ridden sigh, he spelled out what had happened to him years before. Being the sole survivor of a military operation gone wrong, where the cartel leader Andres Porras lost his son. How Jason's "death" had prevented anyone from taking revenge on his family. And how he created this group to both help other people in his situation who had to work one step outside the law and to protect his own family. After Fiona's house was compromised, he was terrified that Porras had learned he was alive and was trying to flush him out, although he had no proof. When he finished telling his story, there wasn't a friendly set of eyes at the table, except for Steve's.

His partner took a sip of coffee and shook his head. "I was as much in the dark about this as all of you were, but after almost five years working side by side with DJ, I still trust him with my life."

"Easy for you to say. You get fifty percent of the profits," Sam replied.

"Is it about the money or his deception or both?" Calvin asked. "Because I can make more money elsewhere. Here I thought I was part of something bigger, helping the little guy, protecting those who needed assistance but couldn't receive it anywhere else." He put his hand up toward Jason. "I need a few moments to think."

Finn stood. "I don't need anything else to make up my mind. It doesn't matter what you say. I'm done. I can't work for someone I don't trust. DJ had five years to establish whether he could trust us with his secrets. Five years. And now that the shit's hit the fan with his wife, he's decided to come clean. That means if Fiona Stirling hadn't been attacked, we'd still be in the dark and our own lives would be at risk from a danger we couldn't anticipate."

Jason understood where he was coming from. Finn had been framed for a murder on a military base to protect someone pretty high up. With no ability to prove his case since the government controlled the evidence, he ended up pleading to manslaughter and getting a dishonorable discharge. His honor meant everything to him and so did loyalty. Losing all of that in the service destroyed him until DJ came along and offered him a fresh start. Since then, he'd spent every day proving himself to those around him. Jason's deception had erased all those years of trust between them.

Jason acknowledged it. "I was wrong. I wanted to protect my family and in the process I hurt you, my new family."

"Save your words." Finn pulled the weapon from his belt and placed it on the table. "I don't have it in me to pull a knife out of my back again." His anger burned behind his eyes, but he held himself under control. He looked over at Noah, his closest friend in the group, the strain on his face evident. "Stay if you want. I won't hold it against you, so don't hold this against me." He shook his head. "Wait until Meaghan hears how all of this has been a one huge lie."

With that, he left the room. The sound of a slamming door echoed down the hall.

Everyone remaining sat in silence. Jason didn't want to believe he'd lost Finn, one of the best things to happen to Fresh Pond Security. Not only would he miss him as a colleague, but he'd miss him as a friend. A friend he'd deceived. It was no use racing down the hall and begging for his forgiveness. Jason respected Finn and understood he had to live in alignment with his morals. Perhaps someday Jason could prove to him that he hadn't meant any harm by hiding his background, but until that day, he had to let him go.

He scanned those remaining at the table. "Anyone else?"

Noah stared at the door Finn had stepped through moments before. "You let us all down. If you can't trust us, what are we doing here? We're not just hired guns. We'd had an understanding that we had each other's backs."

"I agree. And I do have your backs."

"But your wife and kid take priority."

"That's not fair."

"Isn't it?" he asked.

"If you want to know if I'd lay my life down for you, I would without hesitation. I also want to keep Fiona and Matt safe, yes. I owe it to them as they never did anything to put themselves in the line of fire."

Noah's frown remained in place. "It's a lot to take in."

Sam and Calvin nodded in agreement.

The fact that they remained at the table boded well for the future of the group, but someone had to break through the distrust and get everyone one step closer. Jason had no idea how to breach that gap.

Steve leaned back in his chair. "That went better and worse than I thought it would. We still have important details to work out. Number one, should I be with you when you tell the rest of the team?"

"No. It might go better one-on-one. And if they want to kill me, you couldn't save me anyway."

Steve shrugged at the insult. "Okay then. Second, should we call you Jason or stick to DJ?"

Danger was at his door, and he had nowhere to go but through the middle of hell to get out. He regretted not trusting the team with the truth and losing one of his best people because of it. "I don't give a damn what anyone calls me."

"Good enough," Steve replied. "We'll stick to Dickhead for now until this is over."

Chapter 4

The Grasshopper and Gopher Bookstore took up an entire brownstone on Beacon Street. Three floors of perfection. The first floor contained rows and rows of nonfiction books and a cute coffee bar that served the best chocolate brownies in the world. Matt sat in a window seat with his laptop, a chocolate chip cookie and a large hot chocolate with a mountain of whipped cream. He seemed perfectly happy. Fiona sat with him for a few minutes, nibbling on the final corner of the brownie she insisted she needed to calm her nerves. She could handle a lot of things in the world. A violent encounter with a terrorist was child's play, but standing before a large crowd and reading her own words made her sick to her stomach. Sugar and chocolate helped.

"Are you all set?" she asked her son.

"I have been for the past ten minutes."

"Just checking."

He tilted his head in the way teenagers did when they were merely tolerating a person until they left.

"Fine. I'm leaving." She then told him for the tenth time to not leave the bookstore, to keep his laptop with him and to call Janet, her agent, or Meaghan, who should arrive any minute, if he needed anything during the sign-ing. He agreed.

Janet was in town to celebrate the impressive sales of Fiona's newest book and to coordinate Fiona's press tour. She'd dressed in a beige Chanel skirt and white silk blouse—every inch of her announced success. Her three-inch Jimmy Choo platform sandals alone cost more than all the shoes in Fiona's wardrobe. Fiona dressed a bit more casually in a white peasant blouse and jeans. She let her hair and makeup do the heavy work with her image. Red lipstick, perfectly styled platinum blond hair, colored and highlighted two days before, and red leather ankle boots to match her lipstick and nail polish.

Fiona continued to linger next to Matt until Janet tapped her on the shoulder and waved her along. "It's time." She paused and stared at Fiona's face. "Are you nervous? I've never seen you so distracted."

"I'm fine." Fiona didn't tell Janet about the break-in. Janet had a tendency to be overprotective and might have pulled the signing, disappointing both Fiona and her fans. For all her focus on making money, the woman never let a dollar come between her client's mental and physical well-being.

They headed to the back stairs and climbed. The chil-dren's section was on the second floor. A noisy place, but bright-colored and very nurturing. They headed up to the third floor where fiction in every genre was located along with seating for about fifty people. Early in Fiona's career, she'd done book readings to either empty rooms, bookstore staff or an occasional shopper. Her sudden success shocked her as much as it did her publisher. As she climbed higher up the stairs, a line of people twisted around the stairwell, blocking access to the third floor.

"These can't all be for me?"

Janet put her arm around her. "You're a hit. Not only are your readers loving your latest book, but they're discovering your earlier books as well."

Someone in line reached out to her and shouted, "Love your book. Bradley is the hottest hero you've ever written."

"Thanks." She waved and received a bunch more comments from people in line.

When she arrived at the top of the stairs, the room had so many people milling about, she could barely see a path to the microphone. One of the staff of the bookstore waved and directed customers into empty seats. Within minutes, the event was standing room only. For an undercover asset who had always worked behind the scenes, the attention was overwhelming—even more so considering the events a few nights ago. Someone had invaded her space and put her child at risk. She didn't take that threat lightly, but trying to corral Matt into this room and keeping him from leaving in the middle of her reading would be impossible. The best she could do was keep him in the same building in a public place where others could keep an eye on him.

The what-ifs dominated her thoughts again and a thousand scenarios interrupted her focus. The man who had been in her home had not been located. With zero idea about what he was specifically after, she had no idea about the threat level. A botched burglary tended to end at the house with no second attempt since the residents of the invaded space would increase their security. The burglar would just go on to another house. If she were the target, the intruder could show up here in the bookstore. Although that was unlikely with so many witnesses, she had to take everything into consideration.

She'd called Meaghan, who was already in downtown Boston, and would be there in under ten minutes. Fiona took a deep breath. It would all be okay.

The store manager walked to the microphone situated in front of a cozy armchair. "Welcome. We love having you all. Before we get started, can the people standing in front of the stairwell please move. Safety first. If there isn't enough room to see well, we have set up a simulcast in the coffee shop downstairs. I assure you, the author will stay until the last book is signed, so there's no need to worry about missing anything. So let's get started. Our guest today is the bestselling author of international thrillers with a touch of romance—Fiona Stirling. Her newest book, *Wake the Dead*, involves a sexy army officer who is presumed dead after a botched operation in South America. His wife has no idea that she's not a widow, and their second-chance romance melted my heart." The woman placed a hand on her chest and sighed deeply.

"In her former life, Fiona worked for the State Department and helped negotiate several international trade deals. Let's give a big welcome to Fiona Stirling."

The crowd cheered. Fiona waved. Instinctively, she scanned the crowd for anyone suspicious. Mostly women sat in the crowd, mostly relaxed, except for an intense woman talking on the phone in the northwest corner, but she seemed more likely annoyed with a spouse or a child. The manager went over to the woman and asked her to take her conversation outside. After a rolling of the eyes without receiving an ounce of support from the other customers, she finally left.

Fiona took a deep breath, thanked everyone for coming out and introduced her new novel. She read the opening pages with as much personality as she could muster, stopping at the point in the story where an older woman in a bar walks up to the hero and points a gun to his head. The audience visibly reacted to the abrupt ending, exactly as she wanted. They'd be more apt to buy the book if they couldn't wait to learn what happened next.

When she was done, she received a standing ovation. Janet stood to the side and gave her two thumbs-up.

Two staff members brought her to the table where she would conduct the book signing. A line formed in front of it. The signing was going to take hours to complete but she wanted to do it because she appreciated every last reader, despite her hostility toward small talk. Janet went to the back of the table and placed some decadent-looking drink in front of Fiona.

"I thought you could use an iced mocha latte."

"You thought right. Thanks." Fiona took a sip and let the sugar and caffeine motivate her to meet the roomful of readers. "If I've never told you before, I love you."

"Everyone does." She laughed. "You're doing great. Keep up your energy. There's just over a hundred people lined up, some with multiple books."

Fiona glanced at the first woman in line, a thirty-something-year-old holding her newest release and waiting patiently. When Fiona had started writing, her audience was mainly women who were forty and up, but as her books became more popular, her audience changed, or perhaps it expanded, to include a whole variety of new readers.

The exhaustion of the past week hit Fiona like a truck, but she would never let her fans down. She owed everything to them. She took another sip and waved to the woman. "Hi, what's your name?"

Two-and-a-half hours later, she was still smiling and still signing. There were only about a dozen people left. A young woman in a pink crop top and ripped jeans approached. She held a copy of *Wake the Dead* and an envelope.

"Can you sign my book *To Jessie*?" she asked.

"Sure." She signed the book and slid it back to her.

The woman handed her the envelope. Fiona had received lovely gifts from readers over the years so didn't think anything of it.

"Thank you."

"Oh, that's not from me. Some rando told me to give it to you. He said he couldn't wait." She thanked Fiona again and left with the signed novel.

Every nerve in Fiona's body fired. Without inviting the next reader over, she opened the envelope and read the note.

If you want to see your son again, leave right now and meet me at the Mercedes at the front door.

Jason couldn't risk being seen again, but he wanted to remain close enough to help. He'd rather blow his cover and save his wife and son than remain anonymous and not lift a finger to help them. Sure, he had a solid team—although one man short—that was on the job, and he trusted them, but the guilt that filled him over that bastard breaking into her house ran on repeat over and over in his head. He remained in the Expedition illegally parked a block from the bookstore. Inside the bookstore, Meaghan was watching over Matt, while Noah stood guard at the front door. Steve wandered about making sure nothing was out of the ordinary. No one would expect Steve to be anything other than a typical middle-aged Bostonian drinking Dunkin' and hanging out waiting for his wife to get her book signed inside. In reality, Steve's wife worked at city hall and helped the team get out of a lot of hot water as they protected their clients. He also had more skills than anyone gave him credit for. If something went down, Steve would jump in and handle it.

Fiona's book signing had passed the two-hour mark and Jason's patience faded. While part of him felt pride in what Fiona had done with her life, another part wanted the old Fiona back. The one who focused on two things: her work and her family. The work with the State Department offered her the ability to truly affect change in the world. Writing books would be satisfying, but being in the action had always been Jason's preferred place in the world, even one step removed from the military. He took a sip of coffee and froze. Fiona was walking outside. Her expression aloof.

"Noah, this is DJ. Is the signing over?" Jason radioed.

"There's only a few people left in line."

"Fiona is on the move. Do you see her?"

"I have her in my sight now. Damn, she's moving fast."

Fiona pushed through the glass front door, clutching

what looked like a card. Her hair so bright in the sun, it was impossible to miss her. Matt wasn't with her.

"Meaghan, do you have Matt?" Tall, elegant Meaghan Knight had been in law enforcement before joining Fresh Pond Security. After five years of watching guys getting promoted over her, she decided to step into a field where her skills would be better compensated. Her competence made every task better.

"Affirmative."

"Keep him with you. Something's up."

Had Fiona paused for a bit of fresh air after such a stressful event, Jason would have remained exactly where he was, but she strode over to a dark gray Mercedes and yanked open the back door as though she intended to rip the door off the hinges. A man who looked more like an overgrown teenager grabbed her arm and tried to pull her into the car. Her foot braced on the door frame, stopping him from an abduction. Jason jumped out of the Expedition and rushed to the car. Fiona wrestled back and forth trying to free her arm, until someone rushed up from behind her and kicked at her leg until it slid off the door frame, then they pushed her inside. The engine roared to life. When Jason arrived at the car, the door was locked. He could see Fiona struggling, so he punched out the window with his elbow and pulled his wife out through the broken glass, knowing she was getting cut up in the process. There was no other choice. Once the car was out of sight, he couldn't protect her from a much worse experience. He lifted her into his arms, blood dripping from her exposed skin.

Steve rushed to the car and pointed his gun to slow the car reversing, but it spun around, smashing into an

Outback parked on the side of the road. There were too many people in the area to take a chance with a stray bullet, so he lowered the weapon.

Son of a bitch. Jason had let her down again with a whole team surrounding her. Someone had targeted her and would be back, as guys this brazen did not give up. Jason had to gather his family and take them to safety as he should have done before. Not thinking, he carried her to the Expedition and then lowered her to her feet. In the rush to save her, he'd blown his cover wide open. She stared at him, her mouth open, her body frozen in place.

He'd imagined reuniting with her again, a scene filled with tears and warm embraces. Under these circumstances, however, there would be no warm embrace.

They had to leave. Once the police arrived, there'd be too many questions and more exposure for all of them.

"We need to get out of here." He held her by his side.

She pulled back. No tears either. Just laser beams coming from her eyes. "Not without Matt."

He glanced over at Noah, standing next to them. He gave Jason a thumbs-up and pointed inside. Matt was safe. "He's fine. Get in the car."

Twisting her shoulders, she fought for release. "No."

Noah made the mistake of trying to "save" her by shoving her into the back seat. She twisted his arm and flipped him onto his back on the hard asphalt. Steve took the easier way, pointing his weapon at her. His finger wasn't close to the trigger, but Jason wanted to rip his head off anyway for threatening her. His tactic worked, however. She slid into the back seat as he got behind the wheel. Before she could figure out that Steve and Noah weren't going with them, Jason drove off without turning around to look at her. He wasn't sure if they were being followed, so he headed to the Callahan Tunnel, circled around the airport twice, slipped through a secure area and then headed to one of the team's safe houses, the most secure place he could think of.

"Jason? What the hell is going on?" she said, her voice strained.

"I'm here to protect you."

Chapter 5

The whole world tumbled inside out, leaving Fiona unsure of the exact point reality twisted into her dreams. Her arm hurt from the man in the Mercedes yanking it so hard he nearly dislocated her shoulder. She would have worked herself free if the person behind her hadn't slammed her leg. Then there were the slivers of glass in her arm and back and a head wound where she hit the top of the door on the way in or out, she wasn't sure. She reached back and felt a decent-size welt. When she looked at her fingers, they were covered in blood.

"We can look at your injuries when we get you somewhere safe. You might have internal injuries, but the gash doesn't seem large. Head wounds bleed like stink generally."

"I know." She wasn't in the mood for her dead husband to mansplain combat wounds to her.

The self-defense moves she hadn't practiced in years were not exactly there when she needed them. So much for muscle memory. She blamed her pregnancy for twisting her muscles into new forms. One thing for certain, she'd never let those skills go stale again. Despite the possible head wound, the rescue injured her more than the initial kidnapping. Her blood leeched through the outfit she'd carefully picked out for the book signing. Being yanked through broken glass shredded her arms, her back and her blouse. Not that her own safety mattered. All she could think of was Matt. Perhaps he was still with Meaghan. She prayed he was.

She took in her situation. The note, the man in the car dressed in jeans and a gray hoodie and the man who kicked out her legs dressed in jeans and a T-shirt. Then there were the two men fighting off the kidnappers. And Jason.

Her husband.

Her dead husband.

Janet was a great agent, but even she couldn't manage this kind of a publicity stunt. Yet, what were the chances of Fiona writing about a husband coming back from the dead and here he was?

He turned his face partly toward her. There was scarring on his neck and up to his ear—his skin red and white and imperfect—that appeared to have occurred years ago. Her mind analyzed possible situations that would have caused such devastation, and her heart ached over his pain. The tight buzz cut he wore in the military had grown out, but that strong chin, chiseled cheekbones and square jawline in need of a shave were all Jason. She had not one moment of doubt. He was also the same man she'd seen in the hotel room next to hers only days before. The sight should have been a comfort, but something in his reappearance burned away her elation. For years, she'd been alone, caring for their child, holding Jason's love inside her heart. Yet, if this was indeed Jason, he hadn't been lost to her—he'd abandoned her. Left her alone. All the love in the world couldn't sweeten that fact.

She couldn't look at him anymore, giving her attention to the blur of city out the window instead. She'd missed him, cried over him and had memorialized him. His return should overload her with love and compassion, but she felt nothing but a burning pain in her body.

"Are you okay?" he asked, all business.

She stared at him. Was she okay? That was one stupid question. "Sure. I'm perfectly fine. My child is… I don't know where my son is or if he's safe and my dead husband has not only kidnapped me, but has decided to yank me through broken glass and had his friends force me into this SUV at gunpoint. It's a banner day. Oh, and let's not forget someone breaking into my home last week. Were you involved in that?"

"We arrived too late to help you."

"We?"

"My associates."

"There's a descriptive word. Let me guess, you found the redhead with the gun in South Boston hanging out with Whitey Bulger?"

Jason laughed, a sound that almost knocked Fiona from the seat. She'd heard him in her dreams, but over the years she must have changed his laugh a bit, because this laugh hit at her deepest memory of him. Strong, confident and fearless. "Steve's my partner. He's a bit rough around the edges, but he always gets the job done," he answered.

"And the younger guy?"

"Noah."

Noah. The name was too normal for her to hate him

entirely. A normal person with a normal life hanging out with her dead husband.

"He's a former intelligence analyst with some pretty solid surveillance and defense skills." Jason listed his qualities as though he were selling her a car.

"He looks like he lives in a coffee shop, trying to write the next Gatsby."

Jason laughed again. "His appearance lets him get inside places someone less refined wouldn't be able to go."

"Like my book signing." She reached down and pulled off her boots. If she needed to run, she had a better chance in bare feet.

"Why did you leave the bookstore?" Jason asked, his laughter gone, his expression serious.

She buried her emotions and fell back in time, when she was the investigator. Information was power and right now she was powerless. Perhaps he could fill in the gaps. "I received a note."

"What did it say?"

She read it out loud.

If you want to see your son again, leave right now and meet me at the Mercedes at the front door.

The fear that had hit her when she first read the note washed over her. "Are you sure he's safe?" she asked.

Jason nodded. "He was sitting with your neighbor in the cafe."

"How do you know my neighbor?"

"I know everything about you, Fi."

That little statement annoyed her, so she ignored it. "Who wrote the note and why?"

"That's the big question. I promise I won't leave until I make sure you and Matt are safe." The implication was that he'd leave them again. For some reason that angered her even more.

She grabbed a napkin from his console, pressed it over the sore spot on her head and shut her eyes. Everything hurt, especially the memories of her perfect husband. Every word he'd spoken to her about love and their future together had been a lie. Fiona wished she could return to her date with George. He wasn't anything to write home about, but he'd probably never faked his death and abandoned his family. Maybe he had. She couldn't trust anyone right now. The biggest question was why Jason had returned now.

"Were you spying on us?" she said, part question, part accusation, her mind functioning on stress and the iced mocha latte from Janet.

Jason looked over his shoulder at her. Those soft brown eyes had always melted her heart, but they'd have to burrow through the frost that had developed in the past few minutes. "You've been in my field of vision forever."

"That's screwed up. I believed in you, and now I don't know what to believe." She'd dreamed of having him back for years, but not like this. Her traitorous eyes teared up.

"You need to trust me." He reached for her hand. The heat of his touch scrambled her thoughts and for a brief second, she wanted him in the most indecent way possible.

She pulled away and let out a gruff laugh. "That would work if you hadn't lied to me for the past five years."

Jason pulled off the turnpike and drove another few miles until they arrived in a secluded location south of Natick. Fiona didn't recognize anything around her. He drove down a dirt road and ended up at a broken-down wooden shack that appeared to have existed at the time of the Revolutionary War—stone foundation, weather-faded white paint, a red door partially off the hinges.

"Nice place. You've done well for yourself." She wanted the contempt to shoot from her words, yet she'd spent the past five years praying her husband would come back to her. As much as he'd betrayed her, she couldn't hate him.

A car driven by Noah pulled up next to them. Matt was in the passenger seat. The sight of him eased most of her stress. With him safe, she could breathe. For years, she'd tried to shield him from life's dangers, but she'd never envisioned having to physically fight to protect him from real and dangerous threats. The thought terrified her.

He jumped out when the car stopped. "Mom!"

He hugged her, until she couldn't handle the pain. She kissed him on the cheek instead.

Matt stepped back, taking in the blood and cuts and bruises. "You need a hospital."

He was right, but she wasn't sure her tormentors wouldn't wait outside the ER and take her out there. She wouldn't die from these injuries if she cleaned them and rested a bit, although she might need a few stitches for the worst cuts from the glass. She tried to hold it together, but her dead husband had been resurrected and how was she going to explain that to Matt?

"I'll be okay. Just a flesh wound."

"So not funny."

"I'm fine," Fiona repeated.

Jason said something to Noah, then walked over to them.

She didn't have to worry about Matt being devastated by the chaos. He had a serious expression on and took in everything around him, especially the man who had the same shape and color eyes.

"Who are you?" Matt asked Jason, but she could tell from his expression he knew exactly who he was speaking to.

"I'm from a company hired to protect you and your mother." The deep timbre of his voice vibrated through Fiona's heart.

"Who hired you?" he asked.

"Classified."

"Who broke into our house?" Matt was relentless when he wanted an answer.

"A thug from Houston."

The answer shocked Fiona. The police never caught the man. How did Jason have that information?

"Why?" Matt asked, his question exactly the question Fiona wanted answered. *Why?*

Jason shrugged. "I don't know yet."

Matt stood nearly as tall as Jason. He stared him down. "Why should we trust you?"

"Maybe you shouldn't. Don't trust anyone. Follow your gut. If it says you're okay, you might be. But not always. Life sucks that way."

"Seriously?" Fiona interrupted. "'Don't trust anyone,' and 'life sucks' are your answers? That makes sense. Your whole existence is a lie." Her anger accelerated, until her voice boomed across the front yard. For a woman who prided herself on self-control, this was a low point. "Don't you dare think you can return on a whim and offer our son advice as though you had the right."

"Mom?" Matt stared at her as though she'd gone off the deep end. She had.

Jason put his hand up to quiet Matt. "Her comment is valid."

"Dad?" Matt finally asked, but he stepped back from him and crossed his arms over his chest.

Jason sighed. "I can explain everything. I need to get you two inside to safety, then we can talk."

"I thought it was you, but you were dead. They told us you were dead. I was at your memorial. An honor guard handed me a flag. It's in my bedroom. You were dead," he repeated, his voice trembling on the last "dead."

Fiona's anger swelled upon hearing her son's pain. Her life had revolved around protecting Matt after the loss of his father. That his biggest heartache arrived not at Jason's death but at his resurrection stabbed at her more than the shards of glass still stinging her.

Then she noticed Noah, who stood nearby taking in the scene. From his expression, he seemed to know Jason was related to her and Matt, but wasn't prepared for a family showdown.

"Sorry about the body slam," she said to him.

He smiled. "I let my guard down. Totally deserved it."

"You body-slammed him?" Matt asked.

"More like I pushed him down."

Noah laughed. "Sure, make it less impressive than it was."

Jason strode over to him, whispered something in his

ear, something about speaking to Steve, then he slapped him on the shoulder. "We'll catch up later."

"Your friend isn't staying?" she asked.

Jason looked at Noah walking back to his car. "He has a laundry list of issues to deal with."

"All related to the note?"

"Among other things."

After Noah drove away, Jason led Fiona and Matt to the front door. She checked on Matt again, but he wasn't looking for care and affection from anyone. He stayed several arm's lengths away from her, but followed Jason. His father had become a hero to him over the years. One of the good guys, fighting the good fight, lost to evil forces. Now he was back. After the scare at the house and the bookstore, Matt's emotions would be all over the place.

And she had no ability to soothe him while he was focused on his father. She looked at Jason too. He had the same intensity he had whenever he returned from the field. Whatever he'd been doing the past few years, it involved weapons and some motley crew of *associates*.

She'd worked in the gray areas of international relations and from what she'd researched on her husband, so had he. She'd found various foreign news reports about his death. A drug cartel threatening civil war in Colombia attacked a diplomatic mission from the United States. The United States vowed support for the government. But Jason had never been involved in diplomacy, at least not that he'd told her. As far as she knew, he'd never been one for embassy dinners and military parades. He'd preferred the shadow side of the government where any battles he'd been involved in ended up buried in one of a thousand locked file cabinets in a warehouse in Maryland. She'd known he participated in dangerous missions, especially when she found new scars on him as they made love. He'd always acted as though they were minor scrapes. It was all part of being married to him, and she trusted him to keep her and Matt safe, which he was currently doing. At least that was what she thought he was doing, although bringing them to the middle of nowhere would be a perfect place to off the family he never wanted. But that didn't feel right. Even Matt had turned from frosty toward him to fascinated in the fifty feet they walked to the front door.

Jason unlocked the door and stepped aside to let them in.

Matt went inside first. "Damn, this is like Tony Stark's house," he exclaimed.

"Language," Fiona warned him, but couldn't help but agree when she entered a space of white concrete walls with beige leather sofas, and a white marble kitchen with appliances that seemed to have come straight out of *Architectural Digest*. "What the hell?"

"Language, Mom," Matt said, his lips curving into a smile for the first time all day.

Jason leaned against the countertop. "It's a quiet place to work."

Fiona didn't believe him. Had he gone to the dark side and he was in hiding? It was the only thing that made sense. Perhaps he chose money over his family and now worked for the very people he'd spent his earlier years fighting.

When she'd first met him, he'd been a senior ROTC candidate about to embark on a military career. She'd been a graduate student struggling to find a career in a world that preferred men with Ivy League diplomas. They both had big ambitions, and despite frequent absences, soon their lives were incomplete without the other. He'd always made her feel as though she were the most important person in the world, and she'd loved his charm, his clear set of morals and his eye-watering good looks.

Everything had been perfect until he went on that final mission. It should have lasted three weeks, but something went wrong. When he died, his absence destroyed her. If it hadn't been for Matt, she wouldn't have rallied as quickly as she had. Instead of wallowing, she pushed through her grief to raise Matt into a man his father would be proud of.

Jason called her over to a stool at the kitchen island. Now that the immediate danger had subsided, the pain of her injuries roared to life. Wrestling the man in her house, being pulled into a car and then pulled out again through a broken window, as well as the intensity of flipping Noah onto his back, had taken a huge toll on her. Her muscles ached, her head hurt and scrapes and cuts covered her.

Jason rummaged through a cabinet and handed Matt a bag of microwave popcorn. "Can you make this? I'm starving."

Matt nodded and crossed the kitchen to the microwave.

"Want a drink?" he asked.

Matt twisted to face him. "A beer?"

"How about something age appropriate. Look in the fridge. I think there are a few cans of soda there, and then you can watch television while I speak to your mother."

Matt stalled and looked over at her. He bit his lip as he always did when he was unsure of his next move. He stepped toward her, but she waved him away.

"I'll be fine." She nodded until Matt released himself from his indecision and went to the refrigerator.

His concern melted her heart. Fiona had never pushed him to take on the responsibilities of being the man of the house, first, because she was more than capable of handling whatever came along, and also because she never wanted to throw that burden on him. Despite that, he often kept an eye on her, as protective of his only living family member as she was of him. If he had his father back, she had no idea how their relationship would change.

She waved her arm toward the television. "I need to talk to Jason and clean myself up. Can we talk later?"

"Okay." Matt sat down on the couch and turned the television on, far enough out of listening range if she wanted to speak to Jason alone.

Jason placed a large first aid kit next to her on the island. "What hurts?" he asked.

"Everything." She watched him take out alcohol, tape and gauze pads.

He lifted her chin, his face so close that the intoxicating scent of his breath brought her back to their early days, kissing for hours, just because. "You have a scratch on your temple, but it doesn't seem to have broken through the skin." He wiped it with the alcohol anyway.

She pulled back from the burn. "Holy shit."

"Language," he whispered as his thumb caressed her

cheek. "Let me see the damage to your arms and shoulders. It looks like more scratches than actual glass in your arm. The benefits of punching through tempered glass."

She nodded as if in a trance or a dream or a nightmare—she couldn't decide. Shrugging her shoulders out of her ripped blouse, she could feel a few glass splinters catching on the fabric. Without the tempered glass, the injuries would have been deeper and more potentially life-threatening. Instead, she'd ended up with some minor cuts and bruising. She'd be fine. The pain kept her from caring that she was sitting in front of him wearing only a bloody beige bra until his eyes stopped their clinical evaluation and stared at her with a far more carnal assessment.

"I can do this alone in the bathroom," she said, feeling self-conscious. "Do you have tweezers?"

"If I help you, it won't take long at all." He was already picking off the larger pieces with his fingers, and Fiona didn't bother stopping him. There was no way she could reach all of them.

"Maybe I should sneak into a small community hospital, just to get cleaned up," she said, thinking out loud.

"It wouldn't be as safe as here. Relax. We have all night to fix you up."

She glanced around. "This place is a contradiction. Broke on the outside, sophisticated on the inside. Or is it a metaphor for you?"

"I have it for business reasons."

"Business must be profitable." The realization that he was alive was still clouded by her years of grief, but the idea that he'd been out in the world working while she had no idea if he was dead or alive grated on her every last nerve.

"I get by."

He got by living like some superspy in a villain's lair. He could be a villain. She had no idea. He could have lied about their entire relationship all the way back to the beginning of their relationship. Had he even been in the military? Had he been in Colombia when he *died*? She shook her head. She'd done extensive research through government back channels, and according to the classified documents her friend had unearthed, he had been a part of the military and in an operation that went bad in South America. "I won't ask." She wanted to know specifics but didn't want to beg.

His fingers brushed over her shoulder, scraping over several splinters of glass. She sucked back a curse. He continued picking out the pieces and looking for more glass with not so much as an "I'm sorry."

"Ask me anything you want. I owe you an explanation, although to be honest, I never anticipated having to explain anything to you. I thought I'd lost you forever."

"You lost me?" She recoiled from that magnetic pull. She'd been broken for years now, and he was the one grieving?

"Can I help you first? You can crucify me later."

She nodded. "I'm already planning on it." She remained next to him. Love and hate must be identical twins. Her emotions swirled hot and cold like a typhoon. She'd never believed them to be an average couple. They'd had secrets from each other, but they'd also shared love and trust. Without trust, there could be nothing.

He bandaged a fairly long cut on her shoulder. The

incision went deep enough to make her wish he had sutures in his bag.

She swore in a half scream.

"Mom?" Matt looked back over the couch from the other side of the room, staring at her shoulders. He made a face and flinched. "You look bad."

"I'll be fine." She could see blood on a cloth Jason had dabbed her skin with.

"Can you go into the cabinet by the window and grab the bottle of whiskey and two glasses?" Jason asked Matt.

Fiona shook her head. "I'm fine." She didn't want to become alcohol impaired, especially when someone was after them.

"Trust me, this will feel better after a shot or two."

Matt came back with the whiskey and poured the first glass half-full.

"Whoa. Not that much," Fiona said.

"It's fine. I'll drink it. A little less for your mother." Jason placed his own glass next to the first aid kit and handed her the smaller portion. "Bottoms up."

She took it, anticipating a very rough afternoon. She drank a sip and set down the glass.

"I remember you, you know." Matt stood staring at his father.

"You should. You were eight years old when I left. It wasn't so long ago, was it?" Jason spoke with his usual confidence, but there was a cloud over his emotions. Regret maybe, with a side of wistfulness?

"It seems like forever. But I remember playing soccer with you in the backyard. I wasn't very good, but you kept playing with me anyway. I made the traveling team the year after you died. I think they felt bad for me."

"Not true. You have natural speed. A coach can't train that. If the coach were strategic, he would have placed you as a wing and fed you balls from the midfield, balls no one else could catch." He spoke as though he'd been there. And then Fiona bit back more anger. Had he been there? Standing shoulder to shoulder with the other parents, a ghost in her son's life.

In spite of Fiona's turmoil, Matt smiled at his father's words. "Yeah. He did. Maybe it wasn't just because you were gone."

"Don't question your abilities. You have so much going for you. Don't think I haven't kept my eye on you over the years. I couldn't help it. You're my kid. I love you enough to blow up our lives to keep you and your mother safe," he admitted.

Matt's brows lifted. "What do you mean? Mom told me you died in an attack."

"That was what everyone believed. Some bad men wanted what I was delivering. During a fire fight, the cartel leader's son died, then everyone I was with. I only survived because I passed out in a bush and remained hidden until some really nice people took me to the hospital. The cartel leader wanted revenge for his son, but you can't get revenge on the dead. If he knew I was alive, he'd go after my family. I didn't want that to happen."

"Is that who broke into the house last night?" Matt asked.

"I'm not sure, but I'm trying to find out."

"If everyone thinks you're dead, why are they after Mom and me now?"

"I'm not sure about that either, but I hope to get some answers real soon."

Fiona sipped on the whiskey and took in all he said. Someone wanted him dead. And his family. The tension in her chest lifted. Not entirely, but enough to allow her to breathe easier and focus on the man next to her. Maybe he wasn't the monster she'd created in her mind over the past hour or so.

She glanced around the house. Sepia-toned landscapes framed on the walls gave nothing away about his personal life. Not one family photo, not one souvenir from his travels, not one reference to his military career. It was as if he'd stripped his life of any color or life and was merely existing.

"What happens after you fix me up?" she asked. She was asking about tonight and tomorrow and next week and next year.

"I leave you here while I figure out why someone is after you."

Staying here with him was one thing, but remaining in the middle of nowhere alone was not happening. "You're kidnapping us?"

He frowned. "You're more than free to return home and wait for the guys in the car to return with backup."

He had a point. This place had to be better than her house. She couldn't imagine sleeping there while people who had tried to hurt her and her son were still at large.

"What about the man who broke into my house?" she asked.

"He won't bother you anymore."

"You took him out?" Matt's voice rose in excitement.

"He's safely put away until I can figure out what he wanted with you." Jason stood and went to the refrigerator.

Fiona shook her head. "We'll need to inform the police of what's going on."

"No. That would get the press involved and that's the last thing you need. We took care to minimize the burglary and the attempted kidnapping last week. It's for the best."

"Awesome." Matt had those hero-worship eyes that might get betrayed someday.

"No, not awesome." She paused. Jason not only knew where she lived, but he'd been in her house before the police. "Did you take the rest of my lasagna?"

Despite his best effort, his eyes smiled back at her. "That's classified."

Chapter 6

Jason set up an Epsom salt bath for Fiona to ease the smallest of the slivers out of her skin. He'd take care of his own injuries later.

Matt sat in the living room on the large leather couch, eating popcorn and drinking his way through all the soda in the refrigerator. Jason turned on *Die Hard* for him, a classic movie Fiona had never bothered to show him. Jason would never complain about her parenting skills since he'd left her to raise Matt on her own, despite her making helicopter parenting her chosen religion. No doubt he was half to blame. Her parents had both died within a few years of Matt's birth, and when he disappeared, she was completely alone. Losing so much family would set someone up to protect their remaining loved ones with everything they could.

Matt hadn't been allowed to play football like Jason had done in high school. Instead, he played soccer. Fiona had made the right decision. Matt had speed, but not a lot of bulk. He'd be flattened on a football field. Jason had shown up a few times to Matt's games, disguised, of course, to watch him. His son could outrun anyone on the field and had agility and a fantastic right cross.

Fiona would sit on the sidelines in a fold-up red chair with her designer travel mug steaming hot, no matter what the weather. Far too many of the fathers kept their eyes on the Marilyn Monroe of soccer moms. Yet, she never once flirted back. She'd remained focused on Matt and her career and the ghost of her husband. A shroud of guilt wafted through the room and threatened to obliterate him. If he'd found any other way to handle the mess he'd been thrust into, he might have been able to spend every morning at breakfast with his son and every night in bed with his wife. He drank a bit more, just to cut the pain of her not loving him now that he'd returned.

Fiona emerged from the bath an hour later. She came over to the couch dressed in Jason's oversize sweatpants and a T-shirt. Not since she'd dressed in a maid costume for one of their anniversaries had she ever looked so sexy. Perhaps it was five years without being close to a woman or his new proximity to her, but he downed the rest of his whiskey and tried to cool the intensity of his desire for her. His body didn't give a rat's ass about anything but feeling her in his arms again. His heart refused to get close to her when he'd have to disappear for their protection, but then wavered when she looked his way. His head warned him to keep his distance because his body and heart were way too untrustworthy in this situation.

She strode up to him, inches from his lips, her breath sweet and so inviting. After a long sigh that hypnotized him, she shook her head. "I honestly hate you right now. We needed rescuing because you couldn't be bothered to give me a heads-up on some lunatic who wanted to kill your family. I don't know whether to thank you for helping us from something you didn't prepare us for or slap you in the face." The words threw a bucket of ice water over his burning passion.

"Slap away," Jason replied, his chest aching. "I thought I was protecting you by keeping you from the reality of what had happened in Colombia. I was wrong. I should have trusted you."

Her expression fell as she shook her head, then she turned to Matt. "Do you need anything else to eat?"

"Pizza," he said, his eyes not leaving the screen as McClane watched his wife being taken hostage.

Fiona wasn't drawn into the movie at all. "Pizza? We shouldn't leave the house."

Jason's stomach growled. He respected McClane and his focus on doing the right thing no matter the cost. He'd lived the previous five years believing he was doing the right thing for the right reasons, but maybe it wasn't a matter of right and wrong. He did what he had to in order to protect his family and even if another way was better, it was the only path Jason had known to take. A simple solution to a complex problem.

The guilt of his absence in his son's life made him want to spoil Matt. He'd been through enough. "It's fine. I can arrange a delivery."

"You trust someone coming here?"

"I was going to ask Steve to come. He could bring pizza and we could strategize a solution."

"I guess," Matt said, pausing the television. "You trust him?"

Jason nodded.

"More than us?" The question was a valid one, but

he hadn't trusted Steve with his secrets either. He hadn't trusted anyone.

"The difference is that I can't live with the thought of you in harm's way. I care so much for you, I'm willing to sacrifice a perfect life with my family to keep you all safe. He's in a job that has inherent risk. It's what we do." Fiona and Matt shouldn't have to dodge bullets or run from kidnappers. Not because of him.

Matt stared at his father and pondered what he'd said for a minute and sighed. "I guess that makes sense," he said without any conviction.

Jason wanted his son to understand him, to respect him, but lying for five years wasn't a strong base for building such a relationship. They were strangers right now and their relationship wouldn't be repaired in the next few hours. In the middle of this chaos, he didn't have time to forge quality connections. Not if he wanted to keep Matt and Fiona alive. He had to figure out what was going on. He had to find out if Porras was involved.

Matt turned back to the television. *Yippee Ki Yay.*

Fiona waved Jason over to the bathroom. When he arrived, she closed the door for privacy. "Is this Steve guy really trustworthy?"

"He worked for the FBI as an undercover agent at a pharmaceutical company, then moved into the accounting department of an oil company. He left the service before his cover was blown. He seems like an open book but it's all a smokescreen to keep you from knowing anything about him." Steve was goofy enough to get under the skin of most people, which made people open up about things they shouldn't speak about with him. He was the best of the best in his former life and the FBI still used the information he acquired from his assignments.

"That's all well and good, but can he keep a group of bad guys away from us?"

"He's deadly serious when he needs to be. Matt will love him. You may want to kill him after a few hours. He's not your type."

"He isn't?"

"No." Jason was her type. After watching the disaster date she'd had a few nights before, he was even more sure of it. Another part of his subterfuge he'd done wrong was to overly monitor Fiona in her private life. She had every right to find someone new, someone with whom she could create a full life. He didn't have the right to limit her in any way, despite how much it killed him to see her with anyone else.

"You don't know anything about me anymore, even if you have been stalking my movements over the past five years. Now if you'll excuse me." She walked toward him, backing him out of the room.

He didn't move. She stopped when she reached his chest. The scent of the antiseptic he'd placed on her skin stung his nostrils, reminding him of the medical reasons for stepping back. But he'd been dreaming of being this close to her, and the temptation ached inside him. "You're more beautiful than ever."

She lifted her chin, her body leaning into him. "And you lied to me."

An emotional and physical torture he deserved. And until she believed he'd acted in their best interests, he had to keep his distance. "I didn't lie, I omitted."

"The memorial bench with your name on it says otherwise." She placed a hand on his shoulder and leaned towards him, her breath caressing his neck. "Why do you think these guys have something to do with the cartel?"

"Because you told my enemy exactly what he wanted to believe."

"What was that?"

"That I'm still alive."

She shoved him back into the hall. "What are you talking about? I didn't say a word."

But she had. The entire plot of her book was about a soldier on a secret mission in South America who pretended to be dead to protect his wife and two daughters. A bit too close to the facts of their situation to be a coincidence.

"How did you get details of the mission? It was all classified." He knew she had secrets of her own, connections in the government that rivaled his, but she'd never spoken about it.

Her face paled. "It was a story. I made it all up."

"You thought I was dead, and so did everyone else until you wrote a story so close to what happened that people who know something about this may now question if I am indeed alive or not. You still use your contacts, don't you?"

She kept her expression neutral. "That's classified… But I never suspected you were still alive. It was more like wishful thinking." After a moment, she looked at the floor. "I'm sorry, but I filled the holes with a story that healed my heart. There was nothing I learned from official records that gave me any hope you were still alive. Actually, you shouldn't be blaming me at all for something I couldn't have known without you confiding in me. And apparently, I wasn't trustworthy enough for you to give me the truth." She shifted around him and went into the bedroom.

The chance of them rekindling anything seemed like a long shot, so he had to get more serious about keeping them safe. He'd given away his right to a family when he'd decided to hide away.

He checked on Matt, fast asleep on the couch. He needed the rest after so much action. Jason turned the volume down and went to his office.

Finally alone, he cleaned up the abrasions he could reach on his shoulder and then called his team to update them. Steve, Meaghan and Noah appeared on the screen in front of him. Each one had worked extralong shifts over the past week, loyalty he didn't deserve for dragging them into this.

They'd all placed their lives in his hands to join him in a dangerous business. He'd broken their trust. Because of everything that had happened at the bookstore, Jason hadn't had time to tell Meaghan the truth in person. Steve had had to fill her in. From the look on her face, she hadn't taken it well, but at least she was still there and hadn't left like Finn had.

"Thanks to you guys for acting so fast. Fiona and Matt are at the safe house doing well. Fiona has some scratches but nothing life-threatening." Jason waited for a response, but none came. "You guys have every right to be annoyed with me. I was protecting my family, but by not sharing my secret with you, I put everyone at risk. I promise to make it up to you."

"I have so many issues with what you did," Meaghan said. "You need a course in leadership, because keeping such important facts from us hindered us at our job. You owe a huge apology to your family as well. Fiona has become more than an assignment. I value her as a friend. You should have trusted her too."

Jason nodded. "Hindsight is twenty-twenty." He wouldn't deny that he had to earn the trust of everyone at Fresh Pond Security all over again. "But if I had to do it all again, I would have trusted all of you."

Steve interrupted his apology. "Now that your *mea culpas* are done, I located the owner of the car at the bookstore. It was rented to a Federated Security corporate account. Hopefully, they paid for collision damage. Not that they couldn't afford paying for the window you smashed. Federated is one of the best-paying gigs in the field."

"Looking for a new job?" Jason asked, confident Steve would never leave Fresh Pond Security.

"To be fair, the pay here could be better," Steve said, always on the team's side. "We're practically a nonprofit. While we have some higher paying gigs, helping those who can't help themselves is not lucrative. Sure, I go home every night thinking I assisted someone who needed it, but is it enough? The hired thugs at Federated Security have a nice bank account and probably drive something like a Porsche 911. I'm just not sure how they sleep at night."

"Probably on really high-thread-count sheets," Meaghan said.

Steve agreed, but his smile fell as he added, "Once you enter into a job with someone as unscrupulous as Federated, you can never leave—and my freedom is not for sale."

"Exactly," Noah said. "My plan is to retire to the Caribbean in a few years and never pick up a snow shovel again."

"I hope that's a reality for all of us. It's that relentless show of violence and their unlimited resources that are our biggest problems. The question is whether we can keep Fiona and Matt safe until we cut the head off the cartel," Jason pondered out loud.

"Figuratively?" Meaghan asked, glancing back at the samurai sword mounted on the wall behind her.

"Whatever it takes." Jason needed to eat something and rest, as his mind had clouded over with everything that had happened. "Noah, you need a break. Take the next eight hours and get some sleep."

"Sounds good to me." He signed off, leaving Jason, Steve and Meaghan.

"What about me? Should I come over and speak with Fiona?" Meaghan asked.

Jason thought it over. At this point, he didn't want to upset Fiona over another betrayal until she had time to come to terms with her current situation. "Let's wait on that. She's already pissed off at me. Once she settles into her new reality, you can come in and throw me under the bus."

"You should have told both of us."

"I know, but I can only beat myself up so long. We have an active case and pointing fingers won't do a damn thing to keep any of us safer."

She leaned back in her chair and tented her fingers. "I deserve a raise."

"We'll talk about it after."

"That's a shitty negotiating tactic. I heard Finn left.

You're down a man. As the only female in this ensemble, I'm very much needed at this time."

Steve, a man who understood people better than Jason would, leaned toward the screen. "I think your bonus should go to the team."

Everyone on the team made a percentage of the profits at the year-end. This year was their biggest yet, and Jason and Steve would take the biggest share. "Agreed. I put everyone at risk—they deserve a piece of my skin. I'll even send Finn his percentage."

Meaghan smiled. "That seems more than fair, but that's not an increase in salary. So let's meet up after we make sure Fiona and Matt are safe and discuss how much more I'm worth."

He laughed. Meaghan knew her worth and had already negotiated one of the highest salaries of any of the employees, but she had a point. Without her, they wouldn't have a woman for assignments and that was bad business. "It's a deal."

She waved once and signed off.

Steve lingered, his chill disappearing. He'd never chewed Jason out over his bad decision, but he let him know that he had to be straight with everyone forever. Not that Jason planned on continuing his lies. For all his preparation and layers of security, his plan sucked. Had he worked on it with even one trusted colleague, he would have had a solution that didn't involve losing his wife and son.

"You look exhausted," he said.

Jason shrugged. Sleep wouldn't protect Fiona or Matt or the team. He had to understand what they were up against. "I'm good."

"Good to know. I just want it understood that it's your bonus we're talking about. I have to pay for two kids in college."

Jason couldn't argue. He'd put the whole firm's future at risk through his actions. "My secret, my responsibility."

"Agreed. Do you need me to relieve you?"

"That would be great. Can you pick up a few pizzas on the drive over?"

Steve nodded. "Sure, but I pick the toppings. What's your son like. I'll get his favorite too."

"Pepperoni."

"I'm on it."

Jason hung up the phone and rubbed a hand over his head. If Federated Security was somehow linked to Porras, it was only a matter of time before they located Jason and his family.

Chapter 7

The salt bath helped to release most of the slivers of glass out of Fiona's skin and made her far more exhausted than she wanted to be. Although the time said one in the morning, it was still yesterday to her, a day that would not end. She wouldn't sleep for hours, not when danger pricked at her senses. The safeguards her resurrected husband had infused throughout this place only made her more aware of the people after her and her son.

She checked on Matt. He'd curled under a fleece blanket, his socks sticking out of the end. He'd always been tall, like his father, and was wearing one of Jason's old Bruins T-shirts. The yellow shirt fit him almost perfectly, although not entirely in the shoulders, not yet anyway. His breathing seemed steady enough, but the nightmare of that note saying they'd kidnapped him had burned into her memories. If this was all because of Jason, she might never be able to forgive him for placing them in such danger.

She rummaged through the kitchen to find a few crackers and a bottle of wine, but then changed her mind. More alcohol would muddle her thoughts. It wasn't the time to numb her senses. She filled a tall glass with water from the faucet and sat at the kitchen table to go over her situation.

Jason had always been involved in risky operations. Most of the time he couldn't tell her about his job except through vague references and murky descriptions, but surviving a massacre and then "killing himself" with government approval was something else.

A knock on the front door set her guard up again. She started toward the door wishing she had a weapon, but Jason appeared in clean clothes behind her, holding a handgun—from the look of it, some version of a Glock, most likely a 19 or 22. He waved her back and looked out the peephole. The barrel of the gun aimed toward the floor as he opened it wide.

Steve stood in the doorway, three large boxes of pizza in hand. "That will be sixty-five dollars, plus tip if you're feeling generous."

Jason waved him inside. "I'll Venmo you." He pointed to Matt. "It seems like Matt might eat it cold tomorrow."

"The best way." Steve walked to the kitchen island and placed the boxes down. Turning to Fiona, he put out his hand. "I'm Steve Wilson. Nice to meet you under calmer circumstances, Fiona."

She shook his hand, then laughed when Steve looked down for a monetary tip and feigned a frown. "Nice to meet you. I hear you had the luxury of sharing Jason's life these past years." She regretted the bitterness immediately, but the pain that scorched through her wasn't something she could put aside so easily.

Steve nodded, his silent acknowledgment making it easier to like him. "I swear, if I had known of his idiotic plan, I would have driven him to your house personally and thrown him onto your doorstep." He seemed like the type of person to do just that.

"I appreciate your unearned loyalty."

"It's not really about loyalty—it's about doing what's right. Jason took a shortcut, but shortcuts don't always have safeguards built in." Steve went over to the coffee maker to make a pot of coffee. "My recommendation for you two is to get a decent night's sleep so we can hit the ground hard tomorrow."

"I'm not really tired," she replied. Her mind spun through a thousand scenarios for the next day and none of them would create any peace of mind.

"Go ahead, take the bedroom. I'll sleep on a chair in the family room." Jason pointed to an overstuffed chair across from Matt's spot on the couch.

She trusted him, and she trusted Steve, but she wouldn't sleep unless she was near Matt. "I'll stay here. You go and rest in the bedroom."

Jason hesitated until Steve made a gesture for him to leave. So he did. At least he listened to someone. He went into the bedroom, but didn't close the door.

Steve sat at the island and grabbed a slice of pizza. "Want a piece? There's pineapple and green pepper, plain cheese, and pepperoni."

"The last one is Matt's favorite."

"That's what Jason said." Steve bit into a slice of the pineapple and green pepper.

His comment made her pause. What exactly did Jason know about them? Did he have them followed, did he break into their computers or stalk them on social media? The thought of having someone observe her so closely gave her the creeps, even if it had been someone she'd loved once. They'd kept the specifics of their jobs from each other, but then he hid the biggest part of him away from her—his entire existence. The strange thing was that until she saw him, she'd loved him so passionately no one came close to luring her into another relationship. Had she only hated him for a few hours?

"Has he been watching over us all these years?" she asked Steve.

"That's a conversation between the two of you, and if you don't receive satisfactory answers, I promise I'll fill in the gaps. Although I don't agree with the way he went about everything, I trust that he never wanted to hurt you. He deserves the chance to clear the air with you and Matt before someone like me stirs up trouble."

The way he spoke about Jason, Fiona could sense the affection he had for him. For some reason, that made her feel a bit more comfortable with him. Jason didn't trust many people—he never had—but if he trusted Steve, Fiona would too.

"I can say that I was very impressed with the way you handled yourself at both the break-in and the attempted kidnapping. You beat the hell out of Harper. Made our job all the easier."

"Harper?" Fiona asked.

"The man who attacked you in your house. Robert Harper."

More information not handed over to her. She had to treat this whole chaotic mess like an assignment gone wrong. Something she alone could fix, because without all the information, she and Matt continued to be at risk, and she didn't have confidence that anyone else could protect Matt and herself as well as she could. That said,

she'd blown it at the bookstore. Unprepared and acting
on emotion instead of logic. She replayed the events in
her mind: the overwhelmingness of the crowds, the inability to watch Matt and the panic when she thought
he'd been taken. Every decision she made was reactive,
which put her at a disadvantage. She'd even set herself
up to be kidnapped by the men at the car, because she
panicked. That's something she'd never have done in
her prior life.

Self-pity wouldn't solve her problems. Matt's safety
had to be her priority. She took a deep breath and cen-
tered herself. Perhaps she should call in some favors
from powerful players in the government, not relying
so much on Jason. Steve admitted they were supposed
to watch out for her family and had failed.

She shook her head. "I'm glad your job was easier
because I was able to put my own life on the line to protect Matt."

"It's not like that at all. I regret arriving so late."

"Late, but before the police." She wasn't going to ask
how they were monitoring her house. It would add to
her annoyance and she had to rest. She could question
her former husband in the morning. Or was he her current husband? Can a person come back from the dead
and remain married? The circular thoughts gave her a
headache.

The aroma of pizza—melted cheese, tangy sauce and
a crust baked into a golden color—filled the kitchen. The
atmosphere of the room, however, was far from relaxed.

From the living room, Matt's breathing was even and
deep. Every so often, a muffled sigh would drift into
the kitchen, hinting at the stress of the past few days.

She grabbed a slice of cheese pizza and pushed forward with her information-gathering. "So who is Robert Harper?"

Steve hesitated, but she could pull information out of anyone if she wanted to. In this case, she used simple guilt.

She picked up her water and took a sip. "Steve," she began, her voice low, "why was Harper inside my house?"

"We're still looking into it." He focused his attention on the pizza.

"Bullshit."

He met her piercing gaze with a wall of emotional barriers. "Look, Fiona, it's…complicated."

She had all night. She wasn't going to stop until she had some answers she could use to protect them. She leaned in. "Try me. Or was all that 'I'll fill in the gaps on what Jason doesn't say' just a means to placate me."

"The truth is, we know Harper is employed by Federated Security out of Texas. They're a private security team that works for people that prefer living under the radar. We don't know who hired them yet." He was telling the truth, but skipping over something large enough to make him avoid eye contact with her.

"Sounds like you're at a dead end. Or maybe you have a hunch, but it's not confirmed. I'd love to know what that is."

"A hunch? There are so many things to consider. The analysis could take weeks."

"Jason already gave me your background, so don't play dumb. Maybe you, Jason, and your team should explain your part in breaking into my house and cleaning up a crime scene to the police. Trespassing is not a great look for a security guard, or are you a private investigator or are you as corrupt as Federated Security?"

Steve sighed. "You write too many thriller novels."

She'd heard every joke available about her writing. He wanted her to back down. She wouldn't. "You have more information. I need to know who you think is leading this operation." Her voice rose.

"It's no great secret. We don't know."

He needed a kick in the pants to get him talking. She took a bite of the pizza and savored the flavor as she thought through what she knew. This was all related to Jason pretending to be dead. This was Jason protecting them from an attack that not even his security firm could anticipate. Then she walked Steve through it. "Let me try to understand. If you had to guess where these attacks are coming from, I bet your guess would relate to Jason's time in Colombia. Which would mean it was related to whatever happened there. Which would mean that some large-scale drug cartel is involved. Which would mean the resources available to kill me and Matt are endless."

Steve glanced at the open bedroom door. "We haven't been able to connect the two."

"What do you know about the intruder?"

He shrugged. "The intruder is just a hired hand for a bigger fish. From all the information we've gathered so far, everything circles back to his employer, Federated Security. What we can't do yet is link him to Andres Porras."

Fiona frowned, searching her memory. "Why does that name sound familiar?"

"Andres Porras runs a large cartel. Its influence is global and he has the money to make anything he wants happen. From what Jason told me—and it wasn't much—five years ago, he was involved in an operation in Colombia. There was a skirmish, and in the chaos, Porras's son was killed."

Fiona's eyes widened in realization. "So, you're telling me that after all these years, Andres Porras, a man who caused the death of all those soldiers and a bunch of his own men because he's a greedy bastard, is back for revenge?"

"From what Jason told us, Porras lost his son on the day of the ambush. Even if Jason didn't pull the trigger, he's the only one left to blame. If we can link Federated Security to the cartel, we'd know the source of the threats."

The weight of the revelation bore down on Fiona. The loss of a child. A son he sent to battle at a far-too-young age to a fight he couldn't win. A cold fury simmered within her. "So my family might be the target for that man's twisted vendetta? A tiny detail Jason should have shared with me years ago."

"Nothing's proven yet. The intruder might be part of something completely unrelated." Jason came into the kitchen, his hair tousled, eyes a tempest of emotions, growing darker as he stepped closer to them. He stood next to Steve, but focused solely on Fiona. "And yes, I was wrong to keep everything from you. I was stupid. I should have come clean. But I'm here now, and I'm terrified that I've made the biggest mistake of my life. I promise I'll make it up to you. Somehow."

Seeing the only man she'd ever loved fall apart weakened her own anger toward him. She understood his reasoning, but under the same circumstances, she'd have trusted him with the information. "I'm not going to circle back to your deception. There's too much at stake to think about why you did what you did, but I will not be excluded from your plans anymore. Promise me."

Steve said nothing. He waited for Jason's response.

Jason, his eyes red and in need of sleep, nodded. "I promise."

Satisfied, she drank the rest of her water and stood. So many questions needed to be answered, so much preparation she had to do to protect Matt.

Steve pointed her to the bedroom. "Go. You need to be in top form tomorrow and sleeping half-upright won't be beneficial."

She didn't want to displace Jason. He seemed beyond exhausted. "I'll split the bed with you, but you stay on your side."

Jason brushed his fingers through his long hair. It might take a while to get used to his new look, but time together was something she'd wanted since he was declared missing. "I can do that."

She turned back to Steve. "Stay awake and don't blink longer than necessary. Matt needs someone alert enough to protect him."

This made Steve smile. "Yes, ma'am."

Chapter 8

After five years apart from his wife, Jason woke up to her in his arms. Somehow, over the course of the night, their bodies merged into a single, comforting embrace. A position that was both familiar and felt a lifetime away. Jason lay behind her, his arm draped around her waist. His chest pressed gently against her back, their heartbeats syncing as though finally set to the perfect rhythm. Fiona, cradled within his body, leaned her head back slightly, finding a restful place tucked into his shoulder. Her hand rested atop his, fingers entwined. Jason loved how her long, elegant fingers curved toward his, linking herself to him. Their legs tangled gently, feet brushing against one another. The warmth of her body kept him frozen in place. He'd missed her so much.

The guilt threatened to wash over him again. He should let her go, so she could wake easier and not in such an intimate position. He should. In one more minute. Just a minute where he could remember all he'd lost. All of this warmth, trust and closeness; a shared moment of vulnerability and contentment.

He could feel her wake. She turned her head and blinked her eyes open. There was no fear or anger in their expression. She remained completely still, as though she too wanted to stay in this spot forever.

But he'd promised honesty and no deception. This felt deceptive, even if they'd unconsciously bonded in their sleep. He lifted his arm and turned away from her. The chill of the air made the emptiness inside him form into a larger void. "I'm sorry. I should have put pillows between us."

She stretched her arms over her head and turned toward him.

The room felt heavy with unsaid words as Jason looked into Fiona's eyes, seeking a glimpse into her thoughts.

She inhaled deeply. "My mind is a mess when it comes to you," she whispered, emotion evident in her voice. "It's haunted by the past, by memories, doubts and what-ifs. But my body? It recalls a simpler truth."

Jason's gaze held steady, absorbing every word. Each syllable echoed with the resonance of their shared history.

"Both of our bodies," she continued, her fingers tracing a faint scar on his cheek, "remember the connection, the intimacy, the feeling of being one. They don't dwell on the past mistakes and misunderstandings like our minds do."

A soft, rueful smile tugged at Jason's lips. "I feel that too, Fi, as if we're two pieces of a puzzle, perfectly fitting."

She leaned closer, the warmth of her breath caressing his face. "Perhaps we should listen to what our bodies have been trying to tell us. They crave that closeness, that unmistakable bond. I've been without love for such a long time."

He had too. Five years and countless hours staring at his wife mere yards away from him but untouchable.

Time stood still as they considered the implications of their shared longing. With a mutual, unspoken agreement, they both leaned in, guided by the visceral pull that their hearts and bodies never forgot.

His mouth covered hers in a hard kiss, five years of pent-up energy. His tongue caressed her lower lip, and she opened to him. The graduate student he'd kissed in the back of his Oldsmobile for the first time, the beauty he begged to marry him, the bride who took his breath away, the woman who kissed him the night their son was born, the mother who stood holding their young child on the night he left for the last time—he kissed every single one of them. She returned the kiss with the desire of a widow of five years finally back with the man she'd lost.

Their bodies remembered much more than their sleep position. As the sun crept into the spacious bedroom, Jason and Fiona explored old memories, new scars, and experienced feelings so intense they shattered the pain that had encased their hearts.

Fiona's eyelids fluttered open at the soft rays of the morning sun. The weight of the previous night's events pressed down on her chest, heavier than the toned arm that draped over her. Beside her, Jason breathed steadily, his chest rising and falling in a deep sleep. She traced the lines of his face with her index finger, her touch tentative. He was a ghost in her presence and she didn't want to either wake from this dream or have him vanish again.

Memories from the night before flooded her mind. The gentle caress of Jason's fingers, the passionate kisses, the entwining of their bodies. But the euphoria sat side by side with a pang of guilt. Although Jason had been gone—dead, she thought—he'd lied to her and placed her and Matt at risk. Instead of keeping him an arm's-length away from her, she fell into his arms without a moment's thought as to the repercussions for her and Matt. She had zero understanding of how he'd survived, how he hid his presence in the same city and the nature of his new business. For all Steve was a bundle of friendliness, she had no idea about his real background except for what Jason had told her.

Tears pricked her eyes as the most painful memories flooded back—the day she found out he had died, the agony of losing him and the years she had spent grieving, not to mention their son's pain. Yet, she couldn't deny that her attraction and love for him had never died. They had reconnected, reignited a passion that she thought was lost forever, a love she thought she had buried alongside her grief.

But even as the bittersweet reunion cast a warm light into her life, the reality of their situation set her more rational side into overdrive. Someone wanted to harm her family. If it was the Porras cartel, they would not stop until the leader found restitution for the death of his son. That could result in Jason's death or Matt's or her own. Or all of them. The danger they were in was very real.

The weight of Jason's arm now felt suffocating. She carefully slid out of bed, found her clothes and tiptoed to the window. Peering through the curtains, she scanned the surroundings. This place was isolated, but with her own knowledge of such organizations, she understood that no place on earth would be isolated enough to protect them. They had to leave and soon. A plan formed in her mind. They needed to disappear, change their identities and keep Matt safe.

Behind her, Jason stirred. "Fi?" he murmured, voice groggy with sleep, his piercing gaze meeting hers. There was a moment of unspoken understanding, a shared regret over lost time and stolen moments. Before either could speak, a loud banging sounded from the main living area.

"Mom? Dad?" Matt's voice called out, panic evident.

Jason reached for his weapon and was on his feet in seconds. His face darkened. "Steve?" he yelled as he rushed back into the kitchen, pulling his pants back on.

She followed him, her thoughts racing. She should never have left Matt alone.

Without a word, Steve reached for a remote, flipping on access to the security cameras surrounding the house. The living room's large screen displayed the outside. Bathed in the increasing light of the morning, Noah, the man she'd flipped to the ground at the bookstore, was at the door, carrying doughnuts, his car parked a few meters away.

"It's Noah," Steve said.

Jason dropped his gun to his side. Matt, however, remained standing and staring at the television.

The interruption to an otherwise quiet morning made Fiona's spine prickle with unease. Her eyes darted between Jason and Steve, the two men engrossed in whispered conversation. Again, she was an outsider and in this situation, she did not feel comfortable trusting anyone else in the room with Matt's safety, except maybe Jason, but full trust hadn't returned. There were too many questions that needed to be answered and one night of mind-blowing sex wasn't enough to get over that.

She cleared her throat, interrupting them. "We should leave. This place is too isolated."

Jason, her formerly dead husband, gave her a reassuring smile. "We chose this place precisely because it's isolated. We're safe here."

Steve, ever the mediator, nodded in agreement. "This farmhouse is secure, Fiona. It has a hundred fail-safes. No one gets on the property without us knowing."

"You didn't seem to know Noah had arrived."

He lifted his phone showing the same camera angles that were on the television screen. "I had prior knowledge, which was why I didn't come rushing around with a gun in my hand. I turned on the large screen for you."

Jason made a face, one that said a lot about where his head was. Terrified for Matt. He didn't think, because Fiona would bet all the money in her investment account that he had access to the same information on his own phone. That lack of focus would get them all killed.

"Trust us," Steve added. "We're not rookies."

Fiona clenched her fists, her former operative instincts flaring. "Trust? That's what got us here in the first place. You have no idea who we are up against. Until you do, we can't make an effective plan."

Jason opened the door.

Noah had dressed in a crisp white button-down and jeans. He seemed as though he'd just returned from a two-week beach vacation. He lifted the box of doughnuts. "Breakfast, anyone?"

Matt ran over to him and took the outstretched box. "Thanks."

"No problem. Just save me a chocolate glazed."

"No problem." He placed the box on the counter and rifled through them, taking out a marble-frosted one.

Steve strolled into the kitchen and lifted a mug toward Fiona. "Coffee?"

"I need the whole pot." She felt as though she hadn't slept in days, which she hadn't. Instead of taking the night to get rest and a clear head, she'd intertwined her emotions and every other part of her with Jason. The result was a tangle of emotions and hair combined with seriously bloodshot eyes. She hadn't bothered to go into the bathroom to fix herself up, so she took the pause in the activity to slink back into the bedroom and into the bathroom. The face in the mirror looked like she'd had one hell of a good night. Her hair was partially matted on one side and had straightened out on the other. Her face had no makeup but bite marks were on her neck and her lips appeared a bit too swollen. Damn it.

She rinsed her face with very cold water, brushed out her hair and braided the top back, securing it with a rubber elastic she found in a drawer. It would hurt like hell to pull out later, but she functioned better when she was satisfied with her appearance. She didn't have the heart to put on her outfit from the day before, so she remained in Jason's oversize sweatpants and his shirt.

Jason and Fiona glanced at each other as she walked in the room. His hair was as tousled as hers had been, although he didn't seem to care that he was advertising the extent of their reunion the night before. For Matt's sake, she wanted him to go shower and change, or at least straighten himself out. This whole experience could mess Matt up, although dying would mess him up more than his parents having sex. She shook off her insecurities about the night before. They had much bigger things to think about.

Jason leaned against the counter, sipping his coffee black as he always had. A thousand unsaid things bounced between them. He'd watched over her for years, but not enough. Had she known her husband had been in that type of danger, she'd have had a security detail with him at all times. From the look of it, it seemed his team had about five people involved. How did he make an income if he had his resources all on her?

Matt came over to her, a small white frosting mustache under his nose. "How long are we going to stay here? I was hoping to go over to Ethan's house tonight."

"Count out the weekend. I need more information before I can make plans for you going into public or even to school. I guess I can call your teacher and claim you have mono. That will give you a few weeks of Zoom class."

The frown on his face broke her heart. "That's not fair."

"It isn't, but it's the reality." She ruffled his hair and pulled him into a hug.

"Do you know who is after us?"

"I know enough to know they're lethal and relentless." And they could be after Matt. An eye for an eye. The thought churned in her gut, but she couldn't allow it to linger inside her. She had to push back on the emotions so she could do her job. Her job skills had a significant amount of cobwebs over them as was evident from the way she couldn't neutralize the intruder in the house or the men trying to pull her into the car.

Steve turned to her. "Noah can remain here with you and Matt. We'll handle things at the office."

Fiona felt torn. The weight of responsibility bore down on her—she should be protecting Matt, but the office held answers she craved. She had to find out if someone from her own past had caught up to her, or if Porras had hired the men to attack them. Whoever they were, they couldn't care less about her or Matt. "I need more information. Information I can only get if I meet my attacker."

Jason shook his head, chiming in, "We think it's best you stay here, Fi."

"We? Who is we?" she asked, her patience fading.

"The team," he replied.

She carefully controlled the tone of her voice to not sound too aggressive, well, at least not extremely aggressive. "I never hired your team, so as far as I'm concerned, I make my own decisions. If you want to assist me, that would be fantastic, but do not limit my access to information. You lost the right to love and protect when you didn't trust me."

Steve and Noah both stepped back toward the doughnut box, within listening distance, but not in the direct line of fire.

She could and should remain with Matt, but something inside Fiona was restless, a gut feeling that wouldn't be silenced. She looked at Matt, his young face etched with confusion, then back at Jason. "I'm going with you," she said firmly.

The men exchanged looks, their expressions a mix of surprise and concern.

Jason began, "Fi, we thought—"

"I know what you thought," Fiona interrupted. Her mind was a whirlwind, juggling the roles of mother, former operative and wife. "But every fiber of my being

tells me I should be at that office with you. I can't explain it, but I have to be there."

Steve raised an eyebrow, the weight of Fiona's insistence evident. "But Matt…"

Fiona's heart ached, torn between maternal instincts
and the pull of her intuition. "He'll be safe with Noah,
right? I am unable to sit here and wait for whatever the
enemy is planning. If I have some sense of what we're
up against, I'll feel more in control. After leaving me out
of control for so long, you do not have a say."

Matt had always been a smart and competent kid.
As much as her gut told her she had to go out and inter-
view their attacker, she also felt certain Matt was safer
here. She watched as Matt peered at Noah, his unease
at their unfamiliarity palpable. The pang of guilt hit her
hard. She would be leaving her son with a near stranger.

"Look, if anything happens, I need to know we did
everything we could," Fiona continued, her voice heavy
with emotion. "And that means me being at that office."

Jason gave a resigned nod. "All right. But we stay
together."

Steve and Noah agreed.

Matt walked back to his mother, so young compared
to the men in the room, yet he had a calm and perceptive-
ness that gave her hope that everything would be okay.
"Go ahead," he said. "I know it will drive you crazy to
just sit around watching over me. Noah was pretty cool
to talk to in the car on the ride over yesterday. Now that
I have more information about what is going on around
us, I can probably ask better questions."

"Okay." Fiona hugged him tight. "If any harm comes
to you, it will be coming to him as well."

Noah frowned but acknowledged Fiona's maternal need to protect her child.

As the group prepared to make their move, her heart struggled, the love for her son overwhelming her. Every choice had its price, and she prayed she was making the right one.

Chapter 9

Jason and Fiona drove toward headquarters in the Expedition, following Steve in his Tesla. Jason was glad for the private moment with his wife. The night before felt as though he'd been in a nightmare that somehow twisted into a dream and he needed some grounding to convince himself that he had indeed been able to hold his wife in his arms one more time. Holding Fiona close had been a bittersweet reminder of what he had lost. Not that she was acting as though their night together meant anything. The scare of the morning sent her right back into fight or flight mode, not that Fiona was ever in flight mode. She was too focused on Matt's safety to back down. That strong personality had been one of the reasons Jason fell in love with her.

"Are you sure you don't want to stay with Matt?" he asked, hoping she'd stay inside the bunker with their son.

She turned toward him. "I want to make sure that we're not forced underground for the rest of our lives. I didn't spend the past five years raising a strong, intelligent and personable kid to now tell him that he has to dim his light so that no one notices him ever again."

"It won't be that bad. I'll find a way to stop the threat."

"You aren't even positive what threat you're protecting us from. You had five years just sitting in limbo, waiting for someone with a deadly vengeance to find us. If the man in the house had been a sniper, Matt and I would be dead right now. I wasn't anticipating something so sinister arriving at my front door."

Jason had no words to counter hers as she spoke the truth. "I blew it. Somehow, I trusted that they would never find out I was alive. If you could imagine it though, others could too. It was all my fault."

"It was all your fault that you didn't tell me and prepare us, but it wasn't your fault that the assignment you were on had such a tragic ending." She placed a hand on his and sighed. "My anger at you is also fear for Matt. We lost so much when you disappeared. Now he's at risk too. I couldn't bear to lose you again and with him in danger, I'm overwhelmed."

"I'd say let's let the past be the past, but that's a steep order. I promise I'll make it up to you. I'll do whatever it takes to protect Matt and you."

"How about we act as a team. We protect each other."

Jason knew Fiona's past didn't only involve economic treaties, but she never spoke about her job with him except to casually mention far-off places that she'd visited as though she were a travel influencer. Perhaps some of her expertise did relate to criminal organizations and dealing with them. If that were the case, then he would be the biggest idiot of them all by not trusting her with his secret. Somehow it had all seemed so simple five years ago. Disappear and allow her and Matt to carry on without ever having to look over their shoulders at the boogeyman coming after them.

"Agreed," he said as he twisted her hand inside his and squeezed.

"No more secrets?"

"None." He wanted her to trust him as she had in the past. At least while they could still be together. If he couldn't think up a way to take down the entire Porras cartel, his only choice would be to sacrifice himself to save his family.

They pulled up to his office, which on the outside looked like a large storage-unit facility with faded blue paint and rows of white-and-pink impatiens—enough of an effort made for the building to appear cared for but not enough to seem like something special was inside. The building was a master class in deception. He'd always taken pride in creating things that concealed more than they revealed. Fiona scanned the area as they drove through an automatic gate and into an underground garage.

"This setup keeps people less curious," he said.

"I'm not sure. Aren't storage units robbed often?" she asked, always focused on exactly the right questions.

"I'm sure they would be if they didn't have the security system we have around it."

Her brows lifted. "Like the security system you put in my house?"

He bit back his reply. She was right. He'd half-assed the security. Instead of a twenty-four-hour presence watching her house, he'd split up observing her comings and goings with Meaghan. And the alarms that were triggered when the intruder broke inside did nothing but warn them of any current danger without an adequate means to neutralize the intruder until someone arrived.

He parked the car next to Steve's. Fiona followed them to the entrance. Jason watched her face closely as she stepped into the office. The headquarters of Fresh Pond Security included ultramodern offices, an open conference room with an impressive screen covering almost half the wall and a lobby area that held a living wall filled with golden pothos and peace lilies. The lighting and design inside the facility had to make up for the lack of windows. Plants offered a calming atmosphere for a job that called for long hours and strenuous work conditions.

"It's not what you were expecting, is it?" he mused aloud, addressing Fiona but not revealing everything just yet. He wanted to drip-feed the details, to keep her intrigued, to watch her piece the puzzle together.

She turned to him, her eyes reflecting a mix of surprise and admiration. "I was not expecting this at all. I imagined more a Dick Tracy-type office in a brick building with a coat stand where you'd keep your trench coat and fedora."

Steve laughed. "If he had his way, that's where we'd be. This place is better. It's much more space than we could afford in an ordinary office building, and it keeps people from finding us too easily. We tend to meet up with clients at their houses or places of employment in order to get a better perspective on what they are expecting of us and if we want to handle the matter."

"Hidden in plain sight," Fiona said on a sigh. "It makes a lot of sense." She waved her finger across the conference room, the furniture of the lobby and the long hallway of offices. "Must have cost a pretty penny."

"It took us three years to afford this place. Before

that, we worked out of Steve's basement until his wife kicked us out." Jason led her down the long hallway, remembering those first few years where he'd been a mess. He missed his family and had no desire to create anything, much less a successful company. If it hadn't been for Steve taking Jason's idea and creating a business out of it, Jason might still be in a rented hotel room with a bottle of Jack and a death wish.

Fiona followed Jason through what seemed like a technologically advanced office space, although she'd been out of the workforce for a while, so perhaps this was more common than it had been when she'd relied on the government for her perspective.

Steve came up next to them. "You can have the small conference room. We have some information about Federated Security and a list of possible clients who might have hired them."

"A list?" she asked. She had no reason to think her own past had caught up with her, but perhaps she was being naive. She'd done a lot of questionable things in a lot of places to a lot of people, and although she'd never been caught, there might be a file somewhere that would incriminate her. The day she retired from the service, she'd been handed a small pension and a list of federal laws she'd break if she ever spoke a word of her past. Her position with the Department of State had been embellished and her shadow work disappeared. Jason's work in the military, however, had not been scrubbed. She'd easily accessed with her internal contacts why he'd been in Colombia and how the whole assignment had gone up in flames. Perhaps he had other assignments that had also created enemies. There were too many possibilities.

"What about the Porras cartel?" she asked.

Jason frowned, as though the name alone pissed him off. "We can't count them out. Porras has a great business mind, but his ego gets in the way. He'll hunt me down if he thinks I'm alive. But we have no direct proof that they're the ones involved."

"The break-in and kidnapping attempt were not random. Someone is focused on our family."

"I agree. Once we learn who, we can direct all our energy to shutting them down."

Fiona hated waiting for information. She preferred a more direct means of obtaining the intelligence she needed. Perhaps she could find someone to hack into Federated Security's records. It would be safe and would give a decent snapshot of who was paying their bills. Her mind spun with all the different avenues to go down, but felt somewhat assured that Jason had people around him who might be able to obtain the information needed.

A few steps further down the hall, she froze at the sight in one of the offices—Meaghan, the last person she expected to see sitting at a desk here. Meaghan, her hair twisted in a messy bun, looked up and nearly fell back in her chair as she spotted Fiona. *Why the hell was Meaghan in Jason's workplace?*

"What are you doing here?" Fiona asked as her world shattered more and more with each heartbeat. This was her best friend, the one person she trusted to spill her heartache, loneliness and fears for the future. A hundred reasons rushed through her head. She was there being interviewed or perhaps Jason had offered her protection too.

Before Meaghan could answer, Jason stepped forward. "Fi, I was meaning to tell you."

Her gaze jumped between them, a mix of anger and hurt. "Any time before me running into my best friend and neighbor at your workplace would have been a great time to tell me."

Meaghan's deference to Jason told her Meaghan had some sort of connection to him and that nearly knocked Fiona on her ass. There was a knowing between them, as though they'd been through many things together and they understood things about the other a mere acquaintance wouldn't. "Tell me you two aren't together?"

"I work for Jason," Meaghan said. Her unwavering stare directed at Jason, filled with hostility, only added to Fiona's questions.

This was a nightmare. Meaghan knew all of Fiona's flaws and her mistakes and her mishaps and her incompetencies. That she could have been writing those things up in reports and handing them over to Jason for the past five years shattered Fiona's remaining hold on reality. She couldn't breathe. She sat down on a chair in front of Meaghan's desk but missed and crashed to the floor. She struck the back of her shoulder into the corner of the chair. The pain, both new and old, hammered through her.

Meaghan and Jason rushed to assist her.

She lifted her hand, unsure whether she was stopping them or wanting to strike them both down. "Back up."

"Fiona, I was assigned to watch over you, but the friendship was real." Meaghan squatted next to her and remained at her side despite the command.

"Friends don't lie or set up friends with men like George." She swallowed hard and pushed her hair back from her face. "Unless they were instructed to do so by their boss."

It was one thing for her husband to lie to her, but to have her best friend lie too made everything exponentially worse. Fiona pulled herself to her feet. She could use a shot of whiskey to cut through the heartache and the lingering pain from her injuries from the night before. Meaghan whispered something to Jason. Her hostile demeanor directed at Jason only added to Fiona's confusion.

"I feel so bad about everything that happened to you," Meaghan said to her, returning to the other side of her desk as though she'd been placed in time-out.

"I'm sure you do, but I honestly don't care."

"Don't take your anger at me out on Meaghan. She's a workhorse. She's a talented bodyguard and has been looking out for you and Matt this whole time." Jason nodded toward her like a proud parent.

"Stupid me. I thought she worked nine to seven every weekday at an insurance company." Fiona stared at Meaghan. "No offense, but if you're such an amazing bodyguard, then why did I have to fight off some ape of a man in my house and then almost get kidnapped at the book signing?"

Meaghan crossed her arms. "I never left Matt's side at the bookstore. He was safe. I also knew there were three other people watching over you inside and outside the bookstore. As for the break-in, I agree I blew it. I'd been getting lax after years of nothing happening. You had no activity whatsoever. I promise you though, I'll never let my guard down again."

Fiona could see the self-reproach in Meaghan's expression. It was one she'd worn when she let something get by her in the past. "Okay, that wasn't fair. You had a job to do, but I have the right to be angry that I was not included in any of the plans on how to protect me. I'm not that clueless when it comes to security. Right now I have to get my head around a new reality, one where my dead husband is alive and my next door neighbor, the one who nurtured me during my most difficult days, works for him. I'd cried in your arms so many times, and you knew the truth."

"No. I thought your husband was really dead. I only found out that Jason was your husband last night. He went by DJ and never used his actual name. I swear."

Fiona's gut told her Meaghan was telling the truth and the majority of her anger bounced back to him. "So you took me on as a work assignment?"

She nodded. "He hired me to protect your family almost five years ago, but after a few months, I wasn't doing it just for the paycheck from Fresh Pond Security, I was protecting my best friend."

Fiona reached out her hand to Meaghan. They had a solid history and like it or not, she was Fiona's closest friend in the world. In that moment of reconciliation, the significance of her friend's words dawned on her with surprising clarity.

"Fresh Pond Security is the name of your company?" She stared at Jason, overwhelmed by the ping-pong emotions of the past twelve hours. Jason had proposed to her on the edge of Fresh Pond in Cambridge.

Jason shrugged. Although he'd always had difficulty

expressing his deepest emotions, she could see the corners of his mouth fall. "I named it after one of the happiest days of my life."

Her breath deepened. For five years, the love of her life lived a few miles down the road and worked at a place named for their love story. For five years, he watched his wife and son carry on with life without him. For five years, she suffered a depth of heartache she never wished to go through again. "That doesn't make it any better. In fact, it hurts even more. You've screwed with every part of my life. I don't even want to think about the press from the disaster at yesterday's bookstore signing. Janet must be completely overwhelmed with people trying to figure out if I've been kidnapped or if that was a publicity stunt. And don't forget about Matt. Not only have you harmed him psychologically, you also placed his life in danger."

Jason nodded.

Fiona wanted to go back to sleep and wake in a world where she could trust those she loved. And yes, it was hypocritical of her to think such things as she'd never been able to be entirely honest about her occupation with Jason. Her body ached and her concern for Matt grew with each minute away from him, but she had to find out who was after them. From the sound of Steve and Jason's investigations, they still couldn't be certain it was Porras.

She inhaled the sweet smell of the cut gardenias on Meaghan's desk. They had come from her garden, a place where Fiona and Meaghan had spent hours sipping tea and sharing their trials and tribulations. Meaghan's office contained a lot of her personality, the personality she'd allowed Fiona to see. A large laptop that Fiona recognized from her visits to Meaghan's house sat open on her desk next to a bloodred stoneware coffee cup. The paintings on the walls displayed rustic landscapes, one of a farm by a lake and another of a cabin resting next to a wooded stream. Across from her desk, a variety of screens showed an array of information. On one, the news played in mute, another contained a digital calendar and to-do list and a few had surveillance camera feeds. One of Fiona's house, the back and the front. Another house was displayed next to hers. Finally, a man sat on a chair in what appeared to be an interrogation room.

The man in the video seemed very familiar. He had the buff arms and thinned waist of her intruder. Handcuffed to a metal chair that appeared bolted to the floor, he wore medical scrubs, a spot of blood on one of his thighs where she'd stabbed him. His face had been obscured by the darkness and a black mask. Yet here he was.

"Who is that?" she demanded.

"No one you need to be concerned about," Jason said.

Fiona was so sick of being pacified as if she were brainless and defenseless. She'd have protected her identity forever because she had always respected the rules. But not now. Not when her child was being hunted. "Who is that? And don't lie. Is that Robert Harper? Locked up here?"

"Yes," Meaghan replied, not looking over to Jason for permission to hand out information. "He works for Federated Security."

Federated Security out of Houston employed men and women who had no morals. They'd lie, steal and kill if the price was right. Although Fiona had never fully justified her own actions, at least she'd believed at the time she was doing it for some greater cause. One that would make the world safer for the vast majority of people. "I want to see him," Fiona declared, her determination cutting through the thick tension. She needed answers.

"Not a chance. It's not safe, even with him under lock and key." Jason shifted to block her path to the door.

"I need to know why he was there." The weight of her husband's and best friend's combined disapproval might have stopped her before. But not now. Now, she needed clarity, more than ever. "Can I just have a minute?" She sat in the chair in front of Meaghan's desk and put her head in her hands.

Jason and Meaghan stepped out for a minute. She could hear them speaking about Fiona's stability. That was fine. If they thought she was falling apart, they wouldn't anticipate her next move. She slipped behind Meaghan's desk and yanked out the cord to her portable power bank. She slipped the three-foot long cord into the pocket of the sweatpants she'd borrowed from Jason. Her outfit didn't make her appear that intimidating, but perhaps it would make her look a little unstable. That could be used to her advantage.

"I'm done asking for anything," she murmured to herself. No more lies. No more secrets. She was taking control.

She exited the office with a soft, pretty expression. Steve had joined Meaghan and Jason in the hall. They all stared at her as she walked over to them. She focused her request on Jason as he had an abundance of guilt she could manipulate. "After all you put me through, you owe me. I want to talk to Harper."

"What are you going to say to him? He's trained to keep his mouth shut. He won't leak a word without someone waterboarding him and I'm against that practice, personally." Jason stood with his hands in his pockets, trying to appear in control.

Then Steve made a very stupid mistake. "Come on, Fiona. This is not the place to act out your storylines. We've trained for years to handle these situations."

"You're right." She stepped toward him, nodding with all the regret and sadness she held in her heart over the state of her current life. Steve placed an arm over her shoulder, offering comfort. By the time she spun away from him, she had his gun in her hand.

Steve's eyes widened in surprise and Jason yelled out, "Fiona!"

"I need to see Harper. Where is he? And don't think I won't use this. You're already dead, Jason, but your son is very much alive and I intend to keep him that way."

Other employees of Fresh Pond Security had already gathered, drawn by the commotion. No one dared to approach her. She had the upper hand.

Jason granted reluctant approval. "Fine, but I go in with you."

"I want to be alone with him." Her voice strong and unflinching. The gun in her hand brought her back to a time where everything she did risked her own life and took the lives of others, but not once had she been caught. She had a million regrets from that time in her life, but none right now.

Jason protested, "Fi—"

But she cut him off. "Do it."

As the door to the interrogation room opened, Robert Harper looked up. At the sight of her, his lips curled into a sneer. The wound from where she'd stabbed him with the pen kept his leg stretched out in front of him. She stared at it, causing him to remember and feel the pain she'd inflicted upon him.

She turned back to Jason. "Close it. Give me five minutes. I promise, that's all I need."

He didn't have a choice. Not with her waving Steve's gun around in what appeared to be an unstable mindset. Knowing him, he probably didn't believe he could take it from her without someone being hurt. "I'm watching the monitor. If you appear in danger at any point, I'm coming in."

"Fine."

Between the handcuffs, the bolted chair and her skill set, she wouldn't have any trouble.

Once the door closed, Harper started in on her. "Just wait until I get out of here. I will slit your throat and gut your son."

She stormed over to him and stomped the heel of her boot into his knee, dislocating it. His screams lasted a few seconds longer than his ego wanted. When he shut up, she pointed the gun at his head. "Who hired you?"

He stayed silent. She slammed the butt of the gun into his already swollen nose. "Who hired you?"

Blood dripped from his nose, over his lips and down his chin. She pulled out the cord and slipped it around his neck as he fought to get loose.

Her interrogation techniques were ones she had learned in the darkest corners of the world, reserved for the worst of the worst. "You don't get it. I would sacrifice myself for my son without a second thought. Going to jail for murder is nothing." She pulled back on the cord and could feel his breathing slow. "I want a name."

He tried to lift his hand to get her to stop. She loosened the cord and waited. If he didn't say anything relevant, she would tighten it again.

"Andres Porras wants you dead," he muttered, his hostility growing despite his acquiescence. "And your son. And nothing you do will stop him. And if he doesn't kill you, I will."

"You have bigger worries than little old me. Porras is going to want you dead for betraying him. I'm sure it will be slow and painful." She pulled her phone out of her pocket and replayed him giving up Andres Porras.

"You bitch."

"And you're nothing but a stooge. Good luck in hell." She turned and saw Jason.

He must have entered while she was focused on Harper. He stopped at the sight of Harper's face and the blood sprayed over Fiona's clothes.

"I might need a change of clothes and he might need a doctor." She stepped past him into the hall.

Jason approached cautiously. "Fi, what did you—"

"You're right. Porras is after me," she said, her voice low with a mix of fear and rage. "And our son."

As he reached out to her, Fiona stepped back. "Now isn't the time to reconcile." Despite the fact that they had been quite reconciled the night before. "Now that we know who is attacking us, we can make a better plan. There's no hiding from a man like Andres Porras. Matt's in danger," she said, a chilling look in her eyes. "We have to get back to him."

Chapter 10

Jason stared at the bloodstains on his sweatpants and the T-shirt he'd loaned to Fiona. A few drops had sprayed on her face, probably when she broke the man's nose in the same place Jason had broken it only a week before. After the rage she'd carried into the room, brandishing Steve's weapon and ranting about protecting Matt, she had transformed into a calmer state. A very similar state to when she returned from her work trips so many years ago.

When they were married, she'd never exploded in a rage or even shown a higher level of anger. Of course they had had arguments, but neither one of them would ever raise their voice over the loud shout one might make at a crowded bar. The way she'd slipped Steve's gun from his holster, which was located behind his hip, not directly on it, was something a person had to have practiced many, many times in order to pull that trick off with someone trained in law enforcement.

Meaghan, a woman who had spent years with Fiona, also appeared stunned at Fiona's change in temperament and her new skill set. She'd observed Fiona wave the gun around, never once going up to stop her or challenge her. In all of their heads, it seemed there was an intuitive understanding that Fiona knew how the Sig Sauer worked and would use it if she needed to.

As they watched her beat the hell out of Harper, not one of them rushed in to help him. Perhaps the image in front of them seemed too much like a trick of the mind. Fiona was a diplomat and a writer, but here she was breaking a man's nose. When she wrapped the cord around his neck, Steve told Jason to stop her. He agreed and rushed inside the interrogation room as she stepped back from Harper with her phone in her hand playing a recording of Harper ratting out Porras.

Jason, lost in a maelstrom of emotion, felt a strange detachment from the scene before him. He looked at Fiona, her familiar features seeming alien, every contour and line hiding a story he couldn't read. The woman he had vowed his life to, laughed with, cried with, had become an enigma to him. He felt a piercing nostalgia for the days of blissful ignorance, for the moments when he believed he knew every corner of Fiona's soul.

"What the hell?" The words, so small yet laden with anguish, escaped his lips, more a sigh than a question. He struggled to find his footing as though he'd just been caught in the blast radius of an explosion.

Fiona's voice, usually so direct and warm, held a shadow of guardedness as she responded. "I don't want to talk about it. We need to get back to Matt and make a more permanent plan."

Steve's voice broke through the thoughts rushing around Jason's head. "Seems you aren't the sole custodian of secrets, Jason." With an outstretched hand, he accepted his gun back from Fiona. "Don't do that again."

She shrugged. "Don't let it happen again." She turned to Meaghan. "I need to change."

"I have some backup clothes in my office. They may be a bit long on you, but otherwise will fit."

Jason stayed silent while Fiona followed Meaghan back to her office for a change of clothes. She strode away from him with not a flicker of regret slowing her steps. Meaghan matched her pace as though she found Fiona 2.0 even more appealing than the original version. Jason had no idea what he felt except bulldozed.

Sam had tried to get information out of Harper all night. The guy wouldn't say a word to him, not even a nod of the head. Then a few hours later, Harper openly taunted Fiona and when pushed by her, he gave up a client guaranteed to seek revenge.

"To be fair, when Sam had interrogated him earlier in the week, he merely talked to him, while Fiona beat the crap out of him." The violence was extreme. Her entire past as a diplomat now seemed questionable. She flew around the world to negotiate trade deals? Something didn't add up, but she was right. Now wasn't the time to focus on it.

Steve shrugged. "You're not seeing the bigger picture. Sam was doing a job, Fiona was saving her family. Although I will never relax in her presence again. She's got a very specific skill set. Her capabilities seemed even more brilliant when she pulled out her phone with Harper telling her it was Porras who had hired Federated Security. I bet we're only scratching the surface of what she's capable of."

Jason agreed. He called Noah while he waited.

"How is Matt?" he asked, hoping there was some stability in his world.

"He's great. Just kicked my ass in *Grand Theft Auto*."

Jason exhaled some of his stress. "Okay. Look, we now know for sure that the Porras cartel is involved. Be extravigilant and do not open the door for anyone except me, Steve or Meaghan."

"Do you think this site has been compromised?"

"Anything can happen and with their unlimited resources, it's very likely." Which made Fiona all the more correct in saying that they had to get back to Matt.

Meaghan came out of her office.

"Is she doing okay?" Jason asked.

"She's preoccupied with Matt's welfare. She has blinders on for anything else."

Jason nodded. "Steve, can you stay here and get any information on Andres Porras's whereabouts?"

"No problem."

"And Meaghan, why don't you follow us to the bunker. You can give Noah a break and Fiona might talk more freely with you there."

"Or she'll still be furious I kept my relationship to her a secret. It's not like this job allows me unlimited opportunities to get to know people. If I don't hang on to Fiona as a friend, I don't know if I'll get another one in the next decade or so."

"She'll come around."

"She has melted a bit. She complimented my office decor."

Jason saw the worry in Meaghan's expression. He'd always appreciated Fiona having such a decent person as Meaghan around her. The thought that he might have messed that up didn't sit great with him. "There you go. You're back at being best friends."

"I wouldn't go that far, but I have no problem going out there. Want me to leave now?"

"Sure, if you feel comfortable explaining your presence to Matt."

"Absolutely. I'm throwing you under the bus," Meaghan said.

"Go ahead. I seem destined to be run over a hundred times today."

Meaghan strode away as Steve slapped Jason on the back and headed to his own office, leaving Jason alone, waiting for his wife. He checked his watch. They'd been gone for three hours. It was time to go back to the safe house. Perhaps he could call Meaghan to pick up some subs on the way. The kitchen had food, but it was more necessities than luxuries. Cans of soup, pasta, beans and rice. There were some half gallons of ice cream in the freezer, but generally, the pickings were slim.

When the door finally opened, Fiona walked out with a clean face and a short blond ponytail, dressed in Meaghan's workout clothes—bright blue leggings, a concert T-shirt and New Balance sneakers. Her expression had softened more, which eased a bit more of Jason's stress.

"Ready?" he asked.

She nodded.

They walked to the Expedition in silence. She looked quite fit and competent. Had she always been that way and he'd only seen the sexy side of her? Her figure did make a perfect cover. No one would expect the sexy blonde woman to be able to take them down with a kick to the knee in sneakers. She could probably take out an aorta wearing high heels.

They remained in their own thoughts until he hit the turnpike, then she turned to him, her lips tight. "I'm sorry for taking things so far. If anyone comes after you for Harper's injuries, I'll take the blame."

"His employer doesn't want to be caught in a breaking and entering case and if Porras ever hears about his confession, he'll disappear."

"I don't want that to happen. I'm not vindictive."

"Right." He paused and thought about how to phrase his next question. She had certainly hidden something from him. "When did you learn how to torture prisoners?" A bit too direct, but under the circumstances, necessary.

"I took a few self-defense classes as part of my employment." She stared straight ahead at the cars in front of them.

He didn't believe her at all. The inability to trust the person he loved was a bludgeon to his chest. Something Fiona had felt for a day now. "Ever had to use those skills in real life?"

"Occasionally," she admitted. "How long have you had someone interrogating Harper with no answers?"

His employees had worked on Harper for days, but he didn't want to admit his tactics had failed. Sam should have been able to break him without getting them arrested. Fiona crossed over into felony assault. She did, however, get the information in five minutes. As promised. And looking back at what she'd done with more scrutiny, he understood she'd been angry, but never out of control. It was far too easy to label a woman who had strong feelings as someone unable to think through consequences, and she took advantage of such presumptions, gaining access to the interrogation room and Harper.

"It doesn't matter. My people don't beat the hell out of people in our custody," Jason said defensively.

"Don't act so superior. As a private citizen, you can't hold that man against his will. And I didn't initially break his nose, I only compounded an existing injury. Someone between my house and that room must have had a slip of the fist—but go ahead and be upset with my tactics." She glanced at the cut on the middle knuckle of his right hand. She didn't miss a detail.

They didn't speak again for a few miles. They both had their secrets, but most of his were now out in the open. Hers seemed to stretch down an endless hole of lies and misinformation.

He had been happy in the knowledge that he could rush into dangerous jobs that he'd never speak to her about while she worked in the more mild-mannered field of diplomacy. But she'd been in far deeper than he'd ever realized. "I guess we never really knew each other at all."

Fiona hesitated before looking at him. "I wouldn't say that. I know for certain I love the person who sat with me that day in the library. I know you would never do anything to harm our family on purpose, although you did have a massive fail declaring yourself dead five years ago."

Jason sighed, rubbing the bridge of his nose and thinking of his words carefully. "I love the woman I met in school. The woman who had ambition and intelligence and the ability to see straight through me. I love my bride and the mother of our child. It's the person who sat with me for coffee on Sunday mornings who I don't recognize."

Her expression remained soft, almost wistful. "Remember all those times you took off to parts unknown and I kissed you goodbye without knowing if I'd ever see you again?"

"They were the hardest days of my life until now."

She nodded. "Me too. Why did you never tell me what you did when you had to fly overseas on assignments?"

He looked down, his hands tightening and loosening on the wheel. "The information was classified. It would be breaking the law."

She tilted her head, challenging him. "So why would you expect me to break the law for you?"

Jason's mouth opened, but for a moment, no words came.

"You're a hypocrite. And all the assumptions you had of me over the years were the ones you put in your own head. I never told you what I did or did not do when I traveled for work. You created a beautiful fiction for yourself and that worked fine for you and your fragile ego, but don't get all angry at me for being who I am." Her calmness wrapped over him, moderating the tension.

He thought back to conversations where she'd avoided any mention of the country she'd visited or the people she traveled with. Had he opened up his mind, he'd have seen the signs all around them. The congenial phrases in Farsi and Korean she used whenever she met someone who spoke those languages seemed a useful way to connect to people in her field. Did she know those languages more fluently than she let on? She'd once whispered a threat to a man at a bar who had been harassing a young college woman. Whatever she said to him had him rushing out of the bar without a backward glance. Jason laughed about it at the time, although the ability to scare someone double her size had been impressive to him. She'd also shot a perfect set at a carnival with an old BB gun that no one else could aim correctly. The crowd teased her about being lucky, but maybe it was pure skill. Her appearance tended to cause malfunctioning in the brains of most men who met her. Steve could now be included in that group. If Jason had to hire someone who would be completely overlooked as a potential risk, no doubt it would be her. Now that he'd taken off his rose-colored glasses, he could see her as someone with far more abilities than he'd allowed himself to imagine.

"I'm sorry for underestimating you," he said as they arrived at the farmhouse.

"It's preferable to be underestimated at times." She reached a hand toward him. "When we have some downtime, I'll give you an abbreviated version of my CV. For now, let's focus on Andres Porras."

He nodded and scanned the area. Everything appeared as it should. There were some open fields behind the house covered in goldenrod with a small vegetable garden that was tended by the caretaker. Meaghan had already parked her black Corvette next to Noah's car.

When they went inside, Noah and Meaghan were talking in the kitchen and Matt was still on the couch. When he saw Fiona, he stood up and trotted over to her, giving her a hug. "I'm glad you're back."

"Me too."

Before Jason could say anything to his son, the force of an explosion outside the house knocked him off his feet. Fiona pulled Matt to the ground and tucked into the edge of the kitchen as Jason looked at the damage and tried to ground himself.

He yelled into his phone for Steve to send help, as Meaghan and Noah rushed outside, guns raised.

The fortified hideout had been built to hide their clients, not protect them from a bombing. Jason focused on getting Fiona and Matt to safety.

"Stay low." Jason pointed to the corner of the kitchen.

Fiona nodded, as she and Matt remained hunched between the island and the refrigerator. Matt crouched by the island, observing everything. Not once did he lose control in the chaos. His intensity reminded Jason of Fiona.

The sound of multiple shots from outside pushed him to get up and back up his team. He directed Fiona and Matt toward the back of the house. After seeing her performance at headquarters, he wasn't as nervous to send them out alone. He opened a door to a basement. "Turn left at the bottom of the stairs and keep going until you reach the barn. Wait in the back of the Range Rover."

Matt rushed down the stairs.

Before Fiona could follow, a second explosion blew out the wall where the television had been. She hit the floor as debris showered over her. Concrete, brick and electronic parts blocked the door to the basement and Matt.

Jason rushed to the door he'd sent his son through and pushed, kicked and tossed away the wreckage to get through. Fiona was at his side assisting him, and based on her intensity in trying to reach their son, he didn't stop to assess her health.

Once through the door, he rushed downstairs, Fiona

right behind him. The three cars in the barn were all there. A Range Rover, a beat up Ford F-150 and a BMW, but the barn doors hung open and Matt was nowhere in sight.

"Matt?" Fiona yelled out, her panic echoing off the concrete walls.

Jason opened every door of every car, calling out his son's name. "Stay here," he called back to Fiona before rushing outside. The house was in flames as well as the side of the barn. Meaghan's Corvette had bullet holes through the side. The Expedition's tires had been slashed.

"Have you seen Matt?" Jason called out to Meaghan as she hunkered behind a rusted tractor.

"No."

He'd thought Fiona would always be safe with him out of the picture. Instead, he'd left her wide open to attack. If someone had wanted her dead, she would be. The thought tortured him.

Fiona arrived at his side from the house. "He's not inside."

They both whipped around as a helicopter dropped into the field near them. The sound thundered through him and the wind swirled dirt around, making visual observations limited. Two men dressed in black dragged Matt, fighting like a cornered tomcat, toward the bird. Jason ran toward them, but was too late. It lifted off. Once in the air, he couldn't shoot it down. Not with his son inside.

Fiona cried out, "Matt!" Her aching cry stabbed through his heart. This was everything he'd tried to protect them from. He'd been a fool to think he could control such a huge source of evil.

Chapter 11

A whirling haze of emotions consumed Fiona as she watched the last traces of the helicopter vanish into a cloudy sky. Beside her, Jason stood, every line of his face etched with agony.

He lifted the phone to his ear, but before he spoke to the person he called, he glanced over at her and whispered, "I'm sorry."

She didn't respond. No words could fill the gaping hole blown into her by Matt's disappearance. Especially knowing that Andres Porras wanted him for one specific reason...revenge for his own son's death.

Flames roared behind them, consuming the secluded safe house that was supposed to be their sanctuary. Thick plumes of smoke billowed into the sky, yet neither Fiona nor Jason spared it a glance. Material things could be replaced, but Matt's disappearance—that shifted the axis of the world to Fiona. Nothing would ever be the same after seeing her son taken away from her in such a violent way. The fading whir of helicopter blades overhead was an all-consuming focus, its receding noise carrying away their son.

Jason finally turned away from the sky. His gaze met

hers, and for a fleeting moment, the ferocity of their emotions threatened to spill over. His anguish and rage inflamed her own. Under any other circumstance, he would reach for her. She knew that as surely as she knew he would blame himself for this. With one step forward, he could bridge that gaping distance that had grown between them. But not now. This wasn't the time or the place. Their son was out there and that eclipsed everything.

Seeing the love Jason had for his son healed a small part of their brokenness. Not perfectly, but in a way where she could see trying to be with him again. If they could ever get back to what they had. But that time had ended and they had no future until Matt came home.

"They found us," he said, his voice a gravelly monotone. "That's on me."

Fiona didn't want to hear excuses. She wanted her son back by her side. She hardened her shell of a heart and squared her shoulders. "We don't have time for guilt or finger-pointing. We need to pivot, adapt, hit back." Her eyes remained dry as tears were generally foreign to her, but if they weren't, they'd be tears of fury.

He nodded, pushing a torrent of emotions into that well he'd always used to keep life at home more balanced. "You're right. We have to be tactical. They won't see us coming."

Before either could step away from the apocalyptic scene, Jason's phone vibrated. Steve's name flashed across the screen.

"What the hell happened out there? Is everyone okay?" Steve's voice sounded tense.

"No. Matt's gone, airborne. I can't see Noah or

Meaghan." Jason strode back and forth, his eyes scanning the sky, the house and Fiona.

"Check in with them and then get back to the office. We can go over the camera footage of the area and try to pull as much information from the video as possible. Does Kennedy know?"

"I'm calling her now," Jason said.

Fiona had no idea who Kennedy was, but she'd better be someone with a connection to the air traffic control system.

Jason hung up the phone and punched in a new number. "Kennedy, I need you to track a helicopter in the air right now."

Fiona let out a deep breath. His connections were deeper than she'd imagined. She was so grateful. She stepped closer to hear the conversation.

"Where?" Kennedy said, adding no pleasantries. The soft tapping of computer keys could be heard in the background.

He gave her the address and the direction of the flight.

Fiona stared back toward the spot in the sky where she'd seen the helicopter fade from view. From what she saw at the end, Matt had struggled some, but he didn't fight too hard, which was for the best. Fighting trained professionals would result in something broken and maybe a tranquilizer.

Jason put his phone back in his pocket. "Kennedy can find anything in the air or on the water."

"Let's hope they stay in the area. Where are Meaghan and Noah?" She was prepared to run back into the house, but her gut told her they wouldn't be there.

"Noah!" Jason yelled out, voice raw.

She hadn't seen Noah or Meaghan since the first explosion, although gunshots had echoed in the distance until the helicopter disappeared. A dread crept through her. Maybe something had happened to them. She couldn't bear more violence, even from her. She harbored not one regret that she'd retired so early from her government employment. The life she'd created with Matt, being a mom and writing thrillers was more than enough excitement. If she could bring her husband home to live with them, it would be perfect.

Emerging from the smoke and haze around the house, Meaghan, appearing like she'd just climbed Everest, supported Noah, who had a definite limp on his right side. Blood seeped through his clothes from a wound near his hip. The sight gave Fiona flashbacks to a time when blood meant a job well done. The nightmares from that time never left her.

"What happened?" Fiona rushed to him. The bullet had pierced the area above his hip. There was a chance it missed the most important organs, but his chances for a full recovery would be exponentially better in a fully equipped trauma center.

"They ambushed us," Meaghan said, the words growled through clenched teeth. "They shot Noah and got to Matt before I could react."

Noah's legs started to go out, but Jason rushed over to him to hold him up.

Fiona lifted his shirt and saw the raw edges of the wound. She instinctively pressed down to stop the flow of the blood. Warm, sticky and thick, the wound had to be treated immediately.

"Hold on," she murmured, trying to convey strength she wasn't sure she felt. She'd never been great with medical issues, but neither Meaghan nor Jason stepped in. "Can we move him to a car? He needs to be transported yesterday." She could see the shock in his eyes, and she tightened her pressure on the wound as Jason and Meaghan walked him to his car.

"We should be chasing that bird." Noah spoke through his pain.

"You need some hard-core first aid."

"Bullets are just a minor inconvenience," he replied. "As soon as I'm clear, I'm taking down an entire cartel if I have to to get Matt back." His feelings for their son were evident despite only knowing him personally a few hours while competing in a video game.

Jason leaned close to him. "You'll be needed. For now, hang in there. I can't use you until you're fully cleared."

"I'll be fine then. Go. Neither of you will be safe here. They may have someone coming back to finish the job." Noah pointed to the Range Rover in the barn and then said a whole statement to Jason with one nod of his head.

Meaghan paused at the side of her car, a river of oil flowing down the incline from under the hood. Both the engine and the door panels were riddled with bullet holes. "So much for that."

"Take my car. No one touched it. That's why it's better to get a less flashy car." Noah pointed at Jason's Expedition with the flat tires. "You guys have too fine a taste for your own good."

He headed toward his almost ten-year-old Acura, but

lost a step. Jason held him in his arms and helped him into the back seat. Fiona slipped in next to him.

"What are you doing?" Jason said through the open door.

"I'm holding him together while Meaghan drives. Get the Range Rover and meet us at the hospital."

After Meaghan was buckled in, Jason shut the back door.

Fiona scanned everything around her. A calm Noah buckled in with an injury that must be overpowering him with pain, the burning house and barn—the remnants of Jason's plan to protect them. So much for her current life. That chapter had ended and she had no idea what was to come.

Jason ran toward the half-burning barn, his phone to his ear, as they drove away at top speed. A few minutes later, the Range Rover pulled in behind them on the road.

Meaghan spoke without turning around. "We saw two vehicles—looked like a pickup truck and a smaller black sedan—drive away after we ran outside. I'm wondering if they set the blasts as a diversion so the helicopter crew could shuttle Matt away. I'm not positive Matt was the target. They may have been going after either of you."

"I'm not so sure. If Andres Porras lost his son, he could be targeting Jason's son." Fiona could only hope that Matt kept his cool and stayed safe until they could retrieve him.

A medical team waited with a stretcher as they pulled up to the hospital emergency bay. Fiona lifted her hand from Noah's hip and stepped back to let the professionals do their job. She stood in silence as they rushed him inside the automatic doors that slid closed after them.

"You should wash up," Meaghan said.

"I'm a walking biohazard today." Noah's blood had leeched onto Meaghan's borrowed leggings. "I know what I'm getting you for your birthday this year."

Meaghan waved her off. "It's a risk of the job."

They both entered the hospital and a nice woman at the reception desk handed them each a mask and directed Fiona to the bathroom. Meaghan followed. While Fiona scrubbed her hands, Meaghan rinsed off her face.

"So, you're not in insurance?" she asked the friend she knew nothing about.

"Former law enforcement."

Fiona nodded. With hindsight, she could see Meaghan in a uniform. "What made you leave?"

"The town I worked in had a good old boys' club. It was hard to get them to see me as more than a traffic cop. Jason saw my frustration and offered me a job. A very lucrative job. So I took it and have never been happier." She stopped her before they left the restroom. "What about you?" Her expression told Fiona she wasn't accepting her State Department story.

"I can't say, but let's just assume we had similar training." Sort of.

Jason stood by a vending machine, waiting for them. He held two packs of M&M's and a Snickers bar. He tossed one bag of the M&M's at Meaghan and the Snickers at Fiona. "Noah is in good hands. Meaghan, can you wait here for an hour to get an update and meet us at headquarters?"

"You gave me chocolate. I'm at your disposal."

"Thanks. Fiona, we need to go."

She agreed and followed him out to his car. As soon

as she got in, his SUV sped off. "Can we swing back to the bunker? I just want to see if someone left us a way to track them."

"It's swarming with firefighters and police right now and that would slow our investigation. There are more resources available at the office. Steve has been lining up video and Kennedy might have more on the flight path of the helicopter. As for you, you're not leaving my sight. This past day has been a nightmare. Everything I've done to protect you is unraveling." He sped down the road so fast, she had to brace herself on the curves.

If he thought she was going to be tethered to him because he wanted to be in charge, he had another thing coming. She bit back her harshest replies, but her self-control teetered at the very edge. "You're in a nightmare? How dare you come back and destroy my whole life and then ask for pity?"

The road curved through farmlands and past small New England town commons. He zipped around several cars, causing the drivers to send obscene gestures out their windows. The flash of some headlights in his rearview mirror pulled his attention from the past to the present. The isolated location had actually made it a perfect place for an ambush.

A car, some low-to-the-ground sports car, perhaps a McLaren, followed at a distance. There would be no outrunning something with six hundred horsepower, but they had to try.

"Lose them," Fiona told him, needing to have every precaution adhered to so they could focus on Matt and not saving their own hides. He swerved into a field and headed straight across what seemed like soybeans. The car followed, bouncing across the uneven terrain. As they approached the halfway point, a fairly deep brook crossed their path. Jason sped up and after a short liftoff, the front slammed and thumped as though the struts took too much impact. To Fiona's surprise, the SUV straightened out and continued forward until they made it to the road. The car following them stopped before the brook, then backed up and turned around. They'd be long gone by the time it circled the entire farm. Fiona leaned back in her seat and took a deep breath. This was going to be a marathon and she had to treat it as such. The time for panic and hyperventilating had come and gone before she could even contemplate wallowing under all the turmoil.

When they arrived at Jason's office, the place was buzzing with activity. Steve met them at the door. He had an intensity he hadn't worn when Fiona had met him, not even when she was assaulted at the bookstore.

"Kennedy has a fix on the bird," he said without preamble, leading them to a dimly lit room.

"Where?" Jason asked.

"Nantucket Sound."

That wasn't so bad. It was close enough to get there quickly. "That's good, isn't it?"

"Yes and no. We can get to Woods Hole in an hour and a half, but if they're on a boat or get to an airplane, they can go anywhere. We don't have the resources to follow easily."

Steve broke the silence, "We're tracking every vessel around Martha's Vineyard. If Porras is there, we'll find him."

Fiona's eyes sharpened. "And when we do?"

Steve squared his shoulders. "We end this nightmare for your family."

Calvin, their computer wizard, rushed in the conference room. "They've made contact." He placed a printed email in the middle of the table.

Jason reached for it, fingers trembling ever so slightly. Fiona stood by his side, her stance defiant. Jason cleared his throat and began to read aloud.

Jason or should I call you DJ?
Welcome back from the dead. Don't ever think you will outlast or outsmart me. If you want to see your son again, come find me. Alone. I don't like uninvited guests.
—AP

The initials meant the worst thing that could happen had happened. That Andres knew Jason's new identity also meant he could come to their office and hurt all the people on his team. Fiona had to get a better profile on Porras. The only thing she knew about him related to his need for revenge and his quest for domination and power.

Jason looked up, rubbing his temples, the weight of years evident in his eyes. "Andres Porras... I never thought I'd cross paths with him again. When I encountered him in Colombia years ago, it was like looking into the eyes of a serpent. Cold, calculating. He would burn entire villages if he believed someone had betrayed him."

Steve, ever the analyst, added, "It's not just his ruthlessness—it's his reach. I've tracked his finances. The man's got connections in every underworld market you can think of—arms, drugs, human trafficking. His web stretches globally, and the center of it all is him, always making a profit, always staying a step ahead."

"The people I've spoken to about the Porras family say the same thing. You cross Porras, and not only do you pay, but your entire lineage does," Sam added.

Fiona's eyes hardened. "So, we're dealing with a megalomaniac. What's our next move?"

"First, we find out his actual game," Steve answered. "He may want Jason in order to make him suffer the way Andres suffered the day his son died."

She glanced at the bottom of the email and read out the coordinates.

19T 0379904E 459460N

"Matt will be at this location." She typed into her phone. "He's got to be on a boat."

"Why?" Steve asked.

"Because this location is in the center of Nantucket Sound." Fiona fought the urge to rush to the bathroom and expel the limited food she'd eaten in the past few hours. Never had the stakes been so high when doing such a dangerous job. She could lose both Matt and Jason. The thought tormented her and hurt her ability to think clearly.

Jason paced back and forth as he spoke. "He needs me to show up or he can't make his next move. Maybe that's our play. If I go, he'll be focused on me. That could buy us the time we need to locate Matt."

"But it's a dangerous game," Sam interrupted. "Porras will be prepared for whatever we plan. His family hasn't been in this business for decades without intelligent risk management."

"I know," Jason responded. His pace picked up as he rubbed his fingers into his temples. "It's a risk we might need to take."

Fiona could hear the strain in Jason's reasoning. He had always been unflappable in the most extreme situations, but this was his son. She understood. The stakes had never been higher for either of them.

Steve directed everyone to look at the large screen in the conference room as he pulled up satellite images of the coordinates between Woods Hole on Cape Cod and Martha's Vineyard. "There are several large vessels out there. Some container ships, a few mega-yachts lingering before their migration to Florida or wherever they wintered. Wherever he's sending you, we need eyes on the inside before making a move."

Jason focused on the images. Fiona could see the tension in his expression. There were too many choices—and what if Matt was on a small fishing boat?

"I might have the tech we need," Sam piped up. "I made some tweaks on my microdrone. It's discreet, emits minimal buzzing that will be hidden under most engine noise, has some heft to keep it moving through the wind out in the sound and has great visual and audio. Too much rain, however, can knock its capabilities out."

Jason nodded, "Then check the weather. While you handle reconnaissance, Steve, dive deeper into Porras's network. There's always a weak link."

Fiona added, "We need diversions too. Distractions. Porras might be expecting Jason, but he won't anticipate our other moves."

Steve smirked, "Like Trojan horses? We do have some contacts in the area that owe us a favor."

Jason pulled everyone's attention. "All right, here's the plan. I go in as the bait. Sam, you handle tech, make sure we have a constant feed. Steve, contact our allies. We need eyes on the ground and diversions at the ready. Fiona, I need you coordinating from here. It's essential Porras believes I'm alone."

Fiona's eyes met Jason's, his silent plea passing between them. She wanted to disagree, but he had to focus on his assignment—literally being the bait.

She nodded at the plan but had her doubts. Criminal organizations couldn't be killed without a massive defection or an army of law enforcement and even then, they replicated like a Hydra cut down over and over again by the skill of one opponent, thus making the next rounds more and more difficult to win. With Jason and his team working with her, she stood a better chance of helping Matt. They had the resources. She had to understand the game and the rules, and then she'd play to win.

The room was a flurry of activity. Maps, devices and a clear strategy in place. Andres Porras may be a formidable adversary, but he'd now instigated a war. From the look on the faces of the people in the room, this team was willing to go to the ends of the earth to protect their own.

Every action, every step was for Matt, and they would move mountains to ensure his safe return. Fiona would be there with them. Following directions and trusting their orders. And if it all fell apart, she would have her own Plan B to implement.

Chapter 12

Jason remained quiet, trying to release the mountain of stress pressing on him. He had always thought of himself as the one who could remain cool and collected under the worst conditions imaginable, but this was about his only child. If he failed, Matt wouldn't survive. No. Failure was not an option. He had to use all his resources and get in and out with his son. Porras was smart, but Jason considered himself smarter. He also had the best of the best backing him up. They couldn't be found within thirty miles of the pickup point, but they would have the ability to track him and help out if his plan stalled.

"I'd be better in the field," Fiona insisted. An intensity in her eyes said she'd be willing to blow up half the world to get her son back.

But her need for action didn't change his plan at all. He wasn't going to risk Fiona's life on this. He had to handle it alone. He glanced over at the team. They would react in case he was hurt or killed and couldn't get Matt to safety, but Fiona was not going. "You stay here and wait for updates."

She frowned. "I'm more capable than I look."

"I understand, but I'm not ready to do my job and worry about you. Please stay here."

"You don't understand. I would wager I'm more capable than you. I would be an asset. If you had told me what happened in Colombia, I might have been able to help keep us together."

Maybe she was right, but he couldn't count on her understanding of the ins and outs of their team. "Please stay here. I love you too much to lose you."

"That's a lame excuse to exclude me. Love can do amazing things sometimes. It's not a cage. If anything, love should create an environment that expands, not limits. You say you trust me but you want me locked away? You've already forced me into widowhood for the past five years. That decision wiped me out, and now when the stakes are even higher, you want to take away my ability to rescue Matt? I don't think so. So you better start thinking of a plan that involves a cooperative effort. I love you too. We can weather even your prior deception, but only if we start acting like a team again." Fiona reached out, her hand gripping his.

Jason felt her familiar warmth, a reminder that, despite the secrets, the essence of the woman he loved never changed. A woman he couldn't bear to see hurt.

His fingers brushed over her soft skin, grounding him. The feel reminded him of the night before and the trust they'd put in each other, in just existing in each other's company. "We'll get Matt back."

She nodded. "Let me help."

While her intentions came from the right place, he was not going to bring her into a situation where she could be caught in the same hungry lion's den he was headed into while trying to save their son. He couldn't wonder about her safety and remain focused on rescuing Matt too. He didn't care if he survived this ordeal as long as he could make certain his family would pull through and thrive into the future.

He wanted Fiona involved, but at a distance, and yes, he was being a hypocrite, because if the situation were reversed, there would be no way she could keep him from rescuing their son. Yet, his own insecurities blocked him from trusting what his heart and head both told him about Fiona. "Porras will see through any effort we take to minimize the risks. Even the small drone might cause them to just kill Matt and flee. I refuse to let that happen. We have to follow their requirements. The team can work in the background. If I get close to Matt and find an opening in their defenses, I can cause a disruption that will allow backup to board the boat."

"So you go it alone to an isolated place where you have no assistance? And we wait it out until you find a window of opportunity, *if* you find a window of opportunity?" Steve asked, his frown not supporting Jason at all.

"I don't want anything to risk Matt's life." His mind had already started racing, and his thoughts turned darker and darker. The whole mission seemed more and more impossible as he allowed doubt to consume him.

Fiona watched him, her eyes not filled with fear, but with a piercing intensity. "Jason, we need to think this through logically. Going directly to them could be a trap."

He turned sharply, his eyes blazing. "They have our son, Fiona. What choice do I have?"

"You always have choices," Fiona responded. "You need to take a step back. Your reluctance to disconnect from your emotions is limiting your ability to see the

big picture. We have to break every aspect of this operation down in order to understand what the risks are
and formulate ways to reduce those risks."

"We don't have a week to do a whole project analysis on what will work and what won't. I have to be there
in—" he looked at his watch "—three hours. It'll take
me two hours to drive to Woods Hole."

"Figuring out a plan won't take longer than thirty
minutes if the people you've been bragging about to me
are as capable as you say they are. Besides, you can work
in your car to finalize smaller details." She leaned back
in her chair and raised her brows in that way a middle-
school teacher did when handling headstrong preteens.

Steve, Meaghan and Sam nodded in agreement with
her. Fiona had transformed from someone the team protected to a valued member of the team with zero delib-
eration from Jason. In reality, he'd never hire someone
like her. Her background had layers and layers of walls
protecting her from discovery. She'd never disclosed any
of her past work, nor had she ever explained the details
of her actual skill set either during their marriage or in
the past few hours since beating the hell out of Harper.
Too much risk for a fledgling security team to take on.
Yet, here she was, making plans and collaborating with
the team he'd put together. Somehow, their allegiance
had crossed over from him to her.

"Although I don't know your past, as you won't disclose it, I doubt you've ever experienced this scenario,"
Jason said to her.

"You'd be surprised, although I admit my emotions
for the safety of Matt have altered my usual distance
from this sort of thing. What I do know is Porras blames

you for the death of his son," she said. "What makes you think he won't enact the same revenge and kill Matt right in front of you? Once you're there, that's the first thing he might do. Get it out of the way and then head back toward South America."

Jason felt as though she'd hit him with an axe. The possibility of Matt being killed so soon after he arrived on the boat had been on his mind, but hearing Fiona articulate it made it all the more chilling.

She continued, "You charging in there is exactly what they're expecting. I'd bet they also have some pretty decent firepower that would take out a rescue boat or even a helicopter. Why give them what they want?"

Jason hesitated. The immediate rush to save Matt dissipated. "Then what do you propose we do?"

Fiona picked up a pen at the table, tapping it gently over a pad of paper as she laid out her thoughts. "First, we should inform law enforcement. I know we're afraid they'll hurt Matt if we involve the police, but there are ways they can help covertly."

He shook his head. There was no way he was going against their directives without solid assurances that the authorities wouldn't rush in for an arrest without regard for Matt's safety. "It's too risky."

"Riskier than you going in there alone and unarmed?" she challenged.

"What's your second idea?"

"Use a minidrone equipped with a camera as Sam suggested. We'll send it to scout the area first, take stock of what we're dealing with. We need information, Jason." The tapping continued, a nervous tic he'd noticed about her when they were in college.

"And third?"

"Third," she paused, taking a breath, "we negotiate, and while doing so, we use the time to gather as much information as we can to form a tactical advantage. This can be through the police, through surveillance or even through a third party. We cannot just walk—sail—into what could be an elaborate revenge scheme."

He sighed, his eyes meeting hers. "They will not negotiate. They have all the cards. You know this too. If we had something they wanted, besides me, I'd agree with you, but if Porras doesn't get his way, there would be nothing stopping him from leaving tonight."

Fiona moved closer to him. "I concede that point, but if we all put minds together, we may realize we have something they want and would be willing to bargain for. We'll get him back, Jason. And we'll do it by being smarter, not just braver."

With newfound resolve, they turned their attention to enacting Fiona's plan. When the sun disappeared behind the bank across the street, Jason appreciated Fiona's approach. He of all people understood that bravery wasn't about charging into danger—it often involved having the courage to change course, especially when guided by a voice of reason.

When the plan was nailed down into a reasonable operation, Jason drove alone to Woods Hole.

The traffic wasn't too bad and he made decent time onto Cape Cod and into the small community at the southern point. Seagulls soared overhead, their silhouettes contrasting against the moonlight. The docks were mostly empty, save for some fishermen returning with their catch of the day, a line of cars waiting for the next ferry and a few tourists taking an evening stroll.

Jason parked his car in a dimly lit corner, away from prying eyes. His heart raced with a mix of excitement and anxiety. The operation they had planned had to be precise, with no margin for error. He got out of the car, stretched his legs and walked to the dock where a subsequent email from Porras said the zodiac boat would be located.

Hidden between two large fishing vessels was the gray inflatable boat with an outboard motor. A GoPro camera had been rigged onto the motor, to watch the happenings on the water. No doubt he'd locate a tracking device if he took the time to look, but that wouldn't matter. Everyone knew where he was headed.

As he pushed off in the small boat, he set the entire plan into motion. It was a gamble, but so was sailing straight into enemy hands. At least this way, they held a few cards and were active participants in this very deadly game.

The lights from the waterfront shops faded as he traveled farther from shore. The slapping of the water on the bow provided a rhythm to his journey, something to calm his mind as he prayed for everything to fall perfectly into place.

Chapter 13

Fiona didn't want Jason to drive away alone, but knew he'd be monitored as he arrived near the boat. He'd been so focused on rescuing Matt at all costs that he'd let caution and planning fall away. It had been a risk to challenge him in front of his team, but she remembered the days after learning of Jason's death. Her intense grief prevented her from handling her job. The only reason she'd been able to get out of bed had been knowing Matt had lost his father and needed her more than she needed to hide under her covers. The pain of knowing Matt was now in such a dangerous situation made breathing difficult and she too was losing her ability to objectively work out a rescue plan, but like before, Matt would not be saved by her falling apart. She needed to keep it together for both Matt and Jason.

Jason had left a half hour before. That was a decade if he ended up needing backup, but they had to make sure no one saw their involvement. She walked into the conference room, now the control center for the entire operation. The soft glow of computer monitors lit Sam's and Steve's faces. A concentrated energy filled the space as they worked against the clock, finalizing coordinates, updating maps and checking intel.

Meanwhile, in a government building somewhere outside Washington, DC, Kennedy stayed glued to her monitors, tracking every movement on air and on the water. She and Sam stayed in constant communication.

Calvin had remained hidden from Fiona, in his own space, since the technology wasn't so easily transported into the conference room. She located him in a room where screens around him displayed data streams, video feeds and encrypted messages.

"Come on, Porras," he muttered under his breath, "Give me something." With every keystroke, he delved deeper into the web, trying to uncover any hidden trails Andres might have left behind.

"Do you need anything before I leave?" she asked.

"Just for you to get that family of yours back together in one piece. Jason has been a bear for the past year and even with everything going on around him now, he's got a different attitude. A better one."

The news made her focus even more on her task.

She waved and met up with Meaghan. "Ready?"

"Yes." She'd changed into black pants and a black rain jacket.

Fiona was still in Meaghan's yoga pants and T-shirt, although she borrowed a blue hoodie from Noah's office. The word from the hospital was that he would be fine after some exploratory surgery and time off. That he'd risked his life for Matt made her forever indebted to him.

They drove south in Sam's car, a small silver Prius. It had some zip and blended in with the cars around them, as Noah's had done.

"How are you holding up?" Meaghan asked her.

"I'm scared, angry, exhausted and my muscles ache. Otherwise, I'm perfectly fine."

Meaghan laughed. "Sounds like you're ready for our objective."

"The idea of floating out to sea at night isn't my idea of fun, but I can't leave Jason out there alone."

Meaghan parked the car near a private marina, and Sam and Steve pulled up next to them. Sam unloaded the drone, while Steve carried a mini mobile command post with tracking and satellite gear. Fiona stared out at the waves crashing to shore and hoped Jason and Matt were safe. His plan had been to fall upon their mercy or to infiltrate them, grab Matt and somehow leave the boat and return to shore with both of them alive. It wasn't much of a plan, and from what she'd read about that group they would have enough resources to keep a former military operative from taking down a boatload of trained mercenaries. This plan was better, she hoped. There were no guarantees in this business, but risks could be reduced with planning. There was no way Jason had headed into this without a bit of bravado, and that might help him or hurt him. Between their two different approaches, Matt's chances of getting off the boat increased.

Jason had told the rest of the team he had to go to the boat alone. If they were as competent as he claimed, they'd be there as backup without Porras knowing. The only team member she knew, or thought she did, was Meaghan, who was currently focused on loading their small boat with supplies—two extra life preservers, a first aid kit and a few weapons. For just short of five years, Meaghan had lived next door to Fiona and pretended to sell insurance policies. And here she was about to embark on a sea rescue against members of a drug cartel. Fiona was more than a bit impressed. She also felt as though she could confide in Meaghan more. They had similar backgrounds and although Fiona could never disclose what she had done in her past life, she could remain vague and still find connection. She wouldn't be critical of Meaghan for spying on her, as Fiona had hidden her own secrets and would continue to do so. According to Jason, Meaghan had not known her boss was related to her and Matt. She handled the assignment like a true professional and had been as betrayed as Fiona by Jason's lies. It would be interesting working with her as a team.

They exchanged a few brief words, double-checking every last detail of the plan. Meaghan's determination to get Matt back safely gave Fiona the confidence needed to jump back into this world with two feet. Matt's life, and Jason's, depended on her.

Steve approached them with a tablet in his hand. "I've got a live feed from Kennedy's satellite connection. It'll give you both a bird's-eye view of the yacht. I've marked the potential entry points on it. Hold back until Sam can confirm it's the right one with the drone."

"Can Calvin track my phone? I have no GPS," Fiona said.

"A GPS is part of the life preserver. Don't take it off," Meaghan replied.

"What about Jason? Are you tracking Jason?" If Fiona could have microchipped Matt, she would have. Personal liberty meant squat when the person was dead. She shook that thought from her mind and held on as a large wave lifted the dock a few feet higher, then dropped it back down.

"We're tracking Jason. We'd never let him go without something to locate him quickly."

Fiona knew that, but with under an hour to organize this and years on the outside doing nothing to remain in shape or up-to-date, she wasn't quite as capable as she'd been telling herself. That thought scared her the most— that Jason had been right about her. She'd not only be in the way, but her lack of preparation would hinder the rescue and possibly place her husband and son further in harm's way.

"Thanks, Steve," Meaghan said, glancing over his shoulder to look at the screen before taking the tablet from his hands. "This will be helpful. How's the chatter? Anything on the Coast Guard's channels?"

"So far, it's quiet. Calvin is listening to them and will contact us with updates. Be quick. We don't have a big window."

Fiona focused on what they were saying. She had a good idea of the entire team and their jobs within the organization. "We'll stay connected as much as we can. Sam, you've done similar operations on boats of this size. Any last-minute tips?"

"Stay low, keep quiet. These yachts often have more guards than they show. Matt is our priority and Jason. Revenge, justice and any other bullshit you're bringing with you is secondary. Steve and I are going to head out first to give the drone a chance to find openings and learn the situation." He had a calm confidence to him. It reassured Fiona that she was dealing with a highly professional team, although the proof would be in how well they implemented the plan. As she'd seen at the bunker, the element of surprise and unlimited resources could destroy even the most prepared team.

"Once you're ready, signal us. We'll be able to slip in closer and get a better viewpoint." Meaghan slipped on a black life preserver and handed the other to Fiona. "How did you end up with the speedboat?"

In the shadows, a sleek, black speedboat bobbed gently, its powerful engines making the smaller boat seem more like a rowboat than anything tactically useful. Although Fiona would have preferred to be on something a bit larger, a bigger boat would also be a bigger target.

"Seniority. Let's go." Steve, wearing all black like Sam and Meaghan, boarded the larger vessel and Sam followed behind with two silver cases.

After Meaghan hopped on board the smaller boat, Fiona stared at the open water between Woods Hole and Martha's Vineyard. Then she turned east toward Nantucket, an island that wasn't visible from Cape Cod. If she overshot or undershot her direction, they could end up floating out to the Atlantic Ocean and miles and miles of isolation.

Chapter 14

The inky black of Nantucket Sound stretched forever before Jason. Without lights on the zodiac, his main means of navigation were his phone and the lights on the large boat waiting for him. The waves rose and fell, making his stomach reel from the bag of chips and soda he'd grabbed on his way out of the office. As each minute passed, he came closer to his son, but he had no idea whether he'd be able to rescue him. Fiona was right. Without backup, both he and Matt would never make it out of this alive.

Moonlight broke through the cloud cover, offering fleeting, celestial beams over the water, each one a beacon guiding him to the yacht anchored in the distance.

As the yacht emerged from the shadows, two figures signaled him to approach. After another forty yards, the two men came into focus. From their silhouettes, they each carried an AR-15 but wore jeans and surf shirts. Despite blending into the preppy environment, there was no mistaking their purpose on the boat.

"Hold up." The command cut through the lapping waves as Jason cut the engine, allowing the zodiac to drift toward the yacht. The two men moved with military precision, and one climbed down and boarded the zodiac, his hands rough as he searched Jason.

"You won't need this onboard." The second man grabbed Jason's phone from his hand, pulled the battery out and tossed all the pieces into the salty water. He then frisked him for anything else he was carrying. He found nothing.

The welcoming committee then pushed him toward the ladder and told him to start climbing by jabbing the rifle into his back. He scrambled up from his tiny boat, climbing until he reached the rich teakwood deck of the yacht. There was no easy escape from here. He would need backup or a boat. He looked around for Matt, but couldn't see him. Instead, he saw a woman lounging by a hot tub and several more men with weapons lingering about.

Sitting like a king on a lounge chair in the moonlight, Andres Porras nursed a glass of crimson wine. Although Jason had never met the man, he'd done his research in the years since the botched operation. Porras was the reason he had to hide himself away to protect his family. Despite all those years of planning, his nightmare had come to life on a multimillion-dollar ship. Strands of gray threaded through his enemy's otherwise dark hair. When the man's eyes locked onto Jason's, determination masked all other emotions. Determination to bring about his version of justice by causing Jason to suffer as much as he had. His logic was flawed, however, as he'd been the person who sent his son to his death, and Jason had merely been the last person standing at his botched raid.

"Welcome, Jason Stirling." Andres's voice dripped with icy calm. "I've waited so long for this."

Jason remained as composed as he could. "That's a

lot of energy you put into someone who has never done anything to harm you or your family."

Andres tilted his head as though Jason's words made no sense. "You don't believe that. Why else would you fake your own death?"

"To avoid this very confrontation. You want to make up for your own bad ideas. Instead of looking inward, you've decided to lash out at the only survivor of the raid that you set in motion. I never hurt your son. I can honestly say I never even saw him. I'd been knocked out in the IED blast that you set on my unit before any of your men arrived at the scene. My handgun was still in its holster when I woke up in the back room of someone's shop. I didn't hurt anyone that day, but I sure as hell lost all of my colleagues." The memories of the slaughter swarmed through him, crashing loss and pain over his body as icy as the sea below him. If Andres thought he'd get an apology from Jason for merely being at the wrong place, he was wrong. Jason would never forgive that bastard for the senseless murder of so many. That Andres lost his own son in the raid should rest on his shoulders alone, although now was not the time to antagonize him. Not until he knew Matt was safe.

He looked around the deck and found him. Matt, on the floor by the bar, was tied at the hands by duct tape. Otherwise, he seemed unharmed so far. Jason's emotions welled. "Matt!" he shouted and stepped toward him but was immediately blocked.

Andres rose, his pale tan pants and loose white shirt giving off Caribbean vibes. With an easy wave of his hand, he called off his men. "First, we talk." His every word hung heavy in the salty air.

A mental battle waged in Jason's head. The trained soldier in him needed to focus on the enemy, but the father in him could only see the stoic face of his thirteen-year-old son and want to reassure him that everything would be okay, not that he knew what the future held for either of them.

Andres chuckled, the sound hollow. "He's a strong boy. Got in a few good swings at Alex before taking a long nap. Perhaps I shouldn't kill him at all, just take him and raise him as my own. He'd fall into line quickly with the right motivation." He gestured to where Matt was bound.

Matt's eyes burned through Andres. It would take a lot to break that spirit and Matt would either die or lose a significant part of himself in the process.

Jason's voice broke, "Let him go, Andres. This is between us."

Andres leaned forward, eyes sharp. "My family and yours are bound together. My son David's death tied our fates. You could have put an end to this a long, long time ago, but you chose to hide. Luckily, Montana was a fan of your wife's books. Intriguing plots, but nothing that affected me, until her last book. She gave me something I haven't had in a long time. Hope. And here you are. I must thank your wife in person someday."

The considerable implications of Andres's words lingered, a cloud of what-ifs and philosophical meanderings. But the sudden drone of another engine broke their standoff.

Jason walked to the edge, unsure if it was too late to wave them off. Even if it wasn't anyone on his team, anyone innocent caught up in this nightmare would be at risk. Two men shoved him to the ground and secured his hands behind him around a post with mooring line. Matt was seated across the deck, against the edge of a bar.

An urgent shout from the front of the yacht confirmed Jason's worst fear. "Boss! Boat approaching!"

Through the darkness, the faint hum of an engine grew closer. His heart raced, a single thought consuming him: Fiona.

Andres smirked. "Expecting company? I told you to come alone."

Jason met Andres's gaze and tried as hard as he could to contain his alarm. "I don't know who that is." Every fiber in him tensed, thoughts of Fiona dominating his mind. Her safety, her tenacity. Would she attempt to board? He knew damn well she would, and she'd have the whole team supporting her decision. Hell, if they continued like this, she'd be running his whole company before the end of this fiasco.

Andres, with an uncanny ability to read him, raised an eyebrow. "Your backup, perhaps? Or something… more?"

Summoning every ounce of control, Jason met Andres's stare, voice steady. "I told you, I came alone."

Andres smirked, an unsettling blend of amusement and malice. "Then you don't care if I eliminate them." He gestured, and three armed men walked over to the side of the yacht and pointed their rifles in the direction of the sound of the engine.

Fiona's grip tightened on the edge of the boat, her fingers damp with salt water and anxiety. Beside her, Meaghan's face was taut. Fiona could see the police training that had honed her abilities and felt foolish to think Meaghan had ever worked a desk job.

The radio buzzed to life, casting a pale light over Meaghan's face. "Communications to Boat Two. Target located and we have visuals on both Jason and Matt. They're on the main deck by a hot tub. So far, we have confirmed six men, one woman, and Andres are with them." Sam's voice crackled through the speaker.

A pang of fear punched into Fiona. The mere name of Andres Porras and all the violence he'd committed in the name of profit was enough to send shivers down her spine. She tried to picture Jason and Matt held by such predators. The urge to swim toward the yacht and board it rushed through her, but there was no easy way up the sides of such a large vessel and she didn't want to risk Meaghan's life. They were supposed to be following at a distance in an observation role, allowing Steve and Sam to stay far enough away to avoid any aggression or any panicked moves by the crew to get rid of their victims quickly.

Her grip on the sides of the boat loosened as she went through some of the gear they carried. She slipped a small knife into the pocket of her life vest. The roar of the larger craft's engine sounded as though it would drown out their small engine's noise, but if they moved too close, the occupants of the yacht would hear them. "Are they okay?" she asked.

"There's no sign of physical harm, but be ca—" Before Sam could finish, the unmistakable sound of gunfire interrupted the transmission. The bullets struck the water around the boat, sending plumes of water into the air.

"Meaghan, get out!" Fiona yelled.

Without hesitation, Meaghan swung herself over the side, clinging to the boat's edge, the side facing away from the yacht. Fiona needed to pull the gunfire away from Meaghan, so she took a deep breath and dove into the chilling water. She could feel adrenaline pumping through her veins, numbing the cold bite of the ocean. Her life vest fought her body from descending too deep into the water. Her lungs screamed for air as she swam. When she finally broke the surface, the yacht was within arm's reach. From the rifle barrels pointed in her direction, she knew she'd successfully drawn the attention away from the small boat and Meaghan. She glanced back at it. The boat seemed powered by a ghost, motoring away from her in a large curve. Meaghan needed to stay hidden until she was out of sight and everyone on the boat focused more on her. Fiona assured herself that Meaghan would be fine. She had the right mindset to survive anything. There was nothing else Fiona could do for her.

Reaching the yacht, Fiona hoisted herself up the ladder, her movements driven more by urgency than strength. Her body ached from the cold, but she focused on seeing her husband and son and making sure she was able to do something to help them. Standing back in the basement of a storage facility would never have been an acceptable role for her to play in this. Not when so much could go wrong and so much already had. She was still annoyed that Jason had thought he was helping anyone by going at this alone. He had to see that being part of a team was always preferable to being the lone wolf. Even when she'd been sent out on her own to finish her assignments, she'd always had someone looking out for her interests, at least from afar. Without ten other people on the ground around her, she'd never have been able to accomplish all she had.

Two guards greeted her as she arrived on the main deck, their rifles aimed at her, expressions unreadable.

One of the men, attired like a fraternity brother in shorts and a blue linen shirt who had overstayed his welcome on campus by ten years, pointed the cold metal of an AK-15 in her face. "Stop there." He was a bit overcautious. She wasn't going anywhere with so many weapons trained on her.

Another casually dressed man stood next to him. He frisked her and located the knife she'd slipped into the pocket of her life vest. The presence of a weapon, even one only a few inches long, seemed to make them all the more paranoid. They stripped her of the life vest and let her remain standing in dripping wet clothes.

Above them stood a woman dressed in a pale yellow maxi dress with a straw hat over loosely braided hair. She watched silently, her slim figure wrapped in a shawl. Standing to the side, she had a storm brewing behind her eyes. Fiona could tell she was unhappy with the direction things had taken, but there was a resigned set to her shoulders that suggested she wouldn't dare challenge Andres. Without knowing her role in all of this, Fiona couldn't decide how to leverage that emotion. The man behind her, cruelty etched onto his face, caught Fiona's attention. Andres. He was the only man who could stop this. He held up his hand, signaling the others to hold their fire. His piercing eyes assessed Fiona, scanning over her wet hair and drenched clothes.

The yacht's engine roared to life. Meaghan would be safe in the water. Fiona wasn't sure if she'd just signed her own death certificate, but she never second-guessed decisions she'd already made as that wouldn't change them. It was time to understand the situation and bend it toward her will.

"Fiona Stirling," Andres said with the confidence of someone who had stalked her whole family.

She ignored him for a moment while she turned around in a circle, looking for Jason and Matt. She squared her shoulders when she found Matt across the deck. His hands were secured by tape, but otherwise, he had no restraints on him. If she needed him to run across the deck to hide, he'd be able to. He looked scared but determined. She gave him a small wink, a silent promise that she would do everything in her power to make things right.

Jason, on the other hand, wasn't going anywhere. His hands were tied together behind his back, attached to a column for the upper deck. Two burly guards stood on each side of him. They certainly weren't underestimating him, but maybe they'd underestimate her. Jason wasn't too welcoming toward her presence. His whole body was coiled tight, ready to explode at any moment. More anger radiated toward her from him than toward the actual enemy.

She faced her husband's incensed gaze.

"Damn it, Fiona." Jason hissed, a mixture of relief and anger on his face. He'd expected her to remain a safe distance away, but he should know she'd never leave him and Matt at risk. "Why would you put yourself at risk?"

She met his eyes with a fierce determination. "I lost you once already. I won't lose you again."

Andres, leaning against the ship's railing, eyed them both. "Such passion," he mused. "I've watched couples sacrifice each other for nothing but a few thousand dollars. But you two… There's a fire there. It's…touching."

"Honestly, your admiration means zero to me. Just let Jason and Matt go. If you need someone to kill for your little revenge, kill me." If she died saving Matt and Jason, she'd die, not a happy person, but satisfied she did the best she could.

Matt, however, wasn't feeling grateful for her sacrifice. He looked between his parents, torn between his loyalty to them and fear of Andres. She could see his slow, even attempts at pulling apart the duct tape holding his hands together.

Jason's face reddened at her words. "What the hell, Fiona?"

Andres chuckled. "This has become much more interesting. What will Captain Jason Stirling do to save his wife and son? What would happen if he had to choose between them? That would be a very interesting question. And how much love would you two have for each other if your son dies while you both watched? The bond you two share… It's your greatest strength and your most profound weakness." He paused, looking thoughtfully at Jason. "It's like Christmas in September."

"Let them go, Andres. They have nothing to do with this," the woman said. An Instagram perfect beauty, the kind men killed for, she watched Fiona as though she could read the future and it was bloody and bleak.

"And yet, here they are, Montana," Andres retorted with a smirk. He considered Fiona for a long moment, his eyes narrowing. The silence was almost unbearable. Finally, he shook his head. "Sorry, Mrs. Stirling. No deal."

Fiona squared her shoulders. "Jason abandoned us for five years. I doubt losing us now will have an effect on his life. Perhaps you can take one of his colleagues. He was much more attached to them." And not one of them were there to be harmed.

Andres tilted his head with an air of malicious amusement. "Oh, I think you will be more than sufficient for what I have in store for him. Because, as you said, you'd do anything for family and I'm sure he would too." He let the words hang in the air.

The weight of her decision to board pressed down on her, but she wouldn't let Andres see her falter. She met his gaze, unyielding. "Good luck with that."

From the side, Montana spoke up again. "Let her family go, Andres. We've made our point. We have so many bigger issues to deal with back in Bogotá."

Andres frowned, clearly irritated by the interruption. "This is not your business, Montana."

She shook her head and turned away, walking down the stairs to the interior of the boat. Fiona hated seeing her go. She seemed to have a conscience and might have been able to prevent harm from coming to them. It seemed that Andres's obsession with revenge for his son made him blind to everything else around him. He was taking a lot of chances lingering so close to shore. This was not international waters. Regretfully, he didn't seem to have a decent set of advisors with him. He was commanding the crew with his ego and leading himself along with his heartbreak.

One of the Abercrombie henchmen pushed Fiona next

to Matt and wrapped her hands with duct tape in front of her, as they'd done with Matt. Matt had been moving the tape back and forth until the ends twisted over and stuck together, a nightmare to get apart. She'd need a knife to help him.

"Leave it alone," she whispered to him. "You're making it harder to break."

His fidgeting hands froze and from the look on his face, his thought that he would be free vanished and panic rolled in.

She received a sharp smack on the right ear by the idiot closest to her for talking. "Shut up."

She tried to appear apologetic so they'd let her remain there, but another guy walked over and dragged her about fifteen feet from Matt. Now they were all separated. She tried to stay in the moment, but Jason seemed about to blow his top, and Matt was fading under the stress of it all.

Chapter 15

Jason had never been hypnotized by wealth. Once he'd lost his wife and son, nothing seemed to matter except keeping them safe. Now he was trapped in this floating prison, waiting for some super wealthy villain to destroy them all. The dimly lit deck cast long, undulating shadows that melded with the steady rocking of the boat. The silence outside of the clanging of pans from the kitchen and the heavy footsteps of their guards added to the chilling tension aboard the ship.

Jason couldn't pull his hands free. They were tied together behind a thick pole, its cold, unyielding surface pressing against his back. The rough rope dug into his skin with every futile movement he made.

Fiona seemed downright content to sit there and wait for the worst to happen. His anger at her simmered under the dread of what could happen to her. Matt's breathing had become more shallow since his mother appeared. Jason would do anything to prevent them both from being harmed. If the team had followed the plan, they might have backup soon enough.

"Andres," he said, his voice hoarse, "there has to be something, anything, you need. Is it money? Assets? Influence? Just name it."

But Andres, a silhouette against the dim light, smiled at Jason's offer. "You think this is about material wealth, Jason? What did you make last year? Two hundred thousand? How adorable. How much can you offer to me? A used Range Rover or that burned-out house you called home?" He laughed, a hollow, mocking sound that echoed over the waves. "I have riches beyond what you can comprehend. I just need closure on this part of my life so my son will have a sense of closure in the afterlife."

"Hurting my family will never bring closure to this. You sent your son to his death. I had nothing to do with it. Perhaps you need counseling. I can't pay for a private jet, but I'll buy you some therapy sessions. Imagine learning to understand how your own actions affect the world."

Andres stepped over to him. Jason expected an argument—instead, he received a kick in the face. The toe of the leather boat shoe hit the side of his mouth, crushing his teeth into his cheek. He spit out blood onto the shiny deck. He took the injury, thankful it had been focused on him and not on Matt. Time and distance, however, were their enemy. If they went too far out to sea, their chances of rescue would decrease.

A few feet away, Matt stared at Jason's face. No doubt the violence brought the danger they were in to the forefront of his thoughts. His muscles tensed and he tried to slip his hands out of his bindings. Matt's subtle efforts to escape caught the eye of one of the guards, a man no more than in his mid-twenties. With a swift, almost casual move, he kicked Matt sharply in the shin, no doubt spurred on by the violence of his boss. The force of the blow and the sharp pain made Matt cry out. Jason, a person who had held to a very tight code of behavior in the military, wanted to kill that man. After the shock of the attack settled, Matt's eyes narrowed, the intensity almost asking the guard for another blow.

Fiona's eyes, usually so soft and full of warmth, ignited with a fierce protectiveness. Her chest heaved with suppressed emotion, her hands clenched despite being wrapped together in duct tape. Yet, she treaded carefully—any sign of an escape attempt or insubordination would get her beaten up as well.

Jason regretted so many things. Had he gone after Andres years ago, he'd never have had to fake his own death. Instead, he hid like a coward and did nothing but wait. Watching his son get hurt while he was rendered immobile was a torture worse than any physical pain. Andres knew this. Yet, Jason couldn't help trying to help him. "Leave him alone," he yelled out, pulling all eyes toward him.

Andres, a new drink in his hand, had sat down on a lounge chair without the slightest hesitation in his plan. "Every ounce of your pain," he said, savoring each word, "is a gift for my son."

Seeing her son in pain sparked something inside Fiona. She held an arsenal of skills capable of reducing the beast who harmed him into nothing more than a quivering mess, but with her wrists bound, she remained as helpless as Matt. His anguish echoed in her ears, amplifying the rage boiling within her veins. The tape around her wrists was the only barrier holding back the storm of retribution that lurked beneath her restrained exterior. The grimace on Matt's pale face gave her pause. Whatever she did, it would have to be intelligent, deadly and fast enough to not gain the attention of the men surrounding her.

She made a quick assessment of what they were up against. On a boat, in the middle of Nantucket Sound, a mile or so off the coast of Martha's Vineyard. An occasional recreational boat could be seen on the horizon, but not close enough for their occupants to see what was going on. The ferry lane was located farther south, so that wouldn't help them. There were several guards who lingered around Andres. The woman, Montana, and maybe a chef and other staff were belowdecks. There had to be a captain driving the boat, which meant they had too many people to fight off, considering neither she nor Jason had their hands free.

She struggled with the tape, loosening it, but not enough. It was too sticky and any jerky movements would bring too much attention to her, and she'd be no help to anyone dead. Besides, she didn't want to fold over the edges of the tape as Matt had done in his attempts to get free. It would make breaking out of it all the more difficult.

Jason had pulled at his bindings so much when the guard kicked Matt that blood dripped from his wrists. He'd done everything in his power to protect Matt and her from this exact situation and she'd unwittingly written a map for Andres to follow to find Jason. The thought made her sick. Tied to the post with enough guards to prevent him from pulling free, he was completely sidelined. He'd told her several times that this had been the reason he'd hidden himself from the world. He'd done it for Matt and her. She should have respected that. Instead, she'd thrown his concern for them back in his face. Everything he'd warned her of had come true. Yet, she had to be fair to herself too. She'd never have imagined this scenario when he disappeared. She was doing the best she could under the circumstances.

Matt remained passive. No fight, but he didn't have the look of someone who had given up either. He was thinking. Exactly as his father was doing. Going over details, trying to assess the situation. He held himself together not like a thirteen-year-old, but more like a seasoned marine.

"You're an asshole," Jason called out to Andres.

Andres stood up and walked over to Jason. "Your pathetic attempt at saving your son makes this all the more satisfying." He kneed him in the face as he spoke the last word. Jason's head snapped back at the force, leaving him with a bloody nose in addition to a swollen lip. "Can you now imagine waiting to hear from your son, and learning some bastard had gunned him down. He was only seventeen years old."

He stepped toward Matt, presumably to kick him as well. Fiona couldn't yell out to stop him, because that would stir him on. Despite that, her heart raced inside her. Watching Matt suffer was something she'd never be able to tolerate.

Montana returned and Fiona then noticed the large diamond on her ring finger. Fiona had no idea if Andres was married, but Montana's ability to say what she wanted did mean her relationship with him was built on something stronger than sex. "That's enough. I can't deal with blood all over the floor and furniture. Have someone clean this mess up." She waved her hand across the deck. "Come inside, cariño. I'm starving for you." She looked away from the Stirling family and sashayed down the stairs.

"Want me to stand guard over them?" one of his flunkies said.

Porras hesitated. He stared at Jason and then at Montana's retreating figure. It wasn't clear whether he'd been persuaded to follow her or whether he preferred sticking around to shoot his perceived enemies. If Montana was his wife, was she also the mother of the lost son? If so, she carried as much grief as he did, maybe even more because she could do nothing to stop her husband from sending her son into battle with the US and Colombian governments. If Montana could persuade her husband that murdering an innocent family wouldn't honor their son's memory, they might survive this ordeal, but grief was a funny animal, cycling back and forth between anger and sorrow.

Just as Fiona felt a huge relief at Andres following his wife, he turned back. Something had changed his mind, but Fiona had no time to think through what that might be, because he headed straight to Matt and lifted him to his feet. "You are nothing compared to my son, David. He was a man—you are but a boy."

Matt tried to twist away from him, but with his hands tied and Andres's strong hands on him, he didn't stand a chance. Matt scanned everything around him and relaxed for a moment, which was the right thing to do. Fighting Andres would get him killed.

Jason, still tied to the pole, pulled at his bindings, but they were too tight and thick to break free. The wounds from his prior attempts looked painful, but Jason was focused only on Matt. His anger and fear surfaced, as clear as the moon. Her heart broke for him. After missing the past five years of Matt's life, he couldn't lose him now.

Fiona shut her eyes to reduce the tension and clear her mind. Acting out in fear and chaos wasn't the answer. A splash in the water and Jason's screams of pain opened her eyes. She watched the dark sea in horror as Matt broke the surface, struggling to keep afloat. There was no way he'd survive without being able to tread water for a long, long time.

Jason fought, making his wrists bloodier, even though he wasn't able to save him. But Fiona was. She waited for a moment, her heart punching into her chest, gearing her up for the biggest fight of her life. The boat had slowed but was still moving away from Matt and he'd soon be lost to them.

"A life for a life. I feel better, but not one hundred percent." Andres gave Jason the finger and walked downstairs.

"You bastard," Jason shouted, but Andres continued walking away.

When the other men turned away from the railing where they had tossed Matt overboard and toward Jason, Fiona made her move, hopping up on to her feet, racing across the deck and diving over the railing of the boat. Holy crap, it was a long way down. The last thing she heard was Jason screaming for her to stop. Too late. She tumbled around in a most inelegant manner and struck the water butt-first. The cold water woke up all her senses as she submerged and descended lower and lower under the water. Before her momentum slowed, she kicked to the surface, the moon guiding her up. Salt water filled her throat and nose. Her head popped up and she coughed out the seawater and sucked in huge gulps of fresh air. It only lasted a moment until a wave struck her and knocked her back. She didn't have the assistance of the life vest to keep her afloat as she did before, and her tied hands made staying afloat nearly impossible.

First things first, she had to get her arms free. The salt water made the loose duct tape into a far more malleable force. She didn't have time to slowly maneuver her hands through the tape. Yes, the tape was failing in the salt water, but she had to swim back to find Matt. Pulling a leg between her hands and her chest, she yanked her hands away from each other at the same time she jammed her knee between them. The tape split. Her hands were free. She shook her shoulders and glanced over toward the boat. It was much smaller now. They didn't want to see Jason's family die? Cowards. Not that she was complaining. She had enough to handle without someone sitting above her taking potshots.

She did a one-eighty and saw Matt's yellow T-shirt far-off. He was still afloat, but struggling. An athlete like his father, he should be able to kick for a few minutes. Maybe a few minutes had already taken place. She couldn't be sure, as time was rushing through her head at alternative paces—too fast, too slow—and for a moment when she'd first heard the splash, time stood completely still. She swam toward him using the shirt as a homing beacon. One goal. Get to her son.

Although never the best swimmer, she'd done a triathlon once and had a swim instructor teach her how to keep a steady pace without expending all her energy. It was the only way she got through the swim portion.

Stroke, stroke, glide. She stayed underwater until her breath was gone and then spotted her son again. Stroke, stroke, glide. He was so much farther than she'd thought. She should have jumped as soon as Andres threw him overboard, but the chance of his men grabbing her was so much higher and then she wouldn't have had a chance in hell of saving him. Stroke, stroke, glide. She lifted her head and could no longer see him. Her entire body began to fight the cold water, the stress of the waves and the panic of not making it in time to save her son. She still had about twenty strokes to go when she saw him fade under the water. Panic rose, obliterating her rational side. She couldn't let him die, and she was more than willing to risk her own life to save him. She took the biggest breath of her life and dove underwater, hoping she could pull him up in time.

Chapter 16

Jason looked out at the fading image of Fiona with disbelief and anguish. His eyes were transfixed on possibly the last place in the world he would see his wife and son alive. The last thing Jason had seen of them was Fiona's blond hair fanning out over the violent waves as she disappeared beneath the surface of the ocean.

She'd jumped overboard in a desperate bid to save their son. If he'd been able to, he would have done the same thing. Staying onboard would only allow Andres to torture them. Their chances of survival were slim, but they had a chance—at least that's what Jason told himself.

After all this time of protecting them, only to see Matt thrown overboard and Fiona, his heart and his soul, follow him into the icy depths, destroyed him. Time stopped and the world as he knew it became stained with the blood of his family.

A perverse laughter echoed across the deck, turning Jake's blood to ice. Andres, a picture of sadistic satisfaction, stood at the railing edge. "It's quite poetic, isn't it, Jason? Your wife killing herself like that. To be honest, I would have been happy for the men onboard to have had some fun with her. Pity. Well, enjoy the evening. My own beautiful wife is waiting for me."

His amusement was made even more grotesque by the scenario—a chilling testament to his warped sense of justice. However, not everyone aboard the yacht shared Andres's sentiment. Montana, half-hidden in the shadows, listened to his speech with a face white as porcelain. She bore the look of someone witnessing a gruesome accident, unable to look away despite the horror.

She crossed the deck, her steps hesitant, to stand beside her husband. She reached out, touching Andres's arm lightly. "Andres," she said, her voice barely above a whisper. "This…this isn't justice. It's murder."

Her words halted the mirth on Andres's face, yet he quickly resumed his sinister smirk. "This is justice, Montana. David can rest in peace now. Tomorrow, Mr. Stirling can join his family at the bottom of the ocean. And they'll be together for always. I find that somewhat romantic."

"Romantic? It's barbaric." Her voice cracked, her gaze flickering to Jason.

Andres clasped her hand and pulled her away. She followed him without argument, but the temperature in their bedroom would be frigid.

A chilling silence remained on the deck after they left. The waves of the sea rose and fell nonstop, refusing to provide a chance for Fiona and Matt to float peacefully and wait for rescue. Bound to the post, Jason could do nothing but obsess over the fate of his family.

Fiona's heart pounded in her chest as she tried to locate Matt. The frigid water felt like a thousand icy needles against her skin, robbing her of breath. But she fought against the shock, forcing her body to continue on her search. She would not stop until she found him.

Matt was somewhere in this chaotic expanse of water, swallowed under waves. Her focus fought through her panic and all of her maternal instincts toward sacrifice and suffering. A levelheaded mind was so much easier when the task didn't involve one's child.

Salt water stung her eyes as she forced them open, struggling to make out anything in the shadowy depths.

She swam farther down, the weight of the water increasing, pressing on her chest and crushing her resolve. The cold crept into her bones, numbing her. Her body grew weary, her lungs burned for air, her eyes stung. She rose up and took a large gulp of air, fighting off the despair and forcing hope to push her farther than her body wanted to go. Diving down again, she kicked in a circle around the spot where she'd submerged, knowing that the currents were pushing and pulling her in a direction of which she had no control.

But then, she saw it. A spot of color in an otherwise gray and hazy environment. His yellow T-shirt, its vibrant hue contrasting against the darkness of the water. With a renewed surge of energy, she propelled herself toward him, her arms aching with the effort. When she reached him, she saw his eyes wide with terror and confusion, faint bubbles of precious air escaped from his lips as he struggled.

She maneuvered him into a lifeguard's hold, pulling his back against her chest, linking her arms under his. His hands were still tied together with the duct tape. Kicking with all her might, she swam toward the surface, feeling her own breath leaving her. Her lungs screamed, her muscles burned, but she kicked, focused on that shimmer of moonlight to lead them to air.

They broke the surface. She gasped for breath, but held tight to Matt. He coughed, his body trembling. Fiona secured her grip on him, doing her best to calm him despite the wild beating of her own heart.

When they had a moment to release the strain of that first obstacle of drowning, a wave lifted them higher but didn't crest over them. Fiona took that as something positive. The wind had died down and the sea was growing calmer. Yet, looking around her, she had to fight with everything she had to ignite even the smallest flicker of hope. The vast, empty horizon offered little positive to dwell on. Not one distant light, a ship…anything. All she saw was the yacht disappearing toward the open ocean with Jason aboard. Where the hell was the drone and the rest of the team?

Fear chilled her to the bone, but she shifted her mindset back to survival. They were together and she had been able to rescue her son from drowning. Holding on to him, she reassured herself that getting captured had been the best thing. She'd been there when Matt was thrown overboard.

"Hold on, Matt," she murmured, her voice a shaky promise against the storm of emotions inside of her, "We're going to make it. I won't let go."

As the sea rose and fell around them, Fiona and Matt clung to each other. The endless expanse of water offered no reprieve, no floating debris to cling to. The bitter cold was slowly sapping their energy.

She tried to stay calm, tried to keep them afloat, occasionally filling his shirt with air to give them a small reprieve, but his hands had to be free for that technique to be really effective. Her fingers pulled at the duct tape, using the water to help her until she could unravel it. The gray tape was about four feet long, far more than they had used on her—he'd been their only prisoner at the time and they had taken their time to secure his hands. They probably assumed he had more strength than Fiona. No matter. All hands were now free. She shoved the tape into the pocket of her yoga pants. Just in case.

Mathew squeezed his hands together and pulled apart from her for a second. The current moved them farther apart and he struggled to swim back to her.

"That's not going to work." She pulled off her sneaker and between rest periods, untied it.

"What are you doing?" he asked.

"Tethering us together. It's too much effort to try to swim and remain next to each other."

"But what if I start to go down? You'll get pulled down too."

"I won't let that happen." She sounded more confident than she was. If they could no longer stay afloat, she was going down with him. But that would only happen after she did everything under her power to keep them afloat.

In the moments between waves, they took turns resting, supporting the other's weight while they fought to catch their breath, their bodies numb from the cold. Fiona remained positive and as strong as she could for Matt. Their situation was dire—survival growing more and more unlikely as time stretched on—but Matt remained calm.

"Do you think Dad is okay?" he asked.

"He's still onboard, at least he was when I followed you over the railing." She hoped he would survive this. Her gut told her Andres had more in store for him. Jason was a survivor. Hopefully, the team would find the yacht soon.

"I can't believe they threw you overboard too."

"They didn't exactly. I figured the two of us together would have a better chance of survival than only one of us."

He turned toward her. "You jumped?"

"We're a team. That's what teammates do." Fiona looked into Matt's eyes that bore an uncanny resemblance to his father's. "Your dad will be okay without us. For now, let's think about staying above the water and then we can plan his rescue."

"It's hard to believe we finally have him back and all this happens. I wish he'd told us."

"I agree. But your father...he didn't know they'd ever learn he was still alive. He couldn't have known this would happen."

Matt spit out some seawater. "I know, Mom... I don't blame him. I'm scared for him too."

"Have some faith. I've been in worse situations and have come out fine."

"Worse than this?"

"My job was complicated," she replied.

"Mom, I... I knew you did something different when you worked. Remember the Little League coach who wouldn't let me play and you asked him nicely, then he freaked out on you? You literally stood still and stared at him until he got nervous."

"I don't think he was nervous."

"Yeah, he was. He always put me in after that and

never said another word about benching me. I even caught him looking at you whenever I was pulled from the field," Matt said, his voice barely audible against the wind. "You gave up your job just to be with me."

Fiona blinked against the stinging salt water, a shaky smile gracing her lips. "You've made being your mother easy."

She would do anything for her son. Literally anything. If she had a chance to meet up with Andres and his band of thugs, she would make them regret tossing a teenage boy to his death.

Her plans hung in the air. She had to believe they'd get out of there. Otherwise, they might as well just let go and descend to their graves. Cold, tired and scared, they held on to each other in the turbulent sea and reminisced to keep each other awake and alert and able to hold on for a little bit longer. Their plans for the future and shared fear and concern for Jason fueled their will to survive. And as long as they had something to fight for, they could last a little bit longer.

Chapter 17

The more Jason thought about it, the more thankful he was that Fiona had followed him. She was in a position to possibly help Matt. Not that either of them were champion swimmers, but they both had grit and determination and he had to believe that she'd find a way to keep Matt alive. The team should have followed them at a distance and hopefully would come across them, although the darkness made any rescue attempt difficult.

Two of the guards sat at a nearby table, nursing beers and laughing in Spanish about the tough guy who watched his son and wife die from the boat. He didn't bother replying to them in Spanish. The less they knew about his skill set, the greater the chance they'd spill something he could use to escape.

He shut his eyes and tried to rest and think his way out of this nightmare. He definitely didn't want to be like Porras, spending his life on revenge for something he had done. Instead, he plotted various means of escape under a bunch of different scenarios, including being thrown overboard, getting loose and stealing a gun and sending up rescue flares. The mind games helped ease his stress and the fear of losing Fiona and Matt once and for all.

Soft footsteps came up behind him. Montana. She was in a light bathrobe tied at the waist. Her long hair over one shoulder. This was not a meeting he wanted. Her husband seemed like the jealous type, as well as the sadistic type and the asshole type. He didn't want to risk a slit throat for even seeing her.

The two guards glanced over but resumed their conversation. Apparently she didn't warrant any intervention. Which meant she might have more power than Jason had given her credit for.

"Have you eaten?" she asked.

"I'm fine." Jason tried to be as blunt as possible to not push a conversation.

She wasn't taking the hint. She put a drink in front of him with a straw. "It's nutritious. You need the nutrients. I fear you might be here a long time."

He shook his head, not wanting to accept anything from anyone.

"I'm sorry," she whispered. He could hear the distress inside her. Perhaps the memory of her son tormented her even more with the cruelty of her husband.

He could taste the blood from the cut in his mouth and thought of Fiona and Matt freezing to death and maybe worse. "Sorry doesn't bring my family back to safety."

"I know you never hurt David. It was Andres. He insisted he was old enough to be a soldier. He was just a boy. Only seventeen," she admitted, her voice too low for the guards to hear. "Please drink this."

"And if you want to poison me?" Jason said, his voice laced with suspicion.

There was a hesitation in Montana's demeanor. "If I wanted you dead, I would not go through all this trouble. I'd have one of these men shoot you and toss you overboard."

He couldn't disagree and nodded when she offered the drink again. He took a sip through the straw. Some sort of smoothie with mango and banana. The taste hid the taste of his own blood.

Montana wiped away a tear. "I just want my family safe. Like you do."

Understanding bridged the distance between them. They both understood each other on a level no one else on that ship would. Not even Andres with his hyperfocus on all the wrong things.

Jason fought the glimmer of hope that sparkled in the back of his mind. "I don't trust you."

"I'm offering to help," she replied.

Before he could garner any details, Porras came rushing toward them, rage in his eyes. "Montana? What the hell are you doing here?"

"I'm giving humanitarian aid to a prisoner."

"Don't be foolish. He'd just as soon slit your throat than let you help him. Go back to bed."

She backed away from Jason as Porras approached them and fled back downstairs, leaving the smoothie. The two guards were now standing, acting as though they'd been there the whole time.

Porras stood over Jason. "Don't get any funny ideas. She'd help a dog that bit her in the arm." As he walked away, he kicked the smoothie into Jason's leg. The cup turned over and soaked his pants with the golden liquid.

The guards laughed, but left the contents of the cup to seep further into his clothes. They returned to their beers at the table nearby.

Jason tried to move the cup with his leg, and then saw something that most definitely didn't belong.

A nail clipper.

Fiona's body was beginning to shut down. Matt was shivering uncontrollably.

She'd never felt so helpless in her life. The sea tormented them endlessly and the cold was sucking away her energy and her sense. Even her heart was beginning to break down, the potential loss of her son and husband slowing the beating down to a low, sorrowful drumbeat.

Although she'd taught Matt how to tuck in his shirt, blow air into the wet garment, and seal the neck opening with his hands, she knew that this crude floatation device wouldn't help if their minds became muddled with the confusion that accompanies hypothermia. They only had minutes left before the cold took them both.

Her eyes scanned the water, trying to find anything that could help them.

Something swam by her. Something large. She swallowed down her fear to keep Matt calm. "Matt," she said to him in a voice as steady as possible, "stay still."

But it was too late. The sleek form of a shark, illuminated briefly by the soft light of the moon, circled closer.

Matt looked down. She wanted to get between him and the shark, but he was in front of her. As the shark approached, Matt pulled away from Fiona's arms and moved toward the shark, punching it in the snout.

The shark reacted like a chastised puppy, arching back and then circling away from them.

She was speechless, her son having just defied every

bit of advice she'd ever given to him. "That…was incredibly reckless," she choked out, "and incredibly brave."

Matt, breathing hard, looked at his mother. "I saw it on *Shark Week*. I couldn't just let the monster eat us."

Fiona refused to think about becoming a meal for a shark. That was one more threat she wasn't able to control. Instead, she grinned, the release of some of her pent-up tension. Pulling him close, Fiona said, "You handled it better than I would have." She didn't know what she would have done if it had approached her first, but was doubtful she'd thrust a fist toward its face.

They switched positions for a moment, giving her a short rest.

The far-off sound of a motor rose up in the distance. It was dark and impossible to see Fiona, dressed in darker colors. Not the easiest outfit to spot at night. Perhaps the yellow of Matt's T-shirt could catch someone's eye. She wished she still had the knife from her life vest. It would shine if hit by a light.

"Do you have anything in your pockets?"

"I don't know. I had my keys and a few coins. They took my phone."

"Let me see the keys."

He struggled to search for them as he stayed afloat. "They might be at the bottom of the ocean."

"That's okay. I'll get new ones made."

"I have a quarter." He lifted up his hand, clenching something in his fist.

"Perfect." She took it from him. "Can you tread for a few minutes alone?"

"I'll try."

She aimed the flat of the coin toward the boat. It was headed a few hundred feet away from them.

"Wave your arms and try to get their attention."

She screamed toward the boat and Matt waved his arms. The boat didn't turn off course.

Then a spotlight scanned out toward them. Matt, with renewed energy, waved his arms and Fiona aimed the coin toward the light. She had to believe they would see the weak shine off the dull old quarter. This was their last hope. Her arm hurt as she held it up, keeping as much faith in her plan as she could. She could feel Matt losing energy as he went back to treading water.

"This isn't going to work," he said, his voice defeated.

"Don't stop believing. This is our way out of here. I know it."

"Like you knew Dad was dead?"

"I didn't know he was dead. I was told that and acted accordingly. I'm now taking all the information I have and using it to get us out of here. If you think that's absurd, then go ahead and let go of me. You can pull me under and it will all be over."

His legs kicked harder, keeping his weight from dragging her down. "I couldn't. I don't want to die."

"Then don't." She continued aiming the coin toward the boat. It had to work. She was running out of options.

The boat motored away, the lights fading into the distance, but then the spotlight swung back in their direction.

Chapter 18

Jason waited until the two men supposed to keep an eye on him closed their eyes. He then leaned forward and shifted his legs until the nail clipper was by his hip and he could grab for it with his fingers. He took his time and nicked at the rope tying his hands together. When one of the men stirred, Jason slowed his movements to remain undetected. Eventually, the guard returned to sleep and Jason finished the job, pulling the rope apart where it had been frayed.

He had several options. He could hold the sides together and pretend it wasn't broken, but he'd be subject to another beating or a gunshot to his head if Porras became bored of his presence. Those options didn't appeal to him. So he had to escape, but they were too far out to sea for him to dive over the side of the boat and swim to Fiona and Matt. Instead, he had to hide somewhere on this yacht, where no one would find him. He scanned the area. The life raft would be the first place they'd look. The upper deck was all open spaces, except for the pilot-house, and he'd need to move carefully to avoid coming into view of the captain. Although he'd love to take over the boat and send out a distress signal to someone, the men inside the main control room would be armed and not willing to give up control so easily. The main deck where he was located now was also too open for him to hide. He had to sneak downstairs.

The cool breeze in the air gave him the energy to move. He took the rope and tossed it overboard and tip-toed belowdecks. The first landing had a long hallway with what was probably the main bedrooms and the dining area. Jason wouldn't be safe there, so he went below one more floor and passed by the galley, where some-one was already banging pots and pans, preparing for breakfast. Beyond that, a "caution, no entry" sign on a door invited him inside. The door opened to the engine room, a gleaming white and chrome space, heaven for engineers. He could hear footsteps above him in what seemed like a control booth, complete with large com-puter screens high on the walls. That was his destination if he could wait it out until the man inside left. He stayed low and glanced around for a safe place to be close but not seen. There were a few hot-water tanks wrapped in white insulation, double engines and a large generator. He couldn't find any place to hide, except in an access panel in the engine.

The space looked far too small for him, but he had little choice. He opened the hatch. The motor rumbled in a high-priced-sports-car kind of way. The floor seemed clean without any oil or dust and the insulation wrapping the pipes kept the heat contained, mostly. So he ducked inside, his arms and legs pulled tight.

Had Porras held Fiona or Matt as a captive, Jason might have folded to whatever demands Porras made of him, but he had nothing over Jason now. And if Jason had the chance, he'd bring that asshole to justice. For now, he practiced deep, slow breathing and hoped for a miracle.

The confined space became suffocating as the minutes dragged on. His body, pressed against the insulated pipes that weren't burning, but very hot, vibrated under the constant hum of the engines.

Footsteps passed nearby. There seemed to be some urgency in their tempo. His absence might have become known. That would keep him inside this hellish engine for a bit longer. The oily scent of machinery clogged his nose, and his focus was off. But he stayed as still as possible.

He reviewed what he knew of the yacht's layout in his mind. Getting into the ship's communications system was his objective, but not with so many people walking around.

The engines' hum escalated into a deafening roar; the yacht was picking up speed. He had to get out of this space. The cuts and bleeding at his wrists tormented him. But every sharp sting reminded him of watching Matt being thrown away as though he were trash. His stomach roiled with the anguish of what had happened to him and Fiona.

More footsteps, some muffled shouting between men and then footsteps rushing away. He was safe for now.

A rush of energy shot through Fiona as the boat came closer to them. When she caught sight of the silhouette she squeezed Matt's arms. "It's the team. They found us."

His entire demeanor swung from bleakness to elation. The energy shift resonated through his expression and movements. "What were the chances of them finding us?"

"One hundred percent. What is happening now is what-is—let's ignore all the what-ifs. There's no time for that. Look. Steve's waving a towel toward us. And Meaghan made it back on board. We're going to be just fine."

The boat pulled up close to them and Steve reached down, pulling Matt out of the water first. He received a large hug and was immediately wrapped in a towel. Fiona treaded water for another minute until Steve reached for her. The speedboat was higher from the water than the one she and Meaghan had taken out only a few hours earlier, but it also had enclosed areas where they could warm up and get dry.

Once on board, Meaghan ran to her, flung a towel around her and gave her a bear hug. "Damn. Your life vest is on the yacht. We would have flown past you if we hadn't seen something shining from the water."

"They took my life jacket the minute I got on board. Porras thought he'd drown Matt to make Jason suffer, but I was able to dive over the edge after him." She took a sip of water and spit it out over the railing.

"I punched a shark," Matt said through chattering teeth.

"A very brave move, but as a mother, I don't think I could live through a reenactment." Fiona shook her head at the memory. There were too many times she could have lost him. Now that he had a team backing him up, she turned her thoughts back to Jason. "Are you tracking the boat still?"

"We lost the drone when they fired at your boat. One

of them noticed it and took it down. We're following the yacht through Kennedy's systems. We have the specs for the boat and a map of every floor. Now we need to figure out a way to get aboard."

"Did you contact the Coast Guard?"

"Yes, but they're a half an hour out. Kennedy has been monitoring three Coast Guard vessels in the area. Their closest asset is assisting a sailboat that flipped over. Another is still in port in Hyannis, and the last one has to maneuver around the elbow to reach us."

Fiona bit back her frustration. "They're our best chance at slowing their escape."

Her body shivered as she stood with the team. They moved below to the small area inside, while Sam and Steve switched places—Steve now piloting the boat above, Sam sitting at a table helping them think of their next steps. Meaghan went to a microwave and heated up two cups of tea for Matt and Fiona. When Fiona held the warm cup between her hands, she sighed. The heat was wonderful.

"Can we catch them?" Fiona asked.

"Yes, but they'll see and hear us coming and Jason could be killed before we board." Sam tapped his fingers on the nautical map in front of him.

"Can we sneak in, disarm the guards and allow the speedboat to come alongside it?"

"Like you did before? Because that was a cluster-fuck," Sam said with too much truth.

"I admit I drove the boat too close," Fiona said. "But they didn't sink her and you came to my rescue in time."

Meaghan stood next to her. "There's got to be a way to slow them down. Ram them?"

Sam shook his head. "They'll detect us before we arrive."

"Right." Meaghan, her fingers tented together, sighed. "Too bad we couldn't stop the engines."

Sam appeared struck by lightning. He picked up his phone and called someone over the satellite link. "Can we jam their engine and scramble their radar for a few minutes, enough to stall their engine and enable us to slip behind the ship and get aboard?... Doubtful." He looked at Meaghan, then spoke into the radio again. "Okay. I'll ask them and get back to you."

"What did Calvin say?" Meaghan asked.

Sam stood and pointed up to the bridge. "Let's include Steve in this."

They left Matt below, wrapped in a blanket and drinking the tea Meaghan made.

When they reached the bridge, Steve looked over his shoulder. "I have them at a distance, mostly tracking them with Kennedy's guidance and the radar. Any ideas on how to stop them?"

Sam nodded. "We should be able to stall out the boat for about five minutes, but it won't stop, merely glide without engine assistance. Once their computer system runs an override, the engine will click back on and we'll be out of luck. We have literally minutes to get close enough to the boat to board without them seeing us. I doubt they'd let anyone climb up the ladder again, so it looks like the rear portholes are our best bet. The specs I found say that they're just under two feet wide. The rest of the portholes are only one foot and we'd never be able to fit anyone through them. They're located at the stern.

It's risky, but once I get on board, I can cause enough chaos to allow Steve to pull up on the side."

Meaghan shook her head. "You couldn't fit through such a small space, especially in a wet suit. Steve couldn't either. I guess it's me."

"And me," Fiona added.

"No," both Meaghan and Steve said at the same time.

"You can't go in alone," Fiona insisted. "There's too many of them, and you'd never be able to climb up to the porthole without help."

"It's too dangerous. You've already been exposed to the cold water, your body may not tolerate another long, cold plunge during the same night," Steve said, his eyes focused on the radar.

"I'm more than capable of making it back to save my husband. Especially if you have an extra wet suit." She hoped. Part of her wanted a nap and a sleeping bag, but she needed to save Jason.

Steve continued staring ahead at the water in silence. Sam made a face, but Meaghan nodded. It was a slow nod, nothing too enthusiastic, but definitely accepting.

"There are only three people on this boat who can fit through those windows. Me, and I'm already going, Fiona, who has proven she can fight enough to stay alive for at least a few minutes once she's on board, and Matt."

"Matt is not an option," Fiona declared. There was no way he was going near danger again.

"Then we have our team." Meaghan pointed between Sam and Steve. "You guys better carry out the plan to perfection, because we'll be counting on you. Jason will too."

Sam's shoulders dropped enough to let Fiona know he wouldn't be arguing over this anymore.

Steve shrugged. "Fine. It's settled. Be ready in twenty minutes. And you two better not die."

Meaghan gave him a thumbs-up. "We're huge fans of being alive."

Fiona returned belowdecks to check on Matt. He was bundled up and fast asleep on the cot. She kissed his cheek and pulled the blanket under his chin, then leaned back on a large bench at the stern of the boat and stared through the opening to the moon, praying Jason could see the moon too and was safe.

Chapter 19

Sam dropped the dinghy to the side of the rescue boat. The boats smacked each other as they floated along, side by side. As the dinghy tapped against the larger vessel, water splashed onto the wooden bench. Fiona looked over the railing and saw how far down she'd have to climb to get aboard. Having been in the water only thirty or forty minutes ago, she wasn't super keen about slipping back into the cold waves and swimming to a place where they not only wanted her husband dead, but they already thought they'd killed Matt and her.

Sam helped Meaghan down into the smaller boat, their hands linked together. Her entire weight was held by him as he lowered her over the side, not that it appeared to be a problem for him—he had the build of a football player. She remained focused on not falling into the water as she dropped into the middle of the dinghy without making it rock too much to either side. When she was safe, they all turned to Fiona.

"Are you sure you want to go through with this? I can try to fit through the window," Sam said.

She looked him over. There was no way he'd fit through the porthole. It was her or Matt, and there was no way in hell she'd send her son into combat. "I appreciate the offer, but you wouldn't fit. Imagine climbing up the side of the boat, only to end up wedged with your feet waving to the fish and head inside the boat unable to stop someone from using your face as target practice."

He made a face. "Good description, but when you rescue DJ, tell him I offered but you refused."

"Absolutely. We'll disrupt things enough to put everyone else off their guard so you guys can come and save the day." She wouldn't let anything stop her from making sure her non-dead husband was still alive at the end of all of this.

He nodded. "You make a lot of sense. If you have trouble, just contact me through the earpiece. It should work submerged in water."

"Should?"

He shrugged. "We've never had a sea rescue before."

"Good to know." If she and Meaghan were Jason's only hope, she'd better get it in her head that this was her most important mission ever.

"Turn back if you get nervous. It's better to be safe than sorry."

Meaghan called up to them. "Sam, we're grown-ass adults doing our jobs. At least I am. Fiona will be fine with me by her side and if she isn't, you'll have Jason to deal with. Or not. Who the hell knows anymore."

Fiona saw a new side of Meaghan—focused, confident—and yet for this split second, she could sense Meaghan's fear as well. A little fear never hurt anyone during an operation. In fact, she found just the opposite in her years undercover. A reasonable amount of fear made people double-check plans and ensure that safeguards were in place and functional. Overconfidence created gaps in the plan, areas that should run smoothly but without double-checking might result in chaos. The team had enough professionalism to understand the risks involved, try to alleviate them as much as possible and strike out even if things seemed stacked up against them. Although she hadn't met all of the team, those she'd met had impressed her. The love and loyalty they carried for each other showed.

She wished she could give them information that would give them more confidence in her, but she didn't have authorization to release that information. If she ended up in jail because of a security breach, Matt could end up alone. That was not an acceptable outcome. She shook her head and ignored the fact that she might not make it back from this task. Now she had to make sure she didn't let any of them down. They had no idea what she was capable of and yet they trusted that she would at least not get in the way. From her understanding of revenge, Jason needed to suffer a bit longer. No way was Porras going to kill Jason to relieve him of the pain of watching his family die.

That Jason would think she and Matt had been lost after all he'd been through broke her heart. She should have forgiven him when she had the ability to do so. Holding grudges never made life better. Forgiveness was not necessarily an easier path, but it led to better outcomes. A moment of love, of connection, of understanding.

"Ready?" Sam asked her.

She nodded. She was more than ready.

He gripped her hand the way he'd gripped Meaghan's a moment earlier. "Godspeed."

She gave him a nod and a smile in return and then tightened her hold as he lowered her over the side. Meaghan reached up and grabbed her by the waist, helping her down.

"Fiona, this is Steve." He spoke through her earpiece. "Can you read me?"

"Yes." His voice was loud enough to hear, but not biting.

"Meaghan?"

"Loud and clear," Meaghan replied.

They motored away from the bigger craft toward the signal coming from Jason's earring.

"Is there any way of getting a message to him? Like is the earring a communication device as well?"

"We kept it simple. Every one of us has some simple or cheap piece of jewelry that wouldn't attract attention. Mine is a belly-button ring," Meaghan said, lifting her shirt to show off ripped abs and a small diamond hoop in her belly button. "It allows us to track the person, but they can also take it off if they aren't on the job. Most of us leave it on all the time. I prefer having it with me in case a blind date goes wrong."

"Like the one you sent me on?" Fiona asked.

"For the record, George appeared quite upstanding when I met him."

"And the first thing you thought was that he was the perfect person for me?"

Meaghan shrugged. "Hindsight is twenty-twenty, isn't it?"

"I hate to interrupt you both on this interesting conversation, but I have the boat in my sight," Steve called in. "It's probably best for you to swim from here so they don't notice. It's about a quarter of a mile. Are you okay with that? The sound is fairly choppy."

"I'll be okay," Meaghan said. They would be abandoning the boat.

Fiona nodded. She'd rested enough to get some of her strength back and had been wrapped in a large blanket before putting on the neoprene bodysuit. This outfit would have made her time floating at sea with Matt much more comfortable. "Ready."

Meaghan went first, easing into the water over the edge of the boat so as not to tip it too much to one side. "Oh my God, it's freezing."

Not the words Fiona wanted to hear as she psyched herself up. She followed Meaghan into the water, tensing at the cold biting her limbs.

Meaghan swam in such a way as to minimize her time on the surface. Slipping under the water and kicking, then twisting on her back to grab a breath and continuing on. Fiona tried that technique but took in a mouthful of water. In order to make it, she'd have to glide just under the surface like an underwater breaststroke and turn her head at every fourth kick. Not as clandestine as Meaghan, but it shouldn't draw too much attention.

As they drew closer to the boat, Fiona, out of breath and barely keeping up with Meaghan, who seemed part seal, began to panic. Would the window be open still and could she lift herself up into it?

She needn't have worried. They both arrived to find the window still open, although it seemed much farther up than she remembered.

"I'm not sure if I can climb up that high."

"You're going to spring me up there and I'll reach down and pull you up," Meaghan replied.

She explained exactly what Fiona had to do. Float, head down, and maintain stability. "One, two and three."

In one huge movement, Meaghan lifted herself onto Fiona's back, stood up and leaped up to the window. Fiona missed the end of the acrobatic feat as her entire body was shoved underwater. She came to the surface and watched as Meaghan gracefully pulled herself the rest of the way without making a sound.

She twisted around and reached her arm down for Fiona. Fiona needed a second to get her bearings after being pressed underwater and then stretched out her arm. Meaghan had to do all the work because Fiona had nothing to hold on to.

Within seconds, they were both sitting drenched on the floor of a bathroom.

"Towel?" Meaghan handed her a fluffy white towel and took one for herself. "We need to be as dry as possible and a change of clothes will help if we need to fight."

"Montana's bedroom is somewhere on this floor."

"That will be great if Montana isn't inside."

They crept through the hall, hearing voices in the dining area, and slipped into an elegant bedroom that was made for days on the ocean, white-and-blue shells decorating the walls and bed. An entire wardrobe was available to them.

Meaghan, being all legs and small chested, fit into a pair of shorts and a T-shirt while Fiona could wear Montana's sweatpants, but required a sports bra and a tank top to keep herself as comfortable as possible while trying to save her husband. Knowing Matt was safe gave her the confidence to take more chances than she had when his life was in the balance.

A noise down the hall had them both slipping into the small closet together. Meaghan rested her chin on Fiona's head, while Fiona pressed as much of her curves as possible into the wall space behind her. When the footsteps passed the bedroom, they both relaxed for a moment. The footsteps returned and this time the bedroom door opened. From the deep sound of them, they were the larger boots of a man, not Montana's. She'd been in sandals when Fiona last saw her, before Matt was thrown overboard and she followed.

Fiona could feel Meaghan on the verge of a sneeze. There was nothing she could do to prevent it, so she prepared to fight her way out. The door opened and closed again and the footsteps traveled back toward the bow of the boat. Meaghan let her sneeze out in as muffled a manner as possible.

"*Gesundheit*," Fiona whispered.

"*Danke.*"

They slipped back into the room. Fiona hadn't truly gone into a fight situation since Matt had been in elementary school. She took a deep breath and visualized herself as strong and competent with all that muscle memory coming back in the nick of time.

"Ready?" Meaghan asked.

Fiona nodded.

"You can stay here, you know. It's going to be brutal and we're the underdogs."

"Thanks. I'm okay."

Meaghan and Fiona slipped down the hall and past the dining room. Montana sat at one end of a long wood table. Porras sat at the other. They had dishes and flowers and fundamental differences in morals between them. Not that Fiona had time to analyze their relationship; she had to rescue Jason. Meaghan waved Fiona downstairs now that they saw that the route was clear. Meaghan would search for Jason on the main deck. It was better that way, because Fiona would be too invested in saving Jason to focus on her assignment. The longer she stayed apart from him, the better.

As Meaghan crept up the stairs to the main deck, Fiona listened at the engine room door to make sure it was clear.

Chapter 20

Jason's jaw throbbed from the beating, but the pain eased the strain of picturing his wife and son drowning, unable to be saved. He could taste blood in his mouth, whether from a loose tooth or a broken nose, he didn't know. He didn't care. The weight of his despair threatened to destroy him. Nothing on Earth mattered to him more than Fiona and Matt.

Sharing that intimate moment with her only a day before showed him exactly what he'd lost. The love of his life. The only person he wanted by his side. It was impossible to think about how many ways a heart could be broken, but in the past few days, it had been crushed, shattered and destroyed in every way possible. There would be no coming back from this. How did one survive when all hope drained away? The despair edged him closer to a dive into the deep, cold water where he could rest his weary soul near his wife and son. It would be so easy to do.

The engine slowed and then stopped. In fact, the entire room went silent as though something had shut an off switch on the entire vessel. One of the men ran inside and rushed past the engine to the control area. The silence gave Jason hope. His team, with their connections to some of the best technology blocking devices, might have done something to sabotage the ship's controls.

The thought of Steve and the rest of the team carrying on this assignment, more dangerous than anything they'd ever handled together in the past, provided Jason with a reason to hold on in the dusty cramped space. A group of people was out there. They wouldn't let him down, and he sure as hell wasn't going to fail them. While he couldn't wipe away the despair on losing Fiona and Matt, he could function enough to survive. Steve had all the brains, Sam had ingenuity, Meaghan had guts and Calvin had the tech skills. Noah, a man who took a bullet to save Matt, was in the hospital right now aching to get back into the storm with them. These guys deserved Jason's best. He couldn't quit on them or the important work they did. Life wasn't easy. It was tough and challenging and punishing. Yet, as long as he could help make this place better for even one person, he had to go on. His family would expect nothing less.

His back cramped up in the small space, but he remained silent. There was a slight rustle of sound outside the engine room door. When the door opened, a single figure came inside. Barely audible footsteps but the slim figure blocked what was left of the light coming through a porthole.

For a split second, the shape of the shadow appeared as if Fiona had floated right back into his life. The tiny silhouette pushed past his slight view into the engine room, a sliver of an opening from under one of the engines. He tilted his head for a better view. The silent sprite's light hair was wet and pushed behind her ears.

But that couldn't be Fiona. He'd seen her go over the edge, diving into the ocean in an attempt to save Matt.

A shuffle of a man came downstairs from the control room, the actions both sudden and scared. The ghost of his wife pulled something out of her pocket and flung it toward the man. He went down with a thud. Jason couldn't be sure if she killed him, but from the gasping and then silence, she probably had. She then went over to the engine controls and speaking in a whispered voice, responded to someone somewhere.

"Yes… The red one?… Okay, I've got it." The voice was all Fiona.

A moment later, an alarm blared.

With the alarms blaring, Fiona could barely concentrate. She preferred having the ability to hear people come up behind her, but this was an exceptional situation. She scanned the area. The guard who had been at the control panel had blood from the knife in his neck soaking into his blue linen shirt. Fiona hadn't wanted to kill the man, but he'd pulled a gun on her and dodging bullets would have seriously stalled her rescue of Jason, and the gunshots would have alerted the others that someone had infiltrated the ship. She refused to place Meaghan at risk.

The engine remained stalled out with whatever Sam and Calvin had concocted to destabilize the technology aboard the boat, but they'd insisted that she set the fire alarm off to override the generator from starting up automatically. Although she expected someone to arrive soon, she never expected the grate under the engine to open. She pulled out another knife, ready to defend herself, but recognized the rough skin and long fingers of her husband. The area he was attempting to extricate himself from seemed impossibly small for his long body.

She hustled to his side. Touched his arm as if to see if he were real. "Jason?"

"Fi. Are you okay?" He smiled up at her, then twisted his leg from under the quiet engine.

"I was going to ask that of you. How did you get there?" She pointed to the impossibly small space.

"I didn't think anyone would look for me there."

"I definitely wouldn't have." She wrapped her arms around him, knowing it could only last seconds, but gaining strength from the contact with the man who she would risk anything for. "I'm good and so is Matt. Steve found us floating in the water. It was a miracle." She didn't have time to go into specifics. They'd have to reconnect over the details when they were safe and away from Porras and his men.

He lifted her chin and kissed her with an intensity that welcomed her back from the dead and apologized for all the pain he'd put her through. She kissed him back with her own apology for her lost faith in him and a promise to never give up on him. They pulled apart reluctantly.

"Tell Jason we have his back," Steve spoke into her earpiece.

His presence in her ear calmed her. Help was on the way. "Steve and Sam are intending to board the boat in a few minutes," she told Jason. "Meaghan is on deck looking for you."

He shifted toward the side of her face. "You can't get here fast enough, partner." He spoke directly into her earpiece before nipping her earlobe. "Okay, let's go find her."

She nodded and they slipped out of the engine room, making sure they didn't run into anyone in the hall. The loud scatter of men rushing here and there made for a slow, jerky trip from the engine room to the main deck. They slid up the stairs after several close calls but eventually hid behind the bar and waited. What they found made Fiona's blood boil. While she was having a reunion with her husband, Meaghan had been captured and handcuffed to a chair. A very heavy chair that could take her to the bottom of the ocean if someone decided to toss her overboard the way they'd sent Matt.

They must have assumed she was the only one on board, because their urgency was more in getting the boat going than searching for someone. Until the dead man by the control panel was discovered. Several cries for assistance came from underneath. One of the two men standing guard over Meaghan rushed off to see what had happened belowdecks. The other looked out toward the sea, watching over their position, looking for anyone following them.

Fiona and Jason had only a moment to create enough chaos to rescue Meaghan and allow the team to board.

Jason pulled a fire extinguisher off the wall, while Fiona lifted a tray of empty glasses not yet carted away to the kitchen.

"On three," Jason whispered.

Fiona nodded.

Footsteps climbed the stairs. Heavy ones that were probably attached to someone who was heavily armed. Fiona held her breath for a moment and said a quick prayer that luck would fall on her side in this situation.

She looked back at Jason, who mouthed the word

"three." There would be no going back from this. She'd fight to save the people she loved or die trying. There was no in-between in this game. She hustled to the other side of the boat and tossed all the glasses at once onto the floor, then backtracked. She could hear the men scurry over to the area away from her position.

Now she'd have to trust that Jason could fight them back while she released Meaghan. She rushed over to her. Meaghan looked at her, the relief evident. Fiona placed a finger over her lips to keep her silent.

She took out a pin from the knife holster and pulled Meaghan's hands toward her. The sounds of gunshots rang out behind her. She only had seconds. She wedged the pin into the slot, shifted it back and forth and then twisted until she heard a slight click. One cuff opened. That was enough for now. She dropped the pin into Meaghan's free hand, before turning to face whoever was running into the area.

The crew member who had rushed belowdecks had come back, gun in hand. He pointed it in Meaghan's face, then pivoted to Fiona. Fiona held her breath. Meaghan remained calm and kept her hands behind her as though they were still secured behind her back. Fiona lifted her arms up in a surrender. She stepped toward the man, allowed his gun to press into her skin. The proximity would only help her. Remembering how Porras had treated his men when she'd been a prisoner, she worked under the assumption that this guy didn't have the authorization to kill her, and he'd be punished for doing so without a direct order. That second of indecision that passed through him provided her with an opportunity to clasp her hand on the barrel of the gun and twist it in a way that yanked it from his grip.

She turned away from him, the gun now in her hand. With a low drop to the floor followed by a swipe of her leg under him, she dropped him. He landed with a thud on his back, still reeling from her first attack. She stood over him, the gun pointed at his chest.

"Don't move." She stared at the man with such intensity, she left no doubt in his mind that she was more than willing and able to pull the trigger. Meaghan stood by her side, the cuffs now dangling from her finger.

"Cuff him," Fiona said.

Without a word, Meaghan turned the man over on his stomach and yanked back his arms in a move that an experienced police officer would be able to handle in their sleep. She put one on and then secured him to the same pole they'd tied Jason to.

"Where's Jason?" Meaghan asked, a question in her expression.

"He's holding off two other men. I hope." She sped away to where she'd broken the glasses. There was one man on the ground, his head bleeding from what had probably been the fire extinguisher. Jason and the other man were at a standoff. Jason still holding the fire extinguisher and the man holding on to a military grade rifle.

Without a word, Fiona pointed the gun at him, baiting him away from her husband. He took the carrot and turned his weapon toward her. As though in slow motion, she saw Jason call out to her, and could hear Meaghan yelling to her to get down, but there was no moment to contemplate every possible choice, every possible outcome. Instinct, muscle memory, a keen survival instinct.

They all churned together to make the decision for her. She shot him dead before he got to her.

As his body tumbled to the ground, Jason reached her side. He stepped in front of her and took the gun that had only a moment before been pointed in her direction. Meaghan knelt down beside the man and checked his pulse, but the shot had been almost point-blank into his chest. The blood loss enormous. The damage inside not survivable.

Jason pulled her into his arms. "Are you hurt?"

She shook her head. Nothing physical, and she wouldn't allow herself to think of the psychological damage until she had her family intact once again. "I'll be fine. We need to get off this thing."

"Meaghan?"

"I'm fine too," Meaghan said from behind them.

The tension in Jason's face diminished. He rubbed Fiona's back, probably as soothing to him as it was for her. "This whole situation has been more stressful than anything I've been through in my life."

"How adorable. A family reunion." Porras stepped forward and pointed his gun at Fiona.

A sharp, searing pain ripped through her right leg, causing her to gasp and stumble backward. He'd shot her. She clutched her wounded calf, feeling warm blood soaking through her fingers. Panic over Jason's and Meaghan's safety flooded her as she looked up to see Porras, his eyes cold and calculating, continuing to point his gun at her.

"You should have stayed out of this," Porras said, his finger tightening on the trigger.

Fiona refused to let fear paralyze her. With a burst

of adrenaline, she pushed through the pain and lunged behind the bar, praying it would shield her from the hail of bullets.

Jason rushed to her side. Before he could reach her, Porras caught sight of him. Porras sneered as he raised his gun again. This time, it was aimed at Jason. "You can't escape your fate, Jason. You will watch your wife die."

She couldn't see Andres, only Jason's expression. So much hatred and a flickering of fear. Without a weapon, he could do little to protect her.

Yet, in the moment she prayed for his safety, he chose to push away from Fiona and launch himself at Porras, knocking the gun out of his hand. The two men struggled for dominance, fists flying fiercely in a desperate struggle for survival.

Fiona could only watch from the sidelines, the gunshot wound stripping the strength from her. She shredded a dish cloth she located on a shelf to tie above the wound and stem the flow of blood already puddling through her sweatpants onto the floor.

As Jason fought to overpower Porras to her right, Fiona caught a glimpse of Meaghan's struggle. Her friend fought with every ounce of strength and skill she possessed against two men on the deck. The more she fought, the more they came back at her. Blow after blow landed on Meaghan. Her eyes teared up from the pain. Fear for both of them surged through Fiona. Her energy crashed and she watched, helpless to protect them. Jason landed a sharp uppercut to Porras's chin, sending him stumbling backward, momentarily dazed.

At the same time, Meaghan found an opening and

delivered a swift and devastating strike that left one of the men unconscious on the deck.

But before they could fully savor their victories, a second gunshot rang out. Jason stumbled back into a chair. His face paled and his eyes fluttered closed. The momentum sent him careening out of her view. As Meaghan dove on the man who had shot him, Fiona screamed out.

Her heart wouldn't bear losing him again. Summoning every ounce of determination, Fiona stood and faced Porras, fury blocking out the pain burning through her leg. They circled each other, both battered and bleeding, but neither willing to back down. She didn't care if he killed her as long as she could take him out with her and end this senseless attack on her family.

Beside her, Meaghan sent one of the men overboard with a roundhouse kick, then was pushed back into a wall, a fist to her face. Blood dripped from her nose, but she continued to fight, even overpowered.

As Fiona stepped toward Porras, something hit her from behind. She struggled to remain standing, but her strength was draining as fast as the blood flowing out of her leg. The ship blurred around her though she fought to stay conscious, her vision narrowing to only the dark sky overhead.

Before the outcome of their struggle could be determined, darkness claimed her, and she succumbed to the void, praying that Jason and Meaghan would somehow find a way to survive. In the depths of her unconsciousness, time stood still, and her mind drifted through a haze of memories and dreams. She saw glimpses of her old life with Jason—their laughter, their love, their hopes for the future and sweet moments with Matt. A sharp pain shot through her and her mind twisted, conjuring the vivid faces of people she'd been tasked to eliminate when she'd worked for the government. Her sins coming to take her to hell.

Chapter 21

Jason had tumbled backwards into a chair, a bullet skimming his shoulder. He glanced back at Fiona. Her skin had turned a ghastly pale, her leg soaked in blood from the gunshot wound. At the same time, Meaghan fought against overwhelming odds, her luck shifting downward. The pressing need to rescue both of them and get revenge for Porras destroying his family's peaceful existence crashed over him, but he was too outnumbered, at least for now.

His thoughts were interrupted by the roar of engines. Looking out over the stern of the yacht, he caught sight of a speedboat advancing at breakneck speed toward the yacht. Steve was at the helm, with Sam holding a rifle in his hands. For a moment, Jason felt the weight lift off his shoulders, but a gunshot from behind him toward the boat had him terrified he'd lose everyone he cared about today. And each loss would be tied directly to his lie.

The last of the men protecting Porras had turned their attention toward the incoming boat, their own vessel still crippled by the cyberattack. Jason took that chance to throw one of the men overboard and punch another so hard with an uppercut, the man fell flat to the floor, losing his rifle to Jason in the process. Steve never swerved off his destination, despite the gunfire. As the large boat skidded to a stop beside the yacht, Sam leaped onto the lower deck, taking out one of Porras's men in the process. Their timing couldn't have been better.

Jason sprinted towards Meaghan, her face swollen from the beating and slammed aside the asshole using her as a punching bag.

"Thanks," Meaghan breathed, stumbling back and shaking out the impacts. Before Jason could respond, she lunged at the same man. He never saw the punch coming, and with a satisfying thud, he dropped to the deck, knocked out cold by one very pissed-off woman.

Porras and the two remaining guards had fled to another section of the boat, no doubt to reorganize and get more ammunition.

Fiona remained motionless on the ground. Jason squatted beside her. Her pulse carried on as a faint rhythm, assuring him she still had a chance of surviving this, but not for long.

"We need to get Fiona out of here," Jason called out to Sam, who was circling the deck, making sure the area was clear.

After disabling another guard who had wandered into the area, Sam rushed over to help. Together, they carefully lifted Fiona and made their way to the speedboat.

When she was placed behind Steve, his eyes narrowed on her injuries and her weakened condition. As he secured her in a blanket on the floor of the boat, he pointed a handgun and shot over Jason's shoulder. Jason spun around and saw one of Porras's thugs drop.

"Anyone else need medical care?" Steve called out to him.

Jason's shoulder was bleeding, but not too much. He didn't have the luxury to step back, not while Porras was still hell-bent in chasing down his family. He glanced at Meaghan, her face now swollen. She shook her head. He'd never get her off the yacht until she either took out the cartel or died trying.

"Not yet, but we have this. Go. Fiona's losing too much blood to survive much longer."

"I'll get her to the mainland for medical assistance."

Jason paused, afraid to let her go without him, but he had to finish this here and now. "Okay. Take care of her."

"Always." Steve pushed the throttle and turned away from the yacht, reaching top speed toward the mainland.

As the speedboat roared away, Jason turned his attention to the cause of this hellscape. "Porras!" he shouted, his temper seconds from detonating.

Sam waved down from the bridge. He'd taken it over and somehow restarted the engines. Jason could feel the lean of the boat as it turned toward the mainland, following Steve's course. He ran back to the bow and found Meaghan, blood dripping from her nose and a black-and-blue mark on her cheek and under her eyes, pointing a rifle at five men with their hands up and their weapons kicked out in front of them. There were two casualties on the ground in front, and she seemed primed to take out anyone else who stepped toward her. Jason backed her up, using the men's own duct tape to secure them, then scanned the area for anyone else free. Porras was nowhere to be found.

When Meaghan tied up the last thug, Jason descended

into the belly of the ship with Meaghan right behind him, adding to his arsenal as he searched for Porras.

They moved systematically through the ship's quarters. They entered each bedroom, knocking open the closets and bathrooms, checking under every bed. When they reached the galley, Jason caught sight of a man, cornered and looking like a caged animal. Montana was beside him, her expression a mix of fear and defiance. As Jason approached, the man in front of him came into focus. This was a fourteen- or fifteen-year-old boy. Same hair and build as Porras, but slighter. His eyes wore the same tension as Montana's.

Jason's hand clenched around the grip of his pistol. Another son? The thought drained his rage. This would never end. It would cycle over and over again for generations if he didn't find a way to stop it. Another Porras, someone who could hunt down Matt for years. Every fiber of his being screamed at him to pull the trigger, to end the cycle of revenge and pain. But he remembered Fiona's plea from days past. "An eye for an eye will only make the whole world blind," she'd whispered.

He agreed with her. He'd never kill an innocent boy. He couldn't.

Letting out a deep breath, he lowered the gun and Meaghan came around next to him. "I have nothing against you or your son," he said to Montana, his voice cold. "Porras, however, shot my wife and wants to kill my child. Where is he?"

The boy made a sharp move, pulling a gun from behind him. Before he could even point the gun, Meaghan lunged, expertly disarming him. A swift kick to his knees brought him crashing to the ground. Jason moved in, tying his hands behind his back and those of Montana.

Montana didn't fight him. Instead, she dropped her head, a tear sliding down her cheek. "You could have killed him," she whispered.

Jason met her gaze. "I could have. But your husband's cycle of violence ends here."

As they made their way back to the deck, the yacht was eerily quiet. Sam remained on the bridge, on the radio with the Coast Guard. Meaghan led Montana and her son to a seat close to where Porras's men were tied up.

Jason searched for Porras but couldn't see him. Meaghan pointed off the starboard side at the tender with a small outboard motor, almost to the horizon. "He abandoned ship leaving his family and team behind. So much for loyalty," she said loud enough for everyone to hear how their wonderful leader didn't care enough to save them.

"You've got to be kidding me." Jason stared at the boat carrying the man who wanted his family dead now getting away. "Tell Sam to go after him."

But before they could get into a chase, the piercing beam of a spotlight from a helicopter sliced through the darkness, followed by the deep growl of an approaching Coast Guard vessel. Jason wasn't going anywhere until he passed through a whole mountain of bureaucratic BS.

"US Coast Guard. Lay down your weapons and raise your hands!" came an authoritative voice through a megaphone.

Meaghan exchanged a glance with Jason. They knew they were on the side of the law, but the scene—the two of them, heavily armed, with a whole boatload of people tied up—could easily be misinterpreted.

Jason placed his weapon on the deck, raising his hands in surrender. Meaghan followed suit, placing her rifle next to Jason's. The Coast Guard personnel swarmed the yacht, several headed to the men tied up and several others to Jason and Meaghan. No one resisted arrest. Jason tried to explain how they came to be on the boat, but they ignored him and focused on securing the area. They were not interested in explanations. A few moments later, Sam came down from the bridge with an officer, his hands behind his back in handcuffs.

Jason stared at the aftermath of his failure to confront this problem years ago. He should have done something besides hiding out and not protecting all the people who mattered in his life. Matt had almost lost his life and Jason had no idea how much psychological damage this would do to him. Fiona was bleeding so profusely that she might not make it to the hospital in time. Meaghan and Sam both were in handcuffs. And Meaghan had undisclosed injuries she wouldn't complain about because she was that type of person. It was all on him. One hundred percent.

"These guys kidnapped my son," Jason explained to a Coast Guard officer, a stern-faced man with a silver streak in his hair.

"Where is your son?"

"He's with the state police in Bourne," Sam replied.

"He is?" Jason said. He thought they'd transport him somewhere else.

"It was the safest location for him while we came back out to get you."

"You can call them, Officer," Meaghan added, although she received a pretty angry expression in reply.

"And you only contacted us after you took control of the boat?"

Jason was the one who put them in this, so he answered for the team. "We have a lawyer, Barbara Singer." Jason had found Barbara's expertise in criminal law helpful in the early years of the business. She told them what lines they could cross and what lines they absolutely couldn't go near. She would not be happy about this situation. Not at all.

Montana shouted over everyone else, "They kidnapped us. This is all a setup. They killed those men." She pointed to the area where there were several dead men on the deck.

The officer raised an eyebrow, then turned to Jason. "Your lawyer better be damn good." He turned to Montana. "You're all coming with us for questioning."

As the Coast Guard crew began the process of transferring everyone from the yacht to the lower deck of the Coast Guard cutter, Meaghan whispered to Jason, "We have the kidnap demand letter. It'll work out."

Jason nodded, watching the members of the cartel as well as Montana and her son being led away. "As long as Fiona and Matt are safe," he murmured, the roar of the helicopter blades echoing overhead.

As the Coast Guard vessel motored away from the yacht, now commandeered by Coast Guard personnel, Jason, Meaghan and Sam sat next to each other on a long bench, under armed guard. Montana stared out the window while Porras's son wore a stony look of contempt. It wasn't an emotion that would simmer away quickly, but Jason had to believe that he'd soften over time. Not that he was worried about their feelings when Fiona's life could be draining away.

"That was a tough call back there," Meaghan said, nodding towards the kid who almost shot them. Jason had had a shot but Meaghan handled him without having to kill him, even after she'd been beat up by the other men.

"It was an easy call," Jason admitted. "I never want to hurt anyone. Even these assholes. But if they're going for me or someone I love, I'll do what I need to keep everyone safe. Your method was risky, because he could have taken you or me out. Total badass move. I owe you."

She smiled. "I could use a raise."

Sam leaned his head back to rest on the wall. "Combat pay."

Jason nodded. "Fair enough."

But Jason wasn't so quick to claim victory as they were ferried back to the mainland. Porras may have lost his protection, but both Matt and Fiona remained at risk as long as Porras himself was free in the world. His family couldn't survive living under the constant shadow of revenge.

Jason sat with his hands cuffed at a steel table in a gray conference room overlooking the ocean. Last night had seemed like a never-ending nightmare and yet here he was, caught in a state of limbo with Commander Grogan, a man who wanted hard answers from Jason, but refused to offer any news about Fiona or Matt. Jason remained as silent and calm as possible as the officer grilled him over and over about why he'd trespassed on

Porras's yacht. After two hours, Jason's patience wore thin at the Coast Guard officer's continued interrogation.

"My son was being held captive and the ransom note said I had to go out there alone to get him back. So I did." He spoke in a monotone voice as he had repeated this same line about fifty times.

"Alone? Some of your staff at your little security service also headed out there."

"I followed the demand on the note," he replied, not giving Grogan the answer he wanted. "They chose to follow me."

"They went out on their own without orders from you?"

"I did not give an order to follow me." Steve made that call with Fiona's urging.

Meaghan and Sam had been sent to other rooms. Jason warned them on the boat ride back to shore to remain silent no matter what they were accused of. They had enough experience to handle themselves like the professionals they were. Steve would most likely be back at headquarters with Calvin, Noah was still in the hospital and Kennedy had disappeared back into the cubicle where she lived in the Pentagon. The more he thought about it, the more they looked guilty of something. Hopefully, the blown-up house couldn't be pinned on them. They had quite a few murder charges looking straight at them. Sure, it was self-defense, although self-defense while trespassing was a difficult mountain to climb.

His thoughts remained consumed by concerns about the safety and whereabouts of his family. He had to know if Matt was safe, whether Fiona's gunshot wound had been treated in time and if Porras posed any lingering threat to their lives. The unknown gnawed at him. Yet, Commander Grogan wasn't sharing anything. The officer annoyed him. For the moment, Jason was in the dark.

The officer leaned forward, his eyes fixed on Jason, and said, "Mr. Stirling, you and your team took matters into your own hands, and there are definite consequences for your actions."

Jason clenched his jaw and refused to respond. The door to the interrogation room swung open. Barbara, sporting her usual navy suit and annoyed expression, entered the room, plopped a briefcase onto the table and stared down Grogan. "I'm Barbara Singer, Jason's attorney. And you are?"

"Commander Grogan, CGIS."

"CGI what?" she asked, with not even the smallest look of confusion.

"Coast Guard Investigative Service."

"Right." She took a seat next to Jason and said, "How are they treating you?"

"I'm good, but I don't know what's happening with Fiona and Matt."

She turned to Grogan. "Can we have a minute alone?"

He nodded and left the room.

As soon as the door closed, Jason spoke. "Matt is supposed to be with the state police. And I have no idea what happened to Fiona. I last saw her on a boat with Steve, bleeding profusely."

"I understand. Steve contacted me. He's with Matt at Falmouth Hospital waiting for Fiona to come out of the operating room."

"How is she?"

"So far, stable."

"Does she have security?"

"Steve's there, and local police have been notified that Porras is still at large."

It wasn't a perfect scenario, but Matt was safe with Steve and Fiona was stable, so far. But he had to get out of this interrogation room. He had to get to Fiona's side.

About fifteen minutes into their conversation, Commander Grogan returned. He immediately started in on his questioning again.

Barbara turned her shotgun gaze toward the officer. "My client is a concerned father who acted out of desperation to save his son from a dangerous criminal. We intend to cooperate fully, but we also expect his rights to be protected."

The officer hesitated, his composure slipping. "I understand, Ms. Singer, but you have to realize the seriousness of the situation here. Mr. Stirling and his team took the law into their own hands. Two of the guns found on board the ship were licensed to his business. Can you explain that?"

Barbara frowned. "Can you explain why the father of a kidnapping victim is being subjected to a harsh interrogation while the actual villain in all of this is running through the streets of Massachusetts without nearly half as much animosity thrown in his direction?"

Grogan glanced between Jason and Barbara, realizing that the power dynamic had shifted away from him. Barbara goaded him on for a few minutes, then commented on how the press were going to react when they learned that he'd kept a man from seeing his injured son and dying wife while the El Chapo of Colombia was on the loose. Jason knew she was bluffing, because of all the things he'd demanded of her when he'd sent her a retainer was the utmost privacy in all their dealings. His business did very well without any involvement from the press. Commander Grogan, however, did not know she was bluffing.

Barbara pressed on, her voice resolute. "Our priority should be to focus on capturing Andres Porras. My client may have obtained valuable information that can lead to the arrest of Porras and dismantle his criminal network. Jason is more than willing to cooperate fully if he is accorded some decency in this matter."

"Let me speak to my commanding officer," Grogan said before rushing from the room. He'd underestimated her, and it was becoming increasingly evident that he didn't fully grasp the intricacies of the situation.

"That went well. Thanks." Jason appreciated her on his side and hoped she didn't have to help him out of too many more jams, especially ones that involved Homeland Security.

"Give it five minutes. He'll send an underling to release you so he can save face."

Five minutes later, an ensign appeared, who apologized that Commander Grogan had been called to another matter. She handed Barbara and Jason a business card.

They left the harshly lit interrogation room, the weight of the world slightly lifted from their shoulders. Meaghan and Sam were waiting for them. The air outside seemed fresher, the corridors less confining, but Jason couldn't shake the nagging worry that gnawed at him like a persistent itch. Was his family safe?

Barbara must have sensed his unease because she placed a reassuring hand on his shoulder. "I'll drive you all to the hospital. If Fiona's half as stubborn as you are, she'll be fine," she said, her voice steady and calming.

Meaghan laughed. "They're pretty equally matched in that department."

As they stepped outside into the bright, sun-soaked day, Jason couldn't help but feel a renewed sense of determination. The hunt for Porras had begun in earnest, but his heart was torn between locating him and rushing to Fiona's side.

Chapter 22

Fiona's eyes fluttered open, and the sterile white of the hospital room flooded her vision. Her head throbbed, and the pain in her leg was a constant reminder of the gunshot wound she'd sustained while trying to save Jason. She groaned, memories of the terrifying events flooding back.

"Mom?"

Fiona turned her head to see Matt sitting in a chair by her bedside. He looked different now, dressed in gray Massachusetts State Police sweatpants and sweatshirt. Her heart filled with relief at the sight of him, but her thoughts were consumed by the well-being of Jason, Meaghan and Sam.

"Are you okay?" Her voice was raspy as she reached out to touch her son's face.

"I'm okay, Mom," he said, taking her hand as he had when he was much smaller. "Steve took me to the police, and they were pretty cool." He turned his head toward the door and there was Steve, leaning against the door-frame, holding a large coffee cup. He looked as weary as she felt.

"Steve," she said, her voice low. "What's going on? Where's Jason? Meaghan? Sam?"

Steve walked into the room and set the coffee cup on the bedside table. "There's a lot to tell you," he began, taking a seat next to her. "On a good note, Jason, Sam and Meaghan are all alive."

Fiona exhaled as though she'd been holding her breath for a year. "I'm so relieved."

"Don't party too soon. They were caught up in a Coast Guard mission to intercept the yacht. They arrested everyone on board. Everyone, except for Andres Porras. He escaped before anyone could stop him."

"How could he escape in the middle of the ocean?"

"A dinghy. An expensive one with an onboard motor and enough gas to get him anywhere on Cape Cod, Nantucket or Martha's Vineyard. He's on the loose. There's reason to believe he's coming after you and Matt."

Fiona's heart sank at the mention of Porras. He'd done so much damage to her family. And he was still out there looking for them.

"Where's Jason now?" Fiona pressed, her fear escalating.

Steve hesitated for a moment before continuing. "Jason, Meaghan and Sam are all in custody. They were swept up in the investigation of Porras and his operation. It didn't help that our guns were scattered across the ship."

Fiona's mind reeled with the news. Her husband, her friend and Sam, all in custody?

"Don't worry. Barbara is taking care of everything," he added.

"Barbara?"

Steve cleared his throat and nodded, understanding her confusion. "Barbara Singer is an attorney Jason hired years ago for this exact situation," he explained. "Not this exact situation, but something close. She's the best of the best. Intimidating as hell. I sort of feel bad for the Coast Guard officers put in charge of speaking to her."

As Fiona held Matt's hand, she couldn't help but wonder where Porras was headed. It didn't take a whole lot of brain cells to realize he was coming after Matt and her.

A nurse came inside and told Steve that visiting hours were ending. Fiona demanded that Matt get to stay, and the nurse caved for him, only him.

Steve smiled in that way that told her he had everything on his end under control or as in control as he could get it. "I'm going to find doughnuts. I'll bring you back some." He waved and disappeared down the hall.

Fiona had only just met Steve, but in that short time, she understood why Jason had decided to go into business with him. Cool under pressure and he seemed to have an understanding of all the chess pieces in this game. She was grateful for his help.

"Are you really okay?" Fiona asked Matt when they were alone.

He nodded. "I was worried about you and Dad, but otherwise, I'm okay."

She loved that Matt was holding himself together, but he'd need to break down all his feelings eventually as she had after too many situations where blood stained her memories. Her first priority after everything calmed down was to find a decent therapist for him. Perhaps she could enlist her own therapist to give her a good recommendation. She'd need her own double sessions for the next few weeks to get over the immense rage bubbling up inside her.

The hospital room door swung open, and Jason rushed inside. He looked like an impossibly beautiful mess of a man. Rugged, with a steely determination etched into his features, his dark hair hanging disheveled onto his shoulders. Bruises and scrapes marred his gorgeous face.

His clothes were torn and stained with blood, evidence of the gunshot wound to his shoulder that he had miraculously survived. She'd so wanted to believe the bullet hadn't hit anything vital, but she had no idea. That lack of knowledge shook her to her core.

Despite the physical toll, an unwavering determination had him rushing to her side.

"Fi." His voice filled with emotion as he closed the distance between them. He enveloped her in his arms, and she clung to him as if her life depended on it.

She pulled back at the slight wince from him as she touched the wound on his shoulder. "Have you seen someone?"

"I couldn't do anything until I saw you and Matt." His embrace tightened, and he kissed the top of her head, his lips warm against her hair.

She looked up toward him and he kissed her lips. A kiss that reaffirmed their love and their unbreakable bond, a kiss that promised they would stay with each other and never let each other go.

As they pulled away, he turned to Matt, who had buried his head into the phone he was using, most likely to avoid the awkwardness of his parents making out next to him.

"Hey, champ." Jason's voice emitted as much warmth as a man who had been fighting for everyone's life for hours and hours could. He reached out and pulled Matt into a tight embrace. "I'm so glad to see you."

Matt embraced his father back, and Fiona could see the love and relief in his eyes. "I'm glad to see you too, Dad."

Jason straightened up, his expression turning serious. It was a look he had rarely used in their marriage. He'd always been the carefree, lighthearted guy at home and from what she'd heard from his former colleagues, seemed the same at work, until something threatened them, and then his attention became laser-focused. He addressed both of them. "Listen, we can't let our guard down. Andres Porras is headed in our direction. We need to be prepared for anything. How long are you planning on being in bed?"

Fiona didn't have the physical strength to fight off an attacker in her hospital room. "Say the word, and if someone else drives, I'll go anywhere to keep Matt safe."

It wasn't a difficult choice when he was standing over her with so much fire in his eyes and a willingness to do anything for Fiona and Matt. Jason's presence made her feel more secure, but she wouldn't be able to rest easy until Porras was no longer a threat.

Jason's fingers traced the edge of Fiona's hand. The sterile hospital scent hung in the air, but it was overpowered by the overwhelming sense of relief and gratitude. She'd seemed so far gone when he'd laid her down in the boat. Now that he had his family back, truly back with him, he was damned if he would let anyone come between them.

Beside him, Matt sat quietly. Jason couldn't fathom

the thoughts scrolling through his son's head. He'd been through more than anyone his age was expected to endure. And the threat remained as long as Porras was at large. They couldn't protect him from that fact. Keeping the danger hidden from Fiona for so many years never protected her, but made her too complacent. She'd let her guard down at the house because she had no idea such an evil man was headed in her direction. How Jason could make Matt understand the seriousness of the Porras cartel, without destroying what was left of his teenage years, he had no idea.

The exhaustion in Fiona's eyes was undeniable, but all her attention was now on protecting them. Jason had always respected her strength and determination, but he'd never seen her as some savage defender. She'd not only killed someone in cold blood, but she'd never stopped to process it. Instead, she carried on to the next task of saving Meaghan. Someday he'd get the answers he wanted, maybe even deserved, although he couldn't claim any righteousness in the matter of hidden lives.

He leaned in closer to her, and he gently squeezed her hand. "Do you need some rest?"

She shook her head. "Where's the rest of the team? I think they should come to my room so we can make a plan."

"Steve, Meaghan and Sam went to the cafeteria. I can text them to come up."

"Please." She reached back out to Matt. "Stay in this room. No matter what. I don't trust the security in this place."

"We're safe, Fiona," Jason reassured her. "We've

taken all the necessary precautions. There's even an armed guard at the door."

"That won't stop him," she whispered. "I saw the despair in his face when he pointed the gun at me. It's like he will never be forgiven for his son's death until he places the blame on you. It's like the revenge gods will give him absolution on his own bad decision by sending someone else to the grave, only he won't get his son back. That's something that he'll have to just endure for the rest of his life."

"Which makes it even more important that we get the hell out of here." Jason paused and watched as Fiona nodded in agreement. He leaned down to gently kiss her forehead. "We'll find a way to get through this. I don't know what it will be, but we'll find a way."

Fiona smiled for a moment, and then her smile disappeared, and her attention went back inside, scheming, planning and finding a way.

Chapter 23

Fiona lay on the sterile hospital bed, her body throbbing with pain though she concealed it as best she could. The harsh fluorescent lights above cast an unforgiving pallor on the room, adding to her anxiety. She knew she had to keep her mind clear, no matter how intense the pain. She wished she could fade into a drug-induced sleep and wake up when the danger was gone and her leg was healed, but that wasn't an option so she had to let it go. She focused on the small cup of pain medication hidden under her pillow. She'd deliberately kept it out of sight, determined to maintain her mental clarity. In this life-and-death situation, any lapse in judgment could be fatal. Porras was out there, a relentless threat to her and her son Matt, and there was no room for weakness.

Beside her, Jason clutched his right arm. His shirt and whatever he'd tied around it as a makeshift bandage was stained with blood. She could see him slowing because of the pain. His stubbornness kept him from seeking medical attention.

She pressed the button for assistance. When the nurse arrived, Fiona asked to see the doctor. Dr. Gwen Ramirez, an old friend of Steve's from his days at Providence College, had taken over Fiona's care after a personal request from Steve. The head of the emergency department, she could keep an eye on anyone coming and going in the ER.

"Fiona, how are you feeling?" the doctor asked.

"I could be better."

Dr. Ramirez nodded and checked her vitals and the wound.

While she was busy, Meaghan and Sam walked in looking as though they'd both been hit by an eighteen wheeler. Fiona owed them and Noah for helping save her family.

Steve arrived a minute later, carrying a tray of food.

"Gwen, thanks for all of your assistance," he said as he placed the tray on the table next to Fiona.

"No problem. Are you hungry?" She glanced at the decadent tray piled with three slices of pizza, a few brownies, cookies and a doughnut.

"Just feeding the troops."

Jason reached for a slice of the pizza, but Fiona placed a hand on his to stop him. "Did you want the veggie slice?" he asked.

"I want you to get your arm looked at," she said.

"I'm not leaving this room. Not while you're here."

Dr. Ramirez must have understood Fiona's stared request, because she walked over to him and pointed at the blood leeching through his shirt. "Jason, you really should let me take a look at that arm. It's bleeding quite a bit."

Jason hesitated, glancing at Fiona and then Matt. "I'm okay." Typical idiot. He'd pass out in the name of protecting Fiona and Matt.

"You're not okay." Fiona recognized the struggle in his eyes and made the decision for him. "You can't help me if you're injured too. Let her take care of it."

Dr. Ramirez nodded in agreement. "Let me at least look at it. If it's not serious, I can treat it in here so you don't have to leave Fiona's side."

Reluctantly, he agreed. She carefully pulled the clothing from his arm and examined him. Fiona could see him straining to hide his suffering.

Once the doctor was done, she spoke only to Jason. "The scratch on your arm is deep enough to cause some nasty bleeding but not severe enough to warrant more than a stitch or two. Let me call my assistant and we can have it fixed in a few minutes."

"I don't think it's necessary."

"Don't be a baby," Meaghan said, which made Fiona smile. Jason hated being challenged.

"Fine," Jason relented. "If we can remain here while we figure out a few things."

Dr. Ramirez agreed. She called for a physician assistant to bring her what she needed. They worked efficiently, cleaning the wound and stitching Jason up.

As they finished, the doctor offered Jason a reassuring smile. "All done. Just keep it clean and change the dressing regularly. You'll be all right, but try not to get shot again." She looked at Fiona. "You too."

"I'll do my best," Fiona replied, knowing she'd step in front of a gun again if someone she cared about needed her help.

Jason nodded to the doctor. "Thanks. I probably would have left it to fester if I had to leave Fiona alone."

Dr. Ramirez looked over at Meaghan, Sam and Steve.

"I think she would have been in adequate hands either way." As she left the room, she waved to Steve.

"Thanks, Gwen. If you ever need anything, I've got your back," Steve called out to her.

"I don't want to think about what trouble I'd be in to require your assistance." Then she disappeared down the hall.

Don, the physician assistant, remained behind to finish wrapping a bandage around Jason's wound.

Meaghan stepped closer to Fiona. "We're on borrowed time. News crews had caught word of the arrests by the Coast Guard. If Porras doesn't know where we are, he'll know soon enough." She pointed out the window toward several news crews setting up cameras near the hospital entrance.

Fiona glanced over at Matt, who was playing a game on the phone and trying to avoid any eye contact with his mother or father. "We need a plan."

Steve received a phone call and stepped toward the edge of the room to speak with someone. He agreed with whoever was on the phone and only gave one-word answers that showed no indication of the topic of conversation. Then he took a huge inhale and spit out, "Shit. Okay, we'll be prepared."

Everyone's attention turned to him as he ended the call.

"What?" Jason asked.

Fiona somehow knew what was coming. She prepared for the worst, but held her breath until Steve spoke in case it wasn't as bad as she imagined.

"Porras was seen on camera stealing a car in Cotuit. He's headed in this direction."

"What are the police doing about it?" Fiona asked.

"They found the car about ten miles away from where it was stolen. They have no idea where he's disappeared to, but he's within two miles of the Falmouth Hospital."

"We couldn't exactly blast our way out of this hospital without a serious amount of people getting hurt or worse, killed," Fiona said. "It would be better to meet him somewhere less populated. Does he have backup?"

Steve shook his head. "The Coast Guard have both his team and family in custody. Depending on the evidence they have, they could arrest or deport the whole group of them back to Colombia. If they're arrested here, they stand a much lower chance of being able to bribe or threaten the judges. He has nothing to lose if he carries out his plan alone."

Even without his team, Porras remained a relentless threat, and they couldn't afford to lower their guard for a moment. Fiona wished she had more energy. Her thoughts cycled from fear to fury as the pain from her leg sent her mood spiraling and fogged her brain almost as much as pain medications would.

With the armed police officer stationed outside their room, the small group gathered around Fiona's hospital bed.

Steve cleared his throat, his brow furrowed with concern. "I agree with Fiona. We can't stay in this hospital indefinitely. It's only a matter of time before Porras tracks us down. Hell, he could already be here."

"We can't let him find us here," Jason said.

When Don finished with Jason's arm, he joined the conversation. "I could get you discharged, and maybe we can have you leave through the service elevator. Somewhere he wouldn't expect." He stood at the door, not leaving, as though he were more part of the team than a member of the hospital staff.

Sam pulled out his phone. "I'll contact the local police and give them a description of Porras. They can be on the lookout and provide extra security here. If they've been tracking him, we might gain a head start."

"We have a safe house in the area," Meaghan said. "We can get you there discreetly, and it'll be a secure place to hide out."

"Like the last safe house that went down in flames only a day ago?" Fiona asked.

"You may be right. Our security might be compromised."

Fiona looked over at Don. She didn't know anything about him. He could be working for Porras for all she knew, and although that was far-fetched, they needed to keep their plans under wraps in front of him.

"We've arranged a police presence at your residence, Fiona. But it's not safe to go back there," Steve said.

"I agree. I'd prefer to go somewhere no one can connect us to." She glanced at Don, who was now scratching notes on his iPad.

Jason followed the direction of her gaze to Don and nodded. Steve motioned that he understood what she was saying as well.

Jason patted Don on the shoulder. "Thank you. We appreciate your help."

Fiona received a text message from Steve to her and the rest of the team. "'My brother has a cabin up in the mountains, far away from here. It's secluded and secure. We could take you and Matt there until we're sure it's safe,'" she said, reading the text aloud.

Meaghan and Sam both agreed with a thumbs-up emoji. Jason gave a real thumbs-up.

As the group continued to brainstorm and finalize their plans via cell phone, Fiona couldn't help but feel a glimmer of hope amid the uncertainty. They had a fighting chance to outsmart Porras and keep their family safe.

She tried to sit up and nearly fell over with pain. Jason rushed to her side. "If you're not ready…"

"If I'm not ready, I'm dead. We have to get out of here." She winced through the agony of movement and sat up. She pointed to her clothes, but paused as her ears strained to catch the distant echoes of chaos that filtered through the hospital corridor. Shouts, running footsteps and urgent voices signaled the approaching danger. She didn't have the time or energy to battle into a pair of pants.

She turned to Matt, who sat on the edge of her hospital bed, somehow as aware of the danger approaching as she was. "Matt," she whispered, "I need you to hide behind the recliner. Stay quiet, and don't come out until one of us says it's safe."

The fear in Matt's eyes mirrored her own, but he nodded and slid beneath the bed without hesitation. He sadly had experience in hiding now. Fiona reached out to give his hand a reassuring squeeze before returning her attention to the unfolding crisis.

Steve, Meaghan and Sam leaped into action, taking up defensive positions around the small hospital room. Meaghan was by the door, her hand on the handle, ready to bar it if necessary. Sam crouched by the window, his trained eyes scanning the exterior for any sign of trouble.

Jason moved to the side table and pulled a compact, concealed weapon from his back pocket.

"Jason, what are you doing with that?" Fiona asked, with more appreciation than anger.

He smiled. "I thought it might come in handy."

Fiona couldn't argue with the logic, but the sight of the weapon in his hands sent a shiver down her spine. It was a chilling reminder of just how far they had been pushed. He had been told by the Coast Guard to keep a small profile.

Meaghan's voice cut through the tension. "Something is getting closer. We need to be prepared."

Fiona took a deep breath, rallying her resolve. It was difficult turning fierce when her leg felt like a dead-weight and her ass hung out of her hospital gown. "Matt, stay behind the recliner," she said. "Sam and Steve, move the bed. We'll put it in front of the door."

Sam nodded and joined Steve in sliding the heavy hospital bed across the room, positioning it as a make-shift barricade. It wasn't much, but it was the best they could do with the limited resources at hand.

Don, who had turned from a spy wannabe into a trem-bling mess, finally found his voice. "What should I do?"

Meaghan, as always, cool and collected under pres-sure, directed him to a corner of the room by the win-dow, where he would be shielded from the door. "Don, you'll be in charge of calling security to get us additional protection on this floor. Keep your voice low."

With Don settled into his new role, the room was as fortified as it could be. Fiona took a deep breath, her mind racing, her heart pounding, as the sounds of chaos outside the room grew louder, drawing nearer with each passing second. They were ready, but they were defending a fishbowl and had to take into account all the innocent souls around them. And then a loud boom sent the entire room into confusion.

Jason stood near the barricaded hospital room door, his heart pounding as his nemesis arrived like a tornado. The deafening explosion rattled the corridor. He wanted to rush out of the room and put a stop to this once and for all, but Porras could be expecting that. It could all be a trap. Or maybe law enforcement had arrived and had finally subdued him.

He exchanged a glance with Fiona, and their unspoken agreement was palpable. She held her space as though nothing had changed. There was not an ounce of optimism in her expression, but instead a steadfast focus on protecting everyone around them. She had a better mindset. Thinking about being saved would only weaken their position. Innocent lives might already have been taken. At least Matt was safely hidden. Meaghan, Sam and Steve stood beside him, as focused as Fiona. They were ready to confront Porras.

When a loud bang came down on the door, Porras's voice, cold and menacing, punched up the tension. "Open this door or I'll start taking hostages. You have one minute."

Time was of the essence. They needed to make a decision. Fiona appeared both immobile and indestructible sitting up on the bed, her eyes lasered on the door.

"Jason," she whispered, "if he wants us, he can't be focused on anyone else."

He nodded, his mind racing as he contemplated their

limited options. So much for a peaceful stay at a cabin in the woods. This would be the final showdown. "I agree."

Jason signaled to Steve, Meaghan and Sam. "Steve, create a diversion—throw something loud on the floor. Meaghan and Sam, be prepared to act."

Don, the physician assistant, was still relaying information to hospital security. He lowered the phone from his ear and shrank into the corner.

Jason knew this was not the most straightforward defense, but they had few other options. If Porras started shooting through the door, any or all of them could get killed.

While the others prepared to act, Jason addressed Porras through the door. "Let's talk. We don't want anyone else to get hurt."

There was a tense silence, broken by more disruptions outside the door. A woman screamed as though someone had hurt her.

Porras's voice, filled with malicious intent, once again pierced through the door. "Time's up, Stirling. Open the door."

Jason took a deep breath and then nodded at Steve, Meaghan and Sam. Sam pushed the bed back and threw open the door, revealing a hallway filled with a faint haze of smoke. Porras stood in the doorway, holding an AK-15. Steve, tucked into the edge of the room just out of sight of Porras, hurled the food tray to the floor. The clattering noise echoed down the hallway, diverting their attacker's attention. At that same moment, Jason saw his chance and rushed him, while Meaghan and Sam lunged at him from different sides.

The room filled with shouts, grunts and the harsh

clatter of a firearm hitting the floor. Steve rushed forward to help.

"Jason, look out!" Meaghan yelled as Porras slammed his fist into Jason's face.

The blow rocked him to the side, nearly crashing him into the wall. Jason shifted and kicked Porras's legs out from under him. He went down easily. As Meaghan went to hold Porras down, he swung at her, sending her onto the floor. Porras then moved toward Sam, but Sam kicked him in the face, sending his head back into the wall. Fiona called out, pulling everyone's attention for a moment.

Steve stayed out of the brawl, but got hold of the weapon. He pointed it carefully toward Porras, who had had the fight knocked out of him.

With one final push, Meaghan and Sam managed to overpower Porras, pinning him to the ground. Jason and Steve stood over him.

Fiona tossed Jason a white cord. He didn't stop to ask what she'd unplugged to obtain it. He wanted to use it to strangle the bastard, but Fiona was right. An eye for an eye wasn't worth it. Instead, he pulled back Porras's arms and tied him up. In the process, his elbow might have slipped and broken Porras's nose. He wouldn't, however, kill the man.

Breathing heavily, Meaghan picked up Don's cell phone, which was still connected to hospital security. "We need immediate law enforcement in Room 215. Subject is currently unarmed and subdued."

Jason returned to Fiona's side. She'd remained on the bed, almost as though she made herself the most visible person available when Porras came inside. The thought that she'd put herself out there as a target scared the hell out of him, but made perfect sense. She was protecting Matt and Jason and the whole team.

The police arrived, a full-on SWAT unit. According to the officer in charge, Porras had gotten hold of a doctor's white coat and hid his weapon underneath. No one stopped him from entering and by the time he learned the location of Fiona, he was already on the second floor and taking out anyone who tried to slow his approach. Two people were injured, but luckily, no one was killed.

Fiona wanted to leave the hospital immediately after the police left. Dr. Ramirez thought she could move to another room and spend the evening there. They had moved the other patients from the second floor to different rooms and in some cases, different hospitals.

"No, thank you. I'd feel safer at home." She had somehow managed to sneak into the bathroom and get dressed, pulling her bad leg though some large blue scrub pants. Matt assisted her to a wheelchair and they waited until she received an official discharge.

Dr. Ramirez shrugged, knowing she wasn't going to convince Fiona to remain there after so much had happened. "Promise me you'll be back in three days so I can check on the wound?"

Fiona smiled. "I promise." She raised her hand up like a scout.

"Very well. Will there be anyone there to check on you?"

Meaghan nodded. "I'll spend the night on the couch. If she does anything to jeopardize her healing, she'll suffer the consequences."

Fiona burst out laughing and Jason appreciated the humor.

He wasn't sure if he was invited back to the house as well, so he stayed silent for a few minutes. After everything they'd been through, he certainly didn't want to crash her peace.

"Ready?" Fiona asked him, putting her hand out for him to hold.

"Ready for what?" he responded, taking her hand and loving the warmth from the touch of her skin against his.

"To go home."

"I'd thought you'd never ask." And he finally breathed again.

Chapter 24

For four beautiful, perfect, dream-like days, Fiona lived in a bubble with her once dead husband and their son. Jason couldn't stop complimenting the decor of the house, the food on the table, and her flexibility, which was better than it had been when they'd both been younger. Fiona supplied him with just as many compliments. In the years they'd been apart, he'd learned to cook, clean and take care of a place. A far cry from the man-child who held her with the strength of a soldier and loved her every night, but couldn't pick up his socks from the floor or find the dishwasher. He still knew exactly how to turn his wife on in the bedroom, and he made a fabulous chocolate cheesecake. Despite their injuries, they found plenty of ways to reignite their romance. She'd missed being with someone who could take off some of the burden that had been crushing her. She'd missed those strong arms and the way he bit her lip when they kissed good-night, an invitation to so much more. She couldn't wait to spend the rest of their hopefully long lives together.

He and Matt took the time to know each other again. Matt quizzed him on his military service, and Jason was surprisingly open with where he'd been deployed early in his career and many of his assignments later in his career. At least the assignments that weren't still classified. Matt seemed in awe of his father, and Fiona had never been happier.

When Matt returned to school with a bodyguard shadowing him for the time being, Fiona and Jason had time to enjoy one fabulous cup of coffee together before the doorbell rang.

She put down her mug and frowned. The thought of someone breaking up this perfect moment with Jason annoyed her.

"I'll get it," Jason said, strolling to the door with a calm focus and alertness.

Fiona stood up and slipped a perfectly weighted paring knife into her hand. Just in case.

When Jason opened the door, a very tall, middle-aged white man in a navy suit was standing with a forced ease. Fiona knew before the man opened his mouth exactly who he was. CIA. Not field, but an analyst.

He put out his hand toward Jason. "Phil Mayers. I'm looking for Fiona Stirling."

"Why?" Jason did not release his hand and seemed to hold it more securely.

The man tried not to wince, but Jason seemed intent on creating an uncomfortable moment.

Fiona waited for his answer out of his view.

"I'd like to discuss it privately with her."

"I'm here," Fiona said, rushing forward before Jason broke the man's fingers.

Jason looked over his shoulder at her. He had that adorable protective look that had made her fall in love with him so many years ago. But this wasn't his battle to fight. "You can discuss anything in front of my husband." She hoped the man would tell Jason all her secrets.

"Actually, I can't, ma'am."

Jason backed up and allowed Fiona to get closer to Mr. Mayers. "If you need anything…" He slipped the knife out from behind her back as he headed to the kitchen.

Fiona stepped outside with Mayers. "What can I do for you?"

"Director Downes wants to see you."

"Right now?"

"He's waiting at the Four Seasons."

"He still has expensive taste," she said.

"I wouldn't know, ma'am." Decades in a cubicle must have scrubbed the humor right out of this guy.

"When?"

"Now."

It was no use trying to have a normal conversation, so she stuck to the facts. "What room?"

"In the restaurant."

"That's new." She didn't have a choice. If she didn't comply with this demand, she'd receive a less hospitable invitation. "I'm taking my own car. I'll be there in under an hour."

He didn't seem excited about her response, but went back to his car and sat. He'd be following her into the city to make sure she arrived on time.

Jason was standing at the sink cleaning the coffeepot when she returned. "Everything okay?"

"I have to go out."

"Want me to come?"

"Yes, but you weren't invited."

There was a silence between them, but from the look in his eyes, he understood. "I'll head into the office. Want to meet me there when you get out?"

"That would be great." She wrapped her arms around his neck and kissed him.

He pulled her closer to him, pressing his lips harder into hers. The scratch of his chin made her want to stay there in his arms and ignore everyone else in the world. It was Jason who pulled away first. "Stay safe." His finger traced the curve of her jaw, and he pulled her back for one more kiss.

She walked away from him breathless.

Arriving in the hotel restaurant forty minutes later, Fiona strolled inside in a red wrap dress, her hair styled to perfection. Despite the lift in her chin, she felt a deep sense of unease settling over her. Fiona now found herself in the more unsettling presence of a familiar figure from her past.

CIA Director Ron Downes sat at a table in the back of the restaurant. Private, but it provided a perfect view of the room. He held a lowball glass in his hand, most likely containing a Manhattan. He couldn't resist that drink, even at eleven in the morning. His imposing stature contrasted sharply with his controlled demeanor. Ron was renowned for his acute observation skills and his uncanny ability to make swift, precise decisions. Fiona had never been comfortable working under his command in the clandestine force, and she had hoped to leave those days behind. He made kill orders seem as though he were ordering out for coffee. Each success she had had ripped a bit of her soul away from her.

"Mrs. Stirling," he greeted her, his voice as cold and unforgiving as steel. "I've missed having you on my crew."

Fiona shook her head, her expression tainted with suspicion. "After this week, I remember why I chose not to work with you anymore."

Ron leaned forward, his penetrating gaze locked onto hers. "You and your husband have created quite the mess. Gun and murder charges looming over everyone on Jason's team, not to mention the myriad antics from this past week and the years before. They've skirted the law just enough to stay one step ahead of the authorities for several years now."

Familiarity with Ron led Fiona to the unsettling realization that he hadn't convened this meeting merely for a new attempt to recruit her back into service. There was a deeper purpose, an ulterior motive that filled her with trepidation. And it would involve more than just her.

"I'm done, retired, my aim is off, my heart isn't in it anymore, my soul isn't corrupt enough to carry on."

Ron ignored her speech. "You just proved how valuable you still are to your country. I want your skills back in service, Fiona, and occasionally, the skills of your team as well. You're all highly valuable assets to the government."

Fiona hesitated, her mind racing through the potential consequences. "Jason and I have no working relationship. He's not linked to me at all."

"I think he's very much linked to you. You don't give yourself enough credit. He'll do anything for you. And without you, the whole group of them might lose their business license and all spend a bit of time in jail as an example to the good citizens of Massachusetts."

The prospect of working once more with Ron sent her mind reeling back in time to when she'd do anything to keep her family free from her past actions. Blackmail was Ron's favorite game and he never lost. He wouldn't lose this time either, because Fiona would never sacrifice her husband and friends, as he knew.

In their world, the boundaries between right and wrong, legal and illegal, were often blurred. The events of the past week had underscored that reality, and they'd teetered on the brink of catastrophe more times than she could count. If accepting Ron's terms meant safeguarding Jason's team's well-being and protecting her family, then Fiona knew she had no choice but to consider the proposition. Porras could have his team follow up and take out Jason, Matt or her, even from a federal prison. Having Ron's protection would prove useful in the future.

With a heavy sigh, she finally nodded. "I'd have to talk to Jason and Steve. It's not my business. We'd also need guarantees. Not that I don't trust you, Ron, but really, should I trust anyone in my life?"

"Absolutely not. Everyone has a breaking point. Although I've found you to be a particularly difficult person to crack."

"I learned from the best."

Ron smiled at the compliment. "Welcome back to the game."

She drove straight to Jason's office, once a sanctuary, now marred by the events of the past week. With Porras in custody and his main cartel officers behind bars, the immediate threat had been neutralized. Jason's team had returned, their mission accomplished, yet the scars of their recent ordeal still lingered.

Fiona located Jason first. He was at his desk. He jumped out of his seat when he saw her.

"Well?"

"Grab Steve and let's meet in the conference room. We need to talk."

"Both of us?"

She nodded, then turned back to the conference room. She didn't want to delay and she wasn't going to explain this twice. She stood by the window when they both arrived.

Steve, wearing a golf shirt and khakis like an accountant nearing retirement, strolled in and sat at the table. Jason followed, but he didn't sit. He stayed on the opposite side of Fiona and propped one hip on the table.

Fiona couldn't bring herself to speak directly about her shadowy past and the director's demands. Not yet. She steered the conversation toward safer ground. "It seems you guys are doing a great job of building this business. And it's not my place to step in and offer suggestions on how to add more depth to your services."

"But?" Steve asked, his eyes never leaving Fiona's face.

"Have you ever thought of branching out into some more profitable areas of security?" she asked.

"Such as?" Jason moved closer to her, his expression far more hostile than Steve's.

"Maybe adding the government as a client, a silent partner."

"Fi, you've always been so guarded about your past

work. What aren't you telling me? Not that I don't have an idea. I have a very vivid idea."

She hesitated, her gaze locking onto his. "There are things in my past I'm not proud of. Things not even my therapist knows, but I've changed. Yet, there are advantages to going into business with this kind of underground government entity."

Steve leaned forward. "I have got to hear the advantages, because most of our employees are not exactly fans of working for the military or any police force."

"For one thing, the charges about to be brought down on you, Jason, Meaghan and Sam will be dropped."

"Charges? We didn't break any laws." Steve jumped to his feet.

Jason shook his head. "We may have skirted a few things, but we've never had an issue before."

"It wouldn't matter if you broke every law on the books or not. Evidence will materialize, gun permits will disappear from the government database, and there would be prison time." They understood how this worked—they'd both worked in highly classified levels of the government, although most of their work involved assignments on the up-and-up. Ron preferred to work in the total dark. "So anyway, I agreed to their terms."

"Son of a bitch." Steve clenched his fist. "Can we inform the team?"

"Probably not right away."

"So what about you? How are you a part of this?"

"You use me when you need me. Otherwise, I keep my head down in my laptop and write for a living."

After Steve departed, still swearing under his breath,

Fiona walked over to Jason and rested her head in his chest. He kissed the top of her head.

"You retired from a job you hated, didn't you?" He wrapped her in his arms tight.

"I tried."

"And this fiasco brought you back into their sight."

"Sort of. Although they were waiting for a chance to bring me back in."

"You did save Matt by diving off a ship in the middle of the ocean."

"Any parent would have done that for their child."

"Then you snuck back on the boat and saved my life."

"We're married." She looked up into his beautiful eyes. "I'd already lost you once. I couldn't let you die again without a fight."

"Had I known you were such a badass, I definitely would have put my dishes in the dishwasher when we first married."

"You made up for your lack of domestic skills with outstanding bedroom abilities. I'm glad to know you're still so very—" she kissed his lips "—very capable there."

They kissed in a slow, easy way that gave Fiona comfort while also heating up her need for him. He pulled her over to the couch where they stayed wrapped in each other's arms.

"I'm sorry you got dragged into this. I should have made this all go away years ago," he said.

"But it brought you back to me. The price was high, but I have expensive taste." She leaned into his arms and closed her eyes.

"Perhaps we can use our new silent partner to secure better pay for everyone and improve our security systems. This opportunity could keep you in a lifestyle that you deserve." Jason tried to be positive, which Fiona appreciated.

"Or get us killed." She didn't want to live like this forever, always looking over her shoulder, always worried about her family and friends. No amount of money was worth that, but keeping everyone out of prison—that was worth it.

"Do you think they could protect us? We still have to fend off Porras and his cartel members. There were over fifty people involved in his operation at the time of his arrest."

"Downes will send us resources that we'd never be able to acquire as civilians, so there's that. In exchange, we're going to have to handle problems that will make our war against Porras seem like dodgeball." Fiona didn't want to think about the future anymore. It would arrive sooner than she wanted.

Director Ron Downes's proposition loomed over them, and Porras was still very much alive and still intent upon revenge for the death of his son and now the arrest of not only himself, but his wife, his other son and several key members of his entourage. Perhaps they would never find peace.

Chapter 25

One Month Later

Fiona Stirling twirled around like Ginger Rogers in a bright blue chiffon tea-length gown, off the shoulder so her curled blond hair could rest on her bare shoulders. She swirled around again and smiled.

"Beautiful," Meaghan said from across the room. When Fiona had first learned about Meaghan's assignment protecting her, it had felt like a punch to the face. That she'd opened up her heart to this woman who was being paid to remain at her side hurt more than anything. Yet, Meaghan had both taken her job seriously and valued Fiona's friendship. Fiona thought long and hard about that and realized it was possible to do both at once. Her friend looked elegant in a short white dress that revealed annoyingly long legs. With her hair pulled up in a French twist, she seemed every bit the fashionista.

Fiona's mother would be rolling over in her grave at her daughter's refusal to wear white when walking down the aisle again. But Fiona never prioritized other people's insecurities over her own need to be herself. Although she and Jason wanted something a bit different from their first wedding where she wore black, white felt as though she was going backward. So she opted for the pale blue dress and he opted for a light gray suit with a tie matching her dress. The invited guests were asked to wear black or white.

Perhaps Fiona was being a bit superstitious, but she had ended up a widow after she'd worn black to her first wedding. A mourning color wasn't the perfect shade, but at the time she cared more about rebelling against her mother's social demands. For this wedding, she was embracing color and life and fun. Having the wedding at her favorite restaurant, The Oceanside Grill, made the day even more special. The view of the harbor provided an elegant backdrop to the ceremony and dinner.

Matt arrived with his friend Sarah. Both dressed all in black. They looked good together. After everything he'd gone through, it was great he had a person he trusted in his life. He'd changed since his kidnapping. He'd hardened, taking every risk seriously. Sarah, with her sense of humor and ability to roll through life without too much worry, made for a perfect complement to Matt's more serious nature. Fiona hoped he'd get through the adversity with minimal emotional damage, but she was realistic and had already arranged for him to meet with a therapist to air his thoughts about the torture they'd put him through—having his father resurrected and living with a constant threat on his shoulders.

"You nervous, Mom?" he asked as he gave her a hug.

"Nervous? Not a chance. I'm so very happy and excited about starting the rest of my life with your dad."

"He's pretty nervous."

"Is he?" That made Fiona's heart burst with a whole flutter of butterflies.

"He's pulling at his tie and looks like he's biting down on a bullet."

"Good to know."

She called over the waitress who had just arrived with a tray of champagne and asked if she would bring Jason some scotch in a champagne flute. The server thought that would be a great idea.

When she left, Meaghan laughed. "That'll loosen him up."

"Maybe. He's too in control of everything in his life—at least he thinks he is."

"That is a definite personality flaw, although he did hire you, and you're his most unpredictable hire yet." She tipped her glass toward Fiona. "I'm glad he and Steve added you to the roster. Now that there are two women on the ground, we have more standing. And thank you for making sure I had a very generous pay raise."

"You deserve it. The same bullets are flying at you as are flying at the men."

"True. Although I'm better at avoiding them." She shifted back and forth like a character in *The Matrix*.

"Which means, in reality, you should make more than the men on the team. Bullets take a lot of time off to heal." She thought of the intensive physical therapy Noah had done to return to good enough shape to get back into the office, but not yet back into the field. Fiona and Jason had also suffered through weeks of rehabilitation. She told herself she'd start back in small roles at the security agency.

Meaghan's continued friendship made the idea of

working with Jason and the team easier to swallow, although she preferred a life of writing to anything that involved bullets and blood. Ron Downes had made it clear that she would be placed back in service at his discretion. He tended to deal with the assignments that carried the highest risk.

Meaghan tweaked the clip in Fiona's hair, lifting a section just over her ear and twisting it behind in an elegant curl. After they both decided she was perfect, they walked toward the outside deck where the guests and Jason waited for the exchange of vows. They had no officiant and no best man, maid of honor or anyone except them. Instead, they gave all thirty people an intimate role in their public declaration of love toward each other.

Meaghan handed Fiona a simple bouquet of blue irises, before leaving her side and heading to her seat. Fiona walked down the aisle toward her husband, past, present and future. His smile widened as he caught sight of her. And a bit of something else, a devilishness that assured her that they would not only remain together for a long, long time, but they'd each enjoy life so much more with the other by their side. Their relationship had so many new angles and corners and curves in it, but they weren't the same people who had married years ago and they didn't want the same relationship. They wanted something more.

When she arrived at the end of the aisle, she kissed Jason as though a minister had just announced the groom could kiss the bride. Deep, sensuous, a claiming, a promise and an oath between them.

"I owe you my life, all of my love and everything I

own. My purpose on earth is being your partner. I love you, Fi."

She kissed him again, never getting enough of his lips. "Each minute we're together makes my life sweeter and happier. You're my phoenix and I hope this is your final rising."

The crowd clapped and lifted a glass to toast them.

The dinner featured roasted sea bream and beef tenderloin finished with a three-tiered cake that included a layer of Fiona's favorite carrot cake, Jason's favorite chocolate truffle cake and Matt's favorite red velvet.

Janet, Fiona's agent, had flown in from New York City dressed in a Ralph Lauren long black skirt with a white silk blouse. She oozed money, much of it from the profit of Fiona's book. As she sipped champagne, she tried to convince some of Jason's colleagues that they each had a story to tell and she was the person to represent them. None of them took the bait. They preferred a life in the shadows, away from the spotlight. With their new collaboration with the government, they would get their wish.

Barbara also attended with news. She'd received notice from the Justice Department that Montana and her son were deported back to Colombia. Porras and his men weren't so fortunate. They'd been charged with federal racketeering, murder and drug distribution. If found guilty, Porras wasn't going anywhere for a long time.

The risk still lingered, but as Fiona and Jason stepped out into the beautiful day, they both felt unshackled and able to be free.

Until Ron called.

* * * * *

A NOTE TO ALL READERS

From October releases Mills & Boon will be making some changes to the series formats and pricing.

What will be different about the series books?

In response to recent reader feedback, we are increasing the size of our paperbacks to bigger books with better quality paper, making for a better reading experience.

What will be the new price of Mills & Boon?

Over the past four years we have seen significant increases in the cost of producing our books. As a result, in order to continue to provide customers with a quality reading experience, the price of our books will increase to RRP $10.99 for Modern singles and RRP $19.99 for 2-in-1s from Medical, Intrigue, Romantic Suspense, Historical and Western.

For futher information regarding format changes and pricing, please visit our website millsandboon.com.au.

MILLS & BOON
millsandboon.com.au

Romantic Suspense

Danger. Passion. Drama.

Available Next Month

Colton Undercover Jennifer D. Bokal
Second-Chance Bodyguard Patricia Sargeant

Cold Case Kidnapping Kimberly Van Meter
Escape To The Bayou Amber Leigh Williams

LOVE INSPIRED

Search And Detect Terri Reed
Sniffing Out Justice Carol J. Post

Larger Print

LOVE INSPIRED

Undercover Escape Valerie Hansen
Hunted For The Holidays Deena Alexander

Larger Print

LOVE INSPIRED

Witness Protection Ambush Jenna Night
A Lethal Truth Alexis Morgan

Larger Print

brand new stories each month

Romantic Suspense

Danger. Passion. Drama.

MILLS & BOON

BRAND NEW RELEASE!

A hot-shot pilot's homecoming takes an unexpected detour into an off-limits romance.

When an Air Force pilot returns to his Texas hometown with the task of passing along a Dear Jane message to his best friends ex, the tables are turned and she asks him for a favour…to be her fake fiancé in order to secure her future. But neither expects the red-hot attraction between them!

Don't miss this next installment in the Cowboy Brothers in Arms series.

In stores and online October 2024.

MILLS & BOON

millsandboon.com.au

Keep reading for an excerpt of a new title
from the Intrigue series,
COLORADO KIDNAPPING by Cindi Myers

Chapter One

The little girl squealed with delight as she ran across the playground, blond hair flying out behind her. When she stumbled and fell she popped up immediately, still laughing, and resumed her race with her companions. Sheriff's deputy Ryker Vernon, standing just on the other side of the playground fence, swallowed past the catch in his throat and marveled at his daughter's—Charlotte's—sunny disposition. Where did she get that from? Not from her mother. Kim had a decidedly darker outlook on life, one that had led her to eventually leave him and her daughter behind.

Charlotte didn't get her happy personality from Ryker, either. Five years as a law enforcement officer had shown him too much of the bad side of people to make him inclined toward lightheartedness. Yet here was Charlotte, bubbly personality intact despite her mother's desertion and their recent relocation back to his hometown of Eagle Mountain, Colorado.

Charlotte reached the apple tree that apparently marked the finish line of the race and stopped, puffing for breath, her round cheeks bright pink, deep dimples on either side of her smiling lips. She turned and caught sight of Ryker and all but jumped for joy. "Daddy!" she shouted, and took off toward him.

Her teacher, Sheila Lindstrom, caught up with her just as Charlotte raced past the boundary of the fence and, also spotting Ryker, accompanied the child to meet him. He was glad to see the teacher was so diligent. "Hello, Deputy Vernon," Sheila said as Charlotte threw her arms around Ryker's legs. "I didn't know you were picking up Charlotte this afternoon." She tucked a strand of hair a shade paler than Charlotte's behind one ear and smiled up at him in a way that reminded him he was a single man in a small town where the dating pool might be thought of as limited.

He didn't return the smile, and took a step back, hoping to give the impression that he wasn't interested. Not that Sheila wasn't a perfectly nice woman, but he was juggling enough right now, with a new job, a new home and a little girl to raise. He didn't need the complications that came with a relationship. "Charlotte's grandmother will be picking her up, as usual," he said. "I just started my shift and since Charlotte will be in bed by the time I'm back home, I swung by to say hello." He rested his hand on the little girl's head as she beamed up at him.

"That's so sweet," Sheila said, and tilted her head to one side, blue eyes still fixed on him as if he was some delectable treat.

"Ryker! What are you doing here? Is everything all right?"

He and Sheila and Charlotte all turned to see Ryker's mother, Wanda Vernon, hurrying up the sidewalk toward them. Slender and athletic, with dark curls past her shoulders, Wanda Vernon looked younger than her fifty years, but right now worry lines creased her normally smooth forehead.

"Nothing's wrong, Mom," Ryker reassured her. "I just stopped by to say hello to Charlotte."

"Grammie, I found a horny toad at recess this morning, but teacher made me put it back," Charlotte announced.

"You know our wild friends are happier remaining in the wild," Sheila said.

"I know," Charlotte said. "But he was so pretty. He had gold eyes and a gold and brown body with bumps on it. Amy thought he was icky, but I thought he was beautiful."

Ryker hid his smile behind his hand. That was his daughter. She had never met an insect or amphibian or item from nature that frightened or repelled her.

"Horned toads are very interesting," Wanda said. "But it's always best to just look at them, and not touch. You wouldn't want to accidentally hurt one."

"Oh, I would never do that!" Charlotte looked offended at the idea.

Ryker's shoulder-mounted radio crackled, and the dispatcher's voice came through clearly. "Unit five, report to Dixon Pass, mile marker 97, to assist at accident site. EMS and SAR on the way."

Ryker keyed the mike, aware that everyone within earshot had turned to stare. "Unit five responding. I'm on my way." He squatted down until he was eye level with his daughter. "I have to go now, honey," he said. "Can I have a kiss goodbye?"

She responded by throwing her arms around him and kissing his cheek. "Be careful, Daddy," she said.

"I always am, sweetheart. You be a good girl for Grammie and Grandpa."

"I always am!" she echoed.

"Be careful," his mother and Sheila said in unison as he nodded goodbye, then jogged toward his sheriff's department SUV.

He turned the vehicle toward the highway and switched

on lights and sirens to cut a clear path toward the accident. As he passed the preschool he caught a glimpse of Charlotte with his mother on the sidewalk. The little girl was smiling and waving. Some of the heaviness in his heart lifted, as it always did when he was with her. Through all the upheaval in her young life, Charlotte was resilient.

Ryker was trying to follow her example, to roll with the punches life threw at him, or at least do a better job of hiding his bruises.

"IT LOOKS LIKE the vehicle rolled several times before it came to land on that ledge." Eagle Mountain Search and Rescue Captain Danny Irwin stood with the cluster of volunteers on the side of the highway as they peered over the side at the battered silver sedan wedged between a boulder and the cliff approximately one hundred yards below. "You can see pieces of the car that broke off every time the car bounced."

Harper Stanick, a search and rescue rookie, winced as she took in the trail of debris and the battered vehicle. It looked like this was going to be her first body recovery. She had been warned this was part of search and rescue and told herself she was prepared, but still. What would a person look like after enduring that kind of trauma?

"I saw movement!" Paramedic Hannah Richards, who had arrived with the ambulance but joined her fellow SAR volunteers in surveying the scene, pointed at the vehicle. "There's someone alive in there!"

Her exclamation prodded them into action. Danny directed volunteers Eldon Ramsey and Tony Meissner to rig ropes for a rappel onto the ledge beside the car. Harper joined fellow trainees Grace Wilcox, Anna Trent and veteran Christine Mercer in gathering helmets, harnesses, a litter and other gear they would need to stabilize the injured survivor and get them to safety above. Danny radioed to have a medical helicopter land two miles away at the soccer fields in town to meet the ambulance and transport the injured person or persons to the hospital in Junction.

"What can I do to help?"

At the sound of the man's voice, deep and slightly hoarse, Harper fumbled the safety helmets she had been charged with, and had to juggle to keep from losing one. "Careful," Christine said.

"Close the highway, if you haven't already," Danny said. "Clear space on the side of the highway for us to go down and keep everyone back from the edge. We don't want anyone else falling in, or kicking rocks down on top of us as we work."

Harper turned to see who Danny was talking to and this time she did drop the helmets. Seven years since she had laid eyes on Ryker Vernon and she might have thought she was hallucinating him now, except that it made perfect sense for him to be here. Ryker was from Eagle Mountain, just like her. The first thing she had done when she moved back was to snoop around, long enough to determine he had left town, but apparently he had returned. Just like her.

What didn't make sense was that Ryker was now apparently a cop. No mistaking that khaki uniform or the gun on his hip. Ryker, a cop? The motorcycle-riding bad boy who had practically sent her mother into a faint the first time he showed up at their house to pick Harper up for a date was a law enforcement officer?

And damned if he didn't look just as good in that uniform as he had in his motorcycle leathers all those years ago. Better even, his chest a little broader, his jaw firmer. The Ryker she had known had been barely eighteen, still with a bit of the boy about him. This version of him was harder. A man.

"Hey, earth to Harper. Are you okay?" Christine followed Harper's gaze toward the officer who stood with Danny and she grinned. "I take it this is your first encounter with the newest addition to the sheriff's department," she said. "He's pretty easy on the eyes, isn't he?" She nudged Harper with her elbow. "I hear he's a single dad. Maybe when we're done here you can introduce yourself."

The bottom dropped out of Harper's stomach at the word *dad*. Ryker was a father? When? Who?

"Pull your eyes back in your head and focus on the job," Christine said, her voice firm. "You can chase after the cop later."

Harper turned her back on Ryker. "I'm not going to chase after him," she said. "I was just surprised. He reminds me of someone I used to know."

"Must have been a pretty special someone," Christine said. "The way you were staring at him. Like one of those cartoons, where the air fills with hearts."

"Not like that at all," Harper said, and gathered up the helmets she had dropped. Maybe at one time she was that gaga about Ryker Vernon, but those days were long past.

DESPITE HOW FAR the vehicle had rolled and the shape the car was in, three people emerged alive. Ryker watched from a distance as search and rescue volunteers descended on ropes to the ledge and worked to stabilize the vehicle, then cut most of the rest of the car away to reach the passengers trapped inside.

First up was an infant, a living testament to the effectiveness of child safety seats, as he sustained nothing more than a minor cut on his forehead from broken glass. Volunteer Eldon Ramsey carried the baby, still secured in his seat, up to the road, where the paramedics pronounced him perfectly okay then reluctantly turned him over to the Victim Services volunteer, who was tasked with locating a relative or temporary foster parent to care for him until his parents were released from the hospital.

Said parents also both survived, with several broken bones between them. They were brought up one at a time strapped into litters. The technical aspects of the maneuvers required to bring them to safety fascinated Ryker, who would admit to being nervous about heights.

"That was amazing," he said to SAR Captain Danny Irwin after the injured had been transported to the waiting helicopter and the road had been reopened. Accident investigators from Colorado State Patrol had arrived on the scene and were taking photographs and measuring skid marks for their reports, so Ryker had turned to helping the search and rescue volunteers with their gear.

"We're always looking for more volunteers," Danny said. "Deputy Jake Gwynn is on the team."

"Yeah, I hear he loves it," Ryker said. "Unfortunately, I can't commit that much time. I need to be with my daughter when I have time off."

"How old is she?" Danny asked.

"Four. It's just the two of us. And my parents. They're a big help."

Danny nodded. "My fiancée has two kids. They're a little older but I get what you mean about wanting to be there for them. They won't be little forever."

"Hey there! I heard you were back in town." Ryker turned to find Hannah Richards grinning up at him. The two of them had been in the same grade at Eagle Mountain High School way back when.

"Hi, Hannah. It's good to see you. I've only been back a couple of weeks. I'm still getting settled."

"Jake told me you signed on with the sheriff's department," she said. She held up one hand to reveal a modest diamond. "He's my fiancé, in case you haven't heard."

"He's mentioned the amazing woman he's engaged to, but I had no idea that was you."

She punched his shoulder and he pretended to recoil in pain, both of them laughing. "Hey, there's someone else here you need to see," Hannah said. She turned and waved. "Harper. Come over and see who the cat dragged in."

The name itself was enough to set Ryker's heart hammering, but seeing the woman herself made his world tilt for a moment. If anything, she was more beautiful than he remembered—her curly brown hair escaping from a twist at the back of her head, her green-hazel eyes fringed with dark lashes. Kim, to whom Ryker had confided the whole story of his and Harper's ill-fated romance, had prickled at what she interpreted as his too-fond descriptions of his teenage girlfriend. "No one is that perfect," she had protested.

But to him, Harper had been perfect. And she had reminded him of how imperfect he was. "Hello, Harper," he said, surprised at how calm and even his voice sounded. "It's good to see you again."

"Hello, Ryker. I heard you'd left town."

He had heard the same about her. "I just moved back," he said.

She was looking at him, but at the uniform, not into his eyes. "I can't believe you're a sheriff's deputy."

"Neither can I, some days." He was trying to make a joke, but the words came off flat. Hannah was watching them, her face full of questions. Did she remember that he and Harper had dated in high school?

Maybe she hadn't known. Harper's rich parents had pitched such a fit about their adored daughter seeing a guy whose father worked at the town's sewage treatment plant that he and Harper had to sneak around in order to see each other.

He had a hundred questions he wanted to ask her: What was she doing back in Eagle Mountain? What kind of work did she do? How had she ended up volunteering with search and rescue?

Was she okay? Could she ever forgive him?

"I have to go," Harper said, and turned away.

"See you around, Ryker," Hannah said. "Jake and I will have you over for dinner sometime."

"Yeah, that would be great," Ryker said, with less enthusiasm than he probably should have. He stared after Harper. She was still beautiful, all shiny hair and soft curves, but more defined now, the blurred edges of youth replaced by the firm lines of maturity. Not that she was old, but she had been through a lot in the past few years.

She had been through a lot, and he hadn't been there with her. One more failure he was having a hard time getting past.

Subscribe and fall in love with a Mills & Boon series today!

You'll be among the first to read stories delivered to your door monthly and enjoy great savings.

WE SIMPLY LOVE ROMANCE